D0953011

FRONT RUNNER

BY FELIX FRANCIS

Gamble

Bloodline

Refusal

Damage

BY DICK FRANCIS AND FELIX FRANCIS

Dead Heat

Silks

Even Money

Crossfire

BY DICK FRANCIS

The Sport of Queens
(Autobiography)

Dead Cert

Nerve

For Kicks

Odds Against

Flying Finish

Blood Sport

Forfeit

Inquiry

Rat Race

Bonecrack

Smokescreen

Slay-Ride

Knock Down

High Stakes

In the Frame

Risk

Trial Run

Whip Hand

Reflex

Twice Shy

Banker

The Danger

Proof

Break In

A Jockey's Life: The Biography of Lester Piggott

Bolt

Hot Money

The Edge

Straight

Longshot

Comeback

Driving Force

Decider

Wild Horses

Come to Grief

To the Hilt

10 Lb. Penalty

Field of 13

Second Wind

Shattered

Under Orders

FRONT RUNNER

FELIX FRANCIS

G. P. PUTNAM'S SONS
NEW YORK

PUTNAM

G. P. PUTNAM'S SONS
Publishers Since 1838
An imprint of Penguin Random House LLC
375 Hudson Street
New York, New York 10014

Library of Congress Cataloging-in-Publication Data

Francis, Felix.
Front runner : a Dick Francis novel / Felix Francis.
p. cm.
ISBN 978-0-399-16823-9
1. Private investigators—England—Fiction. 2. Horse racing—England—Fiction.
I. Francis, Dick. II. Title.
PR6056.R273F76 2015 2015025077
823'.914—dc23

Printed in the United States of America
1 3 5 7 9 10 8 6 4 2

Felix, qui potuit rerum cognoscere causas
"Happy is he who can discover the causes of things"

—Virgil, *Georgics*, book 2, verse 490 (29 B.C.)

With my special thanks to
Debbie

I was approached by the Sir Peter O'Sullevan Charitable Trust and asked to include a character in my next book as an auction lot at the Trust's Annual Award Lunch in November 2014.

The lot was sold to Mr. Derrick Smith, who bought it for his wife, Gay.

Forty thousand pounds ($60,000) was raised for the Trust by the sale, all of the money going to the six charities the Trust supports: Blue Cross, the Brooke Hospital for Animals, Compassion in World Farming, World Horse Welfare, Racing Welfare and the Thoroughbred Rehabilitation Centre.

I have incorporated both Gay and Derrick in *Front Runner*, but as fictitious characters. I hope they are happy with the artistic license I have taken.

1

The display on the digital thermometer to my left read 105 degrees—105 degrees Celsius, that is, 221 degrees Fahrenheit.

Sweat ran off the end of my nose in a continuous stream and I could feel the heat deep in my chest as I breathed in the searing air.

I'd been in saunas before, but never one this hot.

"So what do you want?" I asked.

My companion in this hellish place didn't answer. He simply stared at the floor between his feet.

"Come on," I said. "I haven't come all this way for my health. It's far too bloody hot in here. You wanted to talk to me, so talk."

He lifted his head.

"At least you're not in one of *these* damn things." He tugged at the black nylon sweat suit he was wearing. As if the heat alone wasn't bad enough.

"Maybe not, but I didn't come here to be slow-roasted."

He still didn't talk. He just looked at me. Dave Swinton, twenty-nine years old and already eight times champion steeplechase jockey. At five-foot-ten, he had a continuous struggle with his weight, that was common knowledge, but owners and trainers were often happy to accept a touch overweight in order to have his exceptional skill in the saddle. And for good reason—the stats showed that he won almost a third of the races in which he rode.

"Off the record?" he said.

"Don't be silly," I replied.

I was an investigator for the British Horseracing Authority, the organization responsible for regulatory control of all Thoroughbred racing in the United Kingdom. Nothing I saw or heard to do with racing could be *off the record*.

"I'll deny I said it."

"Said what?" I asked. "I've been in this bloody oven now for over ten minutes and I'm starting to look like a lobster. Either you tell me why I'm here or I'm gone."

I wondered why he'd been so insistent that we should talk in his sauna. I had thought it was because he needed to shed a pound or two before racing at Newbury that afternoon, but maybe it was actually to make sure that I had no recording equipment hidden about my person. As a rule, I used my iPhone to record meetings, but that was in the pocket of my jacket, which was hanging up on a peg outside, along with the rest of my clothes.

Dave went on looking at me as if still undecided.

"Right," I said. "I'm done." I stood up, wrapped the towel I had been sitting on around my waist and pushed open the sauna's wooden door.

"I lost a race this week."

I put one foot through the doorway. "So? You can't win them all."

"No," he said, shaking his head. "I lost it on purpose."

I stopped and turned to him. I knew most of the Rules of Racing by heart. Rule (D)45.1 stated that a jockey was required, at all times, to have *made a genuine attempt to obtain from his horse timely, real and substantial efforts to achieve the best possible placing.*

To lose a race on purpose was to willfully flout that rule, an offense that could carry a penalty of ten years' disqualification from the sport.

"Why?" I asked.

He didn't answer. He simply went back to studying the space between his feet.

"Why?" I asked him again.

"Forget I ever said it."

"I can hardly do that," I said.

Winding back time wasn't possible. Just as uninventing the atom bomb wasn't ever going to happen.

I looked down at him, but he went on scrutinizing the floor.

"Can't we get out of this bloody heat and talk about this over a glass of iced beer?"

"I can't drink *anything*," he replied sharply without moving his head. "Not even water. What the hell do you think I'm doing this for? I've got to lose two pounds to ride Integrated in the Hennessy."

"Won't you be dehydrated?"

"Usual state for me," he said, trying to produce a laugh. "I've been wasting every day since I was sixteen. I can't remember what a square meal looks like. Nor a beer. In fact, I haven't had a proper drink for years; alcohol contains far too many calories. Not that I miss it much, I don't like the taste." He laughed again, but just once. "Why do I do it? you ask. That's a bloody good question."

He stood up and we both went out of the wooden box into the coolness. I wondered how many people had a sauna in the corner of their garage, not that there wasn't still plenty of room for a couple of expensive cars as well, a silver Mercedes saloon and a dark green Jaguar XK sports coupé, both adorned with personalized license plates.

Dave flicked off a big red switch next to the door.

"It must cost a fortune to heat," I said.

"I claim my electricity bill against tax as a business expense," he said, smiling. "This sauna is a necessity for my job."

"How often do you use it?"

"Every day. I used to go to the one in the local gym, but then they turned down the temperature—something to do with health and safety."

He peeled off the nylon sweat suit and stepped naked onto a scale.

"What the hell is that?" I said, pointing at an ugly purple-and-black ring on his back.

"Something landed on me," he said with a smile. "Hoofprint."

He looked down at the scale.

"I'm still too heavy," he said with a sigh. "No lunch for me today, to go with my no breakfast."

"But you surely have to eat. You need the energy."

"Can't afford to," he said. "According to his bloody owner, if I can't do a hundred and forty-four pounds stripped by two this afternoon, I don't get to ride Integrated, and he's one of the best young chasers in the country. He's incredibly well handicapped for the Hennessy, and if I don't ride him today and he wins, I can kiss good-bye to riding him anytime in the future—maybe start kissing good-bye to my whole career."

He could kiss good-bye to his career anyway if he'd been purposely losing races.

"Tell me about the race you didn't win," I said.

"I need a shower," he replied, ignoring me and going into the house. "*You* can use the one in the guest bathroom, if you like. Top of the stairs on the right."

He bounded up the stairs and disappeared into what I presumed was his bedroom, closing the door firmly behind him.

Not for the first time I wondered what I was doing here.

"Come *now*, Jeff." That's what Dave had said intently down the line when he'd called me at ten to seven that morning. "At once. I need to talk to you. Right now. It's vital."

"Can't we talk on the phone?" I'd asked.

"No. Absolutely not. Far too important. This has to be done face-to-face."

Dave Swinton was one of the very few members of the racing fraternity that I called a friend. Mostly, I avoided social contact with those I was supposed to police, but, two years previously, Dave and I had been stranded for twenty-four hours together by an unseasonal ice storm as we tried to return home to England after the Maryland Hunt Cup steeplechase north of Baltimore. He was there as a guest rider and I had been invited to oversee the introduction of a new drug-testing regimen for American steeplechase horses.

We had ended up spending a freezing night in an upstate country hotel with no heat or light, the power lines having been brought down by the ice. We had passed the night huddled under blankets in front of a log fire, and we had talked.

Hence, I'd come when he'd asked, giving up a precious Saturday-morning lie-in to catch an early train from Paddington to Hungerford and then a taxi to Dave's house just outside Lambourn.

He had dropped a bit of a bombshell with his claim to have lost a race on purpose, but if he refused to elaborate, I'd have made a wasted journey.

I went into his kitchen and gratefully drank down two large glassfuls of water from the cold tap. And still I was thirsty. How Dave could drink nothing after a session in that sauna was beyond me.

I followed Dave's directions to the guest bathroom and had a shower but still had to wait downstairs for more than twenty minutes before he reappeared dressed in a dark green polo shirt, blue jeans and running shoes, his standard work attire.

Whereas most top jockeys still dressed in suit and tie to go to the races in order to impress the owners and trainers, Dave Swinton had long forgone such niceties. Nowadays, Royal Ascot and the Derby meeting apart, racing in general was a more casual affair, and the current champion jockey was the most casual of them all.

"I'm going to Newbury now," he said, picking up a carryall that was lying in the hallway. "I want to run the course before the first."

I looked at my watch. It was coming up on ten o'clock.

"I came by train and taxi," I said. "Can you give me a lift?"

"Where to?"

"Newbury racetrack will be fine," I said. "I'll watch the Hennessy and then take the train back to London."

"Why don't you drive like everyone else?" he said, clearly irritated.

"I've no car," I said. "I don't need one in the city. I'll come with you."

He could hardly say no, but I could tell that he wasn't that happy. Whatever he had decided to tell me at seven o'clock that morning, he had clearly changed his mind since, and half an hour of us together in his car was not on his agenda, friends or not.

"OK," he said grudgingly. "Are you ready?"

HE DROVE THE JAGUAR at speed out of Lambourn up Hungerford Hill, the only sound being the roar of the car's powerful engine, but if he thought I wasn't going to say something, he was much mistaken.

"Tell me about the race you didn't win."

"Please, Jeff. I told you to forget it."

"I can't," I said.

"Try."

He drove on in silence past The Hare public house and on toward the M4 junction, overtaking a line of slower vehicles with ease.

"Which race was it?" I asked.

He ignored me. We turned eastward, accelerating on to the freeway.

"Come on, Dave, you asked me to come all this way because you had something to tell me that couldn't be said on the phone. So here I am. Speak to me."

He concentrated hard on the road ahead and said nothing as the Jaguar's speedometer climbed rapidly past a hundred miles per hour.

"Are you in some sort of trouble?" I asked, although he certainly would be if what he'd told me were true.

He eased up on the power and pulled over toward the left. For a nasty moment, I thought he was going to stop on the hard shoulder and chuck me out, but he didn't. He just drove sedately along in the inside lane at a mere eighty-five.

"Jeff, can I speak to you off the record?" he asked again.

"You know I can't agree to that. This is my job."

"It's *my* bloody job that I'm more worried about."

We took the exit off the freeway at Newbury and I sat and waited quietly while he negotiated the traffic lights at the intersection.

"Look, I'll keep what you say confidential if I can," I said, encouraging him to go on. "But no promises."

He must know that I was obliged to report any breach of the rules to the BHA Disciplinary Committee.

He sighed deeply. "I need your help."

"Ask away."

"I'm being blackmailed."

"Who by?" I asked as calmly as I could.

"I don't know," he said. "Someone who knows more than they should about my financial affairs."

"And aren't your financial affairs in order?"

"Yeah, of course they are." He paused. "But, you know, working out the bloody tax is complicated. Maybe I take a few shortcuts."

"By not declaring certain things?"

"Yeah, maybe. But why should I pay tax on gifts?"

It depended if the "gifts" were actually payments for services rendered.

"How much were these gifts that you didn't declare?"

"Not much," he said. "Not compared to what I do declare."

Dave Swinton was, by far, the highest-earning jockey in British racing. He was the public face of the sport, with a mass of endorsements and sponsorship deals. His was the image that stared out of the *Racing Needs You!* posters of a recent widespread campaign to encourage the young to give it a try. His ever-present green polo shirts had the distinctive swoosh logo of a top sports manufacturer embroidered on the left breast above his name and there were advertising badges sewn onto each sleeve. He certainly earned far more from commercial endorsements than he did from his riding.

"How much?" I asked again.

"About two hundred."

I laughed. "But that's not enough to worry about. Just include it in your next return. No one could blackmail you over that, surely?"

"Two hundred *thousand*."

"Ah." The laughter died in my throat.

"Yeah. But I declare more than a million." He paused as he overtook a line of traffic waiting at some lights, swerving across into the correct lane to turn left at the very last moment. "And then some bastard calls me and tells me to lose a race or else he'll go to the tax authorities and spill the beans."

"And you've no idea who?"

"None," he said. "Otherwise, I'd have killed him."

"I don't think that would be particularly helpful."

"Maybe not, but it might make me feel better."

He drove on in silence until we arrived at the racetrack.

"Which race did you lose?" I asked again as we turned into the parking lot.

"I had twenty-eight rides and ten winners last week, so I lost eighteen races."

"Don't mess with me, Dave," I said. "You know what I mean."

He didn't reply.

He pulled the Jaguar into a space in the jockeys' parking area.

"Do you want my advice?" I asked.

"Not really," he said, leaning his head down on the steering wheel.

I gave it to him anyway. "Go to the revenue and tell them you made an error of omission on your tax return and you want to correct it. Pay the tax. That will be an end to it. I'll try and forget what you've told me."

"And if I don't?"

"Then you'd be a fool. If someone has that information, they will use it. They may not go to the authorities directly, but they will use it nevertheless. Perhaps they will try and sell it to a newspaper. You'd be right in the shit. Much better that you go to the tax man before they do."

"But I shouldn't have to pay tax on gifts. It's not like they were earnings."

He sounded as if he was trying to convince himself rather than me.

"Go and ask your accountant if you need to declare them."

"Bloody accountants," he said, sitting back in the seat. "You don't want to tell them anything if you don't want the tax man to know it. In spite of the fact that it's me that pays their bill, my lot seem to work exclusively for the government, always telling me I can't claim for all sorts of things I think are essential for my job."

"Get a new firm, then. And do it now."

And maybe, I thought, it was one of his accountant team who knew about his tax-return omission who was trying to make a bit of extra cash on the side.

"How much money did the blackmailer demand?" I asked him as we walked toward the racetrack entrance.

"That's what was odd," Dave said. "He didn't ask for money, he just said that I mustn't win the race."

"Which race?"

He didn't answer.

2

Dave Swinton and I were waved through by the Newbury racetrack gateman, who recognized Dave and almost touched his forelock. "Morning, Mr. Swinton," he said without bothering to look at the jockey's pass hanging around Dave's neck. He inspected my authorization more closely. It had my name, my photo and the words *BHA Integrity Investigator* marked in black print. The gateman scowled. No one, it seems, likes a policeman, not even a racing policeman.

"How did the blackmailer contact you?" I asked when we were out of earshot.

"He rang my cell."

"Did you see his number?" I asked.

"It said *Withheld*."

Of course it would.

"What did he say?"

"He told me to lose a race."

"Yes," I said with some impatience, "but what exactly did he say? What were his actual words?"

"He said I had to lose the race or he'd spill the beans to the tax man that I'd received big gifts from owners that I hadn't declared."

"Did he use those precise words?"

"Yeah, near enough."

"He must have told you which race to lose," I said.

"He just said not to win on—" He stopped.

"On what?" I encouraged.

"Never you mind."

"But I do mind, Dave. Goddam it, I'm trying to help you."

"Then forget I ever said it."

He hurried off toward the weighing room and into the safety of the jockeys' changing room. Theoretically, my BHA credentials meant that I could have followed him in there, but I was sure it wouldn't do any good. And it wouldn't help me make any friends. I may have had an absolute right of entry into every part of the racetrack, but such entitlement was to be used most sparingly, if at all. If I invaded their personal space, any moral authority I might currently possess among the jockeys would evaporate faster than ether on a hot plate.

Instead, I meandered around, enjoying the "feel" of the racetrack on the morning of a big race—especially during this relatively quiet time before the bulk of the racegoers began spilling off the special trains, surging through the entrances, filling the bars and raising the expectation level to fever pitch.

It was a while since I had been to Newbury, but it remained one of my favorite courses. The flat terrain gave spectators a good view of all the action from the grandstands, and the long final stretch, with four stiff fences to the finish, provided a keen challenge for both horse and jockey.

The track at Newbury didn't just have a *long* homestretch, it was also very wide. These two features combined to produce a foreshortening optical illusion that made the winning post always appear closer than it actually was, tempting the inexperienced or unwary to make a final effort too soon, only to find that the post was still on the horizon and more patient jockeys were sitting quietly behind, ready to pounce.

Conversely, waiting too long could be a disaster as well. No jockey receives more abuse than one who leaves it to too late and then just fails to get up on a fast finisher.

This was supposedly my weekend away from work, but I was never completely off-duty when on a racetrack. I walked around with my eyes and ears firmly open, watching and listening for anything that shouldn't be there. It was habit, I suppose, and one I couldn't shake off—not that I was trying very hard.

I went through the Berkshire Stand and then on to the betting ring, where the lines of bookmakers were busily setting up on their pitches, erecting their electronic price boards and logging their computers on to the racetrack's wireless network. How things had changed since the days of chalk and the big ledger recording books that had given these men their name.

I went back into the grandstand to warm up and get myself a coffee. I was still desperately thirsty after my stint in Dave's sauna. How he could go without anything to drink at all was beyond me, especially as he was, even now, running around the nearly two-mile-long course in a sweat suit, trying to remove yet another pound of liquid from his system.

The enclosures began to fill quickly as the expected crowd of over seventeen thousand arrived in droves and I wandered among them, listening for any snippets of information that might be useful.

"Jeff Hinkley?" called a voice behind me.

I turned. A shortish, well-dressed man with swept-back gray hair was walking toward me with his hand held out. I shook it warmly.

"Mr. Smith," I said. "How lovely to see you again."

"Call me Derrick, please."

Derrick Smith was a leading owner whose many horses in training had included the great Camelot, winner of both the Two Thousand Guineas and the Derby.

Derrick introduced me to the person he was with, a tall gray-haired man, smartly dressed in a fawn overcoat with a brown velvet collar over a tweed suit.

"Jeff Hinkley, this is Sir Richard Reynard." He said it in a manner that made me think I should know who Sir Richard Reynard was.

I didn't.

"Good to meet you," I said, shaking his hand.

"Are you all set for next week?" Derrick asked.

"Definitely," I said. "Thank you. I'm looking forward to it."

He had asked me for lunch in his box at Sandown on the following Saturday as a thank-you for uncovering and foiling a plot to kidnap one of his horses on the eve of Royal Ascot in June.

"Good," he said.

"Do you have any runners today?" I asked Derrick.

"No. Richard and I are here as guests of Hennessy. Why don't you come up with us and have a drink? I'm sure they won't mind."

"I'm hardly dressed for it." They were in suits but I had on only a sports jacket and no tie.

"Nonsense. You'll be fine."

The three of us rode up together in the lift to the fourth level of the Berkshire Stand and into the large Hennessy Cognac hospitality area, where a champagne cocktail was thrust into my hands.

The room was already half full and many of the faces were known to me.

And I was clearly known to several of them. There were even a few cautious glances in my direction from the few with whom I'd had professional contact—me as an investigator and they as the investigated.

"Godfrey," Derrick called to the chairman of the cognac company, taking him by the arm and forcing him to turn toward us, "have you met Jeff Hinkley? He's the man who saved my horse at Ascot."

Godfrey, or Viscount Marylebone as he was more formally known, was our host. He shook my offered hand with a quizzical look on his face that suggested he was desperately trying to remember the guest list.

I wasn't on it.

"Thank you for the drink, my Lord," I said. "Mr. Smith brought me in with him but I won't be staying long."

Godfrey was not very good at concealing his relief. "Nice to meet you," he said, but he was already looking over my shoulder toward some of his other guests, those who were expected. He moved away toward them. Derrick Smith, meanwhile, had turned away to speak to someone else and had taken Sir Richard Reynard with him.

I took the opportunity to go out onto the viewing balcony. It wasn't often that I had the chance to look over a racetrack from such an exalted position. I was usually down on the lower levels in pursuit of lesser mortals.

There were two men outside braving the cold and they were in earnest conversation, their heads bowed together. The shorter of the two was very angry with the other, as he was making very plain. "You're a total fucking idiot!" I heard him say. "You absolutely shouldn't be here. You shouldn't even be in the country. It's far too risky."

"No one will ever know," said the other man.

"*I know*, and that in itself is bad enough," replied the first.

At that moment, the two seemed to notice my presence and instantly stopped talking. One of them even pointedly turned away from me so I couldn't see his face.

"Sorry," I said. "Don't mind me. I'm just getting some air."

They just stood there, waiting, so I went back inside.

The room was by now getting very full indeed and people were beginning to move toward their places at the tables that were laid for lunch. Time to go, I thought.

I looked around for Derrick Smith and for Lord Marylebone to say my good-byes, but they were both busy talking to others at the far end of the room, so I worked my way toward the exit to leave quietly. Sir Richard Reynard was standing there on his own, next to the coatrack.

"Please say good-bye to Mr. Smith for me," I said to him.

He looked at me and nodded.

As I turned toward the door, I glanced back through the windows toward the balcony. The two men were still deep in discussion, but this time I was able to see both their faces.

I whipped my iPhone out of my pocket and took a quick long-distance photo of them. As I'd lifted the phone, they both happened to look straight at me, so I had a good shot of their full faces.

One never knew when such things might be useful.

HAVING NO LUNCH, added to his run around the course, must have done the trick because Dave Swinton had evidently met his hundred-forty-four-pound target.

At a quarter to three, I watched as he emerged from the

weighing room wearing Integrated's black, red and white colors and went to join the horse's owner and trainer in the parade ring.

The Hennessy Cognac Gold Cup, run at Newbury each year on the last Saturday in November, is one of the most prestigious races on the calendar.

The two steeplechases that every owner, trainer and jockey are desperate to win are the Cheltenham Gold Cup and the Grand National, but the Hennessy would maybe come in an equal third alongside the likes of the King George VI Chase at Kempton Park on Boxing Day, and the Queen Mother Champion Chase.

Hence, the mixture of excitement and anticipation in the Newbury parade ring was palpable, with some owners shifting from foot to foot, unable to keep still in their nervousness as they waited on the grass.

The same was true for the jockeys.

For the up-and-coming, this was one of those days when careers could be made or lost, while the old hands looked worryingly over their shoulders at the young whippersnappers who would cheerfully take their jobs without a heartbeat of hesitation.

Finally, an official rang the bell for the jockeys to get mounted and, one by one, they took their proper places on the horses' backs, completing a transformation from diminutive bystanders to gods.

I stood by the rail as the horses made their way from the ring out to the track.

"Good luck," I called to Dave as he passed.

He looked down at me and smiled but said nothing. I thought he looked unwell, with the deep-set eyes, hollow cheeks and thin lips of one who was undernourished and dehydrated.

This was his fourth ride of the afternoon, any one of which

would have left most normal men exhausted. Dave, meanwhile, had had no breakfast and no lunch, not even a drink of water.

No wonder he looked unwell.

INTEGRATED WON the Hennessy by a nose in the tightest of photofinishes, Dave Swinton employing all his magic to urge the horse to stretch its neck at just the right moment to pip the favorite to the line.

The crowd went wild, and they continued to cheer as Dave maneuvered Integrated into the unsaddling space reserved for the winner, his gaunt pre-race appearance having been banished by a huge smile and a hefty dose of adrenaline.

He was still grinning as he walked toward me on his way back into the weighing room, his saddle over his arm.

"Now, *that's* why I do it," he said. "Bloody marvelous."

"No question of you losing that one, then?" I said.

The smile vanished for a second but quickly returned, although this time it didn't quite reach to his eyes.

"Not a chance."

3

For the second morning running, Dave Swinton woke me by calling before seven o'clock.

"Jeff, I need to talk to you."

"That's what you said yesterday," I replied.

"Yes, I know. I'm sorry. But I *do* need to talk to you now."

"Talk to me on the phone," I said.

"No. It has to be face-to-face."

"Then you'll have to come to London to see me. You wasted my time yesterday and I have no intention of allowing it to happen again."

"I can't come to London," he said. "I've got five rides later today and I need to take a spell in the sauna first. I celebrated the Hennessy with a steak last night and it's made me fat."

Whatever words could have been chosen to describe him, *fat* was not one of them.

"Look, Dave," I said, "there's little point in me coming all the way to Lambourn again unless you're going to tell me what's going on. And I mean everything that's going on. Yesterday was a total waste of time."

"You got to see me win the Hennessy—that wasn't a waste of time." I could visualize him grinning at the other end of the line.

"Yeah, OK. That was good," I agreed. "Well done."

"So will you come?"

I sighed.

"Promise me you have something important to tell me."

"I have," he said. "For a start, I know who it is."

"Who *who* is?" I asked.

"You know, what we talked about yesterday. I know who it is."

I assumed he meant that he knew who was blackmailing him.

"Then tell me now, on the phone."

"You've got to be kidding, mate," he said. "I don't trust these things anymore."

I suppose I couldn't really blame him. Dave Swinton had been one of those whose phone had been previously hacked by a tabloid Sunday newspaper.

"OK," I said with resignation. "I'll come, but you had better not be messing with me again."

"I'm not," he said. "I promise. But come right now. I've a ride in the first race at Towcester and that's at twelve forty-five, so I have to be gone from here by half past ten, absolute latest."

THE TRAINS on Sunday were not as frequent or as fast as they had been the day before, and I had to change at Reading to catch a local that seemed to take forever to get to Hungerford.

There was just one taxi waiting outside the station and I beat another would-be fare down the stairs from the platform to the road by only a little more than Integrated had won the Hennessy.

"I'm going to Lambourn," I said to the loser, a white-haired man with a walking stick, who I reckoned was in his early seventies. "Do you want to share?"

He shook his head. "No thanks, I'm going the other way."

I was half inclined to allow the older man to take the taxi, but I was in serious danger of missing Dave altogether if I was delayed any more. Rather ashamedly, I climbed in and slammed the door shut.

"I'm the only taxi working in Hungerford today," said the driver as we drove away. "He'll be there for quite a while—until I get back, I shouldn't wonder."

Was the driver trying to make me feel even worse? If so, he was succeeding.

THE TAXI pulled up in front of Dave's front door, which was wide open.

I was tempted to ask the driver to wait for me, but then I thought about the old man waiting at the station. So I paid the fare and the taxi hurried away, spinning its wheels slightly on the gravel driveway. Dave would have to give me a lift to a station on his way to the Towcester races.

"Anyone in?" I called through the open door.

There was no answer.

I stepped through the door and shouted again. "Dave. It's me, Jeff."

No reply. Perhaps he hadn't heard me. It was a big house that Dave had once shared with an attractive young wife and the hope and expectation of having children, but she had long ago left him and now he lived alone in this mansion.

I went down the long hallway to the kitchen. That too was deserted.

"Dave," I called again loudly.

Still no reply.

He must be in the sauna, I thought. That's why he can't hear me.

I opened the door from the back hall into the garage and I could instantly feel the heat, and the door to the sauna was open.

I took off my quilted anorak and hung it over the handlebars of a bicycle.

"Dave," I called again. "It's Jeff."

I walked over and put my head through the sauna door. No one was in there.

I was just about to turn around when a heavy shove from behind sent me sprawling forward onto the hot wooden benches.

"Hey!" I shouted. "What are you doing?"

But no one answered. The only sound was of the wooden door of the sauna being slammed shut behind me.

I tried to push it open but it wouldn't move.

"Open the door," I said loudly, banging on it with my fist.

There was no response.

"Dave, please open the door." I used a much more measured and reasonable tone, but still no answer.

I was hot. Damn hot.

I removed the cashmere sweater I had put on to ward off the late-November chill, but it made no difference to the searing heat in my nose, mouth and chest.

The readout of the thermometer on the wall showed 110 Celcius, five degrees hotter than when I had been in this sauna the previous day and that had been almost more than I could bear then.

I pushed hard on the door, but it wouldn't move so much as a millimeter.

"Open the bloody door," I shouted once more. Again, no reply.

I could hear footsteps. Someone was moving about in the garage.

"Dave," I shouted, "is that you? Let me out. It's too damn hot in here."

Again, no reply, but I knew someone was there. I could hear the garage door being opened.

"Let me out," I shouted again, this time banging my fist on the wooden wall of the sauna.

A car engine was started close by, the noise of it suddenly filling the space around me. The smooth hum of the Mercedes, I thought, not the roar of the Jaguar. The volume of it diminished as the car was reversed out of the garage, and dropped considerably more as I heard the garage door being closed again.

"Let me out," I shouted once more while banging on the sauna's door, but nobody did.

My anxiety level rose considerably when I heard the car being driven away—whoever had shut me into this furnace was leaving me here.

I patted my pant pockets, hopeful of finding my phone, but I knew it was in my coat and that was hanging on the bicycle in the garage outside.

By this time, I was sweating profusely and my clothes were becoming wet and clinging to my body. I peeled off my shirt, pants, shoes and socks so that I was wearing only my underpants, but it did nothing to cool me down. If anything, the effort required made me feel even hotter.

I needed to get out of this heat, and soon.

I could already feel my heart pumping rapidly in my chest as it sent blood to my extremities to try to cool my core temperature. Sadly, far from cooling me, the heat from the sauna was making the blood under my skin even hotter and circulation was taking that heat back to my heart, further warming my core and causing the heart to beat yet faster.

It was a positive feedback loop that would be broken only when my heart gave up this no-win struggle and ceased to pump at all or my brain started to cook. Either way, I'd be dead.

I threw myself against the door, striking it with my shoulder, but again it refused to budge. I tried kicking it, to no avail. All that happened was that I became hotter still.

And I was thirsty.

There was a small wooden pail about a quarter full of water on the floor, together with a wooden ladle. I went down on my knees and used the ladle to drink some of the hot liquid. It did little to diminish the dryness of my mouth.

I had been in the sauna for only five minutes or so, but time was already running out. If I didn't get away from this heat soon, it would be too late.

OK, I thought, time for some strategy.

If I couldn't get out, I had to disable the source of the heat.

An open-topped metal box stood in the corner of the sauna, about a foot square and thirty inches high. It was full to the brim with gray rocks, each about the size of a clenched fist, and they were far too hot to touch.

I searched around the side of the box looking for an electric cable, but it was fitted tight to the corner, the power coming straight through the wall.

I tried to move the box but it was too hot to touch, so I kicked at it as hard as I could, which made no impression whatsoever.

And still it poured out heat.

Using my shirt and sweater as oven gloves, I took the rocks out, stacking them on one of the bleached wooden benches. There were twenty rocks and underneath them was a flat metal tray. I tried to get my fingers around the edges of the tray to lift it up, but it was much too hot to touch unprotected and my fingers were too big and cumbersome when covered.

I grabbed my house key from my pant pocket and used it to lever the tray up.

Below were four spiral heating elements much like those found on some electric stoves except that these were positioned vertically, as opposed to horizontally, and each was glowing red-hot.

Try as I might, I couldn't touch them even with my clothes acting as gloves. The heat cut instantly through the material, and one leg of my pants even caught fire. I used my shoe to beat out the flames on the floor.

By now, I was desperate.

If anything, removing the rocks and the tray had made things worse, as I was now feeling the radiant heat directly from the elements.

I was tempted to throw the bucket of water over the elements in hopes of causing a short circuit, but I might need that water to drink.

I picked up one of the rocks and threw it hard at the elements. One of them bent slightly, but it continued to glow.

I tried another rock and then a third. It wasn't enough.

The heat was beginning to overwhelm me and I was getting close to panic.

Calm down, I told myself, *take some deep breaths.*

I tried to take my own advice but the air was so hot it made me cough violently.

I went back to taking small, slow, shallow breaths, Somehow, the coughing fit had helped me to refocus on the matter in hand rather than on the fearsome outcome that awaited me.

I put my socks and shoes back on, stood on one of the benches and tried kicking down on the three rocks that were now sitting on top of the elements. As I did so, I could smell the rubber soles of my running shoes melting.

One of the elements went out and that gave me heart to continue.

I jumped onto the rocks with both feet, bending all the elements down.

There was an almighty flash in the box beneath me and everything went dark. I had clearly caused a short, and a fuse must have blown. The elements went out, but, unfortunately, the light fixture on the wall went out too, plunging the sauna into darkness. But that worry was more than offset by the relief of cutting off the heat.

Not that my troubles were over—not by a long way. For a start, my right leg was being burned by something inside the metal box, my core temperature remained extremely high and my heart was beating so fast it felt in danger of bursting out of my chest.

And I was still sweating buckets.

I quickly climbed out of the box, feeling my way back onto the bench and then onto the floor, where I lay down on the wooden slats. It was the coolest spot.

Gradually, the temperature began to drop.

I noticed it because, unbelievably, I began to shiver.

I searched around in the darkness for my shirt and put it on.

It was now time to get out of this prison.

4

As my eyes became accustomed to the dark, I noticed, in fact, a small amount of light in the sauna.

There was a very small gap around the door and another spot on the far side where the wooden planking of the walls must not be quite in line, allowing through a tiny sliver of illumination.

I held my watch up to the gap around the door. It read ten-thirty. I reckoned I had been in this sweatbox for about half an hour, much of that time with the temperature well above the boiling point of water, and of blood.

It was a wonder that I was still able to think at all.

But think I did.

Why would Dave Swinton lock me in his sauna with the temperature turned up to maximum and drive away? He must have known my life would have been in grave danger. Even if I'd had my phone in here with me, it would have probably taken the police more than twenty minutes to come to my aid. By that time, without me having disabled the heating elements, I would have been dead.

What did he have to gain in killing me?

True, I wouldn't then have been able to report him to the BHA Disciplinary Committee for purposely losing a race, but that would surely be the least of his difficulties with a dead body in his sauna to explain away.

It didn't make any sense.

Now I had to get out of here—maybe before Dave came back to finish off the job properly.

But how?

I tried again to shove the door open, but it didn't move. I threw all my weight against it. Still nothing.

I wondered how long it would be before anyone noticed I was missing.

It was Sunday and the offices of the BHA in London would be closed, not that it would have made any difference. Although I had a permanent desk at HQ, I spent much of my time working away from it and it was hardly unusual for me not to appear there for days, sometimes even for weeks.

A year ago, my absence would have been noted by my then fiancée, Lydia, but not anymore—Lydia was no longer a part of my life.

I suppose it was my own fault.

I had procrastinated and evaded for so long, finding it difficult to commit to marriage, that by the time I had finally got around to it, Lydia was already casting an eye elsewhere.

And I hadn't seen it coming.

I had believed all was well, apart from the fact that I knew she didn't like my job. It had become a source of increasing friction between us. She thought it was too dangerous and maybe she had a point, especially if one considered my present predicament.

But it was not as if she had given me an ultimatum or anything. There had been no *choose between me or the job* stipulation.

I had come home from work one day the previous January to find that she had simply packed up and gone.

She had left me a letter on the mantel to say that she was very sorry but she had met someone else whose job was safer and she was moving in with him—and thanks for a great five years. The envelope had also contained the engagement ring I had bought for her only eight months previously.

I remember having stood there reading the letter over and over in total disbelief. It might have taken me much too long to get around to asking her to marry me, but, having done so, I had been fully committed and we had started discussing a venue and a date for the wedding.

At first, I'd been angry.

But I was angry more with myself than with Lydia. How had I not realized? I was an investigator, for goodness' sake, accustomed to piecing together the reality from fragments of evidence, yet I hadn't spotted what had been happening right under my nose.

I had tried to get her back, but what was done was done, the trust between us had been shattered and there was no going back.

I even spent an unhealthy amount of time finding out everything I could about her new man, a commodity trader called Tony Pickering who worked at the London Metal Exchange in Leadenhall Street, at the very heart of the City of London.

I suppose I was fascinated to discover what Lydia thought he had that I didn't.

Money, for one thing. As a trader he would probably be earning several times what I was getting from the BHA. And he had a family fortune to go with it.

I tried to tell myself that it must have been more than just the money, but, if so, I couldn't see it. I would have found his job deathly boring—buying and then selling derivatives involving thousands of tons of yet to be mined copper for meaninglessly large sums in the hope that the selling price was a tiny fraction above the purchase price in order to make a "margin" and hence a profit.

He never actually saw any copper. The transaction was all on paper or on a computer and may as well have been for buttons, for all it seemed to matter.

How *could* Lydia have preferred him to me?

My wandering thoughts were brought back to reality by the ringing of my cell phone. I could hear it through the wooden walls of the sauna, tantalizingly close yet so far out of reach.

It rang six times, as always, before switching to voice mail.

I wondered who would be calling me.

Faye maybe.

Faye was my big sister, twelve years my senior, who had acted as a mother to me after our real mother had died when I was just eight. She still called me regularly to check that I was eating properly and to make sure I had washed behind my ears in spite of the fact that I was now thirty-two years old and she had more serious problems of her own to worry about.

The phone rang again.

It would be voice mail calling. Great.

THE SAUNA had been well made—far too well made for my liking.

It was a pine cube, each side being about six feet long, set on the concrete floor of the garage.

I tried to lift the whole thing, but it wouldn't move. I couldn't even shift it sideways across the floor.

Next, I tried to separate the walls in the corners, to no effect. I even lay on the top bench and tried to lift just the roof off with my feet, but it wasn't budging, even when I kicked at it ferociously.

All I did was expend a lot of energy and aggravate my thirst.

I had been trying to ration the water in the small wooden pail. I took another tiny sip.

The only movable part of the sauna was the set of wooden slats on the floor, three five-foot lengths of pine held together by three shorter crosspieces. I picked them up and used the slats as a battering ram against the door.

Nothing.

Think.

The door was probably the strongest part of the structure, with all the extra wood used to make the frame. How about one of the other sides?

I started to batter the opposite wall at the point where the thin sliver of illumination was visible, but the slats were too long and unwieldy to be able to get a decent swing.

I switched to using one of the rocks from the heater, searching through the pile until I found one with a nice sharp corner on it.

After ten good hits, I tried to convince myself that the sliver of light was bigger.

I struck the wall again and again, using both hands on the rock to apply as much force as I could. I tried my best to always hit at the same point just beneath the point of light.

After another twenty or so strikes, I took a rest. The wood was beginning to splinter. I could feel it with my fingers.

I went back at it, standing with one knee on the wooden bench to give me a better angle. Over and over I lashed out at the wood until I was sweating again as if the heat were still on.

And now the sliver of light was definitely bigger.

IT TOOK ME nearly an hour to make a hole large enough for me to get a finger through.

I put my eye up to the hole and looked out, but there wasn't much to see, just the far wall of the garage and a space where the Mercedes had been when I'd arrived. But it lifted my spirits no end that I could at last see beyond the walls of the sauna.

I went back to my hammering at the edges with the pointed rock and it wasn't that long before the hole had grown sufficiently for me to get my hand outside.

I then used one end of a floor slat as a sort of crowbar and gradually split the planking farther, both above and below the hole, until there was space enough for me to stick my head out.

By this time the sauna walls had no chance against me. I attacked the hole like a man possessed, kicking away the planking, and before long I was out, standing in the garage.

I walked around to the sauna door.

A garden fork had been jammed between the door and the garage wall with such force that the tines had dug grooves in the brickwork.

I picked up my coat from the handlebars of the bicycle and removed my phone from the pocket.

The missed call had indeed been from Faye.

I held the phone in my hand and wondered what to do.

Should I call the police?

There was no doubt in my own mind that Dave Swinton had tried to kill me, but I was worried that no one else would believe it.

I went over everything again in my head. Was there any way it could have been a mistake or an accident?

I glanced over at the garden fork, still in position holding the sauna door firmly closed. The placing of that had been no accident, no mistake. And the person who put it there had to have been aware that the sauna was switched on.

No one could have driven away from that garage and not have expected the man left in the sauna to die. The fact that I hadn't died had simply been down to dogged determination on my part and good luck.

I dialed 999 on my phone.

"Emergency, which service?"

"Police," I said. "I wish to report an attempted murder."

5

They did believe me—just—in the end.

Initially, two young uniformed policemen arrived in a patrol car. They listened intently as I described what had happened and their eyes widened slightly when I showed them the garden fork. They widened even more when they saw the hole I had made in the wall of the sauna to escape. But it was when they discovered that I was accusing one of the country's most well-known and best-loved sporting celebrities of attempted murder that reinforcements were summoned in the shape of a plainclothes officer who introduced himself as Detective Sergeant Jagger from the Thames Valley Police Major Crime Unit.

"So, Mr. Hinkley," said D.S. Jagger, "why do you think Mr. Swinton wanted to kill you?"

Why did part of me still feel a need to keep confidential what Dave had told me yesterday? I surely was under no obligation to do so. I must be absolved from any promise I had made to him to try to forget what he had said. After all, he had tried to kill me.

"I knew that he had purposely lost a horse race and I think he tried to kill me to stop me saying something to the authorities."

The detective clearly thought it was a poor motive for murder. "Are you really telling me that Mr. Swinton would risk a murder charge over something so trivial?"

I tried to point out to the policeman that purposely losing races was not trivial for a professional jockey, but he wouldn't believe it. And part of me agreed with him. Why would Dave risk a lifelong prison sentence when he knew I didn't have any real evidence that he'd stopped a horse anyway? Especially as I didn't even know which horse or race was in question.

Had he expected to come home from Towcester that evening to find me dead, remove the garden fork and then try to make out that it had been due to dreadful misfortune—he had left me in the sauna alone and I had obviously spent too long in the heat and had been overcome?

"Why don't you ask him that question?" I said.

"Oh, we will," said the detective sergeant. "Just as soon as we find him."

"He'll be at Towcester races," I said, trying to be helpful. "He has five rides there this afternoon." I looked at my watch. "The first race will be in about ten minutes."

"Mr. Swinton, so far, has not arrived at Towcester as had been expected. A request has been made to my Northamptonshire colleagues to detain him if, and when, he arrives."

"Oh," I said. Jockeys had to be at the course at least forty-five minutes before a race they were due to ride in. That put paid to my theory that Dave would continue to act as if nothing had happened and claim my death was just a terrible accident.

I had to go over my account one more time from the beginning while it was written down by a young detective constable. I was asked to read and sign the statement.

"What now?" I asked.

"You are free to go, Mr. Hinkley," D.S. Jagger said.

"Just like that?"

"It is my understanding that you have declined any medical assistance. What else do you need?"

"A lift to a railway station would be good."

He reluctantly agreed and I was dispatched with the young detective constable in an unmarked police car.

"Hungerford, do you?" he asked.

"That would be fine."

He drove in silence out of Lambourn.

"Is there much crime in these parts?" I asked.

"I'm based at Reading," he said. "There's lots of serious crime in Reading." He sounded as if he was pleased. "Rapes, murders . . . all sorts."

"Is Detective Sergeant Jagger from there too?" I asked.

He nodded. "We call him Mick," the constable said with a laugh. "But not to his face, of course. He's my guv'nor."

"Is he any good?"

He chanced a quick look at me.

"Why?"

"I want to know if I can rely on him to catch Dave Swinton," I said. "I don't want to be looking over my shoulder all the time."

"Do you really believe he shut you in that sauna on purpose to kill you?" He didn't sound as if *he* believed it.

"Yes," I said. "I do. Why otherwise would I call your lot?"

"But it seems like a strange way to try and kill someone. Not very reliable."

"Trust me," I said. "If you had been in there with the temperature at a hundred and ten Celcius, you wouldn't have thought so. I was bloody lucky to get out alive."

"Maybe. And I have to admit that bursting through the wall

like that was impressive." He laughed. "Just like the Incredible Hulk." He laughed again.

This policeman had actually seen the garden fork in position and the hole I'd had to make in the side of the sauna to escape and he was still skeptical of the danger I'd been in. What chance would I have of convincing others?

I CALLED FAYE from the train while trying to ignore the strange looks I was receiving from my fellow passengers. Had they never seen a man with a large hole burned in his pants before?

"Hi, little bro," she answered. "How are things?"

"Much the same," I said, deciding not to tell her that someone had just tried to kill me. She would only worry. "How are *you* doing?"

"I'm still alive."

It was the way she always answered that question.

Faye had cancer. To be precise, she had gallbladder cancer, even though she no longer had a gallbladder. That had been removed two years previously.

In those two years she'd had one setback when a scan had shown a small spot on her liver. More surgery and another round of chemotherapy had seemingly done the trick, but, as Faye always said, at her age you never truly survived cancer, you just held it at bay for a while in an ever-decreasing spiral dive into your grave. The slower the descent, the better, but one could never fully arrest the fall.

"But are you having a good day?" I asked.

"Moderate," she said. "Q is out playing golf, so at least I have the house to myself."

Q was Quentin, my brother-in-law, Faye's husband.

"I thought Quentin hated golf," I said.

"He does. But he's trying to ingratiate himself with some judge or other that he's playing with."

Quentin always did something for a reason and never just because he wanted to. I sometimes wondered if he married Faye only because he believed that a Queen's Counsel with a wife was somehow more suitable for elevation to the bench.

"Do you fancy a visitor?" I asked.

"Now?"

"In a couple of hours or so. I'm on a train to Paddington at the moment and I need to go to my apartment first."

"Q will be back by then."

I laughed. "It's OK, you know. I can be civil to him if I try hard enough."

Faye knew that Quentin and I tended to bring out the worst in each other. He thought of me as a dangerously liberal loose cannon, while I considered him to be a dinosaur with outdated views and opinions.

"Come to tea," she said. "It will be lovely to see you."

She hung up and I looked out of the train window as the rural fields began to give way to the urban sprawl of west London.

The events of this morning at Dave Swinton's house seemed somehow surreal and distant. Had I really been so close to death then and yet so far from it now? I felt I should be doing something about it, not simply watching the world go by.

Calling the police had never been my first instinct.

I am an investigator, so I investigate. And I'm not fond of bringing in others to do it for me.

True, attempted murder was outside my normal realm.

I was a senior investigator for the BHA, the British Horseracing Authority, and much of my work over the years had been covert, moving in a world of shadows and secrets, mysterious and furtive, to protect British racing from those who would seek to gain an unfair advantage by dubious means.

Doping, race fixing and unusual betting practices were more my concern, not assault with a deadly sauna, aided and abetted by a garden fork.

But it still seemed strange to be sitting here on a train rather than actually *doing* something. Perhaps I should be out actively looking for Dave, but what good would it do? If the police couldn't find him with all their resources, what chance would I have?

I TOOK a Bakerloo Line train from Paddington to Willesden Junction.

I'd had to move out of the home that I shared with Lydia when it was sold, but I'd rented another place just around the corner, in yet another quiet suburban northwest London street.

I suppose it was laziness on my part.

I'd seen a GROUND FLOOR APARTMENT TO RENT sign outside a house as I'd walked to the local shop for some milk and I'd gone straight in to the realtor and arranged to see it there and then.

I'd moved in the following week, cajoling my stepnephew and some of his friends to carry all my stuff the hundred yards from one abode to the next.

Eight months later, some of the boxes remained unopened in the hallway. I kept telling myself that I ought to sort everything out, but I simply didn't have the heart.

I opened my front door, stepped carefully past the boxes and went into my bedroom to change.

My phone rang.

"Hello," I said.

"Mr. Hinkley," said a voice. "D.S. Jagger here. Have you seen the news?"

"No," I said. "I've only just got back home."

"It would appear that Mr. Swinton has been found. Or, at least, his car has been."

"Where?"

"Otmoor."

"And where is that?" I asked.

"Between Oxford and Bicester. It's mostly a nature reserve. Mr. Swinton's Mercedes was discovered in a remote part of the moor used by the military for firing live ammunition. It has been burned out. It was the fire that attracted attention to the vehicle. Smoke was visible from a nearby farm and the fire department was called by the farmer."

"You're sure it's Dave Swinton's car?"

"Yes, quite sure. In spite of the intensity of the fire, Mr. Swinton's personalized license plate was clearly visible to the senior fireman when he arrived at the scene."

"And Dave Swinton himself?" I asked.

"A body was discovered in the car. At this time, there has been no identification of the remains, but . . ." He tailed off.

"You assume it is Mr. Swinton?"

"That would seem to be the obvious conclusion. Based on what you told us in Lambourn. It will be up to the Oxford Coroner to officially determine the identity of the victim and the cause of death. I thought you would like to hear the news from us rather than from the media."

"Thank you," I said numbly.

"Bloody journalists," the policeman said. "A local news channel was monitoring the fire department's radio and they dispatched a cameraman to the scene. He arrived even before the first engine. It would seem that the personalized license plate, together with Mr. Swinton's unexpected failure to appear at Towcester races this afternoon, has turned a local story into national news."

I sat down on the end of my bed in a state of shock.

"Was it the fire that killed him?" I asked.

"It's too early to say for sure. That will be determined by the autopsy. The flames were very intense and an accelerant appears to have been used."

"Accelerant?" I said.

"Gasoline. Or some other highly flammable substance."

How horrible.

"You will almost certainly be required to give evidence at the inquest," the policeman said, "as you were probably the last person to see him alive."

"Other than whoever killed him," I said.

"We believe it may have been suicide."

"Setting oneself alight with gasoline seems to be a particularly unpleasant way of doing it," I said.

"People who kill themselves often do unpredictable things. *Self-immolation*, as it's known, is surprisingly common in some parts of the world."

But not in rural Oxfordshire, I thought.

I found it difficult to believe that Dave Swinton could have taken his own life in any manner, let alone that way. He'd had such spirit, such joie de vivre.

"What makes you think he may have killed himself?" I asked.

"I'm not saying he did. It is just one of the options. But it has all the hallmarks of a suicide. There's no evidence pointing at anyone else being present; you told us he had problems with his job; he must have known he'd be in serious trouble for shutting you in that sauna, maybe even facing a murder charge; in his own car; at a deserted spot far from prying eyes—suicides generally prefer to do it alone."

It sounded to me like the perfect place for a murder, but maybe that was just the way my mind worked. There may have been other things D.S. Jagger knew but wasn't telling me. I could tell from the tone of his voice that *he* believed it was suicide.

"I am sure someone will be in touch with you soon about the inquest," said the detective as a way of signing off.

He hung up.

I turned on the television.

The news coverage of the fire was the lead story with video images from the scene shown in all their horror.

The rear end of the Mercedes was largely untouched by the flames and the 121 DSS of the license plate was visible in the footage, but the interior of the car was ablaze, with flames roaring out of the open windows on both sides. In the center of the raging inferno, burned almost beyond recognition as being human, sat a figure in the driver's seat.

It was sickening.

The commentary that accompanied the ghastly pictures gave little room for doubt. "A Mercedes with the registration 121 DSS is registered to top steeplechase jockey Dave Swinton, winner of last year's Sportsman of the Year award. Mr. Swinton did not attend Towcester racetrack this afternoon, where he had been expected to ride in several races. Police are treating the death as unexplained, but are not actively looking for anyone else in connection with it at this time."

The media must have been briefed by Detective Sergeant Jagger.

I watched on the screen as two firemen with hoses were shown approaching the vehicle, but it was some time before they made any noticeable impression on the firestorm, such was the intensity of the flames.

My phone rang again.

"Jeff? It's Paul. Have you seen the dreadful news about Dave Swinton?"

Paul Maldini was head of operations in the Integrity Department of the BHA and my immediate boss. It was very unlike him to call me on a Sunday.

"I'm watching it now," I said. "Appalling, isn't it?"

"Really awful," he agreed. "I can't believe it." He paused. "Find out what you can, will you?"

"In what way?" I asked.

"Make sure there's nothing that will come back to bite us in racing."

"Do you think there might be?"

"I've no idea, but it can't be good for the sport for our pinup boy to end up as a human torch."

"No," I agreed.

"So just have a look, will you?" he said. "Root around a bit, in your usual confidential manner, and get back to me."

I wondered how much I should tell Paul at this stage about my conversations with Dave in the sauna and in his car.

Paul Maldini was never the most subtle of men. If I told him that the champion jockey had admitted not winning a race on purpose, he would initiate a full-scale investigation and any chance of having a *Root around a bit, in my usual confidential manner,* would be lost. If I also told him that Dave had actually tried to kill me, he would have had the whole department mobilized and blundering around like bulls in a china shop. The chances of finding out the truth would be lost forever.

I'd probably tell him in the end, but just not yet.

I'd been in trouble before for not telling Paul everything I was thinking or doing right away, but I had good reason to be reticent. He was very good at the day-to-day nitty-gritty of the Integrity Service—checking that runners in races were actually the horses they were said to be, ensuring the smooth running of the drug testing of the winners, checking that trainers and jockeys conformed to the administrative rules for racing and the like. However, he had little or no understanding of the undercover work I was usually occupied with.

Things to him were either black or white, never gray.

I was gaining a reputation for keeping those in racing on the straight and narrow, not by stewards' inquiries and bold publicity after some wrongdoing, but by quiet words and gentle warnings before any formal proceedings were warranted. Not that I didn't write formal reports—I did. But sometimes, to Paul's huge annoyance, the identification of the individuals concerned was somewhat vague and ambiguous.

"I saw Dave at Newbury yesterday," I said to Paul. "We spoke briefly."

"Did he give you any indication he intended to kill himself?"

"None at all," I said. "And we don't know for sure that he did."

"Looks like it to me," he said. "What else could it be?"

Murder, I thought, but didn't say so. "We don't even know for certain that it was Dave Swinton in that burning car."

"Who else would it be?" Paul said. "It was his car."

"I suppose the autopsy will tell us," I said, "if there's enough left of him to work with."

I shuddered once more as the news channel again showed the burning car, even if the TV company had now belatedly edited out the most gruesome images.

"Just let me know if you turn up anything that could be harmful to the reputation of racing."

"OK," I said. "Will do."

He hung up.

I went on watching the news coverage, transfixed by the awfulness of the situation.

The reporters assumed it was suicide, but the big question that they kept asking, and that no one could answer, was *WHY would Dave Swinton kill himself?*

Why indeed? Surely throwing a race was not reason enough, even if he had admitted it to me.

So-called experts were dragged in front of the TV cameras to discuss depression and how a seemingly highly successful person could have so many private demons that it drove him to end everything.

Not that Dave would be the first, not by a long shot. There was an extensive roll of A-list Hollywood actors, best-selling novelists, chart-topping musicians, as well as medal-winning sportsmen, who had all taken their own lives.

There had even been a previous suicide of a top jockey when Fred Archer, the sporting superstar of his generation, winner of over two and a half thousand races and thirteen times champion jockey on the flat, shot himself in 1886, aged just twenty-nine.

But, somehow, the television images made this suicide seem worse than those that had gone before. It had been shown in all its horror and misery.

The pinup boy of British racing—that's how Paul Maldini had referred to Dave Swinton and it was an accurate description.

His death was something that wouldn't send just ripples through racing, it would be a tsunami.

6

Faye didn't look very well when she opened the front door of her house overlooking Richmond Green.

"Are you OK?" I asked with concern.

"You know that I have good days and not-so-good days?" she said. "Well, this is one of the not-so-good, that's all. It's all to do with the drugs I have to take. They make me feel sick."

"I thought you were off the chemo."

"I am. These are drugs designed to boost my red blood count. The chemo does more than kill the cancer—apparently, it's not too good for my bone marrow either." She sighed. "Such is life . . . and death. Anyway, enough about me. What have you been up to?"

"Same old stuff," I said to her. "Nothing very interesting."

Nothing very interesting except someone trying to kill me.

We went through into her kitchen.

"Tea?" she asked. "Or coffee? Or would you prefer wine?"

I looked at my watch. It was twenty past four.

"It's never too early on a Sunday," Faye said, smiling. "I'd like some."

"Great," I said. "So would I."

She took a bottle of sauvignon blanc from the fridge and poured two generous glasses.

"I need this," she said. "Somehow, alcohol helps reduce the feeling of nausea I get from the pills. I often have a brandy if it gets too bad."

"Why don't you take the pills with a glass of brandy?" I said. "Then you probably won't feel sick in the first place."

She laughed. "I can hardly have a glass of brandy to take pills when I wake up in the morning."

"Why not?" I said. "It must be better than feeling ill all day."

She laughed again. "Perhaps I'll try it, though I'm not sure what Q would say."

"Tell him it's medicinal."

"What's medicinal?" Quentin asked, coming into the kitchen.

"Having brandy for breakfast," I said.

"British soldiers in the First World War were given tots of rum for breakfast," Quentin said. "And most of the officers had cases of brandy sent out to them from home. Or whisky. Masses of it. It helped them cope."

"So were they all drunk when they went over the top?"

"Absolutely," Quentin said. "A double ration of rum was issued to the men before they were off. Otherwise, they wouldn't have gone."

"There you are," I said to Faye with a smile. "So you *can* have brandy for breakfast."

"To help me cope?" She burst into tears.

It was a reminder of how close to the edge Faye's life had become, always living in dread of a return of the cancer. Treatment was ever more effective and the statistics were steadily improving, but, deep down, even those patients given the final all clear from the disease lived with the fear that it would get them, in the end. That it would only be a matter of time. This year, next year, sometime—but not *never.*

I waited a second for Quentin to move, but, when he didn't, I went over and put my arm around Faye's shoulders.

"I'm sorry," she said, dabbing her eyes with a tissue. "Occasionally, it all gets to be too much."

"You have nothing to be sorry about," I said. "It's us who should be sorry for making light of something so serious."

Faye took a deep breath. "I'm fine now," she said. "Now, what would you like for tea?"

THE THREE OF US ate hot buttered crumpets, washed down not with Earl Grey but with sauvignon blanc.

I felt the whole situation was unreal. Just six hours ago, I had been fighting for my life and yet here I was genteelly eating crumpets in Richmond upon Thames.

"Quentin," I said between mouthfuls, "what's the maximum prison sentence for attempted murder?"

"Life," he said confidently. "Attempted murder, by definition, indicates a conscious resolve to take someone's life. In fact, time served in jail can sometimes be longer for attempted murder than for murder itself. Some murder convictions occur when there was no desire to cause a death—for example, when the accused only intends to injure but the victim then dies. But intent to actually kill is crucial and is a requirement for an *attempted* murder conviction." Quentin never answered a question in five words if fifty could be used. "Why do you ask?"

"No real reason," I said. "It's just something to do with a case I'm investigating for the BHA."

He lost interest. Racing was not high on Quentin's agenda, as he regularly told me. He considered all sport to be the recreation of the proletariat and not worthy of someone of his standing.

"And how was your game of golf this morning?" I asked pointedly.

"Humph!" he snorted. "What a waste of time."

"Did you win?" I asked, enjoying his discomfort.

"No," he said. "The Lord Chief Justice won, but only because I let him. I had no idea he was so bad at golf. I thought I was the world's worst player, but even I had to four-putt from eight feet on the last green to ensure he won by a stroke."

I laughed.

"It's not that funny," he said. "I was trying to get myself noticed."

I actually thought that Quentin Calderfield, QC, couldn't fail to get himself noticed. He was one of the most successful and flamboyant Queen's Counsels around. QC, QC, was how he was known by everyone at the Bar, but he was also renowned for some of his conservative opinions.

But what he really meant by getting himself noticed was that he was trying to get himself promoted to judge—in his assessment, a promotion well overdue. It seemed never to occur to him that some of his more old-fashioned views on modern life, in particular to do with sexuality and race, may have been a factor in his current omission from the bench.

"And were you noticed?" I asked.

Quentin clearly didn't like the tone of my voice, which, in truth, was slightly mocking. "We will have to wait and see," he said, tight-lipped. He then excused himself and went back to his study.

"I wish you two got on better," Faye said after he'd gone.

"We get on all right," I said, although it wasn't true. "And I'll definitely call him if I ever need a lawyer."

"Do you think that you will need a lawyer?" she asked.

"Probably one day."

She pulled a face at me. She didn't like my line of work.

"Do you want to stay for supper?"

I knew that she was only asking because she felt sorry for me. Lydia's departure had been almost as big a disappointment for Faye as it had been for me. She desperately wanted me to be happy and saw it as her job to get me married off before she succumbed to the cancer. In her eyes, Lydia would have made the perfect sister-in-law.

"Thanks, but no thanks. I'd better get back."

I wondered why I'd said that. My apartment would be cold and lonely. I'd become used to domestic life as a couple and I missed the homey comforts of having a mate, especially one who enjoyed cooking as much as Lydia had.

"You're welcome to stay," Faye said. "We're only having pasta and pesto. I can easily make enough for three."

"OK," I said. "Pasta and pesto would be lovely."

DAVE SWINTON'S apparent suicide was the only topic of conversation at the BHA offices on Monday morning and there was genuine sadness among the staff.

Dave had been popular with everyone in racing, not least because of his famed good looks together with the humility that had accompanied his stunning ability on a horse. The previous December there had been a huge surge of support from the racing community to vote for him in the Sportsman of the Year contest and it had carried him to an easy victory. It was something that had given the whole of racing a boost.

There was not only sorrow for his loss but also bewilderment that he could kill himself, and especially in such a horrendous fashion.

"But why would he do such a thing?" said one of the young female receptionists, who was in tears. "He surely had everything to live for."

I decided not to enlighten her about Dave's attempt to kill me. Not so much out of any sense of not wishing to speak ill of the dead or to add to her pain, but more because I doubted that she would believe me. In fact, I reckoned that no one would believe me, so I kept quiet.

While the collective grief caused others to spill out into corridors and stairwells to share their anguish, I shut myself away in my office and spent the morning studying the videos of all the races that Dave Swinton had ridden in but not won during the preceding week.

I thought back to what he had said to me in his Jaguar at the Newbury races: *I had twenty-eight rides and ten winners last week, so I lost eighteen races.*

Finding the eighteen races was easy using the BHA database and I watched the RaceTech video recordings of each of them.

Dave had finished second in six, third in four and had not placed in the other eight, falling in two of them, once at the last fence when clear in front.

I watched all the available footage, including the side and head-on angles, but there was nothing I could see that indicated that a horse had been prevented from winning on purpose. That was not to say it hadn't happened. Dave Swinton was a genius in the saddle and I was sure that if he had wanted to lose a race deliberately, he could have done so in such a manner that no one would have easily been able to spot it.

I studied the starting prices to see if there was a particularly unusual result, but that line of inquiry wasn't especially fruitful, not least because such was his following among the punters that all Dave Swinton's mounts tended to start at much shorter prices than their past form might warrant. Indeed, of the eighteen horses on which Dave had failed to win last week, fourteen had started as favorites or joint favorites.

I delved further into the archives, looking at the recordings of other races, to compare how his recent mounts had run previously.

After four hours glued to the screen, I came up with three possibles, although I had my doubts about each of them.

The first was at Haydock Park the previous Saturday. He'd ridden a horse called Garrick Party to third place in a three-mile chase. There was little or no doubt that, going to and after the last fence, Dave had tried his best to achieve the best possible result, but the damage had already been done by then.

Garrick Party was a well-known front runner who had won a couple of races before by setting off in front and trying to hold on to a lead all the way to the line. Timeform described him as being "one-paced, with no finishing turn-of-foot."

As far as I could tell from the database, Dave had ridden him in three of his previous runs, including one of the victories. On all those occasions, he had set off in front and established a lead, in one case such a lead that at the halfway point in the race he had been a whole fence ahead of the other horses.

Why, then, at Haydock, had Dave opted to ride a waiting race, holding him up in the pack in a slowly run affair?

The racetrack stewards on the day had called in both trainer and jockey to explain the running of the horse. According to the notes in the file, the stewards had accepted the explanation offered that the horse had been held back due to a concern that the heavy going would have burned him out too quickly in such a long race if he had been allowed to run so freely in the early stages.

But the horse had run exactly in that manner, and won, in a three-mile chase at Fontwell Park in September when the ground had been almost waterlogged and the going was described as "bottomless." And Dave Swinton had ridden it that day too.

The second possible race had been at Ludlow two days after the one at Haydock. Dave had ridden a horse called Chiltern Line and he had become badly boxed in on the final turn and had been forced to drop back to get around other horses. He had subsequently failed to make up the lost ground, finishing second by half a length.

The only thing that made it of note was that Dave Swinton was such a good tactician in a race that getting himself badly boxed in was something almost unheard of. If it had been almost anyone else in the saddle, I wouldn't have looked at it twice.

Had Dave allowed himself to get boxed in on purpose? But if he'd been determined not to win the race, how could he have been sure that he would be boxed in? Perhaps that was the genius of the man.

The third race was the one in which he had fallen at the last fence, even though part of me couldn't understand how anyone, stuntmen aside, would cause a horse to fall on purpose, especially when the fall in question had been such a bad one.

Dave had been well in front on a horse called Newton Creek

in a novice chase, also at Ludlow, when he had asked the horse to shorten and put in an extra stride when coming toward the last fence. The horse had run only once before over fences and was still very green in his jumping. The message for an extra stride got through to him far too late, which then left him perilously close to the fence. Newton Creek did his best to rise but caught the obstacle square across his shoulders, causing Dave Swinton to be ejected forward from the saddle. The horse, meanwhile, completed a spectacular half somersault over the fence before landing heavily on his back.

Dave had been extremely fortunate not to have had half a ton of horse landing right on top of him.

The only reason I was slightly suspicious was that, in my opinion, there had been no need to put in the extra stride in the first place. Again, it was the proven consummate skill of the jockey that made me think that either Dave had not been concentrating properly or he had caused the horse to fall on purpose.

But falls of that nature were almost always nasty, so why anyone would cause one intentionally was beyond me. Maybe it had been out of desperation not to win. Such was the severity of the fall that, according to the stewards' official report of the race, Newton Creek had lain, winded and motionless, on the ground for nearly five minutes. The spectators in the stands must have feared the worst before the horse finally rose to his feet and walked away.

I leaned back in my chair and surveyed the notes I had made.

Was one of these races really fixed? The more I studied them, the less certain I became that anything untoward had occurred at all. But, then, Dave Swinton's skill on a horse was such that it was never going to be easy to spot an intentional indiscretion on his part.

DETECTIVE SERGEANT JAGGER from the Thames Valley Police called me at home at seven o'clock on Monday evening, but he wasn't able to give me much of an update. In fact, he was really only calling to tell me that the police investigation into my attempted murder had been placed on hold pending their inquiries into the vehicle fire at Otmoor.

"The human remains in the car have now been removed and taken to the morgue at John Radcliffe Hospital in Oxford for an autopsy. There is still no word as yet on an official identification. There will have to be DNA tests."

"I'm amazed that any DNA would survive that inferno."

"You'd be surprised," he said. "I know of an instance a couple of years ago where residual DNA testing was carried out on the ashes in an urn of a fully cremated body. To test for paternity, can you believe?"

"Did it work?"

"Yes, it did. Seems they were able to extract enough material from the dental pulp of a tooth that hadn't completely disintegrated."

"So you're confident they will identify the person in the burning Mercedes?"

"I'm certain of it. DNA has already been collected from Mr. Swinton's parents for comparison."

"So you are assuming, then, that it was Dave Swinton in the car?"

There was a significant pause on the other end of the line.

"Are you suggesting that it wasn't?"

"I'm keeping an open mind on the matter," I said. "I feel that Dave Swinton was the most unlikely candidate for suicide I've ever come across. So I just wondered if it might have been someone else."

"That's mere speculation."

"Maybe, but Dave Swinton *had* tried to kill me. Why did he do that? Was it to stop me telling anyone about him deliberately losing a race? But why would he bother if he'd already planned to kill himself?"

"He could have been protecting his reputation for posterity."

"Don't be stupid. His reputation would be in tatters anyway. Better to be known as a race fixer than a murderer."

"He might have decided to kill himself only after he had left you to die in the sauna, by which time it was too late to go back."

"Now who's speculating?"

"But who else could it be?" he asked.

"Don't you have any other missing persons on your files?"

"Several. But none who have the slightest connection with David Swinton's Mercedes. And if it wasn't him in the car, then where is he?"

It was a good question.

7

On Tuesday morning, I caught the nine-thirty train from Kings Cross to Newark and then took a taxi to Southwell racetrack, arriving there just before eleven o'clock.

The first race was not until a quarter past noon, but I wanted to speak to a couple of the trainers before they became too busy dealing with their horses.

One of them was Jason Butcher, who also trained Garrick Party, the renowned front runner that had finished third at Haydock. According to the *Racing Post*, Jason had runners in both the first and third races, so I hung around outside the weighing room waiting for him to arrive.

All the talk was still about Dave Swinton. He had been due to ride at Southwell that afternoon and people were still saying that they couldn't believe he was gone, and much of the talk reflected sympathy for him.

"Poor man, fancy being driven to do that," I heard one man say.

"I reckon it was his continuous dieting that was to blame," said his companion. "Lack of food probably affected his brain. Just like with Fred Archer."

"That was over a hundred years ago," replied the first man. "You do talk such bloody nonsense."

"You mark my words—it was starving himself all the time that was responsible."

He may have had a point. I'd seen firsthand what a struggle it had been. And it hadn't just been the lack of food. Dave Swinton had lived in a permanent state of dehydration. Had that disturbed the balance of his mind?

My thoughts were interrupted by the arrival of Jason Butcher, who came bounding toward the weighing room to declare his runner in the first.

"Jason Butcher?" I said to him as he went to go past me.

He stopped. "Who wants to know?"

"My name is Jeff Hinkley. I work for the BHA."

I held out my credentials and he looked at them.

"I've heard of you," he said. "Weren't you involved in all that extortion business at the BHA a couple of years ago?"

I nodded, slightly taken aback that he knew about it.

"What do you want of me?" he asked.

"Just a short word. I'll wait while you go and make your declaration."

He didn't look especially happy and I didn't really blame him. Just like the gateman at Newbury, no one likes someone in authority, especially someone in authority asking them questions.

I waited outside until he reappeared.

"Now, what's all this about?" he asked with just a slight nervous timbre to his voice.

"It's about Garrick Party," I said. "Specifically, it's about the race at Haydock the Saturday before last in which Garrick Party finished third."

If he was unduly worried, he didn't show it.

"What about it?"

"I understand you were interviewed by the stewards and asked about the running of the horse."

"Bloody ridiculous," he said.

"What was?"

"Dave bloody Swinton." He lowered his voice. "Perhaps one shouldn't speak badly about him at the moment, but he was right out of order."

"In what way?"

"He should have been aware that old Garrick likes to make the running and has a finish only as fast as my grandmother on her walker, but oh, no, he suddenly thinks at Haydock he knows better. Holds the old boy up for a run from the second last. I ask you. The man's a bloody idiot."

"Did you actually tell him how to ride the horse?" I asked.

He raised his eyebrows toward his hairline and lowered his voice even more. "You never *tell* Dave Swinton anything. If you are lucky enough for him to condescend to ride your horses, you have to sit back and watch them run as *he* thinks fit. He reckoned he knows best, and mostly he does. But not with old Garrick, that's for sure—even though he'd ridden him several times before as a front runner and won."

"Did he say anything to you afterward?"

"He made some absurd excuse about thinking the horse would run better in heavy going if he was held up. It was all utter garbage yet the stewards seemed to accept it. Maybe he believed it himself but I'll tell you now he won't be riding old Garrick next time out." He stopped and blushed slightly as he realized what he'd just said. "No, I suppose he won't anyway."

"What did the owner say?"

"Silly old fool. It was his idea to ask Swinton to ride the horse in the first place. Thought it gave him some sort of kudos to have the champion jockey riding his horse. Stupid nonsense. And it's not the first time I blame Swinton for not winning on one of my horses."

"Explain," I said.

"About three weeks ago, he rode a novice hurdler for me at Doncaster, horse called Perambulator. In my opinion, Swinton got the tactics all wrong and left it far too late at the end to make his run. Beaten by a head, we were, but Pram was the fastest finisher by a streak. He'd have won if the post had been just a couple of yards farther away. He should have won that race, easy." There was real bitterness in his voice and I wondered how much he had gambled and lost.

"But things like that happen in racing all the time," I said.

"Well, they shouldn't. Not when you've paid the extra to have the maestro riding for you." His tone was sarcastic and clearly reflected what had been said to him, probably by Dave Swinton himself.

"Extra?" I asked.

"Yeah. The extra cash he demands to ride one of your horses."

"How much extra?" I asked.

"A jump jockey's fee is just over a hundred and sixty pounds for each ride. But if you want D. Swinton in the saddle, it'd cost you the same again in readies. He even has the nerve to call it a present—*Let's just call it a gift, shall we?* he'd say."

I wondered if those were the "gifts" Dave had been referring to when he'd been talking about his taxes.

"And I'll tell you another thing," Jason Butcher said, looking around him to check that no one else was listening, "racing will be much better off without him."

Unlike nearly everyone else, Jason Butcher was obviously not a fan of the deceased champion jockey, if indeed it was Dave Swinton dead in the burning Mercedes.

I WATCHED from the grandstand as Jason Butcher's horse just failed to win the first race, beaten in the mud by a fast-finishing animal carrying fifteen pounds less weight.

The trainer wasn't happy. He stood in the space reserved for second, bunching his fists and looking daggers toward the jockey. He was someone who undoubtedly always blamed the pilot rather than the machine. Not that he was alone. Many punters are convinced that it is the horse's doing when it wins but the jockey's fault when it loses.

I went in search of another trainer, Thomas Cheek, who trained Chiltern Line, the horse that had failed to win under Dave Swinton at Ludlow due to being boxed in on the rails. He had a runner later in the day in the feature race.

I found him sitting with an elderly couple at a table in the Owners & Trainers Bar.

"Thomas Cheek?" I asked.

"Tom," he said.

"My name is Jeff Hinkley. I work for the BHA." I showed him my credentials. "I'd like to ask you a few questions."

He read the word INVESTIGATOR printed on the card and, as was always the case with everyone, he wasn't too happy.

"What about?"

I looked at his two companions.

"It's all right," he said. "I've nothing to hide from Mr. and Mrs. Valdemon. They own Peach of a Day that runs in the fourth."

"I want to ask you about the running of Chiltern Line in a handicap chase at Ludlow on November nineteenth."

"What about it?" he asked. "He finished second behind Taximan."

I nodded. "I watched the race video. Were you happy with the result?"

"I'd have preferred it if he'd won, obviously, but he ran above his rating, so I can't complain."

"Were you happy about the way he was ridden?"

"I suppose so. Dave Swinton rode him." He opened his hands, palms up, as if to say how could he possibly complain about the late champion jockey?

"But the horse was badly boxed in coming round the final bend and had to drop back before making his run."

"I know," he said, "but I'd told Dave Swinton that Chiltern Line liked to run close to the rail. Always does at home, so it may have been my fault he was in that position."

I wasn't completely convinced, but there seemed to be nothing further to say on the matter.

"Well, that's all," I said. "Thank you for your time."

"No problem," Tom said, and Mr. and Mrs. Valdemon smiled.

I began to turn away but then turned back to face him. "Just one last thing. Did Dave Swinton ever ask you for an extra 'gift' to ride your horses?"

He blushed.

"In what way?" he asked, but he knew exactly in what way I was talking about.

"As an extra riding fee?"

"Why would he do that?"

"Look," I said. "I know he asked others. I just want to know if he asked you. It's not against the Rules of Racing." At least, I didn't think so, even though any unregistered payments in cash were always frowned upon, and maybe they did break one or the other of the myriad obscure BHA regulations.

"He called me and said he'd ride my horses, but he wanted an extra hundred and fifty pounds each time to ride them. I said I wouldn't pay that—I couldn't afford it—so I told him I'd get someone else to ride them. But then he said he'd do it for just a hundred, and an additional cut of any prize money."

"How big an additional cut?" I asked.

"As much again as the rules state, paid in cash to him as a gift. I had to get my owners to agree, as they had to pay it."

Mr. and Mrs. Valdemon nodded at me in unison.

"We thought it was worth it to get his services," said Mrs. Valdemon in a soft Black Country accent. "He won two races for us before." She squeezed her husband's hand. "And he should have been riding Peach of a Day for us this afternoon. It is such a dreadful thing to have happened to him, isn't it?"

"Indeed it is," I agreed.

I left the three of them to their drinks and went outside to watch the second race from the grandstand—a not very exciting-looking two-and-a-half-mile novice hurdle race for conditional jockeys.

Inexperienced riders on inexperienced horses—not surprisingly, it was a recipe for disaster.

Southwell racetrack is a flat oval with two long stretches joined by sharp semicircular bends. It is just over a mile around, which means that in a two-and-a-half-mile race the horses have to complete two and a bit full circuits. Hence, the start was between the second last and final hurdles.

The seven runners jumped off fairly well and, as is always the way in novice hurdle races, they clattered their way noisily over the first obstacle.

As they passed in front of the grandstand for the first time, one of them tried to dive back down the chute toward the parade ring and the stables. The poor fresh-faced jockey was caught completely unawares and was unceremoniously dumped onto the turf in full view of the meager crowd, much to the enjoyment of most.

The remaining six continued on their way around the sharp turn and down the back stretch, negotiating the hurdles with little drama.

That was reserved for later.

Two of the young jockeys obviously couldn't count up to three and rode out a finish between them when there was still a whole circuit of the course to complete. Their embarrassment was compounded when they both pulled up and put their arms around each other as if they had just finished the Grand National.

That left four who made heavy weather of the final mile, one horse falling in the back stretch and another unseating its rider at the second last hurdle. So, just two of the seven lasted the course to contest a finish, but at least they did manage to provide some decent entertainment for those in the stands.

In a flurry of hands, heels, elbows and knees, they were finally separated only by a photograph, and, in truth, despite their less than stylish techniques, neither of them deserved to lose. The two jockeys received a good hand as their mounts were led back to the unsaddling enclosure, which is more than could be said for the others, who sneaked back to the changing room in disgrace.

I STAYED to watch Peach of a Day run second in the day's featured steeplechase.

He ran well enough, but the replacement jockey had kept him slightly off the pace for too long and the horse had just been unable to make up the deficit in the run to the line from the last fence.

Mr. and Mrs. Valdemon appeared rather disappointed as they listened to the excuses.

Maybe they felt that paying Dave Swinton his extra "gift" in cash would have been worth it to get the win, if only he had been alive to receive it.

Were they wrong?

Not one bit.

Racing was *all* about the winning.

There were no plaudits for coming in second.

8

"It was definitely Mr. David Swinton in the burning Mercedes. We now have a positive identification of the remains."

"Oh," I said.

D.S. Jagger called me at eight o'clock on Wednesday morning as I was in the shower.

"Did the DNA match?" I asked.

"In the end, we didn't need to resort to DNA. Mr. Swinton had twice broken his right leg in racing falls, once above and once below the knee. On both occasions, surgeons had inserted a titanium plate in the leg. The two plates had serial numbers stamped on them and the numbers matched those on similar plates found in the remains. There is no doubt."

"Thank you for letting me know."

"This call is also to inform you officially that, as a result of the formal identification of the body of Mr. Swinton, there will be no further investigation into the events in the sauna at his home on Sunday morning."

"Yes, I understand."

"But those events may well have had a material bearing on his death and, as the last-known person to see him alive, you will almost certainly be called as a witness at the inquest."

"I didn't actually see him. He pushed me into the sauna from behind and slammed the door shut before I could turn round."

"Nevertheless, you should expect a summons from the coroner in due course."

"Are you sure it was suicide?" I asked. "Burning to death with gasoline is a particularly nasty way to kill oneself." I shivered again at the memory of the TV images of the figure sitting among the flames.

"Is there such a thing as a *nice way*?" he said. "All I can say is that, bearing in mind what he did to you and what you've told us, we are currently not looking for anyone else in regard to the death."

"Is that policespeak for *Yes, it was suicide*?"

"I suppose it is."

"How about the gasoline? Where did he get that?"

"An empty metal gas can was discovered in the burned-out vehicle. It matched a second one found in Mr. Swinton's garage that was full. Mr. Swinton's gardener has confirmed that two such cans were used to store fuel for the lawn mower and that he, the gardener, had filled both the cans the previous week."

So he had taken the gas from his own garage.

"Not much doubt, then."

"No."

He hung up and I stood there, still dripping water on my bedroom carpet.

So Dave had been the body in the car. So much for my crazy theory that it was someone else. But it still didn't make sense.

If he had taken the can of gas from his garage, he knew before he left home what he was going to do. And yet he had still left me to die in the sauna.

Was he such a heartless man?

That was not the Dave Swinton that people knew and loved. All he'd had to do was flick off the electricity. He hadn't needed to let me out so I could stop him.

I'd thought of him as my friend. Had I been so wrong?

And why drive nearly an hour to Otmoor to set himself on fire?

There were plenty of isolated spots on the Downs above Lambourn where no one would have interrupted him.

Had he gone to Otmoor for a specific purpose, perhaps to meet someone?

I SPENT the rest of the day at the BHA headquarters in High Holborn.

The news of the positive identification of the body in the car had been reported to the media and it gradually filtered through the office grapevine. No one was surprised, but it didn't exactly help lift the sense of gloom that had descended on the place.

Dave Swinton had been due to be in the offices that Wednesday for a meeting of the Racing Needs You! campaign. Everyone had been looking forward to it, and a buffet lunch had been planned for the staff to meet him.

It was most unusual for the stars of the sport to make such visits. All too often, they were only present at HQ to face disciplinary panel hearings, and social niceties, such as lunch with the staff, were never on the agenda for those occasions.

Needless to say, after the events of Sunday, the buffet lunch had been canceled, but that didn't stop people speculating on what might have been.

I, meanwhile, went back to watching race videos from the BHA database.

I should have been looking at the other open files on my desk, but I kept being drawn back to the questions surrounding Dave Swinton.

I studied again his rides on Garrick Party at Haydock and on Chiltern Line at Ludlow.

Having spoken to Jason Butcher, I was more convinced than ever that Garrick Party had not been given the opportunity to win the race at Haydock because Dave Swinton had decided not to allow him to run freely as a front runner, as was his forte. That was not to say that the horse would have definitely won if he had been allowed to do so. That was impossible to say.

However, the big question remained: Did Dave make that decision with the express intention of not winning?

The race at Ludlow was less clear-cut. If Chiltern Line's trainer, Tom Cheek, had said that the horse liked to be kept tight to the running rail, it was well within the realm of probability that even a jockey of Dave Swinton's ability could have found himself badly boxed in.

I also pulled up the race at Doncaster in which Dave had finished second on Perambulator.

I could understand Jason Butcher's frustration, as the horse seemed to come from nowhere to within a stride of victory, but there was no evidence on the film to show that Dave Swinton had been in any way at fault. It clearly showed him making continuous efforts to get the horse to quicken from the last fence onward, but he was rewarded by a response only in the last hundred yards or so. A lesser jockey might have had no response at all.

If Dave had lost that race on purpose, then he had been very clever at disguising what he had done.

I leaned back in my chair and stared at the ceiling.

But Dave Swinton *had been* very clever.

Next, I looked up his statistics for the previous full season.

He had ridden in just over nine hundred races in the United Kingdom. At one hundred and sixty pounds each ride, that represented an annual official riding fee income of a little over a hundred and forty thousand pounds. Pretty good, but hardly a huge return for risking one's life on a daily basis. Some Premier League soccer players earned that sort of money in a week.

There was no record of the falls D. Swinton had suffered, but, statistically, a jump jockey could expect to hit the turf on about eight percent of his rides—that is, more than seventy falls in a nine-hundred-race season. So, on average, once or twice a week, every week, Dave would have crashed to the ground at thirty miles per hour, alongside half a ton of leg-flailing horseflesh, and with untold other horses behind him trying to jump onto the space he occupied on the grass.

Bruises, like those I'd seen on his body on the morning of the Hennessy, must have been a constant companion.

Was it any wonder that he'd asked the trainers for more money? I'd have needed a signed blank check and a full suit of armor, not a pair of diaphanous nylon breeches and some wafer-thin featherweight riding boots.

I WENT OUT for lunch at the Old Red Lion pub right next door to the BHA offices and found Paul Maldini propping up the bar.

"Not like you to be drinking at lunchtime," I said to him.

"I'm not," he said. He lifted his glass. "Diet Coke."

"Want another?" I asked.

"Thanks."

I ordered the Diet Coke for him and a lime, lemon and bitters for myself.

"We should have had Dave Swinton in for lunch today," he said.

"I know."

"I couldn't stand being in there." He nodded toward the building next door. "I needed to get out." I was surprised that he appeared visibly upset. "It was my idea, you know."

"What was?" I asked.

"The Racing Needs You! campaign and getting Dave Swinton to be on the posters. I'd invested a lot of time and effort in getting him to agree to be here today."

I knew that Paul had been on the campaign committee, but I had had no idea he'd been the main driver behind it. Would it have been better or worse if I'd told him about Dave's admission that he'd not won a race on purpose? I now wished I *had* told him, as he would find out eventually, at the inquest if not before, and that might be embarrassing.

However, I decided that right now was perhaps not the best time.

"I'm sorry," I said inadequately.

"Yeah, well, these things are sent to try us." He forced a laugh. "And what are we going to do now with the ten thousand glossy brochures we've just had printed, all of them with Dave Swinton's face on the cover and a letter from him inside?"

"Who are they for?"

"Race sponsors. They were due to go out next week to thank them for past support and to persuade them to continue their sponsorship."

"Send them anyway," I said. "With a covering letter saying that racing needs them more than ever now."

He sighed. "I don't know. Some might think it rather crass."

He sighed again.

"It sounds to me like you need something stronger than Diet Coke."

"You might be right, but I'd better not. I've got to go and face the rest of the committee." He didn't sound very happy.

"It's not your fault Dave Swinton isn't here, so don't blame yourself."

"It was *me* who insisted we use him for the campaign."

"And a damn good decision that was too," I said. "Inspired. You weren't to know he'd go and kill himself."

Did I now believe that he *had* killed himself?

"Maybe not," said Paul, "but I still feel responsible. And he was bloody expensive."

I didn't doubt it. I wondered if he'd asked to be paid in cash.

"I'm sure that the rest of the committee will agree that it was money well spent."

"Not all of them will. A couple of members were against the idea from the start, and I'm not particularly looking forward to listening to them crowing *I told you so*."

"Ignore them," I said.

Paul downed the rest of his Diet Coke. "I'd better be getting back. Thanks for the drink. And the encouragement."

He turned with a slight wave and walked out of the pub.

In the five years I had worked at the BHA, that had been the longest and most civil conversation between us. He had constantly treated me as a naughty schoolboy and I had always thought of him as a bit of an idiot.

Perhaps it would be the start of an improved working relationship.

I PASSED that evening in much the same way as I now spent almost every other evening, sitting in an armchair in my kitchen–cum–living room, eating a microwaved frozen dinner off my knees and watching television.

What had happened to me?

I'd never before been one for sitting around doing nothing. I'd been a get-up-and-go person who had purposely chosen a path through life that had been interesting and exciting, even dangerous.

I'd joined the Army straight out of school as an eager eighteen-year-old officer cadet at Sandhurst Military Academy and had spent the next forty-four weeks without a single glimpse of a television set. I'd completed three six-month tours of Afghanistan as an intelligence officer and had survived some scary scraps where only my quick wits and good luck had kept me alive. Even my initial work at the BHA had been challenging, working mostly undercover among the criminal underbelly of racing.

But my promotion to senior investigator status had changed much of that. I'd been given my own office and greater responsibility, but I now had far less freedom to push the boundaries of the law in order to get results. These days, I was far more likely to interview possible miscreants as myself than I was to follow them home in disguise and rummage through their garbage cans in the dead of night.

I was becoming respectable and I wasn't sure I liked it.

And Lydia's sudden exodus hadn't helped.

It had always been me who had been keen to go out, to do something other than sitting at home in front of the television. But when she'd departed, my eagerness for the London nightlife had faded away as well.

If I went out to a bar on my own, I found that I resented the happy couples that surrounded me. And on the few occasions I'd been alone to the movies, I missed the discussion about the film with a companion over a late-night drink or pizza.

It was like a catch-22 situation: I didn't go out because I didn't have anyone to go with, but I didn't meet anyone because I didn't go out.

I resolved to break free from this vicious circle of depression.

I *would* go out.

Maybe tomorrow, or the next day.

9

I spent Thursday cooped up in my office catching up on neglected paperwork, but, on Friday, I escaped to Sandown Park for the first day of the Tingle Creek Christmas Festival meeting, named after the popular horse of the 1970s that had been a Sandown specialist.

These two days of racing were always very popular with the public and I was joined by many others as I walked the mile or so from Esher railway station to the racetrack entrance, some of them wearing bright red Christmas hats in true festive spirit.

I was there specifically to further a separate ongoing investigation into the conduct of a Mr. Leslie Morris, who, according to an anonymous source, had been placing suspicious bets with racetrack bookmakers on behalf of a friend who was an excluded person. The source had also stated that Mr. Morris would be at Sandown that afternoon to do it again.

An *excluded person* was exactly that—excluded from any BHA licensed premises, which includes all racing stables, training gallops, equine pools and, in particular, anywhere on a British racetrack.

Sadly, there was nothing in the Rules of Racing that prevented an excluded person from placing bets, either on an Internet betting site or in a High Street betting shop, but neither of those methods was very anonymous. The Internet sites kept computer records and needed the account holder's credit card details, while all betting shops were now equipped with closed-circuit television that recorded every transaction over the counter.

Until they also started introducing personal CCTV, only the racetrack bookmakers provided a suitable opportunity for someone to place untraceable bets. And it was not uncommon for a single bet of a thousand pounds or more to be made in cash with the racetrack bookies, especially at the big meetings like the Tingle Creek Festival.

Mr. Leslie Morris was a BHA-registered racehorse owner and, as such, was subject to Rule (A)30.3, which states that *a registered person must not associate with a person who is excluded in connection with horseracing in Great Britain unless he obtains the prior permission of the Authority.*

Placing bets on behalf of an excluded person was definitely an association in connection with horseracing and no such prior permission had been granted.

I waited for Leslie Morris near the entrance to the racetrack enclosures.

I knew what he looked like because I had studied the pictures of him in BHA files, but I was sure he wouldn't recognize me even if he had known me beforehand. I had resurrected one of my favorite disguises—long dark wig under a brown beanie, plus a goatee stuck to my face with latex-based glue. For good measure, I had added a pair of horn-rimmed glasses.

I also wore an unremarkable olive green anorak over an open-necked blue shirt and khaki chinos, the perfect gear for spending time in the betting ring.

I was beginning to worry that I might have missed him when he appeared in a full-length dark gray overcoat, brown leather gloves and a blue felt fedora covering his white hair. I smiled to myself. He couldn't have worn something easier for me to follow if he'd tried.

But I had to do more than simply follow him, I had to get close enough to observe which horses he backed and how much he staked.

I followed him in through the main entrance foyer, where he used his racehorse owners' pass card to gain entry.

He turned right and went into the gents, so I hung around outside until he reappeared. I suppose he might have gone in there to meet someone, but I would have been taking too much of a chance to follow him into such a small space and then to be very close to him later in the betting ring.

I kept about ten to fifteen yards behind him as he made his way toward the Owners & Trainers facility next to the weighing room, where there was complimentary food on offer and a cash bar.

The first race was about to start and I walked over to lean on the white rail around the unsaddling enclosure in front of the weighing room as if waiting for the horses to return but all the while keeping an eye on the door of the bar.

LESLIE MORRIS remained inside the Owners & Trainers Bar throughout both the first and second races and appeared again only as the runners for the third were being saddled and taken to the parade ring.

By this stage, I had shifted my position over to the far side of the weighing room to be less conspicuous, and, from there, I was able to observe as he made his way over to the paddock rail and stood close to the point where the horses would leave to go out to the track.

Once the horses had all passed him, he walked through the grandstand and out to the betting ring beyond, with me in close formation behind him.

There were more than fifty bookmakers located in three rows, with more on the rail between the ring and the premier enclosure.

"Come on. Let's be having you," shouted one of the bookies as I walked nearby. "Best value here. Six-to-four the field."

I looked up at his board, with the horse names and the odds brightly lit up in yellow and red lights. There were eight runners in the race and the prices varied from the favorite at six-to-four to a couple of rank outsiders quoted at fifty- and hundred-to-one respectively.

Leslie Morris walked quickly up and down the rows of boards, looking at the offered prices, and I acted as his shadow. Fortunately, he was too busy to notice me, as he was concentrating on the odds boards and also on a red notebook and a small calculator that he held in his hands. He tapped in figures on the calculator and made notes in the book. Try as I might, I couldn't get quite close enough to read what he was writing.

Suddenly, he began moving down the lines of bookmakers, stopping about every second one to make a single bet using high-value banknotes that he peeled from a large bundle of cash he had in his coat pocket. I pretended to make a call on my cell phone while actually taking several photos and a short video of him making the bets.

Even though I wasn't close enough to catch what Morris himself said, I could sometimes hear the bookmaker as he repeated the bet to his assistant, who then logged it into a computer and printed the ticket. Morris wasn't putting money on the same horse on each occasion, that was for sure. As far as I could tell, he was backing most of the eight runners, some of them multiple times with different bookmakers.

It was a slick operation and, in all, he must have placed between thirty and thirty-five separate bets, each with a different bookmaker. He had timed his approach well, when most other punters had already made their selections and gone to watch the race from the grandstand. Hence, making each of his bets took just a few seconds, and by the time the race began, the large bundle of cash in his pocket had reduced to nothing.

I followed him as he also climbed the grandstand steps to watch. With a tiny bit of pushing, I managed to position myself a few steps above and behind him.

The race was a two-and-a-half-mile novice hurdle for four-year-olds and, initially, it was a slow affair with none of the eight jockeys seemingly wanting to make the running from the start.

They popped over the early flight of hurdles at barely a gallop, and it was not until they turned into the homestretch for the first time that a couple of them kicked on and decided to make a proper race of it. The others followed suit, and all eight were fairly closely bunched as they passed the winning post with a complete circuit still to run.

The pace began to quicken as the horses ran downhill away from the grandstand, all of them safely negotiating the first three flights of hurdles, although the two outsiders came under pressure early, their jockeys pushing hard and giving their mounts a few *Hurry up!* slaps with their whips but without any great response.

However, at the last hurdle of the far side, Wisden Wonder, the favorite, hardly jumped at all, crashing through the obstacle and unseating his rider, much to the displeasure of the crowd, which groaned loudly en masse.

By the time they turned for home around the bottom end of the course, the remaining seven were well spaced out. One of them pulled up before the last two hurdles, and the other six finished in line astern, with the winner returned at a starting price of five-to-one.

Leslie Morris had not cheered the winner home, nor had he moved a muscle when the favorite had come to grief. Now he merely stood in the grandstand sorting out his betting slips before moving back to the lines of bookmakers to collect his winnings, making notes all the time in his red notebook.

And the winnings were considerable.

By the time he had collected from eight different bookmakers, Morris had two large bundles of banknotes in his coat pockets. But he didn't hang around to reinvest any of the winnings on the remaining races. Instead, he walked quickly out through the grandstand to the main foyer and exited the racetrack.

I followed him out to the Owners and Trainers parking lot and watched as he climbed into a silver Audi A4 and drove rapidly away. He had departed so quickly that even if I'd wanted to stop him, I doubt that I would have been successful. And he would probably have thought I was trying to rob him.

He'd have been right.

I particularly wanted to get my hands on that red notebook.

MY QUESTIONING of bookmakers about the bets they have taken and paid out on is a delicate area.

Racetrack bookmakers are not registered or licensed by the BHA in spite of the fact that they ply their trade on BHA-licensed property. Rather, they hold operating licenses from the Gambling Commission.

Hence, my authority is severely restricted and not helped by the fact that many bookmakers consider the BHA to be obstructive in not allowing jockeys and trainers to discuss openly with them the prospects of their horses.

In spite of all that, I went back to the betting ring and went up to one of the bookies who had paid out to Mr. Morris.

"How much did the man in the blue fedora win?" I asked.

"Who wants to know?" he replied in a less than friendly manner.

I showed him my BHA credentials with the word INVESTIGATOR and he looked up at my face. "Was it fixed?" he asked.

"Was what fixed?"

"The race?"

Good question.

"Not that I'm aware of," I said nonchalantly. "I'm only interested in how much you paid the man in the blue fedora."

"Three grand," said the bookie. "He'd a monkey on at fives."

A *monkey* was betting slang for "five hundred pounds." At odds of five-to-one, the winnings would be two thousand five hundred pounds. Add back the stake money, the payout was three thousand.

I went to each of the seven other bookmakers Leslie Morris had collected from. Three wouldn't tell me, but four confirmed that he'd had a bet of five hundred pounds at five-to-one. If all eight bets had each paid out three thousand pounds, then Mr. Morris had left the racetrack with twenty-four thousand pounds in cash in his coat pockets.

But how much had he started with?

I went down the row of bookmakers, speaking to each I could remember Morris betting with but not winning. I asked them how much the man in the blue fedora had wagered and on which horse, but none of them could remember. The eight he had collected from had only remembered him because a three-thousand-pound cash payout was a little unusual.

I asked them all if they had taken many bets of five hundred pounds from Morris but it seemed that he had bet varying amounts on the different horses.

One bookmaker told me he knew he'd taken a monkey on the fifteen-to-one shot but couldn't be sure it was from a man in a blue hat. "Punters are punters," he said. "I'm too busy checking for counterfeit notes to worry about what they're wearing." He was also far too busy taking bets for the fourth race to give me any more of his time.

"Come back after the last," he said, but if he couldn't remember now, he would have even less chance in a couple of hours' time.

I asked all the bookies if they'd taken any bets on Wisden Wonder from the man in the blue fedora. None of them thought so, and I certainly hadn't heard him placing one. They all said they'd taken lots of big bets on the favorite from other punters and they were very grateful not to have had to pay out.

Frustrated, I walked back through the grandstand to the weighing room and into the broadcast center, the room from where all the racetrack public address and closed-circuit television coverage was transmitted.

"Can I help you?" asked the technician in charge.

I showed him my BHA credentials.

"I'd like to see the video of the third race."

"Sure," he said. "But not just at the moment. The fourth is about to start and I need to concentrate."

I sat on a stool next to him and together we watched on a screen as the fourth race unfolded.

"We have Channel 4 here today," he said. "They do all the TV production but I have to be sure that the racetrack closed-circuit systems are all working and tied in to their output. And we have our own commentary team separate from them to pipe through the on-course speakers."

I sat patiently as he nervously monitored the bank of electronic equipment, but all seemed to be working well and he relaxed as the race came to a conclusion.

"Now," he said, "how can I help?"

"Video of the third," I said.

"No problem. Just let me make a copy of that race to give to the winning owner."

He put a blank DVD into his recorder and burned the copy before handing it to a waiting official.

"Now," he said, pushing buttons on the equipment, "do you want to see the whole race?"

"Just the last hurdle in the back stretch second time," I said. "Where Wisden Wonder was unseated."

I watched the incident from two different camera angles, at full speed and in slow motion.

The horse had hit the hurdle hard and had pitched forward on landing, stumbling badly and almost going down on its knees. Bill McKenzie, the jockey, had had little chance of remaining in the saddle and had gone past the horse's head onto the turf. He'd even received a kick or two for his trouble.

But I was more interested in what had happened in the run-up to the jump.

Wisden Wonder had been lying fifth of the eight runners at the time and had been closely following the two right in front of him, who were side by side. Wisden Wonder had seemingly not even seen the obstacle until he was upon it. If he'd been given any warning by McKenzie to jump, he had failed to act.

"Is there a problem?" asked the technician.

"No," I said. "No problem."

"The stewards had a look at the same incident after the race, but they didn't seem that bothered. They only watched it once."

"Do you know if they interviewed the jockey?" I asked.

"I doubt it. I think he went straight off to the hospital."

I'd been so engaged watching Leslie Morris collect his winnings that I hadn't noticed what had happened to the jockey.

"I'll take a look at the stewards' report," I said, standing up. "Thanks."

"Anytime."

I left him to his electronics and walked across the weighing room to the medical room.

"Bill McKenzie?" I asked one of the nursing staff, showing her my ID card.

"He's gone to Kingston Hospital," she said. "Possible concussion after a fall."

"How was he when he left here?"

"Conscious," she said, "but confused. The doctor did some concussion tests that all showed negative, but he was still slightly worried about the apparent confusion so he sent him for a CT scan of his head just to be on the safe side. You can't be too sure with head injuries."

"Did he go in an ambulance?" I asked.

She shook her head. "In a car, with my colleague."

Why did I think that it was rather convenient for him not to have to answer any difficult questions about his fall?

10

So do you think he fell off deliberately?"

"I'm not sure that he intended coming right off. Maybe he just wanted Wisden Wonder to blunder badly and lose interest in the race. But I do think it is something worth looking at again."

I was speaking on the phone to Paul Maldini on Saturday morning.

"Are you going back to Sandown again today?" he asked.

"Yes," I said, "I thought I might."

I actually had an invitation to lunch in a private box, but I wasn't going to tell Paul that. He'd want to know who with, and why, and I didn't want to tell him. He may not have approved.

"Is McKenzie riding at Sandown today?" Paul asked.

"That depends on whether the scans showed anything. He's still down in the *Racing Post* to ride, but he won't be if he was concussed yesterday."

All jockeys are stood down from riding for at least a week with concussion, often longer.

"Will you speak to him if he's there?"

"That's up to you," I said. "I'm not sure that I should. If there *was* something dodgy about that race, do we want to show our hand just yet or do we want to investigate further on the quiet? McKenzie will know immediately that something's up if I question him and he would most likely then tell Morris. At the moment, I think we can assume that neither of them believes we are suspicious about that race and I'd really like to keep it that way."

"Why is that so important?" Paul would have gone straight in and questioned Leslie Morris and Bill McKenzie, maybe even calling them in to a disciplinary panel in the offices at High Holborn.

"The tip-off we received stated only that Morris was placing bets for a friend who was excluded. We don't know who his friend is. If we alert Morris now, it becomes far more difficult for me to find out. He would simply go to ground and cover his tracks. We would have no case."

"But he might do it again," Paul said. "The BHA can't be seen to be allowing something that's against the Rules of Racing to happen for a second time, not when we know already it's happened before."

"Then I'd better catch him quickly."

"OK," he said slowly, as if not fully convinced. "You do as you think best for the moment. And keep me informed."

"Will do."

"And you also believe the betting on the race was suspect?"

"I certainly do," I said. "As far as I can tell, Morris backed every horse in the race except Wisden Wonder, which was the six-to-four favorite."

"Mmm, that does sound rather dubious."

"I think it sounds considerably more than rather dubious," I said. "It sounds positively dishonest."

"Do we need to send in the police?"

"No," I said quickly, "not yet. We need to be sure before we do anything." Paul was again for jumping in with both feet. "If we call in the police, I won't be able to investigate anything further—they wouldn't allow it. And we don't want another high-profile race-fixing trial to collapse from lack of evidence. I'm not even a hundred percent sure that Morris did back everything except Wisden Wonder. The bookies were not that helpful."

"They never are."

Paul didn't like bookmakers, although he had to admit that without any betting racing would surely die.

It was the gambling public that ultimately delivered the revenue on which the sport depended. Everyone was trying to back a winner, but it was the losers we relied on.

The only sure way of backing a winner was to bet on *every* horse running in the race and that approach was unlikely to make you any profit.

Suppose you want to end up with a return of a hundred pounds.

On a horse quoted at four-to-one, you would win four pounds for each one you stake, provided the horse won the race. So if you bet twenty pounds with a bookmaker, you would win eighty. You would also get back your stake of twenty, hence the bookmaker would pay out one hundred pounds.

If the horse was at nine-to-one, you would need to bet ten pounds on it so that if it comes in first you win ninety pounds, plus your stake of ten, giving you the hundred you want. For a horse at odds of six-to-four, you would win six pounds for every four pounds you bet, so if you staked forty pounds and won you would win sixty. Add back your stake of forty and you would have your return of a hundred.

In this way, you can calculate how much you would need to bet on each horse to have one hundred pounds in your hand after the race.

It sounds simple.

However, there is a major snag.

In order to be sure of having a hundred pounds after the race, you would have to bet more than a hundred pounds in the first place. You would always back the winner but you would lose money each time. In fact, you would have to bet, on average, about a hundred and ten pounds on each race to receive back just a hundred.

That is how bookmakers make their money. Provided they have done their sums right and posted odds in the correct ratios to encourage an even spread of bets on all the horses, they will take in a hundred and ten pounds for every hundred they have to pay out.

This is why the odds can change as the betting continues in the minutes before the race. If a bookmaker is taking too much money on a certain horse and not enough on another, he will shorten the odds on the first horse to deter further bets and lengthen them on the second horse to encourage bets.

No one in their right mind would stake a hundred and ten pounds on a race to get back only a hundred, but if you knew for sure that the six-to-four shot was *not going to win*, you wouldn't have to bet the forty pounds on that horse. You would only have to stake seventy pounds to be certain of winning a hundred, irrespective of which of the other horses won.

That looks like a good bet—in fact, it's a surefire winner.

If that is what had been going on in the race at Sandown, then to end up with twenty-four thousand pounds in his coat pockets Morris had needed to stake sixteen thousand eight hundred pounds. That gave him a tidy profit of over seven thousand pounds on just the one race—a return on his investment of over forty percent at a time when bank interest rates were at an historic low—and with absolutely no risk of losing his money.

No risk, that was, unless an undercover investigator like me had spotted what was going on.

SANDOWN PARK racetrack on the first Saturday afternoon in December was heaving with people, all of them in great spirits under a sunny sky.

Tingle Creek day had finally arrived and there was huge excitement as the country's leading two-mile chasers were set to go head-to-head. In addition, there were numerous Christmas-themed stalls and festive music provided by a band of badly dressed elves, together with a scruffy Santa.

On this day, I was here as myself, having put the wig, beanie and glasses back in the closet, along with the khaki chinos and the olive green anorak. Instead, I was trying to be respectable in a suit and tie for my lunch engagement in Derrick Smith's private box.

I arrived at the racetrack early, having again taken a train from Willesden Junction to Esher via Clapham Junction. It was highly unusual for me to have such an exciting invitation and I didn't want to be late.

Having arrived early, I used the time to wander around the enclosures, soaking up the atmosphere while also keeping my eyes open for any wrongdoing. Fortunately, there was none I could spot that would keep me from my lunch, so I presented myself as requested at the box at half past eleven.

"My dear boy, come in, come in," welcomed Mr. Smith at the door, extending his hand once again and shaking mine vigorously. "So glad you could make it. Here, have some champagne."

He passed me a glass full of the sparkling golden liquid from a tray being held by one of the waiters.

"Thank you," I said. "It is lovely to be here. You are very kind."

"Nonsense," he said. "It is *I* who should be grateful to you." He put his hand on my shoulder. "Come and meet my wife."

He guided me out to the balcony, where there were already more than a dozen people holding drinks and chatting among themselves.

"Gaysie, darling," Derrick said loudly, causing all the conversations to stop. "Can I introduce Jeff Hinkley? He's the young man who prevented Secret Ways from being stolen at Ascot in June."

All the heads turned toward me.

I wished he hadn't broadcast the fact so openly. It had been an undercover operation, and even those arrested still had no idea that it had been me who had caused their downfall. Without my knowledge or agreement, the BHA chairman had taken it upon himself to inform the horse's owner of all the details, albeit supposedly in strict confidence.

"It's all meant to be hush-hush," I said quietly to Derrick.

"Nonsense," he said. "Give credit where credit's due. Secret Ways went on to win the Coventry Stakes and he's favorite for next year's Guineas. Without you, young Jeff, he'd have ended up as dog meat." He slapped me on the back, smiling broadly.

A slight, very attractive blonde-haired woman came over from one of the groups.

"Mr. Hinkley," she said. "I'm Gay Smith, Derrick's wife."

"I'm delighted to meet you," I said, shaking the offered hand. "It is very kind of you to invite me."

"Derrick was very taken with the idea," she said, smiling at her husband. "He's been singing your praises to anyone who'll listen."

I was beginning to think that accepting his invitation to lunch had been a mistake. I had only done so out of self-indulgence and vanity.

"It was just part of my job," I said.

"And a job well done," Derrick said. "Come on and meet the others."

He introduced me to another of his guests before disappearing off to greet some new arrivals.

"I hear you're Derrick's personal James Bond," said a laughing Alfie Hart, one of the country's top trainers, who I knew by reputation but had never actually met before. "All that cloak-and-dagger stuff must be exciting."

"Not at all," I said. "I'd hardly describe lying in wet ditches or picking through someone's smelly garbage as particularly exciting. Certainly not as exciting as training a Breeders' Cup winner."

He smiled at me and I smiled back. Alfie Hart had trained the winner of the previous October's Breeders' Cup Mile and I could tell he was pleased that I knew.

"I'm surprised to see you at a jumps meeting," I said to him. "I thought you trained exclusively on the flat."

"I do," he said. He looked about him and lowered his voice. "But one never says no to Derrick."

"No," I agreed. And not, I thought, when Derrick has more than a dozen seriously good horses in one's stable.

Alfie went back inside the box to get himself a refill of champagne, but I was not alone for long. Derrick returned with the tall gray-haired man I'd seen with him the previous week.

"This is Sir Richard Reynard," Derrick said.

"We met at Newbury."

"Yes, of course you did. Sir Richard is fairly new to racing and I'm trying to convince him to buy a horse."

"Derrick's just been telling me about your exploits at Ascot," Sir Richard said. "I'm very impressed."

"Thank you," I said, "I was only doing my job."

"And what job is that?" he asked.

"I'm an investigator for the British Horseracing Authority," I said.

"Is there much in horseracing to investigate?"

"Some," I said. "Maybe not as much as some people would have you believe, but enough to keep me occupied."

He smiled. "So is it safe enough for me to invest in a horse?"

"It depends on what you mean by *safe*," I said. "Very few racehorse owners make a positive return on their investment. Most do it for the love of the sport and the thrill of winning races—even if the prize money doesn't usually cover the training fees, let alone the capital outlay."

I could tell he didn't think much of that.

"But Derrick says there are fortunes to be made from breeding."

"Only if you are lucky enough, like him, to have owned a Derby winner," I said. "Almost all male horses in the jumping game are geldings."

"I wasn't considering the jumping game," he said, staring into space.

From the look on his face, I imagined he was visualizing himself leading the winner into the famous Derby unsaddling circles at Epsom or Churchill Downs. It was a fantasy that most owners entertained at some point in their lives yet only a handful of them ever fulfilled it in reality.

"Jeff," said Gay Smith, taking my arm. "Come and meet some friends of ours from the Cayman Islands."

She guided me to the other end of the balcony, where a smartly dressed suntanned couple were standing together holding half-full glasses of champagne. I would have put them both in their early to mid-forties.

"Theresa and Martin," Gay called to them, "meet Jeff Hinkley."

We shook hands.

"Gay says you live in the Cayman Islands," I said.

"That's right," said Theresa. "We have a house on Seven Mile Beach not that far from Gay and Derrick's place."

"Have you been there long?" I asked.

"Ten years now," Theresa replied. "We love it there, don't we, Martin?"

Martin didn't say anything, but I was used to him not replying.

Martin was the man who had turned away from me on the balcony of the hospitality room at Newbury on Hennessy Gold Cup day. The man who was then being told that he was a total fucking idiot.

11

We sat down to lunch just before noon, by which time some other guests had arrived, making twenty of us in all in the box.

"I'm sorry we have to eat so early," said Derrick, ushering everyone in from the balcony. "It's high time they installed some floodlights at Sandown so that racing could be later in the day during the winter."

We were seated at two round tables for ten and I found myself placed between Gay Smith and an attractive young woman in a smart tweed suit who I had been spying from afar ever since she'd arrived.

"Hello," she said. "My name's Henri—Henrietta Shawcross."

"Jeff Hinkley," I replied, shaking her hand.

"Oh, I know who you are," Henri said. "I think everyone here does. You're Derrick's superhero."

"He exaggerates."

"How did you do it?" she asked.

"What?"

"Save his horse."

"I merely uncovered a conspiracy to steal the horse and set a trap to catch the villains in the act. It was nothing very special."

She looked disappointed. "It must have been a tiny bit exciting."

I thought back. It had been far more worrying than exciting, as I wasn't a hundred percent sure that it would happen and I'd mobilized the whole of the BHA integrity team plus several members of the Thames Valley police force.

We had secretly lain in wait outside the Ascot racetrack stables for nearly two hours and I was worried that I'd been wrong and would look foolish if nothing happened. But, thankfully, right on cue, the bad guys had turned up just as Secret Ways was being unloaded from the trailer that had brought him to the racetrack.

One of them had managed to knock over the groom and even had his hand on the horse's halter when the trap was sprung.

In truth, it had been very satisfying and, yes, rather exciting.

"A tiny bit," I agreed with a smile. "What do you do?"

"I work for a recruitment agency," she said. "We recruit chefs, waiters and waitresses for the catering business."

"And is that a tiny bit exciting?" I asked.

"Don't poke fun at me," she said, slightly offended. "I work hard at my job and I enjoy it."

"I'm sorry," I said, "I didn't mean to be rude." Just funny. And it had backfired. "So how long have you known Derrick?" I asked, trying to change the subject.

"I met him for the first time today," she said. "I'm here with my uncle." She pointed at Sir Richard Reynard, who was sitting at the other table.

I must have involuntarily raised a questioning eyebrow.

She laughed. "No, really, he *is* my uncle. I promise you. He's my mother's elder brother. I'm only here because my aunt Mary couldn't make it. She's organizing a Christmas fair in their local church hall, so Uncle Richard asked me to come with him instead."

"The lady doth protest too much, methinks."

"Shut up," she said, laughing and bashing me playfully on the arm. "It's true, I tell you."

"OK, I believe you," I said between guffaws. "But countless others might not."

"What are you two laughing at?" asked Gay Smith, turning toward us.

"Miss Goody Two-shoes here is trying to tell me she came with her uncle while I'm convinced he's actually her sugar daddy."

"From what I've heard," Gay said, "Henrietta Shawcross doesn't need a sugar daddy. And, yes, Sir Richard Reynard is indeed her uncle."

That put me in my place.

"Sorry," I said again.

"Don't be," Henri said. "That's the best laugh I've had in ages."

"Do you know anyone else here?" I asked her.

"A few," she said.

I dropped my voice. "How about the suntanned couple at the other table. The wife is sitting next to your uncle."

"You mean Theresa and Martin."

"Yes," I said. "Exactly."

"Martin's my cousin. Uncle Richard is his father. Martin's the one who's mad keen on racing. He's the real reason why we're all here. Martin and Theresa want Uncle Richard to start owning racehorses. They've roped Derrick Smith in to help them convince him it's a good idea."

I nodded. "Your cousin and Derrick both have houses in the Cayman Islands," I said.

"Yes. I've been there often. It's lovely."

A waitress placed a shrimp cocktail in front of me. I wanted to go on talking with Henri about Martin Reynard, but Gay put her hand on my arm as if to indicate she wanted my full attention.

"So you work for the Jockey Club?" she said, taking a mouthful of the shrimp.

"Sort of," I replied. "Not actually for the Jockey Club, but I *do* work for the racing authorities. I'm an investigator."

"I wouldn't have thought there was enough to investigate for it to be a full-time job."

"There's plenty to keep me busy, believe me, and the other four investigators in my team. There is always someone trying to beat the system and, if it's against the rules, our job is to stop them."

"Is it possible to beat the system without breaking the rules?"

"Absolutely," I said. "And some trainers are very good at it."

"How?" Gay asked.

"It's called *beating the handicapper,*" I said. "Other than those just starting out on their racing careers, every horse in training in the UK is given an official handicap rating each Tuesday depending on how it has run and how those it has raced against have also performed. If a horse runs well compared to others, its rating will go up, and if it runs badly the rating will go down. And the rating is used to determine the weight it has to carry in handicap races."

"So?" she asked, puzzled.

"For a horse to be officially rated, it has to either win a race or it has to have run in three races and be placed in the first six in at least one of them. Suppose a trainer has a horse that has been specifically bred to be good at middle and long distances. He runs it in three moderate sprints over just five furlongs as a young, green two-year-old and, predictably, it doesn't do very well but it does manage to come in sixth in one of them, maybe out of only six or seven runners. So the horse gets an official rating that is very low, but, crucially, it is now qualified to run in handicaps.

"The trainer then doesn't run the horse again until the following year, by which time it has fully developed and is ready to race over a much greater distance. The trainer now places it in a mile-and-a-half handicap for horses with similarly poor ratings and, not surprisingly, it wins easily. If the trainer goes on entering the horse in the right races, it can run up a whole series of wins against moderate opposition before the handicapper *catches up* and raises its rating to a more appropriate value."

"Is that legal?" Gay asked.

"Yes, completely legal. It's simply the trainer playing the handicap system to his advantage."

I looked across the table at Alfie Hart. He was one of the best exponents of the practice.

"How fascinating," Gay Smith said, yet I feared I was boring her as she turned away to talk to the person on her far side.

I finished my shrimp and turned back to Henri, but she was chatting away merrily to another lady beyond her, so I spent some time studying the afternoon's race program. I noticed that Bill McKenzie was still down to ride two horses, one of them in the first race and the other in the fourth.

"Trying to pick a winner?" Henri said. "Do tell."

"Don't ask me, I'm hopeless at choosing winners," I said. "My best tip of the day is to keep your money in your pocket."

"Boring!" Henri said loudly. She received a stern glare from her uncle at the other table.

She blushed.

"Now look what you've made me do," she said to me.

"Don't blame me," I said.

"Why not?" She smiled. "Are you married?"

"No," I said.

"Are you gay?"

"Why do you ask?"

"Most men I know of my age are either married or gay."

"Well, I'm neither," I said. "How about you?"

"That's a secret."

She wasn't wearing a wedding ring. I'd already checked.

She opened her race program. "Come on, pick me a winner."

"Autumn Statement," I said, "in the second."

She looked down at the printed race details.

"Why that one?" she asked, clearly unimpressed by the horse's lowly status.

"He ran on Tuesday at Southwell. I was there and watched the race. He was only beaten a short head by a very good horse that's not running today. His rating is sure to rise considerably this coming week, but he can still run today on the old rating, which means he's very well handicapped."

"I thought you said you were hopeless at picking winners."

"He hasn't won yet and he'll probably start at fairly short odds."

"How about in the first race? Do you fancy Medication? He's the favorite."

"I've no idea, but you had better be quick if you want to make a bet because they're already at the start."

She stood up and rushed out of the box, along with some of the other guests.

I looked up at the television screen in the corner of the room. Bill McKenzie was indeed riding as advertised, which meant that he wasn't concussed. I wondered if the confusion he had exhibited in the medical room the previous evening had been because his mind had been on other matters—like how long he would be banned from riding if anyone knew he had lost the race on purpose.

AUTUMN STATEMENT won the second race by two lengths at the surprisingly long price of six-to-one. Obviously, the betting public hadn't appreciated his potential as much as I had.

"Three hundred quid!" squealed Henri as we watched the finish on the television in the box during our dessert. "I've just won three hundred quid."

"How much did you put on?" I asked.

"Fifty pounds on the nose."

"You're crazy," I said. "Either that or you've more money than sense."

"Maybe I am a bit crazy," she said, laughing. "And what if I do have more money than sense. You're the one who tipped it. Surely you backed it as well."

I hadn't. In fact, I very rarely had any bet at all. Even though there was no rule actually preventing me from gambling on the races, I was concerned that some people might think there was a conflict of interest if I wanted one horse to win more than another. The Authority was meant to be impartial in all matters.

Or maybe it was because my tipping skills were generally so poor and I didn't like losing my hard-earned cash.

"Actually, no," I said. "But I'm pleased for you that it won." I smiled at her.

"You're a strange bird, aren't you?"

"Am I?" I said, slightly taken aback. "In what way?"

"Do you always live within the rules?"

"Rules or laws?"

"Both," she said. "The laws of the land and the rules of convention and polite society."

"Are you implying that you don't?"

"Dead right, I don't. But I'm on my best behavior today. I was warned by Uncle Richard not to make what he calls a scene. Otherwise, he'd be *bloody cross and take me straight home.*" She mimicked an angry male voice.

"And would he then spank you for being a naughty girl?"

She blushed again and, I daresay, I did as well.

"I'm so sorry," I mumbled, hugely embarrassed. "I'm not sure what came over me. It must be the champagne. Please forget I ever said that."

"My," she replied. "You're even stranger than I thought."

How could I have said it? It was so out of character. Had I been trying to break away from the *live within the rules of polite society* classification in which Henri had so accurately placed me? Or, maybe I was just frustrated. Either way, I'd made a complete fool of myself.

I stood up. "I think I had better be going."

"Don't go," commanded Gay Smith from my other side, turning briefly toward me. "I haven't spent enough time talking to you. And we haven't had our coffee yet."

I sat down again slowly and, to add to my discomfiture, Henri was shaking from a fit of giggles.

"Stop it," I said to her quietly.

She took a deep breath and stopped laughing.

"And what are you going to do if I don't? Spank me?"

She started giggling again immediately, this time twice as badly. And giggles are highly infectious. It was as much as I could do not to join in.

The rest of the lunch was a torment as I tried, mostly unsuccessfully, to ignore Henri, who went on sniggering throughout.

Although, to be honest, part of me didn't want to ignore her at all.

I WATCHED the third race from the balcony with Gay Smith and then made my apologies and left, going down to the weighing room and the paddock, to my more familiar surroundings on the racetrack.

"Do come back for afternoon tea after the fifth," Gay had said as I departed. But we'd only just finished an enormous lunch. Many more days like this would see my waistline expand, but I suppose it was better than spending every day trying to keep one's body weight at twenty pounds below what was natural, as Dave Swinton had done.

Even six days after the event, the main topic of conversation was still his suicide. He had been expected to ride Ebury Tiger, the red-hot favorite in the Tingle Creek Chase later in the afternoon, having ridden it on each of its nine previous victories over hurdles and fences.

There was a general acceptance that it had been a good thing for the racing authorities to have canceled all race meetings for the following Monday, the day of Dave's funeral, as a mark of respect for the loss of one of the sport's greats. Very many racing fans had lost their hero, and the *Morning Line* on Channel 4 that day had broadcast such a gushing obituary that all the newscasters had been in tears.

I, meanwhile, was not feeling quite so reverential about the late champion jockey, but, there again, he *had* tried to kill me. And I was still having nightmares about my time in that sauna.

I stood by the rail gazing inattentively at the horses for the fourth race as they circled in the parade ring, my thoughts constantly drifting back to Henrietta Shawcross. The mounting bell was rung and I found myself looking across as Bill McKenzie was given a leg up onto a horse called Lost Moon. No sign of confusion now, I thought, as he gathered the reins and placed his feet in the stirrup irons.

I went on staring at him absentmindedly as I weighed the pros and cons of returning to Derrick Smith's box for tea, and of returning to the giggling Henri.

But, from Bill McKenzie's perspective, it must have appeared that I was interested only in him.

As he saw me watching him, the color visibly drained from his face and he began to shake. I was mesmerized by the effect my presence was causing so I went on staring at him as the horses walked past, McKenzie's head turning slowly to allow him to stare back at me with wide, frightened eyes.

Bugger, I thought.

That had been extremely careless on my part. I had intended to give Bill McKenzie no reason whatsoever to think that I was in any way suspicious of him and yet it had been obvious that I was. But at least it forced my hand. I would now *have* to question him today before he had a chance to concoct some cock-and-bull story with Leslie Morris.

And it was clear that he knew exactly who I was.

Our paths had only officially crossed once before, eighteen months previously when I had investigated an allegation that cell phones were being used in the jockeys' changing-room toilets, contrary to the Rules of Racing.

Even though the finger had not been pointed at any specific individual, I had formally interviewed seven or eight jockeys at the BHA offices, including Bill McKenzie. After an extensive inquiry, I had concluded that the evidence of wrongdoing was merely circumstantial and too unreliable for any disciplinary action to be taken. Instead, a notice had been sent to all jockeys reminding them of their obligation to comply with the cell phone regulations.

Bill McKenzie had undoubtedly remembered.

12

I decided against going back to Derrick and Gay Smith's box just yet and watched the fourth race from the grandstand steps.

The Henry VIII Novice Chase was named for the king who had resided at Hampton Court Palace, just a couple of miles down the road from Sandown Park, even though the racetrack hadn't been established until some three hundred and thirty years after Henry's death.

The race was over two miles and the starting gate was at the far end of the homestretch, so the horses had to negotiate just over one complete circuit of the track.

I looked to my right and used my binoculars to watch as the horses circled, waiting for the starter to send them on their way.

From the stands, Bill McKenzie didn't appear any different from the other six jockeys but his mind must have been elsewhere, as he completely missed the start, Lost Moon being left flat-footed as the others raced away from him toward the first fence.

Two-mile chases are always run at a good pace and Lost Moon was still some ten lengths behind the other six as they came toward the second, an open ditch.

And that is where his race ended.

Trying hard to catch up, the horse overjumped, pitched forward on his knees while landing and crumpled to the turf, tossing his jockey out in front, before rolling right over him. Lost Moon then struggled to his feet before bolting off, riderless, in pursuit of the others. His former rider, meanwhile, was left lying motionless on the grass.

I went on watching the prone figure of Bill McKenzie, ignoring the remaining horses, which galloped up past the grandstands and the winning post for the first time and then swung right-handed down the hill toward the third fence.

Horseracing is the only sport where the competitors are chased by an ambulance. Indeed, the Rules of Racing state that a jump meeting cannot start unless there are at least *three* fully equipped ambulances present, each of them dedicated only to the care of the jockeys rather than being available for the spectators. One ambulance would generally chase the field while the other two would be strategically placed out on the course, with their engines running, to ensure a maximum response time of one minute to any fallen rider.

The chasing ambulance stopped closest to the fence and two green-clad paramedics carrying backpacks ran across toward the prostrate jockey. They were followed by another man in a suit, who I took to be one of the racetrack medical officers—a doctor.

The race, meanwhile, continued apace as the remaining runners safely negotiated the seven quick-fire fences in the back stretch, but I only had eyes for the activity at the open ditch to my right.

I could see that Bill McKenzie was still flat out on the grass with both the paramedics and the doctor kneeling beside him.

As I watched, my line of sight was annoyingly obstructed by a green screen that was put up by the fence attendants to provide the injured jockey with some degree of privacy.

The race itself was beginning to come to a conclusion, the noise of the crowd building as the three most fancied runners jumped side by side over the pond fence and galloped neck and neck into the homestretch.

Fortunately, the open ditch where Lost Moon had fallen was not jumped again in the race, the horses being directed over the adjacent plain fence, so there was no need for any of the obstacle-bypass procedure to be put in place in spite of the fact that Bill McKenzie had still not been removed from the ground.

The three leading horses were all in the air together over the last, and the crowd cheered enthusiastically as they sprinted up the hill to the line in a blanket finish.

Some of those around me began to move down the steps toward the bars and the betting ring, but I and many others stayed precisely where we were, watching events unfold down the track.

The ambulance was driven across to be near the fence and there were worried faces all around me as people feared the worst. Then there was a huge sigh of relief and a spontaneous round of applause as Bill McKenzie appeared from behind the green screen. He had a red blanket draped over his shoulders and was supported by a paramedic, but he was walking toward the vehicle, albeit slowly, clutching his elbow.

People around me smiled and slapped one another on the back. Walking wounded meant no damage to the spinal cord, and injuries elsewhere would heal.

I went through the grandstand, past the parade ring and into the weighing room, showing my BHA pass to the official at the door.

The senior medical officer was in the jockeys' medical room.

"Is Bill McKenzie coming in here or going directly to the hospital?" I asked.

"You can't come in here," the doctor replied pompously while trying to usher me out. "Medical staff and jockeys only."

I handed him my BHA authorization card, which gave me official access to absolutely everywhere on a racetrack, including the jockeys' medical room. He studied the card closely, but I could tell he didn't like it. Yet another example of the seemingly universal dislike of authority. I might have expected better from a doctor.

"What do you want?" he asked.

"To speak with Bill McKenzie."

"I am sorry but that won't be possible." He didn't exactly sound like he was sorry. "That particular jockey will be going to the hospital. The doctor on the course believes he may have sustained a fracture to his left clavicle."

A broken collarbone.

"So is the racetrack ambulance taking him directly to Kingston Hospital?" I asked.

"No. A local ambulance has been called. We can't spare one of ours, not with three races still to run. It will take him from here."

As I had hoped, Bill McKenzie was on his way to the medical room.

"I'll wait for him."

"He's injured," said the doctor. "He won't be able to speak to you."

"Why not?" I said. "He's broken his collarbone, not his jaw."

"Nevertheless, he might be in pain and he's entitled to some privacy."

Not if he'd been fixing races, I thought, but I didn't say so.

IF BILL MCKENZIE had been feeling rough on his way to the medical room, it was nothing to how he felt after he got there. I was the last person he wanted to see as he walked in from the ambulance, again supported by one of the paramedics.

"Oh God!" he said. "Leave me alone, will you? I'm bloody hurting."

He sat down on the side of one of the two beds in the room.

"The transport will be here shortly to take you to Kingston Hospital," the doctor said to him while giving me a disapproving stare. "You will need an X-ray of that shoulder."

"You seem to be making a habit of going to Kingston Hospital," I said, ignoring the doctor's stare. "No confusion this time?"

"What are you talking about?" McKenzie said, but his eyes told me that he already knew.

The doctor gave me another stare but said nothing.

The ambulance to take him to the hospital arrived, the two ambulance staff coming into the medical room with a narrow two-wheeled chair, on which they placed McKenzie.

I stood up as they began to wheel him out.

"You can't go with him," the doctor said firmly. "It's in the BHA list of general instructions for racetrack medical services." He read from the manual: *"Ambulances must not be used as a means of transport for any person other than the ambulance crew, injured Riders and an RMO treating an injured Rider."*

He looked very pleased with himself.

"Unless permission is otherwise granted by the Authority," I added. "I act for the Authority and I'm giving permission. Anyway, I think you'll find that regulation is for the racetrack ambulances, not those from elsewhere." I was also pleased with myself, but *I* didn't show it. "Are you going with him?"

"No," said the doctor. "I have to remain here."

"I will go as your representative," I said, smiling, "to ensure he gets the appropriate care."

"Are you medically trained?"

"I was in Afghanistan with the Army," I said. "All soldiers on operations have basic medical training. I certainly know enough to deliver a broken collarbone to the hospital in an ambulance with two trained paramedics."

I also knew how to stop someone from bleeding to death when their foot was blown off by a land mine—I'd had to do that once too.

BILL MCKENZIE was far from happy when I climbed up into the ambulance after him.

"Can't you leave me alone?" he whined.

The female paramedic in the back looked at me.

"Ignore him," I said to her. "I'm here representing the horse race authority." I showed her my credentials.

"Sit there," she said, pointing at a seat. So I did, as Bill McKenzie himself was transferred from the wheeled chair to a stretcher. Then the doors were closed and off we went.

"Don't I get the bleeding bells and whistles?" McKenzie said with disappointment as the ambulance turned silently into the traffic on Portsmouth Road.

The paramedic smiled at him. "It's not an emergency," she said. "You're not in any immediate danger of dying."

He didn't seem particularly reassured. With good reason.

"Now," I said, "tell me about Wisden Wonder in yesterday's novice hurdle."

"Bloody nag dumped me on the ground and kicked me, didn't he? I've got a right sore head, I can tell you." He reached up with his right hand and touched behind his right ear.

"You fell off," I said accusingly, hoping for a response.

"You try staying on a bloody horse when it doesn't even try to jump. Wisden Wonder was damn lucky not to fall proper and do himself some serious mischief."

"You didn't give him any chance to jump," I said. "I've watched the videos over and over. You covered him up and made him run straight into that hurdle on purpose."

"Now, why would I do that?" he asked. "Do you think I enjoy being thrown to the ground at thirty miles per hour and then kicked for my troubles? It bloody hurt."

I feared I was getting nowhere. If he went on denying it, there would be little I could do. I couldn't actually prove that he'd come off intentionally, although I was sure he had.

"Do you know a racehorse owner called Leslie Morris?"

"No," he said. "Never heard of him."

He tried his best to control his expression, but there was a telltale widening of the pupils of his eyes and an involuntary slight flushing at the base of his neck. He knew Morris, all right.

"How much did he pay you?" I asked.

"No one paid me anything."

"So why did you do it?"

"I didn't," he said, this time in more control. He leaned back into the pillows and closed his eyes. "Can't you get this thing to go any faster? My bloody shoulder's killing me."

"Are you being blackmailed?" I asked.

"Blackmailed?" he repeated with apparent surprise.

"No more questions," said the paramedic bossily to me. She gave Bill a tube attached to a mouthpiece with which to suck in some painkilling gas.

I hoped it might also act as a truth drug.

13

I never did get back to Derrick and Gay Smith's box for afternoon tea, as I spent the next three hours at Kingston Hospital with Bill McKenzie.

The X-ray confirmed that he had indeed broken his collarbone and I silently berated myself for not having fully believed it. Perhaps I would have been slightly more sympathetic if I had realized he wasn't just trying to find another way of avoiding having to talk to me.

In fact, the break was pretty severe, with the ends of the bones overlapping, so surgery was needed to realign them and a plate and screws fitted to keep it that way.

I sat next to him as he lay on a gurney in a curtained-off emergency cubicle while we waited for the on-call orthopedic surgeon to be roused from his Saturday-afternoon slumbers.

"If you are not being blackmailed," I said, "why did you do it?"

"I didn't do anything," he said for the umpteenth time. "I really don't know what you're talking about."

I still didn't believe him.

"The BHA will demand to see your phone records, you know. And those of Leslie Morris. If there's been any contact between the two of you or the slightest bit of evidence that you've been lying to me, well . . . you can kiss good-bye to your career as a jockey. How old are you? Twenty-six?" He nodded. "You'd be banned for so many years that you'd be far too old to come back." I paused. "You have a wife, don't you?"

He nodded. "And a kid. Plus another one on the way."

"What will they do if you lose your livelihood?"

He looked miserable. "Why would I tell you anything even if I was up to no good? You'd ban me anyway. Do you think I'm stupid or something?"

"Actually, yes I do. Otherwise, you would never have got mixed up with race fixing in the first place."

He sighed deeply, which was clearly not a good move as the pain in his shoulder made him wince. "It's not that simple."

"Try me," I said.

He started to cry.

While it was not the response I had been expecting, it was a change from the continual denials he had been spouting since we arrived.

Bill McKenzie was a competent and experienced jockey who was perhaps never going to reach the "superstar" level, but he was doing all right. He was generally more at home on the small Midland racecourses, where he rode frequently for a number of different trainers, although he had recently had rides at some of the bigger tracks as well. He was having his best ever season and currently stood tenth on the jockeys list with forty or so winners from about three hundred rides.

As yet, he had no big-race wins under his belt, but he should still be making a pretty good living from his riding, especially if one added in a share of prize money, plus regular training fees.

If I was right about the fix, Leslie Morris had pocketed about seven thousand pounds from Bill McKenzie falling off Wisden Wonder.

I wondered how much would be the jockey's share.

Half, at best, or maybe a third? Probably even less.

Would he jeopardize his whole career for a couple of thousand pounds?

Did I really think he was *that* stupid?

My thoughts were interrupted by the arrival of the surgeon in blue scrubs and a dishcloth hat, and he was carrying a green folder.

"Mr. McKenzie," he said, studying the folder, "I see that you're a jockey."

He'd hardly had to read that in the paperwork, I thought. The patient was still wearing his britches, and the cut-off racing silks were draped over the end of the couch.

"Is this injury as a result of a racing fall?"

"Yes," said Bill. "At Sandown."

The surgeon made a note in the folder.

"Have you broken your collarbone before?"

"Not on this side," he said, pointing to his left shoulder. "But I've done the other one three times."

"You're crazy," said the surgeon. "Why don't you do something safer for a living?"

"Because I'm no good at anything else," Bill said, and then he looked straight at me. "Racing is my life."

I raised my eyebrows in response. He knew exactly what I was thinking—he was thinking it too.

The surgeon took a thick marker pen from his pocket and drew two big black arrows on Bill's left shoulder, one on his front and the other on his back.

He smiled. "We don't want to open you up on the wrong side, now do we?"

Next the surgeon produced a consent form from his folder.

"How long will I be off?" Bill asked him as he signed.

"Bones generally take six to eight weeks to heal."

"Six to eight weeks! No way. I need to be back sooner than that. I've got a ride in the King George on Boxing Day."

"The plate might help. It will provide the support needed. When I plate a broken hip, I try to get the patient up and standing on it the following day."

"So how long?" Bill asked again.

"A couple of weeks, maybe."

"A couple of days, more like," said Bill with a grin.

"See, you are crazy," the surgeon said again, smiling back at him. "Completely crazy."

I WENT HOME shortly after when they came to pick him up for surgery. I suppose I could have waited for the operation to be over, but it would probably have taken at least an hour and then he'd be woozy for a good few hours after that. Interviewing an injured jockey in an ambulance on the way to the hospital had been one thing but I'd be pushing my luck to be asking him more questions while he lay in the post-anesthesia recovery room.

I let myself into my apartment and sidled past the unopened cardboard boxes into my kitchen–cum–living room.

It was cold, the mercury having plummeted after the sun went down under clear skies. I flicked on the electric fire but kept my coat resolutely on with my hands deep in its pockets.

It was eight o'clock Saturday evening. Just three weeks before Christmas, when any sensible person was out at a party or having dinner with friends.

But not me.

I thought about Henrietta Shawcross.

I hadn't had an opportunity to go back to the Smiths' box to say good-bye to her—or to anyone else, for that matter. I hadn't even been at the racetrack for the main event of the afternoon, the sixth race of the day, by which time I was well on my way to the hospital in the ambulance.

I opened my laptop computer and logged on to the *Racing Post* website to check the results.

Ebury Tiger had won the Tingle Creek Chase, and there were reports of emotional scenes at the trophy presentation when the winning jockey had dedicated the victory to the memory of his dear friend Dave Swinton, who, he said, should rightly have been standing there in his place.

Dave Swinton, alive or dead, was still everyone's knight in shining armor. I would make myself no friends whatsoever if I tarnished that image with talk of him purposely losing races or committing other misdeeds. Like the small matter of trying to kill me.

I also searched the Internet for any mentions of a Henrietta Shawcross.

There were masses of them, and lots of photos too, many in the Bystander section, on the *Tatler* magazine website.

If the images were anything to go by, Miss Shawcross was a socialite of some renown, being photographed at many of the most sought-after events and parties. But there was little actual information about her life in the magazine, just her looking beautiful for the camera lens while cuddling up to a variety of actors, singers and other A-list headliners at glamorous gatherings.

Next, I carried out searches for Sir Richard Reynard, her uncle, and for Martin Reynard, her first cousin.

Both were in shipping. To be more precise, Sir Richard was the sixty-nine-year-old chairman of Reynard Shipping Limited, a company set up by his grandfather, and Martin was forty-two and also a director. And they were loaded. The *Sunday Times* "Top 1,000 UK Rich List" put the Reynard family at number 147, with a combined wealth in excess of half a billion pounds.

Reynard Shipping was almost a household name, and everyone must have seen the trucks carrying containers with REYNARD SHIPPING painted on the side in big white letters. No wonder Derrick had thought I should know who Sir Richard Reynard was.

He would certainly be able to afford to buy a potential Derby winner. In fact, he'd be able to buy a whole stableful of them.

I wondered if Henrietta Shawcross was included in the calculation of the family wealth. Probably.

I sighed. Either way, she was out of my league, that was for sure. That's if she would even speak to me again after my dreadful faux pas at lunch.

I dug a little deeper on the Internet.

For some reason, I couldn't find any recent accounts for Reynard Shipping Limited on the Companies House website. It appeared from their records that the company had ceased to exist some three years previously, although it was quite clearly still trading—their shipping containers were everywhere.

But there was some more detail about Henri.

According to some past newspaper articles, Henrietta Shawcross was an only child. Furthermore, she was an orphan, her parents having died together in a helicopter crash when she'd been just sixteen. Her mother's not inconsiderable fortune, including a twenty-five percent stake in Reynard Shipping, had passed directly to her, to be held in trust by her uncle until her thirtieth birthday, which, I noted, was coming up in February.

No wonder Gay Smith had said that Henri didn't need a sugar daddy.

I went to my freezer and selected a Chicken Madras from a stack of frozen dinners and popped it in the microwave.

I wouldn't go as far as to say that I'd be diagnosed as clinically depressed, but I knew I was pretty miserable. I didn't take antidepressant drugs or anything, and I didn't feel particularly suicidal—indeed, I had fought with all my strength to escape death in Dave Swinton's sauna. There had been no question then of me giving up and lying down to die when it would have been very easy to have done so.

It was just that I considered my life at present as meaningless.

I woke up each morning and went to work in my office at BHA headquarters, or at a racetrack somewhere, or I visited some training stables or an equine swimming pool, or I attended one of myriad other racing venues, yet, wherever I had spent the day, I would return to the solitude and loneliness of my apartment.

I sat in an armchair to eat my dinner and wondered what Henri Shawcross was doing. I may not have been a regular gambler, but I'd bet an arm and a leg that she wasn't eating a microwaved curry off her lap while watching Saturday-night drivel on the television.

I'd just finished my food when my landline telephone rang.

My heart leaped. Could it be her? Asking me out?

No, it couldn't. I hadn't given her my phone number.

"Hello?" I said, answering the call.

No one at the other end spoke even though I could hear some noises in the background.

"Hello?" I said again. "Is anyone there?"

After two or three seconds, the line went dead.

How odd, I thought. I dialed 1471 to get the last number that had called and wrote it down on the back of an envelope that contained my gas bill. It wasn't a number I recognized. I tried calling back, but all I heard was a disembodied voice stating that the number did not receive incoming calls.

No sooner had I put the phone down than it rang again.

I picked it up. "Hello?" I said slowly.

"Jeff, is that you?" said a voice.

"Hello, sis," I said. "Did you call me just now?"

"No," Faye said, sounding concerned. "Should I have?"

"No. It's all right. I had a call, but no one was there. That's all."

"Happens to me all the time," said Faye. "I blame the phone companies. They seem to spend so much of their time trying to sell us cheaper and cheaper broadband that they neglect the phone service."

But the phone service had been working fine—I had been able to hear the background noise. It was the fact that the caller *said nothing* that had been strange.

"Are you feeling any better than last Sunday?" I asked her.

"Much better, thank you," she said. "Brandy for breakfast has helped a lot." She laughed and I wasn't sure if she was joking or not.

"Are you doing anything tomorrow lunchtime?" she asked.

"No," I said.

Nothing other than moping around my apartment feeling sorry for myself.

"Good," Faye said. "Come to lunch. We have some guests and, to be honest, I could do with the help."

"What time?"

"As early as you can. We've got twelve people coming."

"Who are they?" I asked. I didn't altogether trust Faye not to set me up to meet a dozen prospective girlfriends.

"For some reason, Q has decided that it is his turn to host the annual Christmas lunch for the QCs in his chambers, together with their wives. Someone does it every year. It would have been nice if he'd given me a bit more warning. It seems he asked them all ages ago but only sprung it on me last Tuesday."

Suddenly being alone in my apartment with my TV and a microwaved dinner seemed quite attractive compared with spending the day with Quentin's legal cronies. But I didn't want to upset Faye.

"That would be lovely," I lied. "Do you want me to bring anything?"

"Just yourself. We're having a buffet and I've got everything I need. I could just do with some help setting it all out and with the drinks when everyone arrives. Q is so hopeless when it comes to anything practical."

I wondered if I was being asked only because Faye understood how lonely I had become, especially on weekends, and rather than actually needing any real help she was simply trying to include me in something that involved other people, even if they were Quentin's work colleagues.

"OK," I said. "Is eleven o'clock early enough?"

"Eleven would be great. Thanks so much. I'll see you in the morning."

She hung up.

Was the highlight of my day to be acting as a servant to my brother-in-law and a bunch of his barrister friends? I suppose it might make a pleasant change from having someone try to kill me, as had happened the previous Sunday.

I wish.

14

Twice more my home phone rang and no one spoke on the other end. And twice more I dialed 1471 to get the number. Each time, it was different. My gas bill envelope now had all three numbers written on it and each of them, when called back, produced the *No incoming calls* message.

The second call was made as I was getting into bed on Saturday evening and the third woke me at seven o'clock on Sunday morning. I was convinced someone was there, listening, because the line didn't sound completely dead, and at one point I was sure I could hear some traffic in the background.

The calls made me feel a little uneasy, as if someone was stalking me.

And it wouldn't be the first time. Over the years, I had investigated a number of less than agreeable characters, some of whom had taken against me personally for exposing their own wrongdoing. I had been threatened, beaten up and, on one occasion, knocked down by a speeding car.

Most had been attempts to prevent me from carrying out an investigation, but a couple had been out of revenge for getting someone banned from racing.

I couldn't think of anyone in particular that I had recently upset by getting them disqualified or excluded from the sport. There might be, however, somebody who'd ended up in prison as a result of their fraud and was now released and bent on settling an old score.

I would have to just get on with my life as usual and watch my back, as I always did, avoiding dark alleyways and dimly lit multistory parking lots.

MY PHONE RANG once again just after ten o'clock as I was putting on my overcoat to leave for Richmond and my waiting duties at Faye and Quentin's house.

"Hello?" I said.

No reply.

"Who are you?" I asked.

No reply.

"What do you want?"

No reply.

The line went dead. I again dialed 1471 and this time the number was the same as for the previous call. Again, I tried to call it back, but, as before, there was nothing but the disembodied message *No incoming calls.*

Annoying, I thought.

If I'd had more time and it hadn't been a Sunday, I might have contacted the phone company to have my number changed. But it was so irritating to have to go through the whole rigmarole of informing everyone of the change in number. Although, come to think of it, not many people knew my number in the first place.

I'd had the number transferred from the apartment I'd shared with Lydia. Nowadays, the only person who called me on that line was Faye. I tended to use my cell for all work calls, incoming and outgoing, and the only friends who had used the landline phone had departed from my life at the same time Lydia had.

Could it be Lydia? Pining after the sound of my voice?

I thought it most unlikely. The last I'd heard, she and her new man were blissfully happy together. But that had been from a friend of hers who had seemingly wanted to rub my nose in the fact that she had left me, so it might not have been very accurate.

I had a careful check outside as I locked my front door. There was no one hiding in the bushes waiting to attack me.

I was intending to take the train from Willesden Junction to Richmond, but I set off in a direction directly away from the railway station, doubling back along two side streets and retracing my path twice, just to check that there was nobody intent on following me.

There wasn't.

I smiled at myself. I must be getting paranoid.

THE BUFFET LUNCH went off without a hitch and I even found I enjoyed it.

It was a revelation to me to discover that not all the Queen's Counsel in Quentin Calderfield's chambers were as stuffy, bigoted and boring as he. In fact, some of them turned out to be fun, and they were far more proficient at taking the mickey out of their host than I had ever dared to be.

"Come on, Quentin, give us a song, show us your yang side," one of them said, laughing loudly. "All we ever see is your yin."

From the look on his face, I'm not sure that Quentin had ever heard of yin and yang, which was somewhat of a surprise considering he always saw things distinctly as right or wrong, white or black, light or dark, just like Paul Maldini.

Needless to say, Quentin didn't break into song.

"Do you think it's going all right?" Faye asked when I went to the kitchen to fetch yet another bottle of red wine.

"It's fine," I said. "I never realized lawyers could drink so much and still speak so eloquently."

"Practice," she said. "All those liquid lunches they have, then back into court to argue for a man's freedom, or his life. Most lawyers' livers were given a welcome rest when the old Wig and Pen Club closed down. Q used to have lunch there almost every day. He was distraught when it shut."

IT WAS totally dark by the time the last of their lunch guests departed.

Faye collapsed into a deep armchair in the living room. "I'm pooped," she said.

"What a great lunch," said Quentin, slumping down on the sofa and putting his feet up.

"Thank God. it's not our turn every year," Faye said with her eyes closed.

"Right, then," I said. "I'll leave you two and get back home."

"You're very welcome to stay," said Faye. "We're only going to veg out in front of the telly with some cheese and crackers. That's if you'd like the company."

"Thanks for the offer, but I should be getting back. I have things I must do before tomorrow morning."

Did I have things to do? Not really. It was just my silly subconscious telling me that, for some reason, I would be better off on my own—like a leper.

"Suit yourself," Faye said, and she started to get up.

"Don't move," I said. "I can find my own way out. Thank you for a great lunch."

"Thank *you* for your help."

I leaned down and gave her a kiss. "Look after yourself, sis. Getting this tired is not good for you."

"Tell me about it."

I waved at Quentin, who was already half asleep. He briefly lifted a hand in response.

I let myself out into the cold night and walked to Richmond town center across the green. Only when I started down Brewers Lane did I remember about not walking down dark alleyways on my own.

I spun round. No one was following me. Why should there be?

I turned up my coat collar and dug my hands deep into the pockets against the icy northerly wind and made it safely to the station to catch the train to Willesden Junction. Once there, I decided against taking the shortcut home along the gloomy trackside path, rather keeping to the longer, well-lit streets. I did it not out of any worry that it would be me in particular that might be targeted but because there had been reports of several recent muggings on the path during the dark winter evenings and I had no real wish to be added to those statistics.

I checked the deep shadows around the bushes outside my front door for lurking rogues and villains and of course there were none, so I let myself in.

The rogues and villains were already inside.

There were two of them and they were not making a social call.

IT WAS their haste that saved me.

They were waiting for me just inside the front door. One of the men grabbed my arm as soon as I stepped through and slammed me up against the wall, sending my cell phone spinning out of my hand, while the other one tried to make mincemeat of my insides with a thin, sharp carving knife, stabbing repeatedly at my abdomen and chest.

If they had just waited until I'd removed my overcoat, I would have been far more vulnerable. As it was, the thick woolen folds and the twin rows of large bone buttons of my double-breasted, military-style greatcoat, together with my tweed jacket underneath, dampened or deflected the lethal thrusts to the extent that the blade seemed to barely make it through to my skin.

And I fought back with all the strength of the condemned and terrified.

I kicked out at the knifeman, catching him hard in the crotch. Then I flung his accomplice off my arm across the hallway, where he tripped over one of the still-packed cardboard boxes, falling halfway through my bedroom door.

I don't think they had expected such resistance. They must have hoped to catch me by surprise and deliver a mortal wound before I had a chance to respond.

I may not be that big in either height or bulk, but I was once a serving officer in Her Majesty's Armed Forces and I had enjoyed, more than most, the grueling physical regimen of my year at Sandhurst. I had tried to sustain a fairly high level of basic fitness ever since. Even during the recent dark months of my life I had still managed to maintain a daily routine of fifty push-ups and a hundred crunches before bed every night.

So I was strong and agile. And I was angry—bloody angry.

Who did they think they were, breaking into my home and attacking me?

However, in the face of superior numbers, I decided that retreat was probably the best policy, so I ran for my still-open front door. But my two would-be murderers were not giving up that easily and I could both hear and feel them right behind me as I ran out into the street.

I ran down the center of the road, shouting for assistance.

"Help! Help!" I screamed at the top of my voice. "Murder! Murder! Somebody help me."

Not one of my neighbors came to my aid. Not even a curtain twitched. Perhaps I would have had more response if I'd shouted, *Money! Money! Get some free money.*

A car turned into the road at the far end and came toward me, its lights shining brightly. I ran straight down the middle of the road toward it, waving my arms wildly above my head, until it slowed and finally stopped with my legs up against the hood.

The assassins wavered in their pursuit and then took off in the other direction, disappearing into the shadows.

"Call the police," I called breathlessly to the driver of the car.

"Call them yourself," he replied bad-temperedly through his open window. "And get out of the bleeding way, will you? I could have knocked you down, easy. Running down the middle of the road in a dark coat is asking for trouble."

"Someone is trying to kill me," I said.

"Yeah, yeah," he said in obvious disbelief, "and I'm the Queen of Sheba."

I stepped back a pace, unbuttoned and opened the front of both my coat and jacket. The white shirt beneath was blood red and glistening wet in the light from the car's headlights.

"Fuck me," he said.

"*Now* will you call the police?"

15

A police car and an ambulance turned up together, both with multiple bright blue flashing lights that lit up the street and hurt my eyes.

It became clear that a stabbing in a London street was not sufficiently unusual for either the police officers or the ambulance crew to get too excited. In fact, I found the perceived indifference to apprehending my assailants to be frustrating.

"Can't you get the helicopter up?" I urged the police as soon as they arrived.

"Helicopters cost money," one of them replied, shaking his head. "Especially on Sunday evenings."

I was carried on a stretcher, half sitting, half lying, into the back of the ambulance and we set off, with one of the policemen sitting on a chair near my head, just as I had done the previous day with Bill McKenzie.

"My front door is wide open," I said. "The key is still in the lock."

"Don't you worry about that," said the policeman. "My colleague will look after your house."

The paramedic cut my shirt away and raised his eyebrows in surprise.

"You have at least a dozen stab wounds on your torso," he said. "How come you're still alive?"

The policeman suddenly took a slightly greater interest.

"I don't think they're very deep," I said. "My overcoat saved me."

The paramedic placed several electrodes on the bits of my chest with no knife punctures and wired them up to a metal box above my head. Next, he slipped a blood-pressure cuff over my arm. He also attached a sort of bulldog clip to my finger and then inserted a needle into a vein on the back of my hand to set up a drip.

"To stop dehydration," he said when I looked at him quizzically. "You've lost a fair amount of blood."

"So who stabbed you?" the policeman asked.

"There were two of them," I said. "They were waiting for me in my apartment."

"Associates, were they?" he asked in a tone that implied he didn't care much. It dawned on me why.

"No," I said to him. "They were *not* associates and I am *not* a drug dealer. I am a senior investigator for the Integrity Service of the British Horseracing Authority. I *am* the horseracing police and two men have just tried to kill me. I would like, please, to speak to a higher-ranking officer."

The policeman swiftly changed his tune, asking me for a description of the men so he could put out a call.

A description?

"I spent most of the time with my eyes glued to the knife," I said. "I didn't really look at their faces."

"But you saw them well enough to know they were not associates," he said.

"Yes." Funny how the mind works. I couldn't remember seeing their faces, yet I must have. Enough, anyway, to realize I didn't know them.

"White or black?" he asked.

"White," I said with certainty. The overhead light in my hallway had been off, but there had been enough illumination from the one in the open porch.

"Masks and gloves?"

"Gloves, yes," I said. "Leather gloves. But no masks."

"They obviously didn't expect you to survive long enough to provide us with a description."

I was beginning to feel seriously unwell and I was having great difficulty breathing. I leaned my head back on the pillow.

"Blues and twos," the paramedic shouted at his colleague who was driving. "Blood pressure's dropping and his O saturation has fallen below ninety."

I heard the ambulance's siren start up. It couldn't go quick enough, as far as I was concerned.

The medic put an oxygen mask over my nose and mouth, which made me feel marginally better, but I was so tired—I could hardly keep my eyes open.

"Stay with us," the paramedic said loudly into my ear. "Stay with us."

He briefly disconnected the drip from the needle in the back of my hand and replaced it with a full syringe. "Adrenalin," he said, pushing the plunger, but I was barely listening. I was drifting off.

"Don't go to sleep," said the paramedic, leaning over me and putting his face close to mine. "Come on, Mr. Hinkley, you must stay awake."

I forced my eyes open and was not greatly heartened by the worry lines on his forehead as he listened to my chest with a stethoscope.

"I need you to sit up some more," he said, placing his arm around my shoulders and pulling me. The move helped a little, but my breathing was becoming more and more labored as I gasped for air, and still I felt so extraordinarily fatigued.

I was going to sleep and there was nothing I could do to prevent it.

In my last conscious moment before oblivion, I thought with despair, *This is it—I'm dying.*

I WOKE UP lying on a hospital bed with all my senses switching back on at once.

I stared at the light fixture on the ceiling, could hear a beep-beep somewhere over my head that I took to be a heart monitor, and I could smell the typical sweet aroma of hospital disinfectant.

My sensory nerves were fully operational as well, with my chest feeling like someone was driving nails into it. My abdomen was on fire, and my throat felt like it had been rebored with a wire brush.

And I was thirsty.

I tried to speak, but my tongue seemed to be stuck to the roof of my mouth. All that I could manage was a groan.

"Ah, you're awake," said a voice.

I swiveled my eyes away from the ceiling and looked at a

pretty young woman standing at the foot of the bed dressed in a blue nurse's tunic.

"Water," I tried to say through the oxygen mask that covered my nose and mouth. I'm not sure it came out quite right, but she seemed to understand because she nodded and disappeared, returning with a cup and a straw. Nothing ever tasted better.

For a few moments when I'd first awakened, I had wondered where I was, then I remembered everything up to and including the hopeless feeling of impending death that I'd experienced in the ambulance.

I wasn't dead—I was alive and in the hospital.

Unless, of course, this was the afterlife.

I reckoned that it wasn't, not unless this pain constituted Hell itself. I did consider that seriously for a few seconds but came to the conclusion that Lucifer probably was unlikely to have pretty nurses on hand to fetch water for the inmates.

I was still alive and I was glad about it.

"Do you know your name?" asked the nurse, holding the oxygen mask away from my face.

"Jeff Hinkley," I said, my voice still coming out as a croak.

"How are you feeling?"

"I hurt."

"I'll fetch you something for that."

She replaced the mask and disappeared from view, returning in a few moments with a small plastic cup containing some clear liquid.

"Morphine," she said. "This will help."

She held the mask away from my face again and helped me raise my head slightly to drink it down. Only then did I realize that I had a multitude of wires and tubes coming out of the side of my neck below my right ear.

A man came into sight. He was wearing scrubs.

"So, Mr. Hinkley, you're still with us?" I wasn't sure if it was a question or a statement. "I'm Dr. Shwan. It's Egyptian, like *swan* only with an *h*. I'm the doctor that operated on you. You're a very lucky boy. Very lucky indeed. I thought we'd lost you, but we managed to bring you back." He smiled.

He'd called me a boy yet he was hardly older than I.

"I feel like I've been hit by a truck," I said. "I'm so sore."

"I'm not surprised. I had to open both your chest and your abdomen."

"And my throat?" I asked. "That hurts as well."

"We had to insert a tube down your throat in order to ventilate your lungs with oxygen during surgery. Normal breathing isn't possible with the chest wall open. The tube tends to cause some minor discomfort for a while afterward."

It didn't feel minor to me.

"You rest," said the doctor. "I'll tell you everything later."

"Tell me now," I said. I was never one for waiting.

"You have thirteen separate stab wounds, most of which are superficial. Two of them, however, are deep. One penetrated the abdominal muscle wall and punctured your bowel, while the other, the most serious, passed between your second and third ribs on the left side, causing a laceration of the aortic arch just above your heart."

I suppose I *had* asked.

"It is that one that almost killed you," he said. "It caused substantial bleeding into the chest cavity, which compromised your breathing and also filled the space around the heart with blood, giving it no room to beat."

"But I was fine for a while. I was even able to run."

"Yes, but all the time the chest cavity was slowly filling. Only when the blood got to a critical level did you suffer any symptoms. Usually, by then, it's too late to save the patient. You had a cardiac arrest as you arrived at the ER and I had to perform an emergency thoracotomy right there to get your heart pumping again. There wasn't even time to get you to the operating room. As I said, you're a very lucky boy."

"Very lucky to have you around when I needed it."

"I don't know about that," he said with a smile. "Yours was the first chest I've ever opened. I've only ever seen it done by others. I'm an emergency room doctor, not a heart surgeon. But needs must, and it seems to have worked." He made a movement as if to mop sweat from his brow.

I knew from my time with the Army in Afghanistan how extreme situations could require desperate solutions well out of one's comfort zone. And how it takes immense courage not to wait for someone with the right experience but to make the decision to do it yourself because to wait would be to fail.

"Thank you, Dr. Shwan," I said, meaning it.

"Don't thank me yet," he said. "Give it another forty-eight hours or so. A gurney in the ER is not the most sterile of environments to perform heart massage or to repair a major artery. I'm just hoping you won't get an infection. We are delivering antibiotics direct to your heart cavity, yet we can never be sure. And then there's the rupture of your bowel. I repaired that as well, but there's always a chance of peritonitis."

"Well, thank you anyway," I said, "for what you've done so far."

"You need to rest now. Give your body the chance to heal itself."

The morphine was finally beginning to work. I closed my eyes.

"The police are outside and they're keen to speak to you," he said. "I'll tell them they have to wait."

Good idea, I thought. Let them wait.

There would be plenty of time later to think about why I'd been attacked and who would have done such a thing to me.

Twice in eight days someone had tried to kill me.

I just hoped it wouldn't be *third time's the charm.*

THE POLICE in the form of two plainclothes detectives were finally allowed in to question me the following evening, by which time the pain in my chest had subsided a little from an unbearable level 10 to an almost manageable 8.

Thankfully, my throat was nearly back to normal and the oxygen mask over my face had been replaced by two little tubes that jutted up into my nostrils. Hence, two-way communication was much improved.

"Mr. Hinkley," one of the policemen said, "I'm Detective Inspector Galvin of the Metropolitan Police Homicide and Serious Crime Command and this is my sergeant, D.S. Gibb."

They sat down on two chairs, one either side of the bed.

"You've been causing quite a stir," said the detective inspector. "The Commissioner has been getting calls from the chairman of the Horseracing Authority demanding to know who tried to kill his senior investigator."

Blimey, I thought. I hadn't had that sort of response the previous week. Probably because I'd played it down. And also because of the death of Dave Swinton.

"I'm glad somebody cares," I said.

"Tell me what happened on Sunday evening," said the detective.

I went through the whole thing as best I could remember, from the moment I turned the key in the lock of my front door right up to the time of the arrival of the ambulance, and the sergeant wrote it all down in his notebook.

"According to the constable who attended the scene, you told him you didn't know your attackers," said the inspector. "Is that correct?"

"Yes," I said. "Quite correct."

"But you were unable to give him a description of the men."

"I became too ill."

"Can you give me one now?"

I had thought of little else for the preceding twenty-four hours. Over and over again, I had gone through the whole thing in my head trying to conjure up the image of the two faces but with very limited success.

"I was concentrating on the knife," I said. "I know that the men were white and I must have seen their faces well enough to realize I didn't recognize them, but I'm afraid I can't help you."

"Did they say anything?"

"Not that I remember. It all happened so quickly. One of them grabbed me and the other started stabbing as soon as I walked through the door."

"So they were waiting for you?"

"Yes," I said. "I am sure they were. I was careless. I checked the bushes in the front garden and never imagined that anyone would be inside."

The sergeant looked up at me from his notebook. "Were you expecting to be attacked?" he asked.

"Not exactly expecting it, no. I'm just naturally vigilant. And it isn't the first time. Someone tried to kill me only a week ago."

Both the policemen looked at me in surprise.

"Was it the man with the knife?" the inspector asked.

"No," I said. "Not unless he's risen from the dead."

I told them all about being shut in the sauna, my escape and the subsequent discovery of Dave Swinton's body in the burning car. They'd heard about that.

"You can speak to Detective Sergeant Jagger from the Thames Valley Police, if you need to. He's the investigating officer."

D.S. Gibb wrote it down.

"How did the men get into my apartment?" I asked.

"They forced open a window in your kitchen," said the sergeant. "It's now been nailed shut."

They must have come down the lane that ran along the back of the garden.

"Was anything stolen?" I asked.

"You'll have to answer that yourself, Mr. Hinkley, when you go home. There certainly wasn't the usual mess we find when villains have been searching for valuables. No drawers pulled out or anything."

That seemed to confirm that it had definitely been me they were after, not my meager worldly goods.

I leaned back on the pillow and closed my eyes. I was getting tired.

"We will leave you now to rest," said the inspector, standing up, "but we'll be back with some mug shots for you to look at when you're a little better. Is there anything you need?"

"You could contact my sister for me," I said. "She'll be wondering why I didn't call when I got home on Sunday, as I usually do."

I gave them Faye's phone number.

"No problem," said the inspector. "I'll call her as soon as I'm outside."

"Please don't worry her," I said. "Ask her to come in tomorrow."

They started to leave.

"Hold on a moment," I said, opening my eyes again. "There were some telephone calls."

"What calls?"

"On Saturday night and Sunday morning, I received four calls on my landline but no one spoke. I am sure there was someone on the line because I could hear noises in the background, but they didn't say anything, they just listened for a few seconds and then hung up. I now wonder if the calls were made simply to find out if I was there."

"Are you in the phone directory?" the inspector asked.

"I don't really know," I said. "I hardly ever use the landline. It was my former girlfriend who liked it. I just transferred the number to my new apartment when we sold the old one. I need the broadband that comes with it."

"We'll check your phone records," D.I. Galvin said.

"I dialed 1471 each time to get the numbers. I tried to call back, but none of them would receive incoming calls."

"Pay phones, I shouldn't wonder," said the inspector. "Those don't accept incoming calls anymore."

"I wrote down the numbers," I said. "They're on the back of the envelope that my gas bill came in. I left it on the counter in my kitchen."

"We'll look into it," the inspector assured me.

Fine, I thought. Let someone else do the work. I was too tired.

16

Doctor Shwan came back to see me the following morning. The forty-eight hours was up and I hadn't developed a fever. No infection.

"What day is it?" I asked him.

"Wednesday."

"Where, exactly, am I?"

"Critical Care Unit, University College Hospital, Euston Road."

"When can I go home?"

"Soon." He smiled. "Good."

"What's good?" I asked.

"You," he said. "You didn't ask me questions like that on Monday because you were only interested in your body. Now you are well enough to think outside that. I think it's time to remove all the monitors and tubes and send you to a regular ward."

"I want to go home," I said.

"Not just yet," replied the doctor. "We still need to keep an eye on you for a while longer. Your body has suffered a considerable trauma and your breastbone needs to heal some more before you go running around, undoing all my handiwork."

"My breastbone?"

"I had to saw it in half to get to your heart. I joined it back together with stainless steel wire, but the bone needs time to begin to bind naturally before you can put any stress on it."

Too much information, I thought. No wonder it hurt so much.

"So when can I go home?" I asked.

"The earliest would be the weekend."

"Friday?" I said.

He laughed. "Saturday, maybe, but only if you continue to make good progress. And you must promise not to do anything strenuous for at least another three or four weeks. And no lifting anything heavier than a cup of tea. Your abdominal wall needs to heal as well."

The doctor went away, still chuckling to himself, and presently a couple of nurses arrived to disconnect the mass of tubes and wires that sprouted out of various points on my body.

"What are they all for?" I asked.

"Those in your neck include a monitor for measuring the blood pressure actually in your heart and lungs, a tube for taking antibiotics direct to the heart and some pacemaker wires just in case your heart needed an electrical stimulus to make it pump. Then there are three separate tubes in your chest to drain away any excess fluid, a line in each elbow for intravenous infusions, a nasogastric tube that goes through your nose and down your throat to feed you and a catheter in your bladder to assist urination."

Perhaps I shouldn't have asked.

"Plus, of course, the ECG electrodes that are stuck on your torso."

Of course.

Everything was removed other than the single IV in my right arm. According to the nurses, that was so I could receive any fluids and medication without the need for separate injections. I was all in favor of that.

"Now it's time to get you up and walking," said one of them.

They helped me first sit on the edge of the bed and to stand up, hovering on each side of me in case I keeled over. I didn't, and I was soon walking around without any real problems other than the continuous throbbing that went all the way down my front where both the doctor and the knifeman had made their various incisions.

I WAS MOVED from the Critical Care Unit to a regular surgical ward on the ninth floor, where I was allocated a single room close to the nurses' station.

"For better security," I was told.

Security.

Thankfully, murder on a London street has not yet become so commonplace as to be unworthy of reporting. Therefore, with nothing in the media, I had to assume that my two assailants must be aware by now that they had failed to deliver the fatal blow.

They knew they had failed, and, furthermore, they must believe I had seen their faces. So would they try again to complete the job and dispose of the witness?

I wasn't at all sure that being in a single room was the most secure arrangement, especially as the door had no lock. I asked the nurses to leave the door open so I could see them at their desk—and, more important, they could see me.

I also asked them to ensure that any visitors were announced and then accompanied unless I agreed otherwise, although, in fact, the nurses were all so busy that anyone could wander into my room unseen if one was careful to wait for the desk to be unattended, as it was at least half of the time.

Indeed, my first visitor waltzed into my room, unannounced and unaccompanied, about an hour after I'd moved in.

"It's normally *you* visiting *me* in the hospital," she said. "Not the other way round."

"Hello, my darling big sister," I said, smiling at her.

"I told you to move away from Harlesden. It's dangerous up there. Too many robberies. Can't you live somewhere safer, like Richmond?"

"Apartments in Richmond cost more than twice those in Harlesden," I said.

"There can be no price placed on one's safety," she said with gravitas.

How true.

I decided against telling her that I wasn't actually robbed of my wallet and watch and that my attackers would have likely followed me all the way to Timbuktu if I'd lived there.

"Nice room," Faye said, standing by the window and looking out at the spectacular view over London. She turned. "So what happened, exactly? The policeman who called just said you'd been mugged."

"I was attacked by two men," I said in a deadpan voice, trying to play down the drama. "One of them held me while the other one stabbed."

"How many times?" she asked.

I would have preferred not to tell her any of the grisly details, as it would only make her worry, but I knew she wouldn't stop asking until she got the answers she was after and they would be better coming from me than from the doctors or the police.

"Thirteen."

"Thirteen! Good God, Jeff, that's unbelievable."

"You should see my chest and stomach. There are more stitches than in a fisherman's sweater." I laughed.

"It's no laughing matter," Faye said sternly.

"Yes it is," I said. "Be happy that I'm still here to laugh at all."

She didn't look very happy.

"Have the police caught the men?"

"Not that I'm aware of," I said. "I hope they're still looking for them."

I wondered just how hard they were looking. After all, it was only an *attempted* murder, not the real thing. But my attackers had done their best to send me on a journey that would end six feet under and weren't to know that Dr. Shwan would be on hand to open my chest in the nick of time to prevent it.

Surely they were equally culpable whether I had lived or died.

According to the law, as Quentin had said, the maximum term of imprisonment for attempted murder was life, the same as for succeeding, but, in reality, both the effort expended to apprehend and the sentences passed down on the guilty were usually much less.

"How long are you going to be in here?" Faye asked.

"I should be out at the weekend. As long as I don't develop an infection."

"Come and stay with us."

"Thank you, Faye, dear, but I'll be fine at my own place."

She tilted her head sideways and looked at me. "Are you sure?"

"Absolutely," I said. "If this affair has taught me anything, it's that life is more precious than I'd realized. When I thought I was dying, I was in total despair, and now that I've survived I have every intention of living my life to the full. The moment has arrived to move on from Lydia."

"Hallelujah!" she said, lifting her hands and eyes to the heavens. "And about time too."

"Has it been that bad?" I asked with a smile.

"Worse," she said. "Since she left, you've been about as cheerful as a fatted calf at a slaugherhouse."

"Oh, thanks."

"It's true," she said. "Do you realize that you sigh all the time?"

"No."

"Well, you do. It's like being around a penitent monk, but less fun."

"I'm sorry," I said. "Henceforth, I will be happy and jolly. I promise."

"There's no need to go that far. Just be your normal self."

We laughed out loud, and we hadn't done that together for a long time.

FAYE DEPARTED just as D.I. Galvin arrived, this time without his sergeant sidekick.

"Any news?" I asked. "Any arrests?"

"Sadly, no," replied the inspector. "But we have done a check on those telephone calls and, as I suspected, they were all made from public telephones. The first was made from Waterloo Station at eight twenty-seven p.m. on the evening before you were attacked. The second was from a phone at the corner of Parliament Square at eleven thirty-two p.m. the same evening. The other two, on the Sunday morning, were made from the only remaining pay phone in High Street Harlesden."

"But that's only round the corner from my apartment."

"Indeed," he said. "And I suspect you are right in thinking they were checking up to see if you were in. Three more calls were made to your line from that number, one at eleven-fifty a.m., another at twelve noon and the third some ten minutes after that."

"I'd gone out by then."

"As they would have known."

"Is there any CCTV coverage of those public phones?"

"We're looking into that, but I wouldn't hold your breath. Waterloo Station or Parliament Square are our best bet—at least we can assume that the cameras will work there. Even if there are any cameras in High Street Harlesden, they will probably have been vandalized."

Maybe Faye had a point.

"So what else?" I asked.

"Have you remembered anything new about the assailants?" he asked.

"Not really," I said. "Sorry."

"Was the one that stabbed you the bigger or the smaller of the two?"

"The smaller."

I stared at him. "How did I know that?"

"The subconscious mind often knows lots of things that the conscious mind doesn't register until it receives a trigger. How much smaller was he?"

"At least a couple of inches, but he was stocky and made up for his lack of height with width. The other guy was taller but leaner."

"Taller than you?"

"About the same. The knifeman was shorter, but he was also crouching. I remember looking down at his face."

"Glasses? Beard? Mustache?"

"No," I said. "He did have some stubble, as if he hadn't shaved for a couple of days. He was also wearing a dark woolen hat, like a beanie, that covered his head and the top half of his ears."

"Wide face or narrow?"

"Neither one," I said. "Just normal."

I was stunned that I could now remember so much after all those hours of nothing.

"How about the other one?"

I thought hard. "I didn't get to see his face properly."

"Did he also have a hat?"

I tried to picture in my mind the image of him tripping over the boxes in my hallway as I threw him off me.

"I don't know, but he was wearing sneakers—you know, the ones with high ankles and lots of laces."

"Basketball shoes?"

"Yes. Exactly. With white laces."

"What color were the shoes?"

"There was not enough light. I think they were a fairly dark color, maybe red, with white soles. I remember seeing them as he was lying over the boxes."

"How about coats?" he asked.

I tried to recall. "Sorry," I said. "It all happened so fast."

"And the knife? Can you describe that? We didn't find it at the scene."

"It was like a carving knife, with a long, thin blade. I'll not forget that in a hurry. It was very frightening."

"Overhand or underhand?"

"Eh?"

"When he was holding the knife, did it point up or down?"

"Up to start with, but then he shifted it to stab at my chest above my coat."

"Can you remember anything else?"

I tried going over everything once again in my head. "No. Sorry."

"Here," he said, pulling an iPad from his bag. "There are literally thousands of mug shots stored on this. I'll leave it with you. Go through them and see if any of them are your friend with the knife. I'll come back and get it on Friday, but call me sooner if you find him." He gave me a business card with his number on it. "Otherwise, we'll try and get a videofit sorted."

He stood up to go.

"Can I do anything for you?"

"How are things at my apartment?" I said. "It is OK?"

"As far as I'm aware. We have forensics in there today doing a crime scene search for dabs and DNA, although I'm not expecting much. These guys obviously came prepared, but, you never know, perhaps the one you threw over the boxes spat out some saliva or maybe a spot of phlegm was coughed up by one of them while they were waiting for you to get home."

Nice, but at least the police were trying. Perhaps I had been a bit unfair in thinking they wouldn't bother.

"What about my apartment key?" I said. "I left it in the lock."

"We have that. The forensic boys took it this morning to get in and they'll lock up again afterward. I'll bring it with me on Friday."

"Thanks."

"Anything else?"

"Yes. I don't feel particularly safe in here. I've asked the nurses to try and vet my visitors, yet you were able to walk straight in unannounced. How about if my friend with the knife comes back to finish off what he started? If those two thugs were prepared to wait all afternoon in my apartment for me to get home before trying to kill me, don't you think it's quite likely they might just wander into this hospital to have another go? Especially at night when it's quiet. I'd be happier with a twenty-four-hour police guard."

I'd be even happier still with a whole posse of guards and a stab-proof vest.

"I'll have a word with hospital security."

"Hospital security is more concerned about people parking their cars in the ambulance bays than they are about assassins on the loose with carving knives."

"It's the best I can do. I'm afraid I don't have the manpower."

Police budgets are set more to solve crimes than to prevent them. They would happily mobilize a hugely expensive team of detectives if I was murdered in my hospital bed, but they couldn't afford a single man to thwart it happening in the first place. It was madness.

Third time's the charm, I thought. Not if I could help it.

"Have you spoken yet to D.S. Jagger at Thames Valley?" I asked.

"Yes," D.I. Galvin said. "As a matter of fact, I have."

There was something about his tone of voice that set alarm bells ringing in my head.

"What is it?" I asked.

"What is what?"

"You have something to tell me." It was a statement, not a question.

"No."

"I think you have. What is it?"

He lowered his voice as if that made it better. "Their forensics have thrown up something that may indicate that things are not as straightforward as first thought."

"What *something*?" I said.

"You will have to talk to D.S. Jagger. It's his case—at least, it is at present."

"At present?" I echoed. "What do you mean by that?"

"It might be allocated to someone more senior, probably a D.C.I."

Detective Chief Inspectors didn't usually get called in for routine suicide cases, not even those involving high-profile personalities.

"What did the forensics discover?" I asked him again.

"Ask D.S. Jagger."

"I'm asking *you*," I said. "I think I have a right to know. After all, he nearly took me with him."

The detective inspector hesitated. There was no way I was going to let him go away now without telling me.

"Tell me," I insisted. "After all, you and I are in the same business. I am a member of horseracing's police force. We're both detectives."

"All I know is, the Thames Valley forensic team discovered evidence of bodily fluids in the unburned section of the trunk of the Mercedes, including traces of blood from Mr. Swinton."

"In the trunk?"

"Yes."

One couldn't drive a car from the trunk.

Someone else had to have been there and suicide is a solitary affair.

So if it wasn't suicide, was it murder?

17

By Thursday morning, I was more than ready to be discharged. For a start, I was getting fed up with hospital food. And I was not sleeping very well. Not that it was a bad thing—I had one eye always open for a stocky man with a carving knife in his hand.

"Can I please go home?" I asked Dr. Shwan, who popped in to see me at seven-thirty on his way to his day shift in the ER.

"We need to give things a little longer to heal with you resting here," he said.

"I can rest at home," I pointed out.

"But would you? It's only been four days since I had your heart actually beating in my hand. I'll admit you've made remarkable progress so far, but you must give your body a chance to recover from having had both your chest and your abdomen opened or otherwise you'll be back here in worse shape. I've said that you might be able to go home on Saturday, yet that's really too soon. The sutures won't come out until the middle of next week and, while they remain, there's always a risk of infection."

"I'll take that as a no, then," I said.

He smiled and nodded. "You do that."

"Can you give me something to help me sleep? I'm lying awake for hours every night."

"It's not unusual for open-heart patients to complain about having insomnia after their surgery, but I'm loath to give you sedatives. They can slow the healing process. If it's pain that's keeping you awake, we can give you something for that."

"It's not so much pain as the bloody itching of the wounds. It's driving me crazy, especially in the quiet of the night, when it seems to come on the worst."

"Itching is actually a good thing," he said. "It means you're mending. However, try not to scratch, as that can cause infection. When they've healed a bit more, you can use a cream. But not yet. Sorry."

The doctor departed and I went back to studying the ceiling of my room while trying hard not to rub at the incisions on my chest and abdomen.

I was frustrated.

I had promised Faye that I would get on and live my life to the full. Instead, I was stuck here in a hospital room, marking time.

There were things I wanted to do. Not least, finding out who had tried to kill me.

THURSDAY TURNED OUT to be a day full of visitors.

Next to arrive was D.S. Jagger from the Thames Valley Police, who walked into my room unannounced just after nine o'clock as I was looking through some of the mug shots on the iPad.

"Recognize any of them?" he asked. "We've got plenty more of those at Thames Valley."

"None so far," I said, putting the iPad down. "I hear you have some news for me."

"Have I?" he said, pulling up a chair.

"Concerning Dave Swinton's car?"

"How did you hear that?" he asked.

"Through the grapevine."

He wasn't pleased. "I have some *questions* for you," he said.

"Fire away."

"On the morning when you were shut in the sauna, did you actually see who pushed you in there?"

"No," I said. "I told you that I didn't. I was pushed in and the door slammed shut before I could turn around."

"Do you think it could have been someone other than Mr. Swinton?"

"I suppose it could have been anyone," I said. "I assumed it was Dave, but I didn't actually see him. Whoever it was didn't say anything when I called out, even though he had to have heard me. Why do you ask?"

"We now think it may be possible that Mr. Swinton was not responsible."

I waited for him to go on but he didn't, so I prompted.

"What did you find in the trunk of his Mercedes?"

"Plastic cable ties," he said.

It was not what I'd been expecting. "What about them?"

"At least one of them had traces of David Swinton's blood on it. The DNA proved it." He paused, as if deciding whether or not to continue. "The back end of the car was never fully enveloped by the fire. We found bloodstains on the trunk carpet that survived the inferno. These too matched Mr. Swinton. There were also traces of urine in the carpet, although we cannot be sure who it came from, as urine doesn't contain any DNA."

"Are you implying that Dave Swinton may have been tied up in the trunk of his own car with cable ties?"

"Yes, I am," the sergeant said. "That is the possibility we are now investigating. And we are formally treating his death as unexplained."

"Not as murder?" I asked.

"No, not yet. We still have more tests to make on both the car and the ties, and also on Mr. Swinton's remains, before we are sure. Officially, suicide still remains an option."

"But you don't believe it?" I said.

"No."

"Was he even still alive when the fire started?" I said.

"Yes, he was, otherwise we would know for sure it wasn't suicide. There was evidence of deep internal burns that are consistent with him breathing in superheated air and flames. There were also some gasoline residues found in his lungs."

Too much information.

"I suppose he may have been unconscious," I said, wishing for a more agreeable mental picture in my head. "Otherwise, why would he sit meekly in a car while someone else set fire to it?"

"Maybe he was forced into that position. A couple of cable ties to secure his hands to the steering wheel would do it. The plastic would fully burn away in a fire of such intensity. There'd be no trace. If it hadn't been for the prompt arrival of the fire department, we would never have recovered those left in the trunk."

I shivered once again at the memory of the video images of Dave sitting bolt upright in the burning Mercedes. To think that he might have been tied up, alive and alert, while someone poured gas into the car and then set it alight was unimaginably awful.

"Now," he said, "you told me at Lambourn that you thought

Mr. Swinton had tried to kill you because you were aware that he had purposely lost a horse race and he didn't want you telling anyone."

"Yes."

"If it wasn't David Swinton who shut you in the sauna, can you think of anyone else who would want you dead?"

I looked at him and raised my eyebrows. "Why do you think I'm in here?"

He smiled. "Yes, of course. But can you think of anyone who might have wanted both *you* and Mr. Swinton dead?"

It was time to tell the whole truth, not just the edited version.

"Dave Swinton was being blackmailed," I said.

He stared at me. "How do you know?"

"He told me the day before he died, on the way to Newbury races."

"Why didn't you tell me this before?" He was cross and maybe he had a right to be.

"I would have told the inquest," I said as a lame excuse. "I didn't think it was relevant to your investigation if he had killed himself. But now . . ."

His look was enough to tell me that he thought it was relevant anyway.

"Who was blackmailing him?" he asked me.

"I don't know who. But I think Dave had found out. When he rang to ask me to come back to Lambourn on Sunday morning, he said that he now knew who it was. He wouldn't tell me on the phone because he didn't trust that someone wasn't listening to his calls. That's why I went to see him."

"Was he being blackmailed because he purposely lost races?"

"No," I said emphatically. "That's what he was blackmailed *into* doing."

"So what else was it?"

I hesitated.

"Come on, Mr. Hinkley," said the detective impatiently. "Tell me now."

"I really don't want to further denigrate the reputation of one of our sport's greatest ambassadors. It may have nothing to do with his death."

"Let me be the judge of that," he said sternly.

He was right.

Of course he was right. If Dave Swinton had been murdered to prevent him saying who the blackmailer was, then why he was being blackmailed was more than just relevant to the investigation, it was crucial.

"Dave told me that it was to do with taxes. Something about not declaring income from extra payments he'd received for riding in races."

"Did he say how much these extra payments were?"

"About two hundred thousand pounds," I said. "It seems that someone was threatening to report him to the authorities."

"How much did the blackmailer demand?"

"That's what's strange. He didn't want money. He just told Dave to lose a race."

"Mr. Swinton was sure it was a man?"

"He said a man called him and told him which race he must not win."

I could see from his expression that D.S. Jagger thought it a very unlikely scenario. He had made it quite clear previously that he rated the purposeful loss of a horse race as rather trivial, and I suppose it was compared with his daily diet of murders and rapes.

"Who would know about these extra payments?"

"Just about every trainer and owner Dave Swinton rode for. It was general knowledge that he would demand an extra payment over and above the regular riding fee."

"But did they all know that he hadn't paid tax on it?"

"It seems that he always asked for the extra payments in cash. And it doesn't take much imagination to realize why."

"Did Mr. Swinton tell you all of this?"

"Not all of it," I said. "After Dave died, I spoke to a couple of trainers that he'd ridden for. They both told me, independently, about the extra payments. The only thing Dave told me was that he was being blackmailed for not paying tax on some money, not where the money came from."

D.S. Jagger wrote in his notebook. "Mr. Hinkley, you will have to make another formal statement and, this time, with *all* the relevant information included. Do I make myself clear?"

He was still cross with me.

"Perfectly clear," I said.

"I will arrange for one of my constables to come and take it. Will you be in here long?"

"I'm told until Saturday," I said. "But I'm forming an escape committee."

"I'll send my constable tomorrow," he said. "And be sure to tell him everything you can think of whether you believe it's relevant or not."

"Tell him to bring lots of paper," I said. "I'll give him my life story."

"Be serious, Mr. Hinkley."

"I am. If there's one lesson I've learned during my time at the BHA, it's that there is no such thing as an isolated incident. Thoroughbred racing may be one of the largest industries in this country, but those involved—breeders, owners, trainers and jockeys—are like a close-knit family. Everybody knows everybody else and they're all connected by blood, by marriage or by financial dependency."

I wondered if I should tell him about Bill McKenzie and his ride on Wisden Wonder. And maybe about Leslie Morris and his large cash bets. Were they also relevant? Bill McKenzie had told me that he wasn't being blackmailed, but I wasn't sure I believed him. He had definitely lost that race at Sandown on purpose, just as Dave Swinton had at Haydock. Were the two connected?

That's what I should have been investigating this week, not lying in some hospital bed twiddling my thumbs.

NEXT TO ARRIVE was Paul Maldini, although it did take him a while to get in, as one of the nurses had called hospital security when she found him loitering outside my room.

"It must be your shady Italian ancestry," I said with a laugh as he was finally permitted to enter.

"Bloody ridiculous," he said.

"Not at all. I asked them to vet all my visitors. There's someone out there with a long, thin carving knife, and I have no wish to meet him again, thank you very much."

"It's very inconvenient, you being in here," he said, clearly irritated. Paul Maldini was not one for pleasantries like *How are you feeling?* or *I'm glad you're alive*, he was only thinking of the work I was missing.

"I'm not lying here out of choice, I can assure you, and it's better than the alternative."

"What alternative?"

"The morgue," I said. "Seems it was close."

I filled him in on most of the details without making the whole thing too melodramatic.

He was silent for a moment, perhaps thinking, as I was, that my present predicament was not quite so inconvenient after all. At least I would be coming back to the office eventually.

"Do you have any idea who did it?" he asked.

"No," I said. "But it might be the same person who shut me in the sauna last week."

"What sauna?" he asked.

Oops! I'd forgotten that I hadn't actually told Paul about the sauna incident. In fact, I hadn't told him anything about my exchanges with Dave Swinton.

This could be awkward. Not least because I'd already told the police.

"Someone locked me in a sauna," I said.

"How odd," he said. "Where?"

I hesitated.

I'd have to tell him and face the music. "At Dave Swinton's house."

"What were you doing at Dave Swinton's house?"

I took as deep a breath as my stitches would allow. "I think I'd better explain everything from the beginning."

I told him about Dave calling me early on Hennessy Saturday, demanding to speak with me, and of my subsequent trip to Lambourn and Newbury.

Paul's eyes widened when I recounted what Dave had said about purposely losing a race, and his eyebrows almost disappeared into his hairline when I explained about the blackmail. By the time I disclosed the details of my return visit on Sunday morning, including being shut into and then escaping from the sweltering sauna, he was almost apoplectic.

"Why the bloody hell didn't you tell me all this before?"

"When it was reported on the news that Dave had killed himself, it suddenly didn't seem important. Why would I want to tarnish the glittering reputation of our hero with nasty rumors about race fixing and tax evasion when I had no real evidence that either was true?"

"But he himself had admitted it," Paul said angrily. "We should have suspended him from riding immediately and convened a disciplinary panel."

"There you go," I said. "If I'd told you straightaway, it would have been headlines in the Sunday papers."

"But—"

"But nothing," I said, interrupting him. "Just be thankful that it didn't happen, otherwise the BHA would have been blamed for pushing Dave Swinton to kill himself."

That shut him up.

"And also," I said, "instead of reflecting on his stellar racing career, as they rightly did, the obituaries would have been all about his possible connection to fraud and deception. Is that what you would have wanted?"

From the look on his face, perhaps it was.

Paul always considered that anyone who broke the Rules of Racing was personally insulting him in some way. And he didn't take kindly to insults. But maybe it was because Paul individually had invested so much in Dave Swinton as the poster boy of the *Racing Needs You!* campaign and he felt betrayed.

"So why are you telling me all this *now*?" he said in a tone that reminded me of a hurt schoolboy.

"Because Dave Swinton didn't kill himself. He was murdered."

18

Paul stared at me. "Are you sure?"

"Absolutely," I said. "It's impossible to drive a car at the same time as you are tied up in the trunk."

Paul went on staring.

"The police found plastic cable ties in the trunk of the Mercedes with Dave's blood on them." I went on to tell him everything that D.S. Jagger had told me. "And if Dave himself was already trussed up in his car like a chicken, the person who shoved me into the sauna to die is most likely the same person who killed *him*. And it may be the same person who tried again this Sunday with a carving knife."

"But why would anyone want you dead?" Paul asked.

It was the question I had been asking myself over and over.

"Maybe I know something that someone doesn't want me to tell anyone else about."

"What?" Paul said.

"If I knew that, then I'd shout it loudly to everybody so that there'd be no need to kill me to prevent it."

"I don't suppose it has anything to do with McKenzie falling off Wisden Wonder at Sandown," Paul said. "With you indisposed in here, I've asked Nigel to have a look into that. And I've arranged for a letter to be sent to McKenzie summoning him to a disciplinary panel in January to explain his riding of the horse."

I would have much preferred it if Paul had left that for me to deal with later.

I was an advocate of doing the investigating first, preferably furtively and in secret, and then calling the miscreants to account based on my findings.

Paul, meanwhile, tended to believe that the early summons to a disciplinary panel would put the fear of God into the accused and could produce dividends in the form of a confession. He seemed not to appreciate the fact that accomplices, or even the brains behind the scam, might go to ground and never be implicated.

In this particular case, Bill McKenzie was already well aware that I was suspicious of his riding of Wisden Wonder and so I reckoned that no further damage would have been done by Paul's intervention.

We discussed a few of the other outstanding cases that were sitting on my desk, some of which were waiting for me to produce a report, but we kept coming back to Dave Swinton.

"Do you know which race he purposely didn't win?" Paul asked.

"I think so," I said, and I told him about Garrick Party's run at Haydock. "The horse is a well-known front runner with no great finishing speed, but, on this occasion, Dave held him up for a late run that the horse, predictably, was unable to produce. He finished third out of eight."

"At what price?"

"He started as favorite at thirteen-to-eight."

"Did the stewards on that day have him in?"

"Yes. They questioned both Dave and the trainer, Jason Butcher, but they accepted the excuse that the horse had been held up due to the heavy going. But I don't buy it. The horse had previously won twice in the mud, both times from the front."

"Difficult to prove," Paul said.

"Impossible."

MY LAST VISITOR of the day arrived at six o'clock as I was lying in bed having a snooze. Paul's visit, in particular, had tired me out, probably because it had been me who had done most of the talking.

I woke to find myself staring at the beautiful face of Henrietta Shawcross.

My first thought was that I must be dreaming, but I wasn't.

"You are a very difficult man to find, Mr. Hinkley," she said. "And I should know—I've been looking for you ever since you disappeared without a trace on Saturday afternoon."

"Sorry," I said.

"I should think so too." She pulled a cross face that did nothing to diminish her beauty. "Fancy leaving me without even saying good-bye."

"Sorry," I said again.

"And so you should be. I'm not used to men suddenly vanishing without at least asking for my number."

"And do you give it to them?" I asked.

"No. Not as a general rule. But I might have given it to you. If you had bothered to ask."

"Sorry," I said once more.

She removed her coat, placing it over the back of one of the chairs, then she sat down on the other one and looked around her. "What are you doing in here anyway? What's wrong with you?"

What should I say?

"I was attacked," I said.

"Who by?"

"I wish I knew. A couple of heavies with a carving knife."

She suddenly looked concerned. "Were you stabbed?"

"Thirteen times," I replied rather indulgently.

She was shocked and it put her off her stride, but only for a moment.

"Then why aren't you dead?" she asked.

"Luck," I said. "That and a thick coat. Fortunately, I managed to throw them off me and run for help."

"See, you are a superhero after all." She smiled.

"How did you find me?" I asked, but what I really wanted to ask was *Why did you find me?*

"The usual method," she said jokily. "I tried the Internet, you know, on Google, but that failed. I tried those people-finding websites and none of them came up trumps. So I resorted to plan C."

"Which was?"

"I called one of Uncle Richard's racing contacts to find out who, exactly, you worked for. And then I slept with the chairman of the Horseracing Authority and blackmailed him into telling me your whereabouts."

"That seems a tad excessive," I said.

"It worked, though." She grinned.

"Do you ever tell the truth?" I asked.

"Not if I can help it."

"So why did you bother?"

"What?"

"To find me," I said.

She cocked her head sideways. "Maybe I just wanted to."

"Does Uncle Richard know?" I asked.

"Uncle Richard doesn't own me," she said icily. "I do what I want."

I wondered just how true that was. According to what I'd discovered on my computer, Sir Richard Reynard was the sole administrator of her trust fund and the holder of the purse strings—at least, until her thirtieth birthday the following February.

"I'm flattered," I said.

"Don't be," she said, standing up and walking over to the window. "I just wondered what you looked like in a hospital gown." She smiled at me. "Disappointing, to tell you the truth. Dirty pale blue is obviously not your color."

She, meanwhile, was wearing black pants, calf-high boots and a white roll-neck sweater that touched her in all the right places.

"If I'd known you were coming, I'd have worn a clean one," I said. And, I thought, something that did up properly at the back and didn't leave my arse hanging out.

"Don't you have any pajamas or a bathrobe?"

"Nope," I said. "I have absolutely nothing. It seems that everything I arrived wearing was cut off and bagged as potential evidence. I even had to get my sister to go to the hospital gift shop to buy me a toothbrush."

"Isn't there someone who could go and get you something from your home?"

"Are you offering?" I asked.

"Yes, OK," Henri said with enthusiasm. "Give me a list."

"Ah," I said. "There's a problem. The police have the key."

And that was just as well, I thought.

I wasn't at all sure that I wanted Miss Henrietta Shawcross, heiress to a multimillion-pound shipping fortune, letting herself into my tip of a apartment to rifle through my Ikea drawers looking for a long-neglected pair of pajamas.

"Tell you what," she said. "I'll go and buy you something. What do you need?"

"You can't go now," I said. "It's too late. Everything will be closed."

"You're joking. It's Thursday. Late-night shopping, and only two weeks before Christmas. Everywhere will be open until at least nine. What do you want?"

She was clearly excited by the prospect.

"A pair of pajamas, then," I said. "Thanks. And something to go home in would be nice. And maybe a pair of cheap running shoes."

"Shoe size?"

"Nine."

"How about the rest of you?" She raised her eyebrows in questioning amusement.

"Waist thirty-four, chest forty-two, neck sixteen."

"Right," she said. "Don't go anywhere. I'll be back."

She disappeared.

I laid my head down on the pillow and I was laughing.

Never mind Prozac, a dose of Henrietta Shawcross was the perfect antidote for depression.

HENRI RETURNED just after eight and she was heavily laden with smart black-and-gold shopping bags.

She laid out her purchases on the end of the bed: a pair of striped pajamas, a silk bathrobe, some slippers, two shirts, a pair of beige chinos, a double-breasted blue blazer, crewneck sweater, socks, pants, a pair of fine-grain black leather shoes and a full-length navy cashmere overcoat.

Even a tie.

"Where did you get all this from?" I asked.

"New and Lingwood in Jermyn Street," she said. "It's where my father went for all his clothes."

"But I only needed some jeans and a T-shirt from Walmart," I said forlornly, fearful of what this lot would do to my bank balance.

"Nonsense," she replied with a grin. "We can't have you wandering around in just a T-shirt in mid-December. You'll catch your death."

"Fewer references to death, please, if you don't mind. Now, how much do I owe you?"

"Nothing," she said. "It's a gift. My pleasure. And I got you these as well." She handed me yet another smart bag that contained a leather shaving kit, complete with a hairbrush.

"I could do with a shave," I said, rubbing my chin. "It's been four days."

"I actually like your sexy designer stubble," Henri said. "Very George Michael."

I looked right at her and she looked straight back at me. All the right vibes were seemingly in motion.

"Are you playing with me?" I said. "Because I won't take

kindly to you waltzing in here, buying me all these things and then swanning off, never to be seen again."

"And why would I do that?" she asked.

I suddenly felt rather foolish. "I don't know. I just wonder what you're doing here."

"I'm here because I like you," she said, clearly taken aback. "You made me laugh at the races and I wanted to see you again. Is there something wrong in that?"

"No. Of course not. It's just . . ." I tailed off, not knowing what to say next.

"Don't *you* like *me*?" she asked.

"Yes," I said, "I do. Very much. But . . ."

"But what?" she demanded.

"You must have a string of rich boyfriends."

I was saying all the wrong things.

"And what do you mean by that?"

"I've seen pictures of you with all those celebrities, famous actors and such. At fancy parties. You and I don't fit into the same social strata."

"But that's not real life," she said slowly. "That's just fantasy."

"Is this real life?" I asked.

"It is for me," she said with tears welling up in her eyes. "Do you think I'd spend several days looking for you just to swan off and never see you again?" She was hurt. "But I will, if that's what you want."

"No," I said quickly. "That's not what I want at all." I smiled. "I'm sorry."

"Please stop saying you're sorry," she said. "Superheroes never have to apologize for anything." She leaned forward and kissed me lightly on my mouth. "Now, get out of that dreadful gown and put your new pajamas on."

HENRI STAYED until well after the official end of visiting time at nine o'clock.

She had also picked up some smoked-salmon sandwiches from the Fortnum & Mason food court and we ate those, washed down with hospital tap water from the jug on my bedside table.

"I should have brought some chilled white wine with me," she said with a laugh. "I'll remember that next time."

"Tell me," I said, "how did you really find me?"

"I called Gay Smith and asked her for help. She found your home address on the reply to her husband's invitation."

I nodded. "I gave it to him so he could send the badge for the Sandown box to my apartment. I didn't want it to get lost in the mailroom at BHA headquarters."

"Anyway," she said, "I went to your place on Monday evening, but there was no reply, so I put a note through the door, asking you to call me."

"I didn't get it."

"I realize that now. But I wasn't giving up. I tried ringing you at the BHA and someone told me you weren't going to be in this week. I asked them if you were away on holiday. They said no, you were off sick. So I went back to your place yesterday morning and found the place crawling with men in white coveralls, wearing gloves and masks." She paused. "I was pretty upset. I thought you must have died of Ebola or something. One of the men eventually took pity on me and told me that you weren't dead, you were in the hospital, but he refused to say why or which one, so I spent most of yesterday afternoon and all of this morning playing the role of the distraught fiancée, calling hospitals and asking after my lost lover who must either be dead or have amnesia." She laughed. "Do you have any idea how many damn London hospitals there are in the Yellow Pages? You could at least have been in one beginning with *A*. By the time I got down to *U*, I'd almost given up hope."

I stared at her in disbelief.

"You should come and work for me."

19

My friend with the carving knife, and his taller chum with the red sneakers, came a-calling sometime between one and two o'clock on Friday morning, well outside the normal visiting hours.

Fortunately, I was awake.

In fact, I was more than awake, I was up and wandering around in my brand-new silk bathrobe and slippers.

When he'd said it, I hadn't particularly agreed with Dr. Shwan that the itching in my chest was a good thing, yet it had been that itching, together with my desperate urge to scratch, that had woken me and driven me from my bed at the same time my unwanted visitors made their appearance.

The itching saved my life.

The night-duty nurse had suggested that a cup of hot chocolate might help me sleep. Hence, I was standing in the small ward kitchen with her, heating milk in a saucepan, when the buzzer sounded at the main door.

"I wonder who that is?" said the nurse. "The doors are locked at night, but all the staff have key cards. Can you manage a moment?"

"Sure," I said. She went to open the main door while I was left to mind the milk.

Unexpected visitors in the dead of night? Alarm bells started ringing in my head. I flicked off the light and peered around the doorframe of the kitchen.

I recognized the two men as soon as I saw them. It was something about their heights and body shapes rather than their facial features, which, this time, were covered by dark balaclava masks.

One of them was holding the nurse from behind, his arm across her neck, while the other stood in front of her holding the long, thin carving knife in his right hand.

Bugger, I thought. I should have asked for that stab-proof vest.

"Where's Hinkley?" I heard the knifeman ask the terrified nurse.

She nodded toward my room.

The man with the knife disappeared but soon returned.

"Where is he?" he hissed at the poor woman, raising the knife toward her face.

She involuntarily glanced right at me.

I ducked back into the kitchen before the men could turn and waited in the dark.

I saw the knife first, then the hand holding it, as the man edged toward the doorway. But I didn't wait for him to see me.

I picked up the saucepan from the hot plate, stepped forward and threw the boiling milk straight into his face, following it up with a swipe of the pan that made a satisfying clunk as it connected with his nose.

The man screamed, dropped the knife and tore away the balaclava from his burning face, but I wasn't finished with him yet.

I hit him again with the heavy base of the pan as hard as I could on the side of his head and he went down to the floor.

The knife? I thought, looking around me desperately. Where's the bloody knife?

Meanwhile, the other man had tossed the nurse to one side and was now coming across to help his friend. Did he have a knife too?

I didn't wait to check. Instead, I went for him, yelling loudly and wielding the saucepan high above my head. At first, he wavered, then he turned on his red sneakers and ran fast for the exit.

There was a sharp pain in my stomach. I'd done myself some mischief, I was sure of it. I reached down my front with my left hand and could feel wetness on my pajama top.

Blood.

I'd burst some stitches, but I wasn't ready to give up.

I turned back to the knifeman and was greatly dismayed to see that he was neither unconscious nor dead, as I had hoped. Indeed, he was beginning to get to his knees and he had recovered his knife from the floor.

Shit.

I was in no state to fight him off again. The way I was suddenly feeling, I'd have had some difficulty fighting off a fly.

He stood up and looked at me. I looked back, deep into his unfeeling dark eyes.

Underhand, I thought. He was holding the knife underhand, with the point facing up. Would it make any difference? I was not wearing a tweed jacket and thick overcoat this time to protect me, just a pair of striped pajamas and a thin silk bathrobe.

The Grim Reaper was waiting in the wings, about to make his appearance.

The cavalry arrived suddenly in the shape of four scrubs-wearing medical staff running into the ward pushing a cart of equipment. The knifeman took one look at these unexpected reinforcements and obviously decided that flight was the wisest course of action. He grabbed his discarded balaclava, pushed past the new arrivals and scampered in the direction of the stairwell.

"Where?" one of the medics shouted at me urgently.

"Where what?" I asked.

"Where's the cardiac arrest?" he shouted again.

In my chest, I thought.

"What cardiac arrest?" I asked blankly.

"You pushed the *Cardiac Arrest* alarm," he said accusingly.

"I did that," said the night nurse, coming out from behind the nurses' station desk, where she'd taken refuge. "We needed help fast. It was the best I could think of."

Good girl, I thought.

I sat down on the floor. I wasn't feeling at all well.

Oh God, not again.

I ENDED UP back where I'd started, in the ER for repairs.

Doctor Shwan wasn't on duty, so it fell to one of the other doctors to tut-tut about not exerting oneself so soon after open-heart surgery when one is only held together with silk thread and catgut.

"And stainless steel wire," I added helpfully.

I was sent for an X-ray on my breastbone, but nothing seemed to have moved in that department. It was the incision made to repair my bowel that had split open. The underlying muscle wall, thankfully, had remained intact.

"You nearly gave yourself a massive hernia," the doctor said sternly by way of reprimand. "If you had split the internal sutures, as well as the external ones, you could easily have had your guts out all over the floor."

"But I didn't," I said, smiling at him.

My guts had nearly been all over the floor for another reason, I thought, courtesy of my friend with the carving knife.

A UNIFORMED POLICEMAN came to see me as soon as the doctor had finished his stitching even though I was still feeling absolutely lousy and utterly exhausted.

"Call Detective Inspector Galvin," I said.

"Why?" asked the policeman.

"Because I'm not well enough and too tired to tell the story twice."

I closed my eyes.

Why was someone trying so hard to kill me? Three times now, in rapid succession, I'd escaped an untimely death.

I had been assuming that all three attempts were connected. But were they?

Clearly, the second and third had been, but shutting me into a sauna didn't follow the pattern of the other two. Had I simply been in the wrong place at the wrong time at Dave Swinton's house?

The two most recent attempts by the same two men had shown a certain determination to succeed on their part.

It had only been good fortune that I'd been awake and out of my room when they had appeared in the hospital, and I could hardly rely on my luck holding every time they came looking for me.

What was it I knew or had done that was so important it was worth killing me over?

D.I. Galvin came to see me at nine-thirty on Friday morning as I was snoozing, back in bed in my room on the ninth floor of the hospital.

"I told you I needed a guard," I said to him before he even had a chance to speak.

"OK," he said. "I agree. You were right."

"So can I have one now? Those two guys have tried at least twice to kill me. In my book, that demonstrates an undeniable degree of persistence. I reckon they may well come back for a third try."

"I'll see what I can arrange," D.I. Galvin said. "Can you add anything to your description of the man with the knife?"

"He now has a scalded face," I said. "I threw boiling milk at him."

I told the detective everything that had happened from the moment the door buzzer was pushed until the time the knifeman ran for the stairs.

"It seems you gave rather better than you got," he said.

"I had some catching up to do."

"We are trying to establish how the men got in. There's nighttime security in the ER that's meant to prevent members of the public wandering through to the rest of the hospital."

"Surely this place has closed-circuit TV?" I asked.

"All over. It's being looked at even as we speak. Any luck with the mug shots?"

"Not so far, but I'm only about halfway through and there's one or two I now want to go back and look at again. I had a much better look at the knifeman last night than I did at my apartment. I have a vague feeling I've seen his face before."

"I'll leave the iPad with you, then. Give me a call if you spot anyone familiar."

"Talking about giving people a call, is there any chance someone could fetch my phone? I dropped it during the struggle in my apartment hallway and I feel totally lost without it."

"Ah, yes, that reminds me," said D.I. Galvin. "I have your front-door key." He dug in his pocket and placed the key on the bedside table.

"Did you hear what I said? Could someone please fetch my phone?"

"We're finished there now," the inspector replied, not properly answering the question. "Is there no one else who could go for you?"

"I suppose I could ask my sister to go."

"Good," he said, standing up. "You will need to make a formal statement about the incident here last night. Can you write it yourself?"

I nodded. Another bloody statement. And I still had to do the one for D.S. Jagger. "I'll do it later," I said wearily.

"OK. But, in the meantime, keep looking at the mug shots. I'll be back later for the statement."

"How about my bodyguard?" I said.

"I'll arrange for a uniformed officer to be present in the ward's reception area. The nursing staff are demanding it anyway."

Good for them, I thought.

The detective went away and I went back to my snoozing. But about an hour later I came face-to-face once more with my would-be assassin.

HE WAS YOUNGER and had a mustache, but I was certain it was the same man—my friend with the carving knife.

Mug shot number 282.

He was indeed one of those I'd gone back to have another look at, having passed over him before. It was the dark, unfeeling eyes that gave him away, the same eyes I'd stared deeply into when I'd been convinced he was about to kill me. They were not eyes I would forget in a hurry.

Just the picture of him sent shivers of fear down my spine.

"Two-eight-two," I said to D.I. Galvin when I called him using the hospital phone.

"Are you sure?"

"A hundred percent."

"Two-eight-two, you say?" I could hear him tapping it in on a computer keyboard. "Right, got him."

"What's his name?" I asked.

"Lawrence. Darryl Gareth Lawrence. Ever heard of him?"

"No," I said with certainty.

"He was born sixteen July 1978. Originally from Port Talbot in Wales, his last-known address was in Streatham, south London. He's got previous—lots—mostly for violence, including wounding with intent."

"With intent to do what?"

"Cause grievous bodily harm. Sentenced to seven years at Southwark Crown Court in 2008. He was released on parole in November 2012, having served two-thirds of his sentence. According to his record, he's been out of trouble since then, but that only means he hasn't been arrested for anything."

"Well, you can arrest him now for wounding with intent to commit murder."

"I'll get on it straightaway."

He hung up.

In some strange way, I felt slightly safer knowing *who* was trying to kill me. All I needed to know now was *why.*

20

After speaking with D.I. Galvin, I called Faye and asked her if she could fetch my cell phone from my apartment. She came to the hospital at noon to get the key.

"The phone should be on the floor in the hallway," I said. "And the charger as well, if you can find it. That'll be on the countertop in the kitchen next to the microwave."

"Nothing else? How about some clothes?"

"No. I'm fine. I have clothes."

I did think about asking her to get my laptop, but I could do most things via the Internet with just my iPhone. Furthermore, my laptop was somewhere in my bedroom and I wasn't at all sure I wanted Faye exploring more of my home than was absolutely necessary. To be honest, I would have been much happier if the police had agreed to retrieve my phone. I knew that asking my sister to go there was a mistake.

Faye was a naturally tidy person. She had been since childhood, and she had unsuccessfully tried to instill into her younger brother the same culture of neatness and order. Hence, since Lydia's departure and the move to my new apartment, I had resisted all of Faye's attempts to come over to check up on me.

And now here I was sending her there unaccompanied. I must be crazy. But I really needed that phone. And surely whatever the state of the place, sending Faye was better than asking Henri to go.

Only after she had gone did I worry about her security.

What if Darryl Gareth Lawrence and his sidekick were waiting in the bushes outside my front door?

But why would they do anything to Faye? Lawrence had specifically asked the nurse, *Where's Hinkley*? It was me they wanted, not my sister.

Nevertheless, I was greatly relieved when Faye returned about an hour and a half later with my phone plus charger.

"How are things?" I asked.

"It's not very tidy," she said in an accusing manner.

"That must have been due to my attackers. Or possibly the police forensic team."

She looked at me. "I don't suppose either of those would be responsible for the stack of dirty mugs and plates in the sink, or for the washing hung on the back of your sofa, or even for the clothes lying on the floor of your bedroom."

I looked rather sheepishly at her.

"And they surely wouldn't have packed up those moving boxes and left them in the hallway. How long have you been there now? Nearly a year? Isn't it time you unpacked?"

"I will," I said.

And I would. I'd tidy the place too, especially if I was going to entertain a certain Miss Henrietta Shawcross there anytime soon, as I dearly hoped I would be.

"So, are you getting out tomorrow?" Faye asked.

"I'm not sure," I said. "I had to have some of my stitches redone this morning."

"Why?"

"A few of those on my abdomen split open."

"You haven't been doing those push-ups again, I hope," Faye said with a laugh, but she must have seen something in my face because she stopped laughing. "What happened?"

"I had some unexpected and unwanted visitors in the night."

"Not the same men?"

I nodded.

"But that's dreadful. How did they know you were here? And how the hell did they get in?"

"That's what the police are trying to find out," I said. "But at least we now know who one of them is. I recognized him from a police photo."

"Who is it?"

"Someone called Darryl Lawrence."

She stared at me with a blank expression.

"I've never heard of him either," I said. "But he's had lots of previous convictions for violence and has spent time in prison."

"Why is he coming after you?"

"I don't know. I can only imagine that someone is paying him to kill me. The police are searching for him, so we might find out more when they find him."

Faye was distressed.

She had been under the erroneous impression that the attack at my home had been as a result of a random burglary somehow gone terribly wrong. To discover her little brother was being specifically targeted by a hired killer came as an unwelcome shock.

"But who would want to kill *you*?" she asked desperately like a mother wondering how anyone could harm her beloved child.

"That is exactly what I've been trying to figure out."

"It's that bloody job of yours," she said angrily. "Why can't you do something safer? Q has connections and you're smart. I am sure you could get a nice safe banking job in the City."

What Faye meant by the *City* was the *City of London*, the financial square mile at the heart of the metropolis.

"I don't want a safe banking job in the City," I said. "I'd be bored to death. I like what I do."

"It's so dangerous."

Maybe that's why I liked it, but I wasn't going to say so.

Not today.

FAYE STAYED FOR most of the afternoon, sitting quietly reading a book, while I wrote out two formal statements, one for D.I. Galvin concerning the previous night's events and the other for D.S. Jagger about my conversations with Dave Swinton and my twin excursions into his sauna.

"Can I read them?" Faye asked when I'd finished.

"I don't think you should," I said, but I knew I had little or no chance of preventing it. Throughout my life since I was eight, Faye had always been the one *in charge*. And while I might not always do as she wanted—especially in the employment department—she usually got her way. If she was determined to read my statements, she would.

I meekly handed over the handwritten sheets and lay awkwardly on the bed while she sat on the chair next to it, reading them through from start to finish.

"Jeff," she said eventually, "I just can't believe all of this. Is it really true?"

"Every word," I said.

I was prevented from having a further ear bashing by the arrival of the detective constable from the Thames Valley Police.

"I've already written my statement," I said, and I took it from Faye to give to him.

He stood reading it through, then asked me to sign it in his presence. "I'll need to get this typed up properly on a Section 9 form. You'll have to sign again, but this will do for now."

The policeman departed with the folded sheets of paper in his pocket.

"*Please*, will you come and stay with Q and me when you get out of here," Faye implored, almost in tears. "I don't want you going back to your apartment. It's not safe."

"OK," I said, giving in gracefully, "I will. But only until the police catch Darryl Lawrence."

That seemed to satisfy her.

"Anyway," I said, "how are *you* feeling? It should be me looking after you, not the other way round."

"I'm fine," she said. "I'm just tired all the time. It's the bloody drugs."

"You don't have to stay," I said, knowing full well that she believed she was acting as my bodyguard. "There should be a uniformed policeman outside in the reception area to keep me alive and well."

She stood up and went to have a look.

"He's chatting up the nurses," Faye said in a tone that expressed disapproval.

"Sensible man," I said. "At least he's here."

I hadn't altogether believed that he would be.

"I'll go, then," Faye said. "I need to get home and make up the bed in the spare room."

"I don't want to be any trouble," I said.

"It's no trouble." She smiled and gave me a peck on the cheek. "Now, you be careful."

It was a serious instruction.

HENRI CAME to see me soon after six o'clock, wafting in wearing a full-length camel-colored coat with a hood. She looked gorgeous.

"Sorry I'm so late," she said. "I had to finish something at work."

I just beamed. I was so pleased to see her.

Henri removed her coat to reveal a stunning black-and-red tartan dress, with a wide black leather belt, and knee-high black suede boots with stiletto heels.

My heart went all a-flutter. Where was Dr. Shwan when you needed him?

"Wow!" I said.

"Do you like it?" She smiled and did a twirl. "It's all new."

"It's lovely," I said. "Where are you going?"

"Nowhere. I wore it for you."

Wow! again.

"But I had expected *you* to be a bit smarter," she said. "What happened to the jammies I bought you?"

I was again wearing a faded blue hospital gown.

"They're in the wash," I said.

"Had a little accident, did we?"

"Something like that, but not what you're thinking. A few of my stitches burst open and I bled on them."

She looked concerned.

"Surely that shouldn't happen."

"No," I said without elaboration.

"I should have bought you two pairs. Shall I go and get you some more?" She reached for her coat.

"No," I said again, this time more decisively. "Please stay. Unless, of course, you can't speak to anyone wearing a hospital gown."

"I'll make an exception," she said, smiling. "Just this once."

She stayed for two hours, at one point delving into her copious handbag to find a half bottle of Chablis and some glasses, together with some freshly packed sushi.

"Red Cross parcel," she said, giggling.

"The food here's not too bad, except everything is overcooked. And it's pretty bland, as they use little or no salt."

Henri turned up her pretty nose. "I like my salt," she said. "And I can't live without freshly ground black pepper." She produced a small silver cylindrical object from her purse and proceeded to grind black peppercorns from it onto her food. "I'm fed up with going to those big lunch and dinner events at swanky London hotels and not being able to get hold of a pepper mill. They all think you're mad asking for one. So I bought myself this to carry with me."

"Handy," I said.

She popped another piece of raw fish into her mouth and washed it down with some wine.

"I see you got your phone back," she said, nodding at it on my bedside table. "I can call you again now."

"Yes, please do. My sister fetched it for me." I picked it up and used it to take a photograph of Henri sitting on the edge of my bed, looking fabulous in her red tartan dress.

"Let's see," she said. I showed her. "Not bad for an old one."

"Old one?" I said. "You're not old."

"Thirty," she said. "Can you believe I'm going to be thirty in

February? I remember thinking that people aged thirty must be so old they were nearly dead and now I'm almost there myself."

She studied the picture. "At least I can't see any wrinkles yet."

She started flicking through the other pictures on my phone.

"Hey," I said in mock complaint, "that's private."

"Good God, that's Martin and Bentley," she said, looking closely at the screen. "How come you have a photo of my cousin on your phone?"

She didn't ask it in an accusatory manner, she was just interested. I leaned forward and peered at the image. It was the photo of the two men who'd been arguing at Newbury, taken through the window of the Hennessy hospitality area with the racetrack in the background.

"I was snapping the view," I said. "They just happened to be in the shot. It's at Newbury races."

"What a coincidence."

"Who's Bentley?" I asked.

"Bentley Robertson. He's a creepy little lawyer," she said, screwing up her nose again. "He's all work and no play. A bore. Worse, he's a bore who thinks I'm in love with him. I keep telling him that I'm not, but he just winks at me and refuses to believe it. He's a letch. At least, he is toward me. I once quite liked him, now he makes my skin creep." She shivered. "But enough about him. Tell me more about you."

We sat in happy harmony talking about everything and nothing—where we grew up, schools, jobs, likes, dislikes, even our families and our dead parents.

"It was such a dreadful time," Henri said. "Mom and Dad were on their way to pick me up from the sports field at my boarding school. We were going to a family wedding in Lincoln. I can remember being so excited about going in a helicopter."

She paused, and there were tears in her eyes. "They never arrived. I waited and waited for hours, but they never came. Eventually, the headmaster came out to where I was standing to tell me."

A tear ran down her cheek. I reached over and held her hand.

"They clipped a tree in the garden during takeoff. The official report said it was the pilot's fault. He was also killed in the crash, so I suppose it's easy to blame him."

She was silent for a while.

"Sorry," she said, wiping her eyes with a tissue. "I don't do that very often anymore."

"There's no reason to be sorry," I said. "I still cry sometimes over my mother and she's been dead now for twenty-four years. Sometimes, I have difficulty recalling her face. And I haven't been able to 'hear' her voice in my head for longer than I wish to remember."

"What about your dad?" she asked.

"I don't usually talk about him much. He went off the rails after my mother died. He couldn't cope without her. Everything in the house—cooking, washing, cleaning and so on—he left for my sister to do. He started drinking too much and lost his well-paid job with the council because of it. He ended up as an assistant gardener in a local park, but he was usually drunk. He was only kept on due to the kindness of his old council chums who felt sorry for him.

"I actually remember him really well. He *was* drunk a lot of the time, yet he was always kind and loving toward me, even if he wasn't ever particularly happy. He drank himself to death, in the end, although the official cause was pneumonia."

"How old were you?"

"Fourteen," I said. "I can remember his funeral as if it was yesterday."

"Who, then, looked after you?"

"Faye. My sister. She's twelve years older than me. She became my official guardian. I joined the Army at eighteen."

"Which regiment?"

"The Intelligence Corps," I said, making a mock salute. "Two-five-one-nine-eight-two-four-one, Captain Jefferson Roosevelt Hinkley, at your service."

"Jefferson Roosevelt?" she said incredulously. "You've got to be kidding."

"I am not," I said in my most superior tone of voice. "My parents clearly admired dead American presidents."

Henri laughed.

"Don't you start," I said. "I was endlessly bullied at school because of it."

But at least it had taught me to fight and that had always been an asset, not least during the previous night.

21

After constant badgering, the doctors finally agreed that I could go home on Sunday morning. I think they were glad to see the back of me—I know the nurses were. They didn't appreciate having a potential killer on the prowl.

To be honest, and for the same reason, I was grateful when Quentin arrived in his BMW to drive me to Richmond rather than to my apartment in Harlesden.

I'd been in the hospital for a whole week, but, in many ways, it seemed longer.

I was eager to get back to work in spite of the dire warnings I'd been given by Dr. Shwan about having to take things easy for a while. In particular, I wanted to continue my look into Bill McKenzie's riding and the gambling habits of Leslie Morris, and to rescue the investigation from the desk of Paul Maldini.

Was it just eight days since I'd met Henrietta Shawcross at Sandown Park races? It seemed that I had known her forever.

She had come into the hospital on Saturday afternoon and we

had watched the Channel 4 coverage of racing at Cheltenham and Doncaster.

"I'm sorry I can't stay late tonight," she said. "I'm going to a dinner at the Dorchester. It's the Christmas party for all our UK staff and their wives. We do it every year."

"For Reynard Shipping?"

"Yes. I promised Uncle Richard I'd be there."

"Will your cousin Martin also be there?"

"Oh, yes. He's the host tonight. That's why he's over here."

"From the Cayman Islands?" I asked.

"From Singapore. He has a place in the Caymans, but he spends much of his time in Singapore running our operation there, although he was here for most of the summer restructuring the UK business. He's our new managing director now that Uncle Richard is taking things a bit easier."

"Well, I hope you have a great evening," I said. "Much better than staying here."

"I doubt that," she said. "The Christmas party always turns into a nightmare. Everyone drinks too much and then they start telling me what they really think of us."

"Which is?"

"That we don't pay them enough, we have too many Asia-based staff and that the company makes the Reynard family too much money."

"And does it?" I'd asked.

"No. My great-grandfather took a job as a stevedore on the London Docks after returning from the battlefields of France in 1918. Her started his own ship-loading business in 1920 and, since then, it's been the Reynard family that has built the business up to what it is today, so why shouldn't we enjoy the spoils?"

It sounded to me like something she was well used to justifying.

"Everyone who works for us is well paid. We certainly have no trouble recruiting from our competitors. And, these days, our main hub is in Singapore, so we are bound to have lots of Asia-based staff, aren't we?"

"Are you much involved?"

"I sit on the board as a non-exec director."

"But you work full-time elsewhere?"

"Yes," she said.

I had been desperate to ask her why, but I said nothing. She would tell me if she wanted to. And she did.

"I run a recruitment agency in Fulham," she had said finally.

"You told me at Sandown that you worked *for* an agency, not that you ran it."

"I didn't want to brag. I set it up about six years ago after a friend complained how difficult it was to get catering staff for her kids' parties and it's sort of blossomed from there into quite an enterprise. I now have six full-time employees, including me, and literally hundreds of people on our books. Clients come to us with their requirements and we act as the middlemen, putting them together with our self-employed chefs, waiters and waitresses. We do all the contract work and arrange payment to the staff. And we charge the clients a fee for doing it all."

"Sounds great."

"It is," she'd said, beaming. "The agency makes a healthy profit and it's all because of me rather than my family."

I could see how important that was to her.

"I've just started a section recruiting entertainers and magicians for events."

I could do with a magician, I thought, to make Darryl Gareth Lawrence disappear.

FAYE FUSSED around me like a mother hen, insisting that I sit on the sofa in their living room with my feet up.

"Can I get you anything?" she asked.

"Nothing, thank you."

I had talked Quentin into going home to Richmond via Harlesden to pick up some things from my apartment.

"Will it be safe?" he'd asked.

"What has Faye been telling you?"

But my safety was indeed a big concern.

Twice I'd made Quentin make a detour in the journey up Harrow Road toward Harlesden while I watched to see if anyone was tailing us.

Satisfied that there wasn't, I'd still made him drive slowly past my apartment three times until I was sure that no one was waiting in the bushes for my arrival.

Remembering what had happened last time, I'd been even more wary as I'd put the key into the lock, stepping back from rather than through the open front door as I'd done before.

There'd been nobody lurking inside, with or without a carving knife.

Quentin had parked the car on the road outside and come in with me to carry my stuff. It was also the first time he had been to my new apartment and I don't think he'd been particularly impressed as he'd stepped over the boxes in the hallway.

"You're even more untidy than Kenneth and that's saying something."

Kenneth was his son by a previous marriage.

I'd gathered up my laptop computer and some more clothes, which I'd stuffed into a carryall.

I'd never realized how happy I would be to get into Quentin's BMW and drive away from my home. Not that it had stopped me from insisting that he make two complete circuits of Hanger Lane gyratory to check we weren't being followed.

"You're paranoid," Quentin had said.

"You would be too, if you were me. There have been three failed attempts on my life in the last two weeks alone. I have no desire for another that succeeds."

I wondered if he was now having second thoughts about having me stay at his house.

ON MONDAY MORNING, with my phone and laptop fully recharged, I sat at Faye's dining-room table and started making calls and replying to the backlog of e-mails that had accumulated in my in-box.

I was back in business.

I e-mailed Paul Maldini asking for an update of where things stood with respect to Bill McKenzie and requesting that the investigation be handed back to me.

His response was less than encouraging. A date had been set in the middle of January for a disciplinary panel hearing into the running of Wisden Wonder at Sandown, and also into the betting pattern of Leslie Morris on the same race.

"But who's to say that the investigation will be complete by then?" I said to Paul when I called him.

"We can always postpone the panel if we need to."

Maybe, I thought, but it seemed like the wrong way around to me. I was a firm believer in doing a full investigation first, preferably without the target knowing that his behavior was being looked into.

"Has anyone interviewed McKenzie or Morris?"

"Not yet," Paul said. "But they will have both received the letter by now requiring them to attend the disciplinary panel. They can be questioned at that time. They have also both been told to produce their phone records for the past six months."

So Morris would, by now, know that we were on to him. That was a shame. It meant that there was little hope that we would ever learn the identity of the mysterious excluded person for whom he had allegedly been placing bets. Not unless he'd been foolish enough to use a phone to call Morris that was registered in his own name.

Increasingly, all dodgy betting conspirators, together with most other villains and terrorists, used pay-as-you-go cell phones. Bought for cash, with a false name, and thrown away immediately after use—tracing who had made a particular call was almost impossible.

I logged on to the BHA database remotely, which told me that Mr. Leslie Morris was a sixty-six-year-old retired accountant and that he was the registered owner of one moderately rated racehorse.

An accountant. Now, was that a coincidence?

I also used the database to look up where he lived.

The address on his owner registration was in Raynes Park near Wimbledon, just down the A3 from Sandown Park races and only a handful of miles from where I was in Richmond.

I wondered if paying Mr. Morris a visit might be helpful. He'd probably be on the defensive at the official panel and would most likely have a lawyer with him to advise what he should say and, more important, what he should not say. At home, alone, he might be less guarded, especially if I caught him unawares.

"Do you ever use a local taxi company?" I asked Faye.

"Where do you want to go?" she asked in reply.

"I need to go and see someone," I said.

"Not to do with your work?"

I nodded.

"But you're meant to be resting and recovering, not working."

"I only want to go and speak with him," I said. "I'm not going to chase him anywhere."

At least, I hoped not.

"Where does he live?" Faye asked.

"Raynes Park."

"I'll drive you, if you like," she said. "I'm not doing anything else."

My first instinct was to say no. My work was my work and my family was my family. I didn't mix the two. Largely because Faye would not have approved of everything I did in my work. However, the way things had been going recently, I thought it could be reassuring to have someone waiting for me outside when I went in to see Leslie Morris.

"OK," I said. "That would be great."

TO SAY THAT Leslie Morris was not pleased to see me would be an understatement. As I introduced myself as a BHA investigator, he tried to close his front door, but I had my foot against the frame, preventing it.

"Move your foot," he demanded through the six-inch gap.

I didn't budge. "No."

"What do you want?" he asked without releasing the pressure on the door.

"I want to talk to you about Bill McKenzie's riding of Wisden Wonder at Sandown."

He didn't ask me *what* it was about Bill McKenzie's riding that I was interested in. He knew.

"I don't want to talk to you," he said. "Now, remove your foot."

I still didn't budge.

"Aggravated trespass is against the law," he said.

"So is defrauding the betting public," I replied.

There was no response other than an increased pressure on the door.

"You'll have to talk about it sometime," I said. "Or shall I pass the file over to the police? The Fraud Squad won't just put their foot in your door, Mr. Morris, they'll break it down and then they'll arrest you. Is that what you want? Do you fancy a cold night in a cell shared with some drug addicts?"

He was rattled. I could see it in his eyes.

"Mr. Morris," I said. "This is your last chance. Either you let me in now or you had better go pack your toothbrush and get ready for the arrival of the boys in blue. It's your choice."

I was pretty sure that the police would not be sufficiently interested to hotfoot it to his door with an arrest warrant, and they certainly wouldn't have put him in a cell with anyone else, but was Leslie Morris prepared to take the risk?

Obviously not, as he slowly opened the door wide.

"Who is that?" he asked, looking over my shoulder toward Faye, who was sitting in the car parked in his driveway.

"My assistant," I said. "She'll wait there for me."

He led me through to the kitchen.

"Now, what is all this about?" he asked, nervously pushing his fingers through his white hair while trying his best to exude an air of innocence.

"How well do you know Bill McKenzie?" I asked.

Again, movement in his eyes indicated a rising degree of concern.

"I've heard of him," Morris replied. "I've seen him riding, of course. But I don't know him personally."

"That's strange, because he seems to know you."

More concern.

"I can't think how," Morris said. "I don't believe he's ever ridden my horse."

I'd already checked for that in the BHA records.

"Tell me about the bets you made at Sandown Park races on the Friday of the Tingle Creek meeting," I said, changing tactics.

There was a distinct tightening of the muscles around his eyes and his breathing became shallower, sure signs that rising concern was nearing the slide into panic.

"I don't know what you're talking about," he replied, trying his best to control his breathing.

"You made multiple bets on the race where Wisden Wonder was the favorite."

"I think you must be mistaken," he said.

I took my iPhone out of my pocket and showed him one of the photographs I had taken on that day at Sandown. It clearly showed him in his distinctive blue fedora handing over a substantial wad of cash to a bookmaker. In the background, plainly discernible, was a bookie's brightly lit price board showing the names of the eight horses in the race including Wisden Wonder, offered at six-to-four.

"I am not mistaken," I said slowly. "You made over thirty large bets on that race. I watched and filmed you."

I looked around, hoping that his little red notebook in which he'd recorded his bets would be conveniently lying on the kitchen countertop. No such luck.

"But not a single one of your bets was on the favorite," I said. "Why was that?"

Now he was really anxious. He showed all the signs of increased adrenaline in his system—wider pupils, bunched muscles, rapid breathing. His body was ready for fight or flight, but his mind was still in control.

"I obviously didn't think the favorite would win," he said calmly. "And it wasn't good value at such a short price."

"I think you are lying to me, Mr. Morris. I think you knew that Wisden Wonder wouldn't win because you had paid Bill McKenzie to ensure it didn't. Then you backed every other horse in the race knowing that whichever of them won, you would make a handsome profit."

He said nothing.

"Whose money did you use?" I asked.

He looked slightly baffled by the question. "What do you mean?"

"I calculated that you wagered nearly seventeen thousand pounds on that race. Where did you get that sort of cash?"

He seemed genuinely surprised that I knew the amount.

"It was my money," he said.

I looked around me again. Mr. Leslie Morris may have lived in a fairly sought-after part of London suburbia, yet there was nothing about his house or its contents that indicated he would have had seventeen thousand pounds in spare readies lying around to wager on the horses.

The original covert tip-off had indicated that he was placing bets for an excluded person.

"I don't believe you," I said. "Who's your banker?"

"I tell you, it's all my own money," he said again with more confidence. "I used the lump sum from my pension fund."

"How did you know that Wisden Wonder wasn't going to win?"

"I didn't," he said.

"Don't hand me that nonsense," I said with annoyance. "You and I both know you wouldn't risk your pension money unless you knew for certain that the horse wouldn't win. Do you take me for an idiot or something?"

He said nothing.

"So how did you know that, Mr. Morris? How much did you pay Bill McKenzie to make sure he didn't win?"

He still made no reply.

"Saying nothing won't help you at the disciplinary panel," I said. "Your racing days would be over for good."

Disqualification as an owner and exclusion from racing premises for a minimum of ten years was the least he could expect, maybe even for longer. Racing and the BHA were not very good at forgiveness, even for those who admitted their guilt and helped to implicate others.

"Did you know Dave Swinton?" I asked.

Full-blown panic now appeared in his eyes.

"I met him once," he said, his voice sounding higher in pitch owing to the tightening of the muscles in his neck. "He rode my horse at Ludlow last May."

I'd also checked that on the BHA database and he would have known it.

"His death is such a terrible loss for racing. I liked him."

"Did you know him professionally?" I asked.

"And what do you mean by that?" he said, regaining some of his confidence.

"Were you his accountant?"

"No," he said, "I was not."

"I'll check, you know," I said.

"Check away," he replied. "I worked for a small three-man outfit here in Wimbledon. I'm sure the likes of Dave Swinton would be represented by one of the big London firms."

"Were you blackmailing him?"

"I've had enough of this rubbish," he said suddenly. "Get out of my house. Right now. Go on, get out." He was almost shouting as he ushered me down the hallway toward his front door.

I was in no position to argue with him as standing my ground may have resulted in a physical assault, something my poor damaged body could ill afford.

"And don't come back," Morris shouted as I walked out toward the car.

"I'll see you at the disciplinary hearing," I called back in valediction.

"I doubt that," he replied.

The words sent a chill down my spine. Had he said it because he would not be attending the hearing or because he believed I wouldn't live long enough to be there myself?

"Not a very successful visit, by the look of it," Faye said as I got back into her car.

"No," I agreed. "Let's go."

I had been in Morris's house for less than fifteen minutes but I was exhausted. I leaned my head back on the head restraint and closed my eyes.

"You need to rest," Faye said as we drove away. "You must regain your strength."

She sounded like a character in a Jane Austen novel speaking to the victim of a nasty fever. But I think she was right. I did need to regain my strength if I was going to discover who was trying to kill me.

22

But I want to see you," Henri said on the phone at Monday lunchtime. "I'll come to Richmond after work."

To be honest, I'd tried to put her off, although I wasn't sure why.

Perhaps I was worried about what Faye would think of her. Or maybe it was because Quentin could be so abrupt and offhand that I didn't want Henri to be offended to the point of never coming back.

"What's your sister's address?"

I told her. Of course I told her. It had been two whole days since she had kissed me good-bye in the hospital on Saturday and I was desperate to see her again.

"I'll be there sometime after six," she said.

"Lovely."

I SPENT most of the afternoon either on the phone or at my computer.

First, I called Paul Maldini at the BHA offices.

"How did we find out that Leslie Morris would be placing bets at Sandown on Tingle Creek Friday?" I asked.

"We received a tip-off," Paul replied.

"From whom? And what sort of tip-off was it?"

"I think it came from a CHIS."

A CHIS was a covert human intelligence source—a racing insider who provided information of possible wrongdoing to the BHA. They were crucial to the integrity of racing. Some were stable staff who had concerns over the legality of things they saw happening and who then approached the authorities in confidence for clarification. Others were employees of bookmakers concerned about the probity of their practices.

Once established, a CHIS would be nurtured and cherished, made to feel important and encouraged to pass on any snippet of information that might be useful to the Authority.

"Yes, but which CHIS?"

"I don't know. It was anonymous by the time it reached my desk."

"Try and find out for me, will you?" I said.

"Why?" Paul said. "The information was accurate."

"That's partly why I want to know who provided it. How was the informant aware something was going on unless he was also somehow involved? We were also told he was placing bets on behalf of someone else, an excluded person."

"What about it?" Paul said.

"Morris claims he used his own money."

There was a long pause on the other end of the line while Paul worked out, first, that I must have spoken to Morris and, second, whether he approved or not.

"I'll get back to you," Paul said.

I started searching on my computer. My main problem was that I didn't really know what I was searching for.

Paul Maldini phoned back almost immediately.

"It was an anonymous call to RaceStraight."

"Dead end, then," I said.

Anyone could make such an anonymous tip and there was no way of us knowing who. The RaceStraight reporting line was operated by an independent body and they weren't allowed to say who had called them even if they knew.

I went back to my computer and used the BHA database to watch the videos of all the races in which Bill McKenzie had ridden for the month leading up to his ride on Wisden Wonder at Sandown. I was trying to spot anything suspicious.

In all, there were forty races, twenty-three of them over hurdles, fifteen steeplechases, and two National Hunt flat races. In those forty, Bill had had three winners and five seconds. In addition, he had fallen twice and been unseated once.

The difference between a *fall* and an *unseated* being whether the horse itself actually falls to the ground or the jockey simply comes off its back while it remains upright. Both result in the jockey landing on the turf at high speed and from a great height.

I studied his riding in all the races and with only one did I have the slightest question.

McKenzie had ridden a horse called Pool Table in a three-mile novice chase at Cheltenham in mid-November on the same day as the Paddy Power Gold Cup. It had started as hot favorite at a price of eleven-to-eight but had finished second of the six runners, beaten two lengths by a much longer-priced competitor.

The only reason I was even the tiniest bit suspicious was because Pool Table had hit the third last fence in exactly the same way that Wisden Wonder had at Sandown.

Pool Table had been lying third in the approach to the fence, tucked up very close behind the two leaders. He blundered badly, crashing through the stiff birch, and was lucky not to have fallen. However, his momentum, critical at this stage of the race, had been totally lost and he was unable to make up the deficit in the run up the famous Cheltenham hill to the finish line.

The fence in question was on the run downhill toward the turn into the homestretch, where the runners were racing almost directly toward the crowded grandstands. Even the broadcasted television pictures were head-on at this point, where the horses were traveling at their fastest as they made their bids for victory.

It would not have been easy for anyone to spot what actually happened.

Only on the RaceTech camera footage, taken from behind, was it possible to see that Bill McKenzie appeared to have made no effort to invite his mount to jump, just as he had failed to do with Wisden Wonder in the hurdle race at Sandown.

According to the BHA database, Bill McKenzie lived near Wantage, not far from Lambourn. If I had been feeling better, I'd have taken a train, there and then, to go to see him. He probably wouldn't be at the races, not if he was nursing a broken collarbone.

Maybe I'd go later in the week.

I WARNED FAYE that I had a female friend coming to visit, but that did little to ease my nerves at what she would think of her.

My ever-caring sister did her best to extract information but I was playing my cards very close to my chest. If there was one thing I'd learned in the Intelligence Corps, it was how to keep things to myself.

"I met her at Sandown races," I said finally when pressed. "We sat next to each other at a lunch."

"And you like her?"

"Yes."

"And is she keen on you?"

What could I say? Henri had been keen enough to spend several days trying to find me at University College Hospital.

"I think so."

"Good," Faye said, smiling broadly. "I look forward to meeting her."

I WAITED FOR Henri in the living room, unable to resist the urge to stand at the window so I could watch her approach across Richmond Green. I was like a child impatient for the arrival of Santa Claus.

She arrived at half past six, again wearing the full-length camel-colored coat with hood, this time over a white lace-front blouse and black pants.

I opened the front door before she had a chance to push the bell, eager to have the chance to spend a few moments together with her before I took her in to contend with Faye's inquisitive gaze.

"You look great," I said, taking her coat and hanging it on the stand in the hall.

"Hardly," she said. "These are my work clothes. I've spent most of the day as a waitress."

"You've been waitressing?" I asked incredulously.

"What's wrong with that?" she said. "The waitress I'd booked was hit by a cyclist who ran a red light, so I stood in for her."

"Where?"

"Some offices in Covent Garden. It was a boardroom Christmas lunch for the directors of an Australian travel company. I also provided the chef."

I wondered if any of the travel company directors appreciated that they had been served their turkey and mince pies by someone on the *Sunday Times* "Rich List."

"Well, you still look good to me," I said, but I'd probably think she looked great in burlap.

"Nice shirt," she said, stroking my back.

I smiled at her. She had bought it.

We went through to the kitchen.

"Faye," I said, "this is Henrietta Shawcross."

I think Faye was impressed. The two certainly hit it off well, helped along by a couple of glasses of sauvignon blanc.

Quentin arrived at seven o'clock and he too took an instant shine to Henri. He kept saying that he had some reading to do, but he never went off to do it. Instead, he sat and chatted, in the most genial manner I have ever seen from him, while never taking his eyes off Henri.

"What are you doing for Christmas?" she asked me.

Christmas was something I had been trying to ignore for months. Faye had asked me almost every week since August if I'd like to spend it with her and Quentin and every time I'd been vague in my response, unwilling to set anything in stone, and not at all sure that Christmas at the Calderfields' was my idea of a fun time.

Three years ago, Lydia and I had stayed with them for four nights over the holiday and Quentin had become more and more grumpy with every meal. Never again, we had agreed.

Up until last week, I had seriously considered taking to my bed and staying there from Christmas Eve right through until New Year's Day, missing all that dreadful bonhomie, mulled wine and repeat TV showings of *It's a Wonderful Life* or *Miracle on 34th Street*.

Maybe I'd have risen briefly to attend Kempton races on Boxing Day, but, otherwise . . . no thanks.

However, my near-death experience, combined with my joyous meeting with Henrietta Shawcross, had slightly softened my view of the festivities.

"Nothing," I said. "How about you?"

"I'm going away," she said, "with my uncle and aunt."

Disaster, I thought.

"Can you come too?" she asked excitedly.

"Where are you going?" I asked with a certain degree of trepidation, ever wary of my bank balance.

"The Caribbean."

"I ought to be at Kempton on Boxing Day."

She looked disappointed. "Surely you're allowed time off to recuperate?"

"Of course he is," Faye said, "but he won't take it. He never takes his vacation time. I'll bet he's not taken one day off all year. He even works on Saturdays and Sundays."

"I didn't work last week," I said in mild defense.

"But you were in the hospital!" Faye said in astonishment. "You can hardly call that a holiday. And I know for a fact that you had meetings with people from your office."

"Only one meeting," I said sheepishly.

Faye rolled her eyes. "Do you see what I have to put up with?" she said to Henri, who laughed. Even Quentin laughed.

"What's this?" I said. "Be Nasty to Jeff Week?"

"She's only trying to get you to come away with me for Christmas," Henri said.

I looked at Faye. "Are you?" I knew she had been working on the assumption that I would, in the end, agree to stay with her and Quentin.

"Absolutely. I think it's a great idea."

So did I.

"But what will your uncle Richard say?"

"I mentioned to him last night that I might ask you. He remembers you from Sandown. He liked you. In fact, he seemed very keen on the idea of you coming with us."

"OK," I said with a grin. "I'd love to."

"THE CARIBBEAN?" Paul Maldini sounded more surprised than annoyed when I called him first thing on Tuesday morning.

"Yes," I said. "For Christmas and the New Year."

"Are you well enough for such a journey?" Paul asked.

"I reckon so," I said. "At least, I will be by then."

"What about your investigations?"

"They will all wait," I said. "I've been told that I need to have a good rest in order to fully recover."

I wasn't going to tell him that it had been my sister who'd told me.

"But how about all this Wisden Wonder business?" he asked. "Who will investigate that, ready for the disciplinary panel?"

"There's plenty of time to get things done when I get back. Don't worry. I'll take some of my vacation. I've got loads of days left. It won't cost the BHA anything."

That seemed to placate him somewhat.

"What if I need to contact you?" he said.

"My cell will be on and I will try to pick up my e-mails."

"Well, I suppose it's all right," he said reluctantly. "When do you go?"

"Sometime next week."

Detective Inspector Galvin called my cell phone at lunchtime.

"We've found Darryl Lawrence," he said.

"Good," I said. "That's a huge relief. Where was he?"

"At Victoria Tube station, just after eight-thirty this morning."

"What does he say?"

"Nothing. He's dead."

"Dead!"

"He fell in front of a train."

"Suicide?"

"Possible," he said. "But I'd say it was unlikely. The northbound Victoria Line platform was extremely busy, totally packed full of commuters, with more coming down the escalators from the rail station every second. In my experience, suicides prefer to do it when it's quieter, even deserted. I'd say it was more likely to be an accident. Or murder."

"Which?"

"Can't tell, at present. Those nearby are in shock. I understand that no one the Transport Police have spoken to so far saw anything suspicious, but that doesn't mean it didn't happen. The traveling public are generally useless as witnesses. It's as if people go into a trance when they travel on a train."

I knew exactly what he meant. Following someone on the Tube was dead easy. Most people never looked beyond the end of their noses, largely out of fear of attracting the attention of a potential mugger or rapist.

"So where does that leave us?" I said.

"There's still his accomplice to find. Any further thoughts on what he looks like?" He sounded bored.

"No," I said. "Any luck with the CCTV at the hospital?"

"Nothing useful. His face was covered, so it's difficult to get a positive ID. And there's not much more we can do."

It was pretty clear that he was signing off on the investigation. I suppose I couldn't blame him. On average, there were more than a hundred murders each year in London to be solved. I was just thankful that I hadn't been one of them.

"Are you still in contact with D.S. Jagger at Thames Valley?" I asked.

"Not lately. Is there anything new?"

"Not that I'm aware of," I said. "But it wasn't by chance that Lawrence and his chum tried to kill me. They knew me by name and I feel it may be tied to the previous attempt to kill me at Dave Swinton's place."

"Does D.S. Jagger know you think that?"

"It's in my statement."

"Then I'm sure he will look into it."

It didn't sound very positive to me.

Coordination was one of the major problems with having so many different police forces: Thames Valley were investigating the Swinton death, British Transport Police would be responsible for looking into the Lawrence incident at Victoria, and D.I. Galvin himself was a member of the Metropolitan force.

The only common denominator seemed to be *me*.

I WENT HOME to my apartment on Wednesday morning despite the urging of Faye to stay a while longer in Richmond.

"I need some clean clothes," I said.

"I *do* have a washing machine, you know. Or I could fetch some for you."

"Faye, my darling, the man who was trying to kill me is himself dead. It will be perfectly safe for me to go back home now."

I wondered if I was trying to convince myself as much as I was her.

"But you said he was a paid killer," she said in desperation. "How do you know there won't be someone else paid to kill you?"

Good point.

"I'll be careful," I said.

Hence, I made Faye drive slowly past my apartment twice in order for me to check that there was no one lurking outside my front door.

It did nothing to ease her state of anxiety.

When I was finally satisfied that there were no miscreants hiding in the bushes, she parked outside and helped me carry my stuff, being careful first to check that nobody was waiting for me within.

Faye went into every room. The place was deserted.

Nevertheless, she was reluctant to leave and I had to shoo her away, assisted, in the end, by a traffic warden who threatened to give her a ticket if she didn't move her car.

I stood on the sidewalk and waved at her as she drove off, wondering if I was doing the right thing. But I couldn't hide away in Richmond forever. I had to confront my fears and get on with my life because if I didn't, I'd have no chance of finding out who was behind it all and why.

I FINALLY UNPACKED the boxes, removing things slowly, piece by piece, from where they lay in the hallway so as not to carry anything heavy. I also washed the stack of dirty dishes in the sink and cleaned the place from one end to the other, including removing slimy fingerprint powder from all the surfaces in the kitchen and hall.

After three hours' work, interspersed with several lengthy rests, the apartment looked almost presentable, but I was exhausted. I slumped down into an armchair in my living room and put my feet up on the freshly polished coffee table.

I really did need to get my strength back.

My landline phone rang.

I stared at it. Not again.

"Hello," I said gingerly, picking it up.

"Just checking you're all right," said Faye over the line.

I breathed a sigh of relief. "I'm fine," I said. "I've been clearing up. You wouldn't recognize the place."

"But you're meant to be taking it easy."

"Don't fuss," I said. "You hate it when I fuss over you."

"That's different," she said. "I don't need to be told to take things easy. You do."

"OK," I said, admitting defeat. "I promise to take things easy."

One should never make promises one can't keep.

23

I was following Faye's instructions and was taking things easy at home, my feet up on the sofa, watching highlights of cricket from Australia, when Detective Inspector Galvin telephoned around lunchtime on Thursday.

"I think we may have Darryl Lawrence's accomplice in custody," he said. "I'm not certain, but his height and shape fit the man in the hospital CCTV images."

"That's great," I said. "But can you hold him on such flimsy evidence?"

"Currently, he's under arrest on suspicion of the murder of Darryl Lawrence. CCTV footage at Victoria shows him entering the Tube station with Lawrence and leaving it again on his own after the incident."

"Does it actually show him pushing Lawrence under the train?"

"Sadly, no, but we do have a couple of eyewitnesses. The Transport Police have now handed the case over to us. We've arranged an old-fashioned lineup for this afternoon. Would you come and see if you recognize him from the attack at your apartment?"

"Where?" I asked.

"Charing Cross Police Station. Come to the main entrance on Agar Street at three o'clock."

"I'll be there."

Charing Cross Police Station is built in a triangular shape with a fully enclosed courtyard in the middle. Eight men were standing in a line across the center of the courtyard, each of them holding a card with a number on it from 1 to 8.

"Now, take your time, sir," said the uniformed police sergeant who'd accompanied me outside. "Walk down the full line and have a good look at each man. If you recognize anyone, please go back and touch him on the shoulder or you may come and tell me his number."

I started walking slowly along the line of men, looking at their faces.

All of them were of roughly the same height and build, and each was dressed in everyday clothes and a balaclava. None of them was conveniently wearing red sneakers.

But I didn't need that clue. I easily recognized the man who had held me in my hallway as Darryl Lawrence had repeatedly thrust his knife into my torso. Even though I'd been unable to provide D.I. Galvin with a description at the time and I'd said that I couldn't remember what he looked like, I knew him instantly. He was holding card number 3.

I went on down the whole line, looking closely at each of them in turn. I was quite certain that I had never seen the other seven men before.

I went back to number 3 and touched him on the shoulder.

"Are you sure?" asked the sergeant.

"Positive," I said. "This is the man who held me in my apartment while I was being stabbed."

The man had previously been standing up very straight and looking into the distance well above my head. Now he moved his eyes down to meet mine. They were cold, like ice, with no emotion in them whatsoever. Eyes are sometimes described as the windows to the soul. If so, this man had no soul at all. The windows were black and uncaring.

I wondered what was going on in the brain behind them.

He said nothing as he was led away by two burly constables back into the building.

D.I. Galvin, who had been watching the proceedings from the far side of the courtyard, now walked over to join me.

"Well done," he said. "You picked out the right one."

"There was absolutely no doubt," I said. "What's his name?"

"Gary Banks. He has previous convictions for violence."

"How about the other two witnesses?" I asked. "Did they pick him out?"

"One did, one didn't."

"Is that enough?" I asked.

"Probably not. But identification on its own is never enough."

"Does that mean he'll walk?" I asked with concern. I didn't fancy Mr. Banks coming after me again. "I'd feel a lot safer knowing he's locked up."

"That will be up to the CPS and the magistrates. We do have a little bit more on him—the hospital CCTV images and the fact that he was arrested wearing red sneakers with white soles and laces might help."

"I looked for those," I said with a smile.

"That would have been a bit too obvious. We needed you to

pick him out without those to help you." He smiled back at me. "And we will continue to interview him, of course. So far, he's replied *No comment* to every question he's been asked, but we'll see. We have a few alternatives to try."

"Thumbscrews?" I asked.

"Only verbal ones, sadly."

ON FRIDAY MORNING, I caught a train to Ascot races for the first day of the last major meeting before Christmas. It had been almost two weeks since I'd been on a racetrack. That had been at Sandown on the day before I'd been stabbed.

That was also where I had first met Henrietta Shawcross, the day of the giggles over lunch in Derrick and Gay Smith's box.

Thirteen days ago.

In some respects, it felt like much longer; in others, like only yesterday.

I hadn't seen Henri since she'd been to Richmond on Monday evening and I'd spoken to her only on the telephone for a few minutes.

"I'm sorry," she'd said when I complained I was being neglected. "It's my busiest time of the year. Everyone is having Christmas parties and needing staff. I've worked solidly every day this week, and every evening except Monday. All I want to do afterward is go home and go straight to sleep."

Sleep, I'd thought.

All I wanted to do was "sleep" with her.

"We will spend lots of time together next week," she'd said.

"Shouldn't I be booking my flights?" I'd asked.

"Don't worry, I've done all that. We leave on Wednesday."

"Where to?" I'd asked.

"The Cayman Islands."

It all seemed surreal as I struggled up the hill to the racetrack on a typical December day of dampness and wind. The Cayman Islands seemed as far away as the moon.

I had to stop at least twice to rest.

I was beginning to wish that I had heeded my sister's advice to take things more easily and to watch racing on the television.

But there was nothing like actually *being* where the action was happening. On television, one saw only what the producer decided was relevant, whereas I preferred to look elsewhere, perhaps to see what someone didn't want me to.

I went through the racetrack entrance turnstiles using my official BHA pass and made a direct line for the coffee bar on the concourse level of the imposing grandstand. It wasn't so much a drink that I needed but a place to sit down. The walk up from the station had tired me out more than I'd thought it would.

Now, you must *be careful,* the nurse had said at the hospital clinic the previous morning when I'd gone to have the stitches out. *We don't want you back in here again, now do we?*

No, I'd thought. We don't.

As I was sitting, drinking my coffee, my phone rang. It was D.I. Galvin.

"Banks has been charged with manslaughter," he said.

"Why not murder?" I asked.

"He says he didn't push Lawrence under the train on purpose. It was an accident."

"And you believe him?" I asked with sarcasm in my voice.

"Of course not. But we were in danger of getting nothing and having to let him go since our time was almost up. Everything was circumstantial. The fact that the second witness couldn't pick him out rather negated the one that could. He wasn't saying anything at all, so we offered him a deal and he took it."

"I didn't think plea bargaining was allowed in the UK."

"It wasn't like one of those U.S. deals. There was no mention of a specific sentence or anything. We simply gave Banks the opportunity to agree with us that Lawrence's death was manslaughter, not murder. His solicitor must have thought we had a stronger case than we actually did because he advised Banks to agree. He has since been chatting away, telling us all about how in the crush on the platform he only slightly nudged his dear old friend Darryl, who then stumbled accidently, falling under the train.

"It's all a load of old hogwash. Banks knows it, the solicitor knows it and I know it. But it does mean that Banks has confirmed his association with Lawrence and that was crucial for your case. What the solicitor doesn't know is that we are now going to arrest Banks for the attempted murder of you—twice over. We'll see what he has to say about that."

"Ask him if he knows a man called Leslie Morris," I said.

"Why?"

I told him briefly about my inquiries into the fixed races and how Morris had placed the suspect bets at Sandown.

"The attempts on my life may have been to stop me investigating."

"OK," he said. "I'll try it."

"Will Banks be taken into custody?" I asked. That was far more important to me than anything else at the moment.

"Sure to be."

"Well done," I said. "Please keep me informed."

"Will do."

He hung up.

With Lawrence dead and Banks in jail, I suddenly felt a lot safer.

PART OF THE REASON I'd come to Ascot was because I thought I'd detected a pattern in the races that had been lost on purpose.

Dave Swinton had ridden Garrick Party at Haydock Park in a lesser race on the day of the Grade 1 Betfair Chase. The same had been true for Bill McKenzie's ride on Pool Table on the same card as the Paddy Power Gold Cup. True, Wisden Wonder's race at Sandown had been on a Friday, not a Saturday, but it had been the first day of the Tingle Creek Festival and a sizable crowd had attended, plus there had been a large number of bookmakers in the betting ring.

Someone trying to bet seventeen thousand pounds in cash would have stuck out like a sore thumb at, say, Newton Abbot on a Wednesday, when the seagulls would have outnumbered the genuine punters, and there would be only a half-dozen or so bookies to bet with. But among a big crowd, and with some serious money about, no one would raise an eyebrow.

Were there more races than just the three I had spotted? Were more jockeys involved than just Dave Swinton and Bill McKenzie?

I had spent most of Thursday afternoon researching race results and watching video recordings. I was looking for favorites that hadn't won on days when large crowds would have been present.

Somewhat surprisingly, it was quite common for even very short-priced favorites not to win. Looking back for the past four months, I found seventeen horses that had started at odds shorter than two-to-one that had failed to win a race on the same card as the week's main feature.

My list included two at Newbury on the same day that Dave Swinton had won the Hennessy Gold Cup on Integrated. One of those, Global Expedition, had started the Grade 2 Long Distance Hurdle at the incredibly short price of seven-to-four-on and had then finished a bad third of the six runners, well beaten by seven and eighteen lengths.

It was the first time Global Expedition had not won in his seven starts over hurdles and I remember the result being a considerable shock. However, I had been at Newbury that day, had watched the race live and hadn't noticed anything questionable about the horse's running at the time.

I studied the video of the race over and over again, but however many times I watched it, and from whichever camera position, I couldn't establish that the horse had been deliberately prevented from winning by its rider. The jockey appeared to have made every effort to stay in touch with the leader, yet to no avail.

I concluded that there was nothing suspicious. Global Expedition simply hadn't performed on that day in the same way as he had in the past.

Perhaps the horse had been feeling a touch unwell or was merely not in the mood to race. Racehorses were not machines. If they always ran exactly as their ratings suggested, racing would quickly die as everyone would pick the same horse to back.

It was the healthy dose of unpredictability that made racing so exciting.

But there had been another heavily backed loser that had run on Hennessy day, in the first race, a two-and-a-quarter-mile novice handicap chase.

Electrostatic had started as the six-to-four favorite, but not only did he fail to win the race, he failed to jump even two of the thirteen fences. He'd been pulled up immediately after the first with, as the jockey claimed, a saddle that had slipped to the side.

The racetrack stewards had questioned the trainer about the care that had been taken when saddling the horse. The trainer had blamed the starter's assistant, who had supposedly tightened the horse's girth at the start. He, in turn, was adamant that the girth had been both tight and secure.

The jockey, Willy Mitchell, had told the inquiry that he'd had no alternative but to pull up Electrostatic. He would have fallen off if the saddle had slipped any farther, perhaps causing some of the other runners to be brought down.

No action had been taken by the stewards other than to warn both the trainer and the starter's assistant to be more vigilant of the problem in future and to commend the jockey for his quick reactions in preventing a serious incident.

I watched the video of the race, many times and from every available angle.

There was no doubt that in some of the TV images the saddle had slipped to the left, but they were taken long after the horse had stopped. It was impossible to tell if the slipping had occurred prior to the horse being pulled up. The footage seemed to show that the saddle had been in the right position as the horse had taken off at the first, although I couldn't be sure it hadn't moved on landing, as that wasn't shown.

Was it just my suspicious mind or had the jockey moved the saddle on purpose only after he'd pulled up at the most conveniently distant point from both the start and the grandstand?

There was no real way of knowing without confronting Willy Mitchell and hoping for some sort of reaction.

And, hence, the real reason I had come to Ascot was that Electrostatic was declared to run in the two-mile novice chase, the second race of the day, and Willy Mitchell was again down to ride. All the morning papers had suggested that the horse would start once more as a short-priced favorite, his failure on his last outing being put down to just bad luck rather than any deficiency on the animal's part.

ELECTROSTATIC LIVED UP to his past form and his high-voltage name, winning the second race at a canter.

I'd wandered around the betting ring beforehand, but, as far as I could tell, no one was placing large bets on all the horses other than the favorite. There was certainly no blue fedora visible. No sign at all of Mr. Leslie Morris.

Perhaps the summons to the disciplinary panel and my unwelcome visit to his house had frightened him away. Paul Maldini would be pleased.

Willy Mitchell was all smiles as he unsaddled the horse in the space reserved for the winner.

"No slipped saddle this time, then?" I said to him as he walked past me into the weighing room to weigh in.

He looked at me and the smile disappeared from his face faster than a bargain TV on Black Friday. Willy Mitchell knew exactly who I was. He'd also been part of my investigation into the misuse of jockeys' cell phones.

"No," he managed to say. "Not this time."

"Come out and see me," I said. "After the presentation."

There was a slight touch of panic in his eyes. Not that it was necessarily an indication of wrongdoing. It was the sort of panic that sweeps over everyone, myself included, when a police car comes up behind you when you're driving. It was a reaction I was quite used to generating in the innocent as well as in the guilty.

Willy came out wearing a thick-padded gray anorak over his racing silks.

"I have a ride in the fifth," he said. "I can't be long." He looked out at the parade ring, where the horses for the third race were circulating. "Is there some place more private? I don't want to be seen talking to you. Especially not by my gaffer."

His *gaffer* was the trainer for whom he rode, the trainer of Electrostatic.

"He doesn't have a runner in this one," I said.

"Maybe not, but he'll be around here somewhere."

We went into the stewards' room.

In the media, Willy Mitchell was often referred to as one of the up-and-coming young jockeys. Sadly for him, he had been up-and-coming for some time now, ever since he was seventeen, and he was in some danger of being relabeled as come-and-going. But he was still only twenty-one. Being the retained jockey for a horse as good as Electrostatic might just be his ticket to the big time.

"Tell me about the slipped saddle at Newbury," I said to him.

He was clearly very uncomfortable talking to me.

"What about it?" he asked with only a very slight tremor in his voice.

"How did it happen?"

"I don't know," he said. "The girth, obviously, wasn't tight enough. My saddle started sliding left as I was jumping the first fence. I tried standing on the right stirrup, but it wouldn't go back."

I didn't say anything, I just looked at him.

In spite of the coolness of the room, he started sweating. "It's true, I tell you."

I didn't believe him. But I still said nothing. I let him do his own digging.

"Why would I do it on purpose?" he said. "You've seen what a great little novice old Electro is. I reckon he'll win the big novice chase on the Thursday of the Festival at Cheltenham. Why would I jeopardize my ride on him for that?"

Indeed, why would he? Was I wrong?

"I've studied the video of the race at Newbury," I said, "together with the footage that was not broadcast."

He sweated some more. He wasn't to know that it showed nothing suspicious.

"Do you know a man called Leslie Morris?" I asked, trying to pile on the pressure.

He thought for a moment.

"Never heard of him," Willy said confidently without so much as a flicker of the eyes. If he did know Morris, he was a much better liar than I took him for.

Instead of adding to the pressure, I'd just released it.

"Don't you have a young family?" I asked, but I already knew the answer. I'd done my research.

"Twins," he said, nodding.

He looked like a child himself, hardly old enough to have kids of his own.

"What about them?" he asked.

"Must be expensive," I said.

I also knew that Willy didn't have that many rides, certainly not on horses as good as Electrostatic. In fact, he'd had only fifteen rides in the preceding month, including the one at Newbury. He was riding two here this afternoon, but that was a rarity. Usually, it was a maximum of one ride per day—if he was lucky. That didn't leave much to live on, not after traveling expenses and valet fees.

"You can check my bank balance, if you like," he said more confidently. "I've not received anything I shouldn't have." He laughed. "Chance would be a fine thing."

I thought back to what Dave Swinton had said to me during our journey to Newbury races on the day before he died.

"Willy," I said slowly, "are you being blackmailed?"

He stared at me for what felt like an age without moving so much as a single muscle in his face, not even a blink.

Finally, he turned away. "Can I go now?" he said.

"Is it to do with tax?" I asked.

He turned back to face me.

"Tax?" He laughed. "I hardly earn enough to pay any tax."

"What is it, then?"

"Nothing," he said. "Leave me alone."

He pushed past me to the door.

He had as good as admitted to me with that stare that he was being blackmailed. I suppose I couldn't really blame him for not telling me why. If he was prepared to lose a race when riding the best horse he'd ever been on, with all the possible consequences for his career, then it must be something that he was very determined to keep a secret.

I wouldn't have told me either.

IN A STRANGE WAY, I was pleased when Willy Mitchell won the fifth race as well. I don't suppose that he'd had many *doubles* in his career, and even the sight of me standing by the unsaddling enclosure couldn't wipe the smile from his face entirely.

I left him alone to enjoy his success.

But I'd be back.

24

On Saturday I went again to Ascot for the second day of the pre-Christmas meeting.

I had briefly thought of asking Henri if she would like to come with me, but I'd quickly dismissed the notion.

I was always working when on a racetrack. Even the day at Sandown when I'd first met Henri, my work had been the higher priority—I had gone off to the hospital with Bill McKenzie rather than accepting Gay Smith's invitation to go back to the box for tea.

That day, it had been a difficult decision, and the right one, as it was again now.

"I couldn't come with you anyway," Henri had said when I'd called to explain why I wasn't asking her. "I'm going to a wedding in Kent."

"As long as it's not *your* wedding," I'd said with a laugh.

"There's no chance of that."

I hadn't been quite sure what to make of that answer, but it was not the right time to delve deeper into the matter, and definitely not when on the telephone.

I wandered down to the Ascot weighing room still thinking about her and looking forward to spending some decent time with her in the warmth of the Caribbean. I wondered if we were going to Martin Reynard's place in the Cayman Islands. Henri had said that she would be away with her uncle and aunt, so it would be quite likely that her cousin would be there too.

Bill McKenzie was standing on the terrace in front of the weighing room and he was clearly not happy to see me.

"How's the shoulder?" I said.

"Mending slowly."

"I thought you'd be resting it at home."

"I don't want any of the trainers to think I'm going to be out for long," he said. "Out of sight, out of mind." He wasn't even wearing a sling. "I need to be back in good time for the King George."

That would be just three short weeks after the fall at Sandown. His surgeon had been right—he was crazy.

"Do you fancy a quiet talk over a drink or a sandwich?" I asked.

"What, with you?" He sounded incredulous.

"Yes. With me."

"Now, why would I want to do that?"

"Because, Bill, I may be the only friend you have." He didn't look like he believed it. "There's a disciplinary hearing next month and, as far as I can tell from the evidence, you're going to lose your jockey's license for a very long time, maybe forever. Then it won't matter whether the trainers see you or not. You won't be riding. You won't even be allowed on a racetrack."

He looked miserable.

"Is that what you want?" I asked.

"Of course it bloody isn't."

"So speak to me," I said. "Tell me what's going on."

"I can't." He was again almost in tears.

"Come on," I said in my most persuasive tone. "Let's go and find a quiet place to have that drink and a chat."

I steered him not to a bar but to the elevators, which took us up to the private hospitality area of the Ascot Authority, the organization that operates the racetrack on behalf of the Queen, who owns the place.

As I had suspected, even though there were some guests, the hospitality area at a jumps meeting was far from full and I was able to secure a table in a quiet corner, well away from where the others were enjoying a champagne reception near the viewing balcony.

I went over to the waitresses' station and one of them poured me a couple of glasses of white wine.

"I can't have anything to drink," Bill said. "I'm having enough trouble with my weight as is. Lack of riding is making me flabby."

"Drink it," I said, handing him one of the glasses. "You need it."

And, I thought, it might loosen his tongue.

He drank it down in just a few large gulps and I waved to the waitress to bring him another.

"Tell me what's going on."

"I can't," he said pitifully.

"Are you sure you're not being blackmailed?" I asked.

He took a gulp of wine from his new glass.

"No." He sighed. "Not for money anyway."

"Is someone making you ride to lose?"

He didn't say anything, he just nodded slightly as if not voicing the admission somehow made it less damaging.

"How?"

"I love my wife," he said gloomily. "She's five months pregnant and I absolutely adore her. And Oscar, my son. He's now nearly two."

"I'm sure you do," I said, not immediately realizing the significance.

"I don't want to lose them," he said, looking down at the table with tears running down his cheeks.

"Why would you?" I asked.

"There are some photos," he said. "This man calls me and says he'll send them to my Julie unless I lose the races."

So he *was* being blackmailed after all.

"What are the photos of?"

He looked up at me. "What do you think?" he said. "Me and a girl."

"Have you seen them?"

"No. I don't want to. But the man swears he has them."

"Where and when were they taken?" I asked.

"In May," he said. "I went to Paris to ride in the Grand Steeple-Chase. I was in a hotel near the track and I got picked up by some girl in the bar. The next thing I know, it's morning and I'm waking up in bed next to her and both of us are stark naked. I must have had more red wine than I'd realized because I don't really remember much, but this geezer on the phone says he's got some graphic pictures of me and the girl having sex."

"Didn't you ask to see them?" I asked. "He may be bluffing."

"Does it matter?" he said. "Even if he just tells the missus that I've been sleeping with some French floozy, with or without pictures she'd hit the roof and I'd be out on my ear."

"Was it a setup?"

"Yeah, 'course it was. I remember being flattered by her attention. It seemed harmless enough. And I was a long way from home. At first, we were just laughing and chatting. And drinking. Then she was all over me, kissing me and such. I never intended screwing her or anything, but . . ." He tailed off.

"Whose bed?" I asked. "Hers or yours?"

"Mine. Upstairs, in the hotel. I don't even remember going up to the room, let alone doing anything with her when I got there." He put his head in his hands. "I'm bloody finished, aren't I? My job's going down the Swanee over this Wisden Wonder business. And my marriage will be in ruins too. I might as well go kill myself."

He downed the rest of his wine.

"Come on, Bill," I said. "There's no need to talk like that."

"Isn't there? My life's over either way."

I felt sorry for him because it did rather sound like he'd been specifically targeted.

"I'll see what I can do for you," I said. "In the meantime, tell me about riding Pool Table at Cheltenham. Was that another race you were told to lose?"

He hung his head as if in shame. "That was the first time."

"How were you contacted?" I asked.

"By phone," he said. "I got a call at home one night when I'm watching TV. My missus was there in the room with me. It was bloody awful. I couldn't believe what the man was saying. My mouth went completely dry, and I remember going hot and cold all over. I started sweating and such. I was convinced Julie must be able to tell just by looking at me. I've never felt so wretched in my whole life."

"Was it by phone every time?" I asked.

"It's only been *twice*," he said. "Stopping one, that is. Not twice with other girls. That was just the once, and I'd give anything for that not to have happened at all."

"Do you know who it was who called?"

"He didn't give his name," Bill said.

There was something about his tone of voice that made me think he did know.

"Was it a man called Leslie Morris?" I asked.

He looked up at me sharply.

"When I asked you about him before, you said you'd never heard of him. But you blushed, so I knew you were lying. So was it Morris who called you?"

He looked down again at the empty wineglass in his hand.

Then he nodded. "He didn't actually say so, but I think it was him."

"Why did you lie to me about knowing him?" I said.

"Because I was worried about what he might say to you."

"Have you known him long?" I asked.

"Only since May. It was his bloody horse I went to Paris to ride. Morris called me out of the blue after Aintree. He was dead keen for me to go—paid my fare and everything, although, at the time, I couldn't think why he bothered. Useless nag finished last."

So Morris had been lying about that too. Bill McKenzie had indeed ridden his horse, but in France. I silently berated myself for not having checked the French records as well as those for the UK and Ireland.

"So Morris was over there with you?"

"Yeah, together with his son. Nasty piece of work he is, I can tell you."

"Does Morris know about the girl?" I asked.

"I reckon he might."

I believed there was no *might* about it. I'd wager my life savings that not only did Morris know about it, he'd set it up. He'd probably arranged for the girl to get McKenzie drunk or, more likely, to slip him a mickey. Rohypnol maybe.

Easy.

Help him up to his room, remove all his clothes, lie him on the bed with the naked girl in a few compromising positions on top, snap a few photos just to be sure, and, presto, he had cause for blackmail and control. Rohypnol even caused temporary amnesia as a side effect, so he wouldn't have remembered much, just enough not to question that it had happened.

Bill probably never even had sex with the girl. He'd have been incapable. But how would he be able to convince his wife of that?

"Who else knows?" I asked.

"No one," he said. "I've not mentioned it to a soul before you. Please don't tell anyone." He was begging me. "I don't want Julie finding out."

"There may be nothing for her to find out about," I said. "If you don't remember anything happening, then it's quite likely that nothing actually did happen. Especially if you were unconscious."

"I talked to the girl in the first place," he said gloomily.

"If every wife divorced her husband simply because he'd talked to some girl, there'd hardly be a single marriage left intact."

"You don't know my Julie. She can be very jealous."

More the fool her, I thought. But, then, I wouldn't have wanted Henri chatting up some other man at the wedding in Kent.

I wondered what she was doing right now.

"I was determined not to go through with it," Bill said, bringing me back from my daydreaming.

"With what?" I asked.

"Stopping Wisden Wonder from winning. I'd done it once with Pool Table and I told the man that that was enough. But he says that I should think very carefully before I subjected my wife to such distressing news." Bill laughed forlornly. "I told him it wasn't bloody me who would be subjecting her to the distressing news. He just replied that I should have thought about that before I fucked another woman."

I could appreciate his dilemma.

"I did consider trying to win the race anyway and to hell with him. If I'd won, perhaps it would screw the man good and proper. And if I didn't, it wouldn't matter. Because at least I hadn't stopped the horse on purpose."

"So why didn't you try and win?" I asked.

"I didn't want to risk it. The man would have sent the pictures to Julie." He put his head in his hands again. "I even tried to get *you* to stop him."

"What?" I said, surprised.

He looked up. "I tried to get the BHA to stop him by phoning that anonymous tip-off line. I was hoping you might arrest Morris or something. Then I'd be off the hook, so to speak. But I saw him standing by the paddock exit at Sandown as I was going out on Wisden Wonder, all bold as brass in his bloody hat. He didn't say anything, he just glared at me. It gave me the bloody willies, I can tell you. So I made damn sure I couldn't win. I fell off."

"Why did you tell the tip-off line that he was placing bets for an excluded person?"

"I was hardly going to say that he was betting on a fixed race, was I, not when I was the bloody fixer? Don't be crazy. I tried to think of something that the BHA would have to act on. Something that would prevent him from being allowed into the racetrack. Something that wouldn't implicate me."

But it *had* implicated him.

It had been Bill's telephone call that had alerted me to what was actually going on.

The irony wasn't lost on him.

"I suppose that was a bloody stupid idea."

25

The following morning, having checked in the *Racing Post* that he wasn't riding at either of the day's two race meetings, I went to the village of East Hagbourne hoping to find Willy Mitchell at home.

My taxi drew up outside Mitchell's place at noon. Willy was strapping his twin girls into their seats in a battered old Ford that stood in front of a modest-looking house.

"Can you please wait?" I said to the taxi driver. "I may be a while."

"Be as long as you like," he said, reclining his seat. "The meter's still running."

Willy Mitchell wasn't pleased to see me.

"We're just going out for Sunday lunch," he said.

"I won't keep you long."

His very young-looking wife came out of the front door carrying two plastic bags. She was little more than a girl herself.

"Look after the twins for a minute, will you, love?" Willy said to her. "This is about work. I won't be long." He looked at me. "You'd better come inside."

Mrs. Mitchell looked quizzically in her husband's direction, but he said nothing more to her. He just led me through the front door and on into their kitchen, where we stood on either side of a small table.

"Now what?" he said.

"I'm on your side, Willy."

"I doubt that."

"It's true, even if you don't believe me."

"What do you want?"

"Who is blackmailing you?" I asked.

He didn't say anything. As before at Ascot, he just stared at me.

I waited.

"Who says I'm being blackmailed?" he asked eventually.

"You do," I replied. "It's what your body language is shouting at me."

He went back to saying nothing. I waited some more.

"I'm trying to help you," I said.

"Then go away and leave me in peace."

"I can't do that," I said. "Either talk to me now or you'll end up at a disciplinary panel at the BHA and you will lose your license to ride."

"If I talk to you, I'll lose my license anyway."

"Not if *I* can help it," I said. "Willy, I know that you are being forced to do something you don't want to. You are not alone. There are other jockeys in the same position as you. I don't want any of you punished. I just want the blackmailer."

"Come on, Willy," called a female voice from down the hall. "Hurry up or we'll be late."

"All right, Amy, love," Willy shouted back. "I'll be there in a minute." We heard her go back outside. He looked at me. "We're going to her mother's place. She likes us there on time."

"I'm sure she'll wait," I said. "Now, who is blackmailing you?"

He sighed. A big, heavy sigh that had all the weight of the world. He slumped down onto one of the kitchen chairs.

"I don't know," he said, looking down at the table. "I really don't know."

"What hold does he have over you?" I asked.

He lifted his eyes to my face. There was fear in them. "I can't tell you that."

I thought about Bill McKenzie and the sex photos.

"Have you been sleeping with another woman?" I asked.

"No," he said emphatically, standing up and bunching his fists. "How dare you!"

"OK, OK," I said. "Calm down."

So it wasn't tax and it wasn't adultery.

"Willy, we *have* to go." His wife came down the hall into the kitchen and she was quite cross.

"Where does your mother live?" I asked her.

"Didcot," she said flatly.

"Then, Mrs. Mitchell, why don't you go on alone with the children. I'll bring Willy there shortly in my taxi. I have to go to Didcot anyway to catch the train back to London."

She didn't like it. She looked at her husband.

"Good idea, love," Willy said, clearly not giving her the support she was hoping for. "You go on. You know how much your mom is looking forward to seeing the girls. I'll be there soon enough. In plenty of time for lunch."

She opened her mouth as if to say something but closed it again, turned on her heel and marched out. She slammed the front door behind her.

Willy went to go after her. I moved to block his way.

"Tell me what you know," I said to him, "and I'll do my best to get you out of this mess with your career intact."

He stared through me as if I wasn't there.

"How did the blackmailer contact you?" I said. "Was it by phone?"

His eyes refocused on my face and he nodded. "A man called me here one night out of the blue."

"What did he say?"

"He asked me if I loved my twin girls," he said. "I ask you. What sort of question is that? Of course I love them. I absolutely adore them and I'll do anything for them."

He paused. What father wouldn't?

"And?" I said, encouraging him to go on.

"The man said I had to do what he asked or he would make sure that I'd lose them. He'd have them put in foster care."

His voice broke, and there were tears in his eyes. He was really nothing more than a boy.

"That's ridiculous," I said. "No one can arrange to have other people's children put in foster care just like that."

There was a long silence.

"You don't understand."

"Tell me, then," I said.

There was another long silence. He audibly sighed.

"Do you know what the registry of sex offenders is?" he asked.

"I've heard of it," I said.

He sighed again.

"I'm on it."

Now it was my turn to be dumbstruck. There was no mention of that in his BHA file.

"Four years ago, I was convicted of having sex with a child."

I stood and stared at him, waiting silently for him to go on.

"I was seventeen and the girl was fifteen. She became pregnant—that's how they knew we'd done it. At first, they said they wouldn't prosecute me, but I refused to promise not to see her again." He looked up to the heavens. "Bloody silly, that was. Anyway, I was found guilty and sentenced to three months' juvenile detention, which was suspended. I was also put on the sex offenders list for five years. I'm still on it."

"What happened to the girl?" I asked.

"I married her," he said. "You've just met her. Amy was pregnant with the twins. We were so much in love and everything was going brilliantly until this happened."

"Why is someone able to blackmail you over it? The information must already be in the public domain."

"The man on the phone said that unless I did as he wanted, he'd fix it for another girl of fourteen to make a complaint to the police that I'd been having sex with her." He swallowed. "I told him that was a lie. He said it didn't matter. With my record, social services would believe it and they'd take the twins away. The man told me I'd never get to hold my little girls again."

He was in tears once again. Whether or not the threat was real, Willy Mitchell clearly believed it..

"Does Amy know about this?" I asked.

"No," he said quickly. "Well, of course she knows about the registry and all that. She was in court when that happened. She told the judge we were madly in love and that we were getting married as soon as she turned sixteen, but he took no notice." The judge would have been bound by the law, I thought, and a suspended sentence had been quite lenient. "But she doesn't know about the call from the man or about the race at Newbury."

"Isn't it time you told her?" I said.

I DROPPED HIM at his mother-in-law's house before going on to the railway station.

"What will happen to me now?" he'd asked me in the taxi.

"Nothing for the moment," I'd said. "But call me straightaway if the man contacts you again." I gave him my business card.

He'd nodded. "OK."

"Tell me," I'd said, "how did you pass the criminal records check?"

The BHA would have done such a check as part of their *fit and proper person* test before issuing him with his first license to ride.

"I got my jockey's license when I was sixteen. Before all this happened. One of the advantages of being only seventeen was that my name was never revealed in the press. Ever since, whenever I've applied for a renewal, I've answered no to the question on criminal proceedings."

Which was also a breach of BHA regulations, but that was the least of his problems.

"LUTON?"

"Yes," Henri said on the phone when she called on Sunday evening. "We have to check in at Luton Airport on Wednesday morning at eight-thirty."

"I'll take the train from London."

"OK," she said. "I'm coming with Uncle Richard. We'll pick you up from the airport railway station at eight o'clock."

"I didn't think flights across the Atlantic left from Luton."

"Ours does."

I hadn't seen her for six whole days. It felt like six months.

"You do still want me to come, don't you?" I asked.

"Of course I do," she said earnestly. "Why on earth did you say that?"

"It's just that we have hardly spoken this last week, even on the phone."

"That all ends at lunchtime on Tuesday," she said. "That will be my last event for the year, thank goodness. After that, I'm all yours. I promise."

It sounded delicious.

"OK," I said. "What do I need to bring with me? Suit, tuxedo?"

"Good God, no," she said with a laugh. "Shorts and T-shirts, mostly. It's very casual. But bring some long pants and a couple of decent shirts to go out to dinner."

"Do I need a jacket and tie?" I asked.

"You shouldn't."

"I'll pack them anyway," I said.

Smart clothes were a bit like nuclear weapons—better to have them and not need them than to need them and not have them.

"Don't bring too much," she said. "There's a weight limit on luggage. We can only take one suitcase each."

Flying from Luton Airport and a luggage limit of only one suitcase.

I had visions of us being cramped together on a knees-to-the-chest charter flight for ten hours. But as long as I was with Henri, I wouldn't mind a bit.

As I put down my cell, it rang again. This time it was Detective Inspector Galvin.

"I thought you would like to know that Gary Banks was remanded in custody by the magistrates," he said.

"Thank you," I said.

"He was charged with both the manslaughter of Darryl Lawrence and the attempted murder of you. He is due back in court next week, but that will be a formality. You can rest assured that he will now stay behind bars until his trial."

"When will that be?" I asked.

"Sometime next year," he said. "The date won't even be set for months yet."

That was a relief.

"Did he say anything?" I asked.

"He blames it all on Lawrence. Claims he didn't know that Lawrence had a knife with him. He says he thought they were there just to rough you up a bit."

"He definitely knew about the knife when they came to the hospital to try and finish the job."

"He says it wasn't him with Lawrence on that occasion."

"But he was wearing the red sneakers."

"Indeed," said the inspector with a slight laugh. "I'm afraid our friend Mr. Banks is not very bright. He just talked himself into more and more trouble."

"I assume that you asked him *why* they were after me."

"He said he doesn't know. Lawrence was the brains behind it, if you can call it *brains*. Lawrence just told Banks what to do."

"How about the phone calls to my landline?"

"Lawrence made those, apparently. Just as you thought, they were trying to find out where you were. It seems that they'd been waiting for you to appear outside Sandown racetrack on that Saturday afternoon. Banks told us they were planning to *do* you on your way back to Esher railway station. But you never turned up."

I'd departed from the racetrack in an ambulance on its way

to Kingston Hospital with Bill McKenzie and his broken collarbone.

"What did Banks say when you mentioned Leslie Morris?" I asked.

"He swore up and down that he's never heard of anyone called Leslie Morris," said D.I. Galvin. "But, then, he would, wouldn't he?"

Perhaps he *had* been telling the truth.

The timing didn't fit.

Bill McKenzie hadn't known that I was interested in him until he was leaving the parade ring on Lost Moon for the race in which he'd be injured. Even if he'd wanted to, he hadn't had a chance to contact Leslie Morris before he'd gone to surgery. I knew because I'd been with him all the time.

Morris would have been unaware that I was at Sandown that Saturday. So if *he* hadn't told Lawrence and Banks to wait for me outside the racetrack, *who* had?

And how would they have known what I looked like?

Even if Morris had spotted me following him on the previous afternoon, which I knew he hadn't, then Lawrence and Banks would have been looking for a man with long dark hair, a brown beanie, glasses and a goatee.

If so, it would appear to be a very poorly thought through plan for murder.

The chances of knifing the wrong man to death as a result of misidentification seemed enormous.

No, they had to have known exactly what I looked like.

"Did you ask Banks how they would recognize me outside the racetrack?" I asked the inspector.

"Indeed I did," he said. "It seems that they followed you to the racetrack from Esher railway station earlier in the day."

I silently berated myself for not having spotted a tail. I was the one who usually did the following and I knew all the tricks. I should have noticed.

"But how did they know what I looked like then?"

"According to Banks, you were pointed out to them."

The hairs on the back of my neck began to stand up. It was my turn for an adrenaline rush. Fight or flight. The body's natural response to fear. I had been pointed out to a pair of killers without me having the slightest notion of why and it frightened me badly.

"Who pointed me out?" I asked, forcing my voice box to relax.

"Banks says he doesn't know. Just a man."

"Didn't he give you a description?"

"He claims he never met the man. He only saw him from afar. Lawrence spoke to him inside the station while he, Banks, had been told to wait outside."

"He must be able to give you something," I said. "Was the man young or old? Tall or short? Fat or thin?"

"He says he doesn't know, but I'm not sure I believe him. He claims that only Lawrence knew who the man was."

And Lawrence was conveniently dead.

26

On Monday morning, I caught another train from Paddington, this time to Reading, where I took a taxi to the police station for a booked appointment with Detective Sergeant Jagger.

"Now, how can I help you?" he said when we had both sat down in one of the interview rooms. We were accompanied by a detective constable with a pen and notebook.

"I think it's more about how I can help *you*," I replied.

"I'm all ears," he said.

"A lot of it was in the statement I gave to your colleague. But I now have more to tell you."

I told him everything about my investigation into the race fixing, from my meeting with Dave Swinton in his sauna on the morning of the Hennessy Gold Cup right up to my conversation with Willy Mitchell on the previous day. I told him of the dubious bets made by Leslie Morris and of my visit to Morris's house in Raynes Park. I left out the actual identities of McKenzie and Mitchell, referring to them only as *Jockey A* and *Jockey B*. I also skipped over the true reasons why they were being blackmailed.

"You know who these jockeys are, of course?" he asked.

"Of course," I confirmed. "But I'd like to keep them out of it."

There was a brief moment of silence, bar the scratching of the constable's pen in his notebook.

"Are you sure that Mr. Swinton told you that he was aware who had been blackmailing him?"

I thought back to the conversation. Dave had been reluctant to say anything of substance on the phone. But I was sure.

"Yes," I said. "He told me on the morning that he died. He said that he knew who it was. I presume he had found out at Newbury races the day before, or maybe on the Saturday evening. Either way, he wouldn't tell me the person's name over the phone. He said he didn't trust them after being a victim of hacking a few years ago. That's why I went back to his house that Sunday morning."

"He hadn't known who it was when you spoke to him on Saturday?"

"No," I said. "He told me that he'd kill him if he knew."

The detective raised his eyebrows. "Do you think Mr. Swinton might have set a trap for the blackmailer on Sunday morning? One that went badly wrong?"

"I suppose it's possible," I said. "I tend to think that saying he'd *kill him* was only a turn of phrase rather than an actual threat. Dave was ruthless in his riding, even aggressive, but he was a gentle soul underneath. That is why I was so surprised when I thought he had left me in his sauna to die."

"Do you believe that the same person is blackmailing the other jockeys?"

"Yes," I said, "I do. Otherwise, it would be too much of a coincidence."

"The world is full of coincidences," the detective said. "Trust me, that's something you learn very quickly in my business."

"So are you now going to arrest Leslie Morris?"

"You say Mr. Morris is a retired accountant?"

"Yes," I said.

"Well into his sixties?"

"He's sixty-six."

"Do you think a sixty-six-year-old would have the strength to overcome a young, fit jockey like Mr. Swinton? And would he also have the strength to lift him into and then out of the trunk of a car?"

These were good points.

"But whoever it was had to have had an accomplice with him anyway," I said. "To drive another car. Otherwise, how did he get away from the burning Mercedes? You can hardly hitch a ride in the middle of Otmoor. And how did he get to Lambourn in the first place?"

"But who was that accomplice?"

"One of the jockeys told me that Morris has a son and that he's a nasty piece of work. And there's also Darryl Lawrence and Gary Banks to consider."

"Are those the men who attacked you at your apartment?"

"Yes," I said. "It seems they met a man at Esher Station who pointed me out to them as their target. Maybe that was Leslie Morris, although I'm not sure how it could have been. But if it was, then together they would easily be strong enough to lift Dave Swinton into the trunk. Lawrence is now dead and Banks is in custody for killing him. You had better speak to Detective Inspector Galvin."

"I will," he said. "Thank you, Mr. Hinkley, for your assistance."

He stood up.

"Is that it?" I said.

"Is there anything else you have to add?" he asked.

"No. But . . . you don't seem to be very interested."

"I will have discussions with my colleagues," he said. "I will also speak with D.I. Galvin and other officers from the Met. We will act on your information, be assured of that, but we can't just go in and arrest someone, with all our guns blazing, until we have considered the matter further. We have to be pretty sure before we detain anyone under these circumstances, not least because we would have only twenty-four hours to question him and complete our investigation before we would be required to either charge him or release him. We like to line up all the ducks before we start shooting at them."

"And in the meantime," I said, "I have to go on watching my back?"

"That would seem to be a wise course of action. My constable will type up what you have just told us into a formal statement. Can you wait here while he does that so you can sign it?"

"Yes," I said. "No problem."

"Good." He started to leave but then turned back to face me. "Oh, yes, one more thing, Mr. Hinkley. I *will* need the names of those other two jockeys. They'll both have to be interviewed. And *you* don't want to be the one arrested today, now do you, for obstructing the police?"

There was no humor in his voice whatsoever.

"WHAT THE bloody hell have you been telling the cops?"

Willy Mitchell wasn't happy with me. He called me early the following morning as I was packing my suitcase for the Cayman Islands.

"You promised me you'd keep what I told you confidential."

Actually, I hadn't, but I decided now was not the time to say so.

"All I told the police was that you were being blackmailed. I absolutely did not tell them why."

"Well, they bloody know," he shouted over the line. "I had some cop on my doorstep here at seven o'clock this morning and all he talked about was the effing sex offenders registry."

D.S. Jagger had assured me that he would act on my information, but I hadn't expected his approach to be quite so insensitive.

I had discovered for myself the previous morning that Detective Sergeant Jagger was neither the most tactful nor the most considerate of men. He was only interested in making an arrest. He didn't care what collateral damage was done to people's lives in the process and he made no allowance to mitigate it.

He had obviously looked up Mitchell's conviction on the police computer and favored the *bull in the china shop* approach, just like Paul Maldini. I didn't think it was likely to encourage Willy to cooperate.

"I'm sorry," I said. "I had no choice. I was threatened with arrest for obstructing justice unless I gave him your name."

"I wish I'd never told you anything."

"But you did," I said. "And surely that makes you safer. Now if the blackmailer gets some girl to go to the police and complain about you having sex with her, they will know it's a lie."

"Will they?" He didn't sound like he believed it. "Why, then, has this bloody cop been going on about how I'm a danger to society? He says I should have been chucked in jail and the key thrown away. He kept calling me a pedophile. Poor Amy is still in floods of tears over it."

It was, as they would say in American football, "unnecessary roughness."

"He was just trying to frighten you into revealing something that you didn't want him to know."

He grunted.

"So *what* did you tell him?" I asked.

"Same as I told you," he said, "but I don't think he took much notice. He treated me all the while like something that he'd picked up on his shoe. But I'm not the bloody villain here. I'm the victim."

The BHA might disagree.

After all, he *had* failed to win a race on purpose.

I THOUGHT it was prudent to call Bill McKenzie and warn him that he too might be getting an unwelcome visit from D.S. Jagger. It had the potential to be far more damaging for his marriage than it would have been for Willy's.

I was too late.

Jagger had already been there. He had obviously gone straight from Mitchell's place.

"Oh, thank you very much," Bill said ironically. "You may well have destroyed my marriage."

"I'm sorry," I said.

But it had been him who had been with another woman, not me.

"Has your wife found out about the photos?" I asked.

"No, thank God, but she insists on knowing why that policeman was here. She claims she has a right to know if I've been accused of something. I told her that I hadn't—I was just helping them with their inquiries. But now she wants to know what those inquiries were about."

"What did you tell her?" I asked.

"Nothing," Bill said. "Hence, we're not talking to each other at all at the moment. It's dreadful."

"Tell me, Bill," I said. "Did you speak to Leslie Morris after riding Wisden Wonder at Sandown?"

"No," he said. "Of course not."

"Did you speak to him at all during the Tingle Creek meeting?"

"I've only ever spoken to him in France. Not before and not since. And I never want to speak to him again."

I HAD BEEN invited to spend Tuesday evening with Faye and Quentin, to join them for a sort of Christmas dinner, before I went away.

I spent some of the afternoon wrapping presents for them—Jo Malone perfume for her and a silk bow tie and matching handkerchief for him. It made me think about some other presents I should be taking with me to the Cayman Islands.

I wondered how many of us there would be. Uncle Richard and Aunt Mary for sure, plus Martin Reynard and his wife Theresa. How many others?

I left early for Richmond and occupied a constructive hour in a department store in the center buying a selection of ties for the men and silk scarves for the ladies—three of each so I'd have some spares. They would be easy to pack, and nice and light for the luggage weight limit.

In addition, I looked for something for Henri and that was far more difficult.

What did you buy for someone on the *Sunday Times* "Rich List"?

Any sort of jewelry would definitely be out. There was nothing I could afford that would even come close to what she had probably inherited from her mother.

I searched around in vain for quite a while, finally deciding in desperation on some Chanel N°5 Parfum. Lydia used to wear it all the time. And I liked it.

I ARRIVED AT Faye and Quentin's house at seven o'clock sharp, as instructed.

The place looked wonderful, with a tall twinkling Christmas tree in the hallway. Faye had gone to town with the decorations, and the living room and dining room were adorned with scented candles, festive swags and row upon row of Christmas cards hung on strings between the ceiling beams.

"It's lovely," I said to her, giving her a kiss on the cheek.

"Thank you," she said. "Ever since this bloody cancer took control of my life, I've wondered if each Christmas will be my last. I'd hate to go out on a fizzle."

I smiled at her and rubbed her shoulders. I hadn't realized she thought that way. Perhaps I shouldn't be going away.

No one but the actual sufferer fully understands what a diagnosis of cancer really means. It isn't just the body that's affected, it's the mind as well. Even when it appears to be beaten, as in Faye's case, it still has an all-encompassing and persistent presence, forcing one to make difficult choices and confiscating one's free will. It is the enemy within, the fifth column, forever ready to rise up and strike unless forcibly restrained at every turn.

"Come on," Faye said, snapping us out of the moment. "Let's open a bottle of bubbly."

QUENTIN ARRIVED HOME as we were on our second glass.

"What a dreadful day," he said as he came into the kitchen, where Faye was cooking the dinner and I was sitting on a barstool watching her.

I gave him a flute of champagne, which he drank down in one long slurp.

"God! I needed that," he said.

I refilled his glass.

"What was dreadful about it?" Faye asked.

"Oh, nothing important," he said, taking another sip of champagne. "It just never ceases to amaze me how juries can come up with some of their verdicts. I've spent ten whole weeks explaining to them in the minutest detail how the defendant was as guilty as sin of fraud and tax evasion and they take a mere forty-five minutes to acquit him. I think jury trials are a joke in fraud cases. The average man off the street doesn't understand the complexities and, hence, won't convict irrespective of how persuasive the facts are. They've been talking about changing it for years but nothing happens."

"What had he done?" I asked.

"He claimed he was not subject to UK capital gains tax on the proceeds of the sale of his printing company. He maintained that he was a tax resident of the Channel Islands at the time of the sale, but it was blatantly not true. How the jury couldn't see he was lying is beyond me."

"OK, you two, that's enough legal talk," Faye said firmly. "This is family time."

She produced some delicious canapés and Quentin opened another bottle.

"I can't have too much to drink," I said in mock protest as he refilled my glass. "I have to be up early to get to the airport."

"Off to a hot Christmas," Quentin said. "Sounds a bit odd to me."

"They must have them all the time in Australia," I said. "I suppose you get accustomed to what you're used to."

"Will you still have roast turkey for Christmas lunch?" Faye asked.

"I have no idea. In fact, I have no idea of anything about this trip except that I have to be at Luton Airport at eight o'clock tomorrow morning."

"Luton?" Faye said. "I'd have thought it would've been Heathrow."

"So did I," I said, "but apparently our flight departs from Luton. I just hope there's decent legroom. It's a long way."

"When are you back?" Faye asked.

"January the third," I said. "We leave on the second and fly back overnight."

"I do hope you have a lovely time," Faye said warmly.

"I feel rather guilty at leaving you," I said.

"Don't be silly. Q and I will be fine. Kenneth is coming here for lunch on Christmas Day itself, so that will be great fun."

Quentin didn't look like he thought it would be any fun at all, but I couldn't worry about that. I was so excited at the prospect of spending the next eleven days with Henri that I could hardly sit still during dinner.

27

I was outside Luton Airport Parkway railway station in good time at ten minutes to eight on Wednesday morning when my cell phone rang.

I thought it was going to be Henri, but it was Detective Sergeant Jagger.

"Having spoken to the jockey Bill McKenzie and having checked his phone records, we have now arrested Leslie Morris on suspicion of blackmail."

"Great," I said. "Thank you for letting me know."

"My superior officer, D.C.I. Owens, now heads the inquiry into the death of Mr. David Swinton. He wants to interview you himself concerning the events in Lambourn on the morning that Mr. Swinton died."

"When?" I asked with some trepidation.

"As soon as possible. Can you come to Reading today?"

"I'm afraid that's out of the question. I'm currently at the airport and am flying to the Cayman Islands for Christmas."

"Hmm." He didn't sound very happy at that news. "When are you back?"

"Not until the third of January," I said. That didn't seem to please him much either. "But I have nothing more to add than I have already given you in my statements. Are you charging Morris with Dave Swinton's murder?"

"At present, he is being interviewed only concerning the blackmail of Mr. William McKenzie."

"Well, if I were you, I'd also ask him about the blackmail of Dave Swinton and Willy Mitchell."

"All in due course, Mr. Hinkley. All in due course. One doesn't need to rush these things."

I wondered if it gave them more time to hold Morris in custody if they arrested him for each offense in turn.

"Have you searched Morris's house?" I asked.

"Not yet, but it will be later today."

"See if you can find a small red notebook," I said. "It contains the records of all his bets on the dubious race at Sandown and that should be enough to prove Morris knew beforehand that McKenzie wouldn't win."

A large black Range Rover drew up in front of the station with Henri waving at me through the back window. I waved back.

"Look," I said to D.S. Jagger, "I've got to go now. I'll call you from the Cayman Islands tomorrow. I can speak to Chief Inspector Owens then, if he wants."

A smartly dressed chauffeur climbed out of the driver's seat and loaded my suitcase into the Range Rover's trunk. I, meanwhile, climbed in the back next to Henri.

There were two other people already in the vehicle.

Sir Richard Reynard was sitting in the front seat, and there was another woman in the back with Henri.

"This is my aunt Mary," Henri said.

"I'm so pleased to meet you," I said, shaking her hand.

"Me too. I've heard much about you from my husband."

The driver climbed back in and drove off, but we didn't go to the regular passenger terminal. Instead, we went to the other side of the airport to the private aviation center, where a Reynard Shipping–liveried twin-engined jet aircraft awaited us. We even drove out in the Range Rover, across the concrete apron to the base of the aircraft steps.

It suddenly dawned on me that we were going to the Cayman Islands not on a knees-to-the-chest charter flight but on a private jet.

No wonder I hadn't had to book my own ticket.

Henri grinned like a Cheshire Cat. "I didn't think you knew."

"But why only one suitcase?" I asked.

"Uncle Richard and Aunt Mary always have at least two each, while lesser mortals like us can have only one. There's not that much room in the hold, and if the aircraft's too heavy, we have to make two fuel stops instead of one."

"Where?" I asked.

"Last time, it was Bermuda. I think it depends on the winds."

"Who else is coming?"

"Martin and Theresa were meant to be with us, but Martin had to go on ahead over a week ago. I don't know if Theresa will be coming."

We found out soon enough as another vehicle drew up beside the Range Rover and Theresa Reynard got out of one side while Bentley Robertson, the creepy, lecherous lawyer, got out of the other.

"Oh God!" Henri said. "What's *he* doing here?"

Traveling with us, it seemed, as we watched his single bag being loaded into the luggage hold alongside ours. Henri was not at all pleased, and I could tell from Bentley's unfriendly stare that he was just as unhappy about my presence as I was about his.

"Please keep him away from me," she said.

"I'll do my best."

We went on board the jet.

The interior was laid out with no luxury spared. There were ten passenger seats in total, each of them cream leather armchairs that wouldn't have looked out of place in a stately home.

"How the other half live," I said quietly to myself.

The ten seats were laid out in three distinct sections, with one on either side at the front, then a group of four—two each side of a table facing one another—and finally four more at the back in two rows coach style.

Henri went straight to the very back and sat in the seat nearest the window while beckoning me to quickly take the one next to her. I knew why. In this way, she was protecting herself from having to sit next to or opposite Bentley Robertson.

She needn't have worried.

Bentley came on board and immediately sat in one of the seats at the table. He spread out papers from his briefcase and concentrated only on them.

Theresa Reynard boarded and sat down next to Bentley. My suspicious mind went into overdrive wondering if there was a sexual rapport between the two of them. There was just something about their body language that shouted *lovers* at me.

"Do you think Martin and Theresa's marriage is OK?" I asked Henri.

"Yeah, I think so," she said. "Why do you ask?"

"I just wondered why Martin went on ahead and Theresa didn't go with him."

"I expect she was too busy Christmas shopping," she said, smiling.

Sir Richard and Lady Mary Reynard came on board and sat

in the two seats at the very front. And then we waited. There seemed to be no urgency to close the cabin door and get going.

The reason became obvious after about ten minutes when a chauffeur-driven limousine pulled up at the steps. I watched through the window as Derrick and Gay Smith climbed out of the vehicle and came on board as their copious luggage was shoe-horned into the aircraft's hold. Clearly, no one had informed *them* of the one-bag limit.

Gay and Derrick greeted Sir Richard and Lady Mary with polite kisses, then came through the cabin to the two seats in front of Henri and myself.

I stood up in the aisle.

"Hello, Jeff," Gay said with a broad smile. "What an unexpected pleasure."

She gave me a peck on the cheek while Derrick shook my hand. "We are just hitching a ride back home," he said. "Sorry we're late."

It was clear that the Smiths were the last of the passengers to arrive, as there was now some activity up front with the main door being closed and the engines started.

"Do you always travel like this?" I asked Henri.

"I wish. The trust is so tight with *my* money that I'm usually in coach, although I have been on this baby a few times. But not so often that I'm not really excited every time."

I was excited too. Extremely. And it wasn't all to do with flying on a private jet. I'd be excited to be anywhere with Henrietta Shawcross.

WE ACTUALLY REFUELED at St. John's in Newfoundland, where the outside temperature was a balmy minus seven degrees. Needless to say, all eight of the passengers remained warm and cozy in the cabin rather than choosing to venture the hundred yards or so across the icy windblown tarmac to the airport buildings.

After forty minutes, we were on our way again.

I could get quite used to this, I thought, as I was presented with yet another plate of delicious food prepared by the onboard steward.

"More champagne, sir?" he said.

I felt it would be churlish for me to say no after he'd gone to all the trouble of opening the bottle.

"Lovely," I said, and he poured more of the bubbles into my glass.

Henri giggled and I held her hand.

I'd left my troubles behind in winter-gripped England, and there were eleven days ahead of warmth and sunshine in the company of a gorgeous girl.

What could have been better?

With every sip of Veuve Clicquot, I could feel the strength and vigor returning to my body.

Little did I realize how much I would need it.

WE LANDED ON Grand Cayman nearly twelve hours after leaving Luton. It was almost four in the afternoon, the local time being five hours behind that at home.

Suddenly, my senses were full of first impressions—the bright colors of the buildings, the intensity of the tropical sunlight, the flatness of the country, the freshness of the ozone-filled sea air and, of course, the warmth.

"Where are we staying?" I asked Henri as we waited to have our passports checked by the Cayman Island immigration officials.

"Uncle Richard and Aunt Mary are staying at Martin and Theresa's place, but I imagined that you would rather be somewhere on our own."

She imagined right.

"I've rented an apartment in a condominium just down Seven Mile Beach from them."

"Sounds perfect," I said. "How about Bentley? I hope he's not sharing it with us."

Henri pulled a face. "If he is, I'm going back to England."

In the end, Henri had to put her foot down when her uncle suggested that it might indeed be a good idea for Bentley to stay with us in our apartment since it had two spare bedrooms, adding that he could *keep Henrietta in order.*

I wasn't sure if he was being serious or not. Henri thought he was.

"No," Henri said firmly. "Absolutely not. If he can't stay with Martin, he'll have to find a hotel."

"But it's Christmas," said Sir Richard. "There won't be any hotel rooms free."

"Then he'll have to sleep on the beach," Henri said without the slightest note of compromise. "What's he doing here anyway?"

"We have a board meeting tomorrow, remember?" Sir Richard said. "I assume you did get the papers?"

She nodded.

Much to Henri's relief, Theresa announced that Bentley would be staying in their guest cottage, with Sir Richard and Lady Mary taking the guest suite in the main house.

Maybe I was completely wrong, but why did I suspect that Theresa had arranged for Bentley to be in her guest cottage because it was a convenient location for a clandestine assignation between them?

THERE WERE three luxury cars waiting for us outside the private terminal. One for Derrick and Gay to take them to their home, another for Sir Richard and Lady Mary—both with chauffeurs—and the third with Martin at the wheel, waiting for Theresa and, it seemed, Bentley.

Martin got out of his car and greeted his parents and his wife, giving Theresa the smallest little peck on the cheek. Hardly a greeting for a loving couple, I thought. Not one that had been apart for more than a week.

He steadfastly ignored me, pointedly not shaking my offered hand.

"You can ride with us," Sir Richard said to Henri, but it was quite clear that with two large suitcases each, there was hardly enough room in the car for them both plus their luggage.

"It's fine," I said. "We'll get a taxi."

"It's only about ten minutes away," he said.

Henri and I hailed one of the island's many taxi minivans for the short journey to the Coral Stone Club, a three-story condominium complex nestling between two much taller buildings off West Bay Road.

Henri picked up the key to the apartment from the manager's office while I supervised the unloading of the bags by the taxi driver and paid him using some of the dollars I had obtained from my bank.

"If I was allowed to lift anything, I'd carry you over the threshold," I said to Henri as we went in.

"But it's not our own home."

"It is for the next eleven days," I said. "And that's good enough for me."

The apartment was on the ground floor and stretched right through the building on the southern edge of the complex. Painted lemon yellow, with white-and-blue furnishings, the open-plan kitchen and living area was bright and cool, but it was the view through the large picture windows at the far end that was totally breathtaking.

The spectacular Seven Mile Beach was just a few steps away, complete with archetypal desert island coconut palms growing at lazy angles out of the brilliant white sand. And, beyond that, the dazzling turquoise blue Caribbean Sea shimmered and danced as it reflected the rays of the late-afternoon sun as it began to dip toward the western horizon.

"Wow!" I said.

Henri opened the sliding door and we went outside together onto the beach.

"Wow!" I said again as I looked either way at the mile upon mile of soft white powder.

"It's not really seven miles long," Henri said. "Only about six."

Long enough, I thought.

We went back inside.

"I've told Uncle Richard we would go up to Martin's house for a drink with them at sunset."

"What time is that?" I asked.

"Just before six."

I glanced at my watch. That gave us almost a full hour.

I looked at her and she looked back at me.

"Are you thinking what I'm thinking?" she said, grinning.

28

Even though Henri and I had known each other for almost three whole weeks, this was our first time, and it was a journey of discovery and delight, of tenderness and love, with moments of primeval rawness and desire.

For me, it was like a reawakening of my emotions after almost a year of abstinence, a release of sexual tension that sent multiple shudders through my body.

"Wow!" It was now Henri's turn to say it. "You sure needed that."

I certainly did.

Afterward, we lay entwined on the bed, our naked skin glistening wet from the exertion. So much for my promise to Faye to take things easy.

I snuggled up to Henri, happy and content, and also rather relieved that my aerobics appeared not to have reopened any of my various incisions.

"Come on," she said, sitting up. "Don't go to sleep. It's nearly time to confront the family."

"What did Martin say when you told him I was coming with you?" I asked, not moving.

"I didn't tell him," she said. "I only asked Uncle Richard. He's the one who matters. Even though Martin has taken over as managing director, Uncle Richard is the chairman and he's still very much the boss."

"Martin didn't seem particularly surprised to see me at the airport. He just ignored me."

"Perhaps Theresa told him. I had to ask her if it was all right to bring you to Christmas lunch. It's at their place."

She rolled off the bed and I watched as she walked into the bathroom. What a fabulous sight.

I heard the shower start and I soon joined her under the spray.

"That was more lovely than I had ever imagined," I said.

"For me too," she replied.

We embraced again and kissed in the stream of water, causing me to shudder once more with pleasure.

"And we still have eleven nights left."

THE SUN was only just above the horizon as Henri and I walked hand in hand along the beach about two hundred yards to Martin and Theresa's house.

If I'd thought the apartment at the Coral Stone Club was spectacular, then the Reynard residence was beyond compare. The two-story building had been constructed in an L shape, with both wings angled toward the beach to give the maximum number of rooms a view of the sea. And it was vast.

In the inside apex of the L was a terrace containing a kidney-shaped swimming pool surrounded by white sail-like sunshades stretched horizontally on stainless steel frames.

As far as I could see, it was the only private house on this part of the beachfront, with condominiums stretching away, cheek by jowl, on either side. Not that the Reynards were overlooked. Several towering casuarina trees provided both privacy and shade for the terrace. And that is where we found the others, sitting in a semicircle close to the pool, looking out to sea.

"Ah, there you are," Sir Richard said. "You've nearly missed it."

We watched as the sun appeared to go straight down into the sea, staring until the very last tiny piece of the fiery disk had vanished for another day. It was the most dramatic sunset I had ever seen.

"No green flash," Sir Richard announced. "Not that I could see anyway."

"Green flash?" I said.

"Sometimes when the sun finally disappears, you can see a flash of green," he replied. "At least, that's what people say, even though I've never seen it myself. It's said to be due to the sunlight refracting through the earth's atmosphere, but I rather think it's just an old wives' tale."

"It's perfectly true," Theresa said. "It happens all the time."

I wondered if she actually believed it or was just being contrary to wind up her father-in-law.

"What would you like, Henri?" Martin asked.

"White wine, please," she replied.

"Beer do you?" Martin said to me without any warmth in his voice.

"Great," I said. "Thanks."

He stood up and went inside the house, soon reappearing with a glass of white wine for Henri and an opened green beer bottle for me.

"It's Caybrew," he said, handing it to me without once looking at my face. "It's the local lager."

"Lovely," I said.

I took the bottle and drank a welcome mouthful of its cool contents.

Even though the sun had only been down a few minutes, it was already getting quite gloomy.

"We'd best all go in," Theresa said. "The mosquitoes and sand flies are at their worst when it's getting dark."

"Are mosquitoes a big problem here?" I asked.

"They were once," she said. "It was so bad that everyone had to cover up and wear nets over their faces. But, nowadays, the government sprays to keep them in check. But there are still a few about, and the best way to avoid being bitten is to be indoors at dusk. So come on, everyone, I've got some smoked salmon waiting."

She rounded us up like miscreant children.

We went inside to their cavernous living room that sat in the middle of the L, stretching right up through both floors to an octagonal cupola perched high at the point on the roof where the two wings met.

"It was designed to keep the house cool," Theresa said with a smile as she saw me looking up. "The windows in the cupola can be opened to let out the hot air, although we tend to use the air-conditioning most of the time anyway."

It was certainly cool in the house compared to outside.

And it wasn't just the temperature of the air.

Martin and Theresa were fighting.

Not that they were shouting at each other or anything. Indeed, they were not even talking. But, nevertheless, there was a flaming fight going on between them, conducted exclusively with body language.

No one else seemed to have noticed, but I had been trained

by the Army to read the body language of Afghan tribal elders. They would smile at you and speak sweet nothings in your ear while at the same time blowing your brains out with an AK-47. "Never look at someone's mouth when they are speaking to you," my instructor had said. "Always look into their eyes. If their smile doesn't reach the eyes, watch out."

Theresa's smiles were never getting close.

HENRI AND I didn't stay long. The time change meant we were dog-tired and ready for bed by eight o'clock. It had been a long day and I'd been up for nearly twenty hours.

"We can't go to bed just yet," I said as we walked back along the beach in the dark to the Coral Stone Club.

"Why not?" she replied with a giggle.

"I mean, we can't go to sleep yet. We'd be awake again in the middle of the night."

We managed to stay up until nine, chancing the mosquitoes and sitting outside on the patio to share a bottle of white wine that the management had kindly placed as a welcome gift in the refrigerator.

"How long have Martin and Theresa been married?" I asked.

"Eleven years," Henri said. "I was a bridesmaid at their wedding. Why?"

"I was just wondering. Do they have any children?"

"Theresa is desperate to have one. Martin had a son by a former wife and I know it bothers her. She's had loads of tests and tried all sorts of fertility treatments. But no luck so far, and they're both getting on. It must be hard for them, as Martin's younger brother has four."

"Is *he* involved in the family firm?"

"Not at all. He's an artist and hates anything to do with it." She made it sound like a failing. "He and his wife live in some godforsaken place in the Scottish Highlands with no electricity. I haven't seen them for years."

"Do you ever see Martin's son?"

"All the time. His name's Joshua. He's fifteen now. Martin supports him financially, and he comes to stay with them at weekends when they're in England and also during the school holidays. He's been here to Cayman as well, often, but sadly not for Christmas this year. It would have been nice to have some kids around." She laughed. "Perhaps you and I will have some."

We looked at each other. Were we really that serious?

I WOKE IN THE DARK and it took me a moment or two to remember where I was. Then I heard Henri's rhythmic breathing beside me. I smiled. It was Christmas Eve in the Cayman Islands and all was well in my life.

A little while later, I heard Henri stir.

"Are you awake?" I asked quietly into the blackness.

"No," she replied.

I snuggled over to her, searching for her body with my hands in the super-king-sized bed.

"What time is it?" she asked.

"Time for sex," I replied.

"Oh, goody."

IT WAS STILL DARK when I went into the kitchen to make us some coffee. The digital clock on the stove told me it was ten minutes to six, ten to eleven back in the UK.

When I went back into the bedroom, Henri was sitting up with the light on, reading.

"What's so interesting you have to read it in the middle of the night?"

"Papers for the board meeting. I've had them for over a week now, but I haven't even looked at them yet. Uncle Richard would be furious if he knew."

"What time's the meeting?"

"Ten o'clock."

"Why is it taking place here?" I asked.

"Because this is where the company has its registered office. Martin moved everything here three years ago when he became managing director."

No wonder I hadn't been able to find any recent accounts for Reynard Shipping Limited at Companies House.

"Why?" I said.

"Partly because this is where he lives."

"I thought you said he spends his time in Singapore."

"He does, but this is his official home. Even though Cayman is not an independent country—it's an overseas territory of the UK—Martin and Theresa have what they call *status* here. It's like Cayman citizenship."

She turned over another sheet of paper.

"Of course, the company move was also done for tax reasons. Reynard Shipping was a British company and was therefore paying UK corporate taxes on all its worldwide profits. The whole lot. Our competitors, meanwhile, were mostly based in Singapore or Hong Kong, which have far lower tax rates than the UK. Hence, we had become noncompetitive. We even began losing money. So Martin moved the company registration over here to take advantage of Cayman's tax laws."

"Very wise," I said.

"We still pay UK tax on our UK profit, of course, through our UK subsidiary. That's fair enough. But not on everything else as well."

It all sounded eminently sensible.

I left her to read the board papers and went into the kitchen to call Detective Chief Inspector Owens, D.S. Jagger's senior officer, as I had promised.

"Ah, Mr. Hinkley," he said when I was finally put through to him. "Thank you for calling."

"Have you charged Leslie Morris with murder?" I asked.

"No," he said.

"How about his son?"

"So far, we have been unable to locate Mr. Andrew Morris."

"You mean he's gone missing?" I said.

"It would appear so," agreed the chief inspector.

"Have you charged Mr. Morris Senior with anything?"

"Not yet. He's out on bail, pending further inquiries. He has to report back to us on fifteen January."

"But surely you must have enough on him to charge him with blackmail."

"Mr. McKenzie is no longer being very cooperative," the chief inspector replied. "He maintains that he might be mistaken about the times of the calls made to him demanding that he lose the horse race—times that we know from the records match calls made to his phone from Morris's number. He now says he's not sure it was Morris who was blackmailing him."

Unbelievable.

I would have to have words with young Bill.

"Mr. Hinkley, what I really wanted to talk to you about is your visit to Mr. Swinton's house on the morning of his death."

"Yes?" I said. "What about it?"

"At the time you gave your first statement to D.S. Jagger, you were under the impression that Mr. Swinton himself had locked you in the sauna. Is that correct?"

"Yes," I replied.

"We now believe that it might have been, in fact, the action of a third party."

"Yes," I said again. "I know."

"At the time, why did you think it was Mr. Swinton?"

"I thought he was the only other person there, so it had to be him."

"But what was it about Mr. Swinton's character that gave you reason to believe that he was capable of such a thing?"

"Dave Swinton was the most competitive person I have ever met," I said, "and I've met quite a few in racing. He would do almost anything to win a race, even if it was not entirely within the rules. He considered that life itself was a series of games and that winning was all that mattered. That's why his marriage broke down. He was never prepared to lose an argument and he would never admit he was wrong even if he knew he was. Some people thought he was arrogant, and he was, but I'll tell you, without that arrogance, he would never have been half the jockey he was."

"Does that mean you didn't get along?" asked the D.C.I.

"Not at all," I said. "Dave and I were friends, but I still thought him capable of locking me in the sauna if he thought it would help him to win—whatever game he imagined we were playing at the time. Although, I have to admit, I was surprised and disappointed when I assumed he'd left me there to die. Why is all this relevant?"

"I like to get inside the character of the murder victim," the policeman said. "To try and think like him. Somehow, it helps me to understand the reasons someone might want him dead."

It sounded like mumbo jumbo to me.

"The reason someone wanted Dave Swinton dead was because he'd found out who was blackmailing him," I said. "Plain and simple. And that person was Leslie Morris."

"But what if Mr. Swinton was blackmailing Morris in return?"

"Is that what Morris told you?" I laughed.

I could easily believe that Dave had tried to blackmail the blackmailer. He would have considered it another game to be won. But the stakes had clearly been much higher than he'd imagined.

"It would seem that Mr. Swinton somehow discovered that it was Morris who was blackmailing him. Swinton obviously couldn't report it to us, as it would expose his own wrongdoing, so he attempted to silence Morris by telling him that if Morris spilled the beans about the unpaid taxes, he, in turn, would tell us about the blackmail and they would go down together."

It sounded to me *just* the sort of thing Dave would have done.

"I think that Mr. Swinton may have also threatened Morris with violence. Certainly Morris says he was afraid of that. Swinton must have figured out that Morris, a diminutive sixty-six-year-old retired accountant with a heart condition, couldn't be a serious threat to him physically."

"But he hadn't factored in the son?"

"Just so," he said. "From what I've gathered, Mr. Andrew Morris has always been very protective of his father and has been in a few scrapes over it."

"Well, I hope you find Andrew Morris soon," I said. "And, preferably, before I get back to England."

"We are afraid that he may have already left the country. We are currently checking airline passenger lists."

Surely he couldn't have followed me to the Cayman Islands?

No, I told myself. Don't be silly.

29

Henri went to her Reynard Shipping board meeting at nine-thirty, collected by her cousin Martin, while I called Bill McKenzie.

"What's all this nonsense about you telling the police you're not sure if it was Morris who was blackmailing you?"

"I'm not sure," he replied almost in a whisper.

"You were pretty sure when I spoke to you before."

"That's as may be," he said. "But now I'm not."

"What's changed?"

"Nothing," he said. I could hear the nervous timbre in his voice even from four and a half thousand miles away.

"Has Morris contacted you?"

"No," he said, but I knew he was lying to me from the slight hesitation before he answered.

"What did he say?"

"Nothing," he said again.

"Did he promise to give you the pictures if you didn't help the police?"

There was a long pause, which was answer enough.

"You're stupid," I said. "Do you really trust him? The only way to stop your wife seeing those pictures is to get Morris locked up."

"And how long would that be for?" he said. "A year, two maybe? Then what? And you can still arrange to have things sent from prison, you know."

He was right.

"But even if he sends you a set of prints, he'll still have the original image files. He could print some more or send them to your wife in an e-mail."

"I'll have to take that risk."

Bill McKenzie was in a very deep hole whatever he did. I suppose I couldn't blame him for wanting to accept a ladder from the very man who'd put him down there in the first place.

"Bill," I said. "I'll have no chance of saving your jockey's license unless you cooperate."

His only reply was to whimper down the line.

"Your best course of action is to bite the bullet and tell your wife about your French adventure. Then Morris would have nothing on you."

"I can't," he said. It was more of a plea than anything.

"It would be much better coming from you than from Morris. I'm sure your wife will forgive you when she knows you were drugged and set up."

"She won't," he said. "You don't know what she's like."

That made me wonder if his marriage was even worth saving. But there was his child to consider, and another on the way.

HENRI RETURNED at half past twelve.

"Good meeting?" I asked.

"It was OK," she said. "Our board meetings are never much

more than rubber-stamping anyway. Most of the day-to-day decisions are made by the management board. The main board is just there to ratify them. Much of today's meeting was taken up with the recent sale of our Hong Kong–based operation to a Chinese consortium. Uncle Richard thought it was a good time to sell off some of the company's assets. The money involved is mind-blowing."

"No need to cancel the private jet just yet, then?" I said flippantly.

"No."

"Who's on the main board other than you?"

"Uncle Richard and Martin, of course, plus a couple of directors appointed from our law firm over here. But those two don't say much."

"How about Bentley?"

"He's not actually a board member. He's the company secretary and takes the minutes."

"It must be interesting for you being a director of such a big organization," I said.

"Not really. It's all rather boring and mundane, to tell the truth. The others don't take much notice of what I say even though I do know what I'm talking about. Even though I run my own business in London, I think the others just look upon me as a token female on the board. Uncle Richard effectively makes all the decisions anyway."

"But you are a shareholder?"

"Yes, that's true. We are still a hundred percent family-owned business. My mother and Uncle Richard used to run it between them, so I suppose I'm now there to represent my side of the family. The main board only meets three times a year and I don't usually get to all of them."

"Are they always here in the Cayman Islands?"

"Mostly, although I prefer it when we meet in Singapore. We stay at Raffles and I absolutely love it there. But we have the major meeting of the year here. It also acts as the company's annual general meeting. That's what we did today." She gave me a cuddle. "What have you been up to in my absence?"

"Chilling out and making a few work phone calls," I said.

"You shouldn't be working," she said in mock crossness. "You're meant to be on holiday."

"You've been working," I pointed out.

"That's different." She smiled. "Now I'm hungry. What shall we do for lunch?"

"You know the place better than I do."

WE LAZILY WALKED next door to the Ritz-Carlton Hotel and split a club sandwich and a Caesar salad at their pool bar, washed down with an excellent bottle of Côtes de Provence rosé.

"So what's on the agenda for the rest of the day?" I asked.

"I'm afraid I've agreed for us to go with Uncle Richard and Aunt Mary to the traditional Christmas Eve carol singing in the garden of the Governor's residence. That's at seven. We could go out for dinner afterward, just the two of us, or we could just go back to bed." She giggled and stroked my hand.

"What happens tomorrow?" I asked.

"We have champagne with a few friends at noon, followed by a traditional family Christmas lunch. Both at Martin and Theresa's house. Then we laze around for the rest of the afternoon, complaining that we've eaten and drunk too much, before we eat and drink even more in the evening. Then we might watch a movie. Much the same as in England."

"Sounds great to me."

"Martin asked me if you were a diver. He always goes out diving early on Christmas morning. It's a sort of ritual. He wonders if you would like to go with him."

It seemed strangely out of character for him to ask me.

"I was taught to dive by the Army," I said, "but that was ten years ago at Sharm el-Sheik, on the Red Sea. I haven't done it now for ages."

"Shall I tell Martin you'd like to go?"

I had to admit that I was quite keen..

"Do you think I'm well enough to go diving?" I said.

She laughed. "I'd say you were quite well enough, if your exertions in the night are anything to go by."

"I won't be able to carry the tanks when they're out of the water."

"That's no problem. We always have a divemaster and a safety officer with us on the boat. They'll help you."

"Will you be coming?" I asked.

"If you want me to," she said. "As long as you don't plan to go too deep. Otherwise, I'll stay up on the boat while you and Martin dive."

"OK, then. Yes. I'd love to go."

THE CAROL SINGING on the lawn in front of the Governor's official residence was delightful. And it was packed with a mixture of expatriate British families and local Caymanians.

Sir Richard and Lady Mary picked Henri and me up from the Coral Stone Club and we drove about half a mile down West Bay Road.

Government House was an elegant colonial-style bungalow

set among mature trees, close to the beach. A uniformed Cayman Island policeman stood guard at the gate, but there was no other sign of significant security. Indeed, the white-painted wall to the road was only about five feet high, and, on the beach side, there was simply a low white-painted picket fence, along with a couple of notices requesting that passersby should respect the Governor's privacy.

"Who is the Governor?" I asked Sir Richard as we walked into the garden, which was lit up with strings of festive lights, attractively wrapped in spirals around the tree trunks.

"The current one is a chap called Peter Darwin," he said. "The Governor is nominally appointed by the Queen, but it's actually decided by the Foreign Office in London. It's often the final posting before retirement for a career diplomat—a swan song in the sun. Peter is about halfway through his term."

"What's his role?" I asked.

"He is Her Majesty's personal representative in the Cayman Islands."

"So he's quite important, then?" I said.

"Formally, Peter calls me *Sir Richard*, but I call him *Your Excellency*."

That was one sort of answer.

I took a glass of thick red liquid from an offered tray.

"What is it?" I asked Henri.

"Cayman rum punch," she said, also taking one. "It's the national drink. Either this or frozen mudslides."

"Frozen mudslides?"

"A cocktail made from ice, vodka, Baileys, Kahlúa, chocolate syrup and cream, all blended together. It's absolutely brilliant."

"And incredibly fattening," I said.

"It was first created here on the Cayman Islands at The Wreck Bar at Rum Point. They're famous for it."

"In spite of not having any actual rum in it?"

"Shut up!" she said, punching me playfully on the arm.

Martin and Theresa arrived and came to stand with us under the royal poinciana trees as we listened to a large choir made up of children from all the islands' schools singing a selection of the best-known Christmas carols. Everyone joined in for a rousing rendition of "Hark! The Herald Angels Sing" as the finale.

One and all were in celebratory mood, wishing each other *Merry Christmas*, as the crowd began to disperse back to their cars.

"Jeff," Sir Richard called. "Come and meet the Governor."

He introduced me to a short, slim man with dark wavy hair that was just beginning to go gray at the temples.

"Delighted to meet you, Your Excellency," I said, shaking his hand.

"Please, call me Peter. I'm not one for formality, especially not on Christmas Eve. This is my wife, Annabel." He indicated the blonde-haired woman with a small mouth and large blue eyes who was standing next to him.

"Thank you for your hospitality," I said to her.

She shook my hand and smiled at me. "Is this your first time in the Cayman Islands?"

"Yes," I replied. "But I hope it won't be my last."

"That's what everyone says," the Governor said. "It's very good for the tourist trade."

"Is it the islands' main source of income?" I asked.

"It's certainly important, but our financial services industry is much bigger," he said. "There are over two hundred and fifty separate banks operating in Cayman. We have almost ten thousand different investment funds licensed to trade here. And we are one of the world's largest insurance centers, with over seven hundred insurance companies registered."

"All of them trying to avoid paying taxes?" I said.

"Financial institutions and companies will always base themselves in the most tax-efficient jurisdiction," he said as if lecturing me. "If it wasn't here, it would be somewhere else where conditions were favorable, such as Bermuda or the Bahamas. All Cayman financial services are fully compliant with both U.S. and European directives and regulations."

It sounded to me like a line he had used often before.

"No suitcases full of dodgy cash, then?"

"Absolutely not," he said. "It is far more difficult to launder illegal money here than almost anywhere in the world. That, sadly, is a reputation that the Cayman Islands has unfairly acquired from the past. Nowadays, it is simply not true."

I believed him. Thousands wouldn't.

The Governor and his wife moved on to some of their other guests.

"Come on," Henri said to me. "Let's go and have some dinner."

As we were walking out of the garden, we met Derrick and Gay Smith, also on their way back to the road.

"Weren't those children great?" Gay said. "I love hearing choirs sing."

We all agreed with her.

"Jeff," Derrick said. "Would you and Henri like to come for drinks on Boxing Day?"

Henri and I looked at each other and we both nodded.

"We'd love to," I said. "Where and what time?"

"Come to our place around six," Derrick said. "Then we could all go out to dinner afterward at the Calypso Grill."

What could be more Caribbean? I thought. All else it needed was the "King of Calypso" himself, Harry Belafonte, singing "Day-o" from "The Banana Boat Song."

"Henri, you know where we live, don't you?" Derrick said.

"I think so," she replied uncertainly. "I'm sure we'll find it."

30

Christmas Day dawned sunny and calm and Henri and I were out on the beach by seven o'clock in our swimsuits and T-shirts. Even though the sun had only just peeped over the eastern horizon, the temperature was already in the mid-seventies, which gave every indication of a very warm day to come. As Quentin had said, it really was going to be a hot Christmas.

We walked up the beach toward Martin and Theresa's place and found the dive boat was already there with a hive of activity going on around it. Bags of diving gear were being loaded on board from the beach, along with eight scuba air tanks. Martin Reynard was directing operations while two other men appeared to be doing all the work.

"Morning," said Martin as we approached. "Merry Christmas."

Henri gave him a kiss on the cheek.

"This is Truman Ebanks," Martin said, pointing at a large dark-skinned man standing on the sand. "He's our divemaster. And also Carson Ebanks." Martin pointed at the man on the boat. "He's the captain and our safety officer."

Truman was passing the gear to Carson.

"Good morning, gentlemen," I said. "Are you brothers?"

"No, man," said Carson in a deep, resonant voice.

"I thought both being called Ebanks . . ."

He laughed. "Lots of people hereabouts are named Ebanks. Those that ain't Boddens." I loved the way his local accent gave the words a rhythm, almost as if he was singing them.

"I suppose we must be related somehow," Truman said with a similar lilt, grinning with his large white teeth showing brightly against his dark face, "but from way back."

The equipment was almost fully loaded when Bentley came walking down the beach to join us.

"I thought I'd come too," he said to Martin. "Just for the ride."

Henri clearly wasn't happy.

"Fine," Martin said. "Let's get going."

I thought for a moment that Henri wasn't going to come, so I took her hand and squeezed it. She smiled at me and shrugged her shoulders in acceptance.

"OK," she said.

The dive boat consisted mostly of a single flat platform that ran right through from bow to stern, with the driver situated in the center, a bench down each side with tank holders behind it and an overhead awning that provided shade to most of the boat. The bow had been run aground on the sand and Martin, Bentley, Henri and I now climbed a short ladder to get on board. Truman then pushed us off the beach into deeper water.

The trip out was wonderful, with the movement of the boat causing a refreshing breeze to blow into our faces, keeping us cool.

From out at sea I could assess the whole sweep of Seven Mile Beach, with its array of hotels and condominiums stretching away into the distance in both directions.

"Do most people live near the beach?" I asked Henri.

"Nowhere is that far away," she said, "but this is certainly the busiest end. Three-quarters of the whole population live in George Town or West Bay. Most of the eastern half of the island is just deserted mangrove swamp."

"Here you are, Jeff," Martin said, placing a blue mesh bag full of gear by my feet. "All you need is in here. Take the yellow guest tanks. Yellow makes it easier for Truman and me to keep an eye on you."

"OK," I said. "Thanks."

All the scuba tanks I had ever used before were uniformly boring gray aluminum that came with the dive boat, but here we had eight smart, brightly painted ones, two each in white, yellow, red and light blue. There's personalized license plates, of course, but I'd never come across personalized dive tanks before. The red ones had HENRI painted in large black letters down them, the white had MARTIN, the blue had THERESA and the yellow GUEST.

Bentley, it seemed, really was only there for the ride, as he obviously wasn't planning on getting wet. He hadn't brought any swimming trunks with him.

"Where are we diving?" Henri asked. "I don't want to go too deep."

"The wall first, then *Kittiwake* after," Martin said. "It will be good to do *Kittiwake* without the usual mass of tourists getting in the way. No one else dives on Christmas Day."

"What is *Kittiwake*?" I asked him.

"The USS *Kittiwake*. It's a retired naval ship that was deliberately sunk here in 2011 to provide an artificial reef and a dive site."

"Sounds interesting," I said. I'd never dived on a wreck before. "How deep is it?"

"It sits on the seafloor at about sixty feet. But we're going to do a wall dive first. That will be a deeper yet shorter dive."

Like every diver the world over, I'd heard of the *Cayman Wall*, that point where the shallow shelf on which the island sits ends and the surrounding deepness begins. It is characterized by an abrupt and almost vertical falling away of the seafloor down into the Cayman Trench, the deepest part of the Caribbean at a depth of over twenty-five thousand feet. But, of course, we would only be exploring the very top of the wall.

"I'll skip the first dive," Henri said. "It's too deep for me."

I watched as Martin and Truman began to pull on a wet suit each.

"Do we actually need a wet suit?" I asked. "I've done all my diving in the Red Sea without one."

"It may be hot up here in the sunshine," Truman said, "but it's still wintertime. The water will be cool a hundred feet down."

I pulled the wet suit out of my mesh bag and started to put it on.

"I must have a photo," Henri said, laughing, as I grappled with the black neoprene outfit that was none too big for me. She took my iPhone and snapped away as I struggled to pull up the long zipper at the back.

"Very funny," I said to her, pulling a face.

I felt like the Michelin Man.

"It's Theresa's," Martin said. "It's the largest spare I could find."

Even though Theresa was only an inch or so shorter than I, she was considerably less substantial around the waist. But I managed to do it up, in the end, with some extra help from the giggling Henri.

Next out of the bag came a BC, a buoyancy compensator, a

short jacket that has an air bladder between the inner and outer layers, which, when connected to a tank, could be filled with air to make a diver neutrally buoyant so that he neither floated up nor sank down but remained level in the water as if weightless.

I attached the BC to one of the yellow tanks and connected the regulator to the valve, checking that the pressure in the tank was well above twenty-five hundred pounds per square inch. The pressure gauge, together with a depth indicator, was housed in a console about eight inches long that was attached by a length of high-pressure hose to the tank's valve.

I next tested the two mouthpieces, breathing through both the primary one and the emergency alternate.

All seemed fine.

It had been several years since I had last been diving and I was pleased that at least I hadn't forgotten how to set up the equipment.

"You'll need a weight belt," Truman said to me. "The air trapped in the neoprene will make you float otherwise."

"You'd just bob round on the surface like a cork," said Martin, laughing. "Ten to twelve pounds should be enough."

I attached several rectangular lead blocks to a two-inch-wide belt and placed it around my waist. Next, I tried on the flippers and the mask.

I was ready.

The hum of the engine dropped away as we arrived at the first location and the boat was tied to one of the colored buoys that mark every dive site in Cayman waters.

"Have fun," Henri said as Carson carried my heavy gear over to the boarding ladder. I had decided that going down the ladder was a more preferable means of entry for my still-delicate abdomen to jumping off the side.

I sat on the bottom step, put on the BC, flippers and mask and slipped gently into the clear blue Caribbean water. Martin and I were acting as dive buddies, hence we would constantly check each other for safety reasons, but after so long a break from the water I was pleased that Truman the divemaster was also coming with us.

As we descended the buoy's anchor line, I equalized the pressure in my ears by frequently holding my nose and blowing air into my sinuses. We arrived at the bottom almost at the point where the sandy floor disappeared over the top of the wall into the abyss.

"Remember to continually check your depth," Truman had told us in the pre-dive briefing. "It is far too easy to go over the edge and down too deep. One hundred feet maximum. Bottom time no more than fifteen minutes."

I reached around for the hose to the console and looked at the depth reading on the indicator. Seventy feet. Theoretically, therefore, I could go some thirty feet down the wall face, but I was happy staying up near the top where there was plenty of bright coral.

Truman had also told us to be aware that we were diving in a designated marine park and that we should not touch or remove anything. But looking was all I was interested in doing anyway.

What a delight it was to be down here exploring a world so different from the one above the surface that it could have easily been on another planet yet was, in fact, just a few short yards from life as we knew it.

Back in the 1940s, Jacques Cousteau had perfected the open-circuit scuba equipment we were now using, solving the problem of a diver having to inhale air at a low pressure by attaching a gas regulator to a highly pressurized tank. But he probably had no idea at the time that he would also be creating a whole new leisure industry.

The ability to breathe underwater must have been a dream of human beings since they first walked on dry land and here we were doing it.

I checked the pressure in my tank. It was fine, a little below 2000 psi.

I looked around for Martin.

He was below me, his white tank clearly visible against the darkness beneath. He and Truman were some way down the wall, but I was happy remaining close to the lip. I was enchanted by the multicolored anemones swaying in the gentle current and by the shoals of black-and-yellow-striped sergeant major fish and the beautiful cobalt blue angelfish as they nibbled away at some invisible food on the surface of the coral.

Truman swam up to join me and placed his thumb and index finger together to make a circle in the universal dive signal for *OK*. He was asking if I was all right. I answered in the affirmative by repeating the signal. He pointed at his watch and then held up his open right hand. I repeated the OK, indicating that I'd understood. Five more minutes.

I again checked the pressure in my tank. It had now dropped to 1700. To be on the safe side, it needed to still be above 800 when I surfaced.

No problem.

After five minutes, the three of us ascended slowly toward the surface, stopping for prearranged decompression safety stops at forty and twenty feet. The last thing any of us wanted was to get the bends, the agonizing, hugely dangerous and potentially lethal condition that can occur when a sudden reduction in pressure causes bubbles of gas to form within the body in the same way that they do in a bottle of fizzy drink when the top is rapidly unscrewed.

"That was fabulous," I said to Henri as I sat on the bottom step of the ladder to take off the heavy equipment. "I'd forgotten how much fun diving could be."

She used my iPhone to snap more pictures of me.

"You'll break the lens," I said, laughing.

When the three of us were back on board, Carson maneuvered the boat the few hundred yards to the *Kittiwake* dive site, where we again tied up to the buoy.

"I'm definitely coming with you on this one," Henri said, opening her dive bag. "I'm not staying on the boat again with Bentley. He didn't take his lecherous eyes off me for a second while you were under. I kept moving away to the other end of the boat and he kept following me." She shivered with disgust.

So Henri and I would be dive buddies on this dive, with Martin pairing up with Truman.

I helped Henri zip up the back of her wet suit. Whereas I looked like I was bursting out of mine in all the wrong places, she looked fantastic, with the tightness of the neoprene showing off her amazing curves to perfection.

"Wow!" I whispered in her ear. "I could go down with you all day long."

"Stop it," she said quietly. "Don't give Bentley ideas."

It wasn't me who would be giving Bentley ideas, her wet suit would have done that. He just sat on the opposite bench, watching us, and I wondered what was going on in his head.

I switched my BC from one yellow tank to the other while Henri attached hers to one of the red ones. Soon we were set to go.

"Bottom time for this dive will be a max of thirty minutes," Truman said, briefing us. "You may go inside the wreck, if you want, but be careful not to snag your gear on the hatches. And don't go in on your own in case you get stuck. Maximum depth is sixty-four feet, so no decompression stops are required. Nevertheless, rise and surface slowly. Have fun, everybody."

Carson again carried my BC and tank to the steps and I was soon descending once more into the magical and alien underwater world, following Henri down the buoy's anchor line.

We swam away from the line and the shape of the ship soon came into view.

The USS *Kittiwake* had been a submarine rescue craft for the U.S. Navy and had served all over the world since being commissioned in 1946. Perhaps its most memorable task had been to recover the black box flight recorder from the ill-fated *Challenger* space shuttle, which had blown up over the Atlantic during launch in January 1986.

Now *Kittiwake* sat rather forlornly on the sandy seafloor, its superstructure already beginning to show the effects of the marine life that had begun to colonize the gray steel hull.

Henri and I first went into the ship's bridge through the windows from which the glass had been removed. Then we ventured deeper into the vessel, moving down companionways to the lower decks. At one point, we were even able to surface in a compartment where there was an air pocket.

It was an eerie feeling, moving through these watery spaces where once over a hundred men had lived and worked, past the mess hall where the tables at which they had eaten still remained in rows and bolted to the steel floor, along the corridor of the officers' quarters and into the captain's cabin.

I checked my watch. We had been down now for fifteen minutes and I had developed a splitting headache that was thumping away behind my eyes. I reckoned I must not be used to the continuous pressure changes in my nasal passages.

I went on following Henri deeper into the structure, but I was beginning to feel decidedly unwell.

I grabbed Henri's flipper and indicated that I would like to go back to the surface by first pointing at myself and then putting my thumb up. At first, she thought I was liking the dive and giving it the thumbs-up, but soon realized something was amiss when I next rotated my hand horizontally from side to side at the wrist and pointed at my head.

We exited the ship through one of the holes that had been cut in the hull and started to go up slowly.

But halfway to the surface I was attacked by a giant sea monster that swallowed me whole and blacked out my world entirely.

31

I woke up lying on my back with a man kneeling beside me, forcing a plastic mask tightly over my nose and mouth.

Oxygen mask, I thought knowingly. I'd had one of those on before—in the hospital, in London.

Was I back in the same hospital?

No. I couldn't be. I was all wet and I was lying in the sun.

So where was I?

My brain was scrambled and drifting, like the swirling of fog.

Was I drunk? I couldn't remember being drunk. Then again, I couldn't remember anything.

I tried to move, but my limbs seemed to have minds of their own.

"Thank God, he's awake," said a female voice from somewhere over my head.

Henri, I thought. That was Henri. I recognized her voice. And it was Carson who was fitting the mask.

Suddenly, the fog in my head cleared and I could remember everything, including the sea monster.

"What happened?" I tried to say. The mask was so tight on my face that I couldn't properly enunciate the words.

"Just you rest, man," Carson said. "You have the bends, man. We're getting you ashore real quick."

The throbbing in my head continued in perfect time with my heartbeat. I also felt sick, waves of nausea washing over me every few seconds.

I was lying on the platform of the dive boat with a rolled up towel under my neck. Henri came and kneeled down next to me and opposite Carson. She took my left hand in hers.

"You really frightened me," she said.

I'd really frightened myself.

"What happened?" I tried to say again.

"You passed out as we were on our way up and then you started sinking back down again. I grabbed you and hauled you up to the surface, forcing my alternate airline into your mouth to breathe through. I thought your own tank must have emptied. Luckily, there was enough air left in it for me to inflate your BC, which kept you up. Carson dived into the water to help pull you out."

"I banged the hull to alert the others, man," Carson said. "Now on our way to the nearest beach. I called an ambulance, man. It'll meet us there."

Good old Carson, man.

I NEVER DID get to eat my traditional Christmas lunch at Martin and Theresa's house. Instead, I spent the next hour and a half in a pressurized hyperbaric chamber at Grand Cayman Hospital breathing one hundred percent oxygen. And then I was kept there for most of the afternoon for observation.

My time in the chamber had certainly made me feel better.

The headache slowly faded away to nothing and the feelings

of nausea went with it. By the time I was allowed to see Henri, I was itching to get out of the hospital.

"Don't be so impatient," she said. "The bends can be nasty."

But how could I have had the bends? I had checked the dive depth tables myself. Both dives had been well within the recommended limits, especially since I'd chosen not to go down as far as a hundred feet in the first one. There was no way I should have had any problem with decompression sickness.

And I'd had the headache long before Henri and I had started to ascend to the surface. That's when the bends would have surely happened. And without a headache as a warning.

HENRI WENT BACK to Martin and Theresa's house for the noontime champagne with friends.

"I promise I'll come back later," she said to me as she left. "I'll bring you some turkey."

A little while after she'd gone, a doctor in a traditional white coat came to see me.

"Not the best way to spend Christmas Day for either of us," he said.

"I'm sorry," I replied.

"It's not me you have to apologize to," he said. "I was always going to be on duty here today. But our phlebotomist is a different matter. You may need to buy her a drink for giving up an hour of her Christmas morning."

"*Phleb* who?"

"Phlebotomist," he said. "Someone who takes blood."

"Ah." I could vaguely remember someone sticking a needle into my wrist just before I was placed in the hyperbaric chamber.

"I asked her to come in to do an arterial gas test on your blood."

"And?" I said.

"The results show that you had severe carbon monoxide poisoning."

"Carbon monoxide?"

"Yes," he said, "and you're lucky to be alive. You had over thirty percent of carboxyhemoglobin in your blood when you arrived here. It would have been even higher before you were given oxygen to breathe on the boat."

"Is that bad?" I asked.

"Normal levels are about *one* percent."

Maybe I didn't look sufficiently alarmed.

"Let me explain," he said. "Oxygen is constantly needed by your muscles and brain in order for them to function. When you breathe normal air, the oxygen molecules in your lungs latch onto the hemoglobin in your red blood cells and are transported around your body. But if you breathe air that is contaminated with carbon monoxide, then the CO molecules attach to the hemoglobin instead of the O_2 ones, forming carboxyhemoglobin. And that prevents the blood carrying oxygen. Hemoglobin is two hundred times better at absorbing carbon monoxide through the lung walls than it is oxygen, so it's very serious, even at low concentrations."

"Wouldn't I be able to taste it?" I asked.

"Carbon monoxide is odorless and tasteless. People die of it all the time without ever knowing it, especially in tents and trailers when they use heaters without proper ventilation."

"But how did it happen on a dive?" I asked.

"I suspect you were breathing from a tank that was contaminated with carbon monoxide," he said. "I had my doubts when you first arrived. The ambulance staff said you had the bends, but you didn't present the usual symptoms. Decompression sickness is referred to as *the bends* because the agony in the joints tends to bend people over. But you were pain-free. That's why I arranged for the arterial gas test. Fortunately, treatment for the bends and for CO poisoning are exactly the same—one hundred percent oxygen in a hyperbaric chamber—so that's what we did, even before we had the test results."

"Thank you," I said. "But how could such contamination happen?"

"Easily. In the past, it was quite a common problem, but people are usually more savvy and careful these days, so such accidents are now rare. Air compressors are used to fill the tanks and most are driven by gas engines. If the air intake valve for the tanks is placed too close to the exhaust of the engine, then you can partially fill the tank with carbon monoxide. That would be enough."

"So I wasn't eaten by a sea monster," I said, mostly to myself.

"Eh?"

"Nothing," I said. "I must have been hallucinating. I imagined I was being eaten alive by a sea monster."

"The brain does funny things when it's starved of oxygen."

"But how come I'd been underwater for more than twenty minutes and was fine, apart from a headache, and passed out only as I was coming up to the surface?"

"That is quite normal," he said. "It's to do with the increased partial pressure of oxygen that compensates at depth. It reduces as you ascend and hence the manifestations of the poisoning become more apparent."

I didn't understand, but at least the doctor seemed confident that he knew what he was talking about.

"Will there be any lasting effects?" I asked.

"There shouldn't be," he said, "not after breathing pure oxygen at high pressure, as you did in the hyperbaric chamber. It drives the carbon monoxide out of your system. We'll keep you here for a few more hours just to be sure, but I'm pretty certain you'll be able to go home later."

The doctor went away and I laid my head back on the pillow.

Carbon monoxide in a contaminated dive tank.

Take the yellow guest tanks, Martin had said to me on the boat. Had that been because he had known that one of them, or even both, had been purposely contaminated with poison gas?

Or was I just being paranoid?

Perhaps it had just been an unfortunate accident, as the doctor had suggested.

Maybe. But I'd spent far too much time in hospitals recently. And being stabbed thirteen times certainly hadn't been accidental.

HENRI CAME BACK at two o'clock with a large tray holding two plates, over which there were metal covers.

"I couldn't eat my Christmas dinner at Martin's place, not without you being there, so I brought it to have with you here."

She removed the plate covers with a flourish, like a magician revealing a white rabbit. Underneath were two large platters overflowing with roast turkey plus all the trimmings.

Henri even produced a pair of Christmas crackers from her handbag.

"How lovely," I said.

I didn't have the heart to tell her that just an hour previous I'd been served an identical Christmas lunch from the hospital food cart. But that one hadn't been particularly tasty and, fortunately, my half-eaten attempt had been retrieved just five minutes before Henri arrived.

This one was much better, and, to my great delight, Henri had also smuggled in a thermos full not of hot coffee but ice-cold chardonnay, which we drank out of plastic hospital glasses.

We pulled our crackers and put on our paper hats.

"Why did the bicycle fall over?" Henri read from her joke slip.

"No idea," I said.

"Because it was two-tired."

We both groaned.

"What's yours?" Henri said.

"What is Good King Wenceslas's favorite pizza?"

"I don't know."

"Deep-pan, crisp and even."

More groans.

"That's even worse than mine," Henri said.

I actually think it was the best Christmas lunch I'd ever had, which I put down to the company rather than the ambience of the surroundings. I didn't want to spoil it by suggesting to Henri that her cousin might have tried to kill me, but it was she who brought up the topic of the dodgy tanks.

"One of the doctors here at the hospital called Carson Ebanks to tell him that you didn't have the bends after all. It seems you were poisoned by carbon monoxide from a dive tank."

I nodded. "The doctor told me that too."

"He called Carson to demand that all his dive tanks be immediately emptied and refilled with clean air as a precaution to stop it from happening again."

"But the tanks we used didn't belong to Carson."

"I know," she said. "They were Martin's and he had filled them himself using his own compressor. That, exactly, is why Carson called us."

"Did anyone else suffer any effects?" I asked. "Did you have a headache or anything?"

"No, nothing. And Martin seemed to be fine as well. I don't know about Truman Ebanks, but he used his own tanks anyway."

"We should get the tanks tested for carbon monoxide," I said. "Including the ones we didn't use."

"It's too late," she said. "As soon as Martin got the call from Carson, he went straight out to his diving store and opened all his tanks to empty them. He even removed the valves and washed the tanks out. He said he didn't want there to be any chance that someone else would be poisoned."

How convenient, I thought.

I looked at Henri and raised a questioning eyebrow.

"You surely can't think that Martin poisoned you on purpose?"

"It was *he* who told me to use the yellow tanks," I said. "And it was *he* who invited me to go diving with him in the first place, when he'd been anything but welcoming beforehand."

"Yes, but . . ."

"But what?" I asked.

"Why would he do such a thing?"

Why indeed?

"GOD, I'm so dreadfully sorry," Martin said. "I can't think how it could have happened. I'm so careful when I fill the tanks for the very reason that I know how dangerous the engine exhaust fumes can be."

He really did sound quite apologetic. And almost believable.

He was standing in the center of the living room of our apartment at the Coral Stone Club, having walked down the beach from his house. It was five o'clock and I had been there about half an hour, having been discharged from the hospital.

Henri and I were sitting next to each other on the sofa in front of him.

Should I come straight out and accuse him of poisoning me on purpose?

Perhaps not just yet.

"It was strange how none of the other tanks was affected," I said.

"Yes, I thought that," Martin replied. "You must have been unlucky. I'm always careful about placing the compressor outside in the open, with the engine exhaust downwind from the air intake, but maybe the wind shifted direction, or something, when that particular tank was being filled."

Or something, I thought. Like purposely turning it around.

"Who knew I would use the yellow tanks?" I asked pointedly.

"The yellow tanks are my guest tanks. They are the easiest to see and I generally give them to the diver who I think needs the most watching. In this case, that was you. If Bentley had been diving, he would probably have had them."

But Bentley hadn't been diving. He'd brought no trunks with him.

"Who knows that?" I asked.

"It's standard practice. At least, it is for me." He paused, but he wasn't finished. "Are you seriously suggesting that you were in some way specifically targeted? That someone gave you a contaminated tank on purpose?"

I just looked at him as he built up a head of steam.

"That's preposterous. How dare you!" He looked fit to explode.

"I'm sure Jeff didn't mean that," Henri said, stepping in to try to defuse the bomb.

But I *did* mean that. However, it seemed diplomatic not to continue with that line just at the moment.

"At least I'm fine now," I said, smiling at him. "Fully recovered."

He was only a little placated. He turned on his heel and stomped back out to the beach without another word.

Bloody cheek, I thought.

His contaminated dive tank had nearly killed *me.*

On purpose, or by accident, it was still *his* fault.

Surely it was I who had the right to be angry, not he.

But Henri was cross with me as well.

"You simply can't go around accusing people like that," she shouted at me as soon as Martin was out of earshot. "What evidence do you have?"

"I was poisoned," I said. "There's no doubt about that. It was one of Martin's yellow tanks, filled by him, which was responsible. No other tanks appear to have been contaminated. It was Martin who made sure I used the yellow tanks. And, on top of that, he has since emptied the tanks and washed them out so that they can't be tested for carbon monoxide. OK, I'll admit the evidence is circumstantial, but . . . what else am I meant to think?"

"That's ridiculous," she said. "Why on earth would Martin

try to kill you? It just doesn't make any sense. He would be risking everything."

But Martin was not averse to taking risks.

What had Bentley said to him on the balcony at Newbury?

You're a total fucking idiot! You absolutely shouldn't be here. You shouldn't even be in the country. It's far too risky.

32

An uneasy truce was established between Henri and myself, helped in part by the Chanel N°5 Christmas present, which she adored.

"It's my favorite," she said, kissing me. "Thank you so much."

However, she was still cross with me, not so much for my initial accusation but for then not agreeing with her that it was ridiculous and for not apologizing to Martin.

We had been invited by Theresa to go up to their place for a light supper and some Christmas games. I was not really in the mood for party games. And especially not for Murder in the Dark.

"You go," I said. "I'll stay here and watch television. I could do with the rest." I leaned my head back on the sofa and put my feet up on the ottoman.

"I'm not going without you," she said adamantly. "I'm not letting you sulk here like a spoiled schoolboy. So move your blooming arse and get yourself changed."

I was still wearing the baggy tracksuit I'd been lent by the hospital to come home in.

"OK, you win." I dragged myself upright. "Do you know what happened to the shirt I had with me on the boat? And also my cell phone is missing."

"Sorry, I've no idea," Henri said. "I was too busy worrying about you. But I'm sure they're safe somewhere. Carson Ebanks probably has them."

I hoped so. Even though I occasionally backed up everything from my cell to my laptop, I hadn't done it for a while, and I'd hate to lose the photos taken on this trip.

AS IT WAS GETTING DARK, we walked along the road to the Reynard residence to avoid being bitten by the sand flies on the beach.

Martin's welcome was less than enthusiastic, and his anger simmered just below the surface for most of the evening. He pointedly did not offer me a drink when we arrived even though he poured a glass of wine for Henri.

Fortunately, Henri noticed, giving me her glass before fetching another for herself. It saved a minor diplomatic incident.

I didn't care. I could cope with his spiteful little actions with ease. He wasn't likely to walk up behind me and blow my brains out, as I'd suspected of some of the hosts with whom I'd been a houseguest in Afghanistan. At least, I hoped he wasn't.

Remarkably, no one asked me if I was all right. In fact, the morning's incident was not spoken of at all. It was as if the whole thing had never occurred. I soon realized that it was not just my poisoning they weren't going to talk about, none of them wanted to talk to me about anything. Apart from Henri, they were even avoiding eye contact. I put it down to their embarrassment that such a thing could happen to a guest, but, nevertheless, I found their behavior somewhat bizarre.

Only Theresa said anything to me and that was to ask if I'd enjoyed my Christmas lunch.

"Yes, thank you," I replied. "Very thoughtful of you."

"I'm sorry there was no Christmas pudding with it," she said. "That was still steaming when Henrietta left." She forced a smile. "But you can make up for that tonight. There's plenty left over."

During yet another awkward gap in the conversation, I asked if anyone knew the whereabouts of my cell phone.

There was a collective shaking of heads.

"Then does anyone have Carson Ebanks's home telephone number?"

Martin reluctantly gave me the number, and I called it, using the phone in the kitchen.

"Sure, man," said Carson in his deep, resonant voice. "I got it."

That was a relief.

"Your shirt too, man," he said. "You OK now?"

"Yes," I said. "Fully recovered. Thank you."

"Had me worried there, man," he said. "First person to pass out on me." He sounded anxious. "I keep oxygen on the boat, man, in case. First time I used it."

"What happened wasn't your fault," I said to him. "In fact, it was your prompt action in giving me the oxygen that probably saved me."

I could hear his relief over the phone line that I wasn't blaming him.

"Where do you live?" I asked. "I'll come by to pick up my phone."

"No, man," he said. "I'll bring it. You staying with Mr. Martin?"

"No, I'm at the Coral Stone Club," I said. "Unit number one."

"I know it, man," Carson said. "I'll get the phone back there."

"Thank you," I said, and hung up.

"Any luck?" Henri asked me when I went back to the others.

"Yes. Carson Ebanks has my phone and my shirt. He's going to drop them back to the apartment."

"Great."

THE ATMOSPHERE improved little throughout the evening as we ate some supper and then played charades, each of us, in turn, drawing a book, film, song or play title from a hat and trying to get the others to guess it by mime alone.

I thought there was going to be a slightly awkward moment when I drew Agatha Christie's *A Murder Is Announced* out of the hat, but no one else seemed to notice.

Sir Richard was particularly good at guessing, even getting the tricky title *True Grit* from some rather strange and obscure miming by Bentley Robertson. I could easily understand how Reynard Shipping Limited had grown to be the market leader under his astute leadership. There seemed to be nothing going on that escaped his sharp and insightful scrutiny.

Hence, I couldn't imagine that he was unaware of the ongoing antagonism directed at me by his son—an antagonism that intensified in direct ratio to the amount of red wine Martin consumed, which was considerable. But Sir Richard made no attempt either to stop it or to apologize to me in any way.

In contrast to her husband, Lady Mary was not the sharpest needle in the sewing basket, getting hopelessly confused by the game and being totally unable not to speak when she shouldn't.

But even she was not as affable toward me as she had been in the Range Rover at Luton Airport.

Bentley wasn't being very pleasant either. He took every opportunity to put me down. Whenever I made a wrong guess, he would roll his eyes and make some comment or other about how stupid I had been. But at least I could understand the reason why *he* was so ill-disposed toward me—*she* was sitting next to me on the sofa.

I had what he wanted.

What I couldn't fathom was why Martin had been so blatantly unfriendly ever since I'd arrived on Cayman.

It couldn't only be because I'd accused him of purposely poisoning me with carbon monoxide, although that in itself would have probably been enough, and it certainly hadn't helped.

There had to be more to it.

Perhaps he didn't approve of me as the boyfriend of his cousin.

But he'd actually been unduly hostile toward me right from when we'd been first introduced by Gay Smith on the balcony of the box at Sandown, which had been before I'd even met Henri.

Everything pointed to the fact that it must have something to do with me overhearing him being so crudely castigated by Bentley at Newbury. Perhaps he was embarrassed that I'd seen him being spoken to in that manner by someone I would consider his subordinate.

MY SHIRT and phone were waiting for us on the doorstep when Henri and I arrived back at our apartment just before midnight.

Our truce from earlier was still holding and we went to bed and converted it into a full-blown peace treaty.

But I couldn't get to sleep afterward.

Henri, meanwhile, went straight off and was soon snoring gently beside me. I continued to toss and turn for what seemed like an age before finally getting up and going through to the kitchen to make myself a cup of tea. Perhaps that would help.

I put on some shorts and took my tea outside to the beach. It was a beautiful night, with an almost full moon casting nighttime-sharp shadows of the palm trees on the sand. I walked down near to the water's edge.

I was troubled.

Coming away for Christmas with Henri's relations had been a mistake. My presence now seemed to be resented by all of them. Maybe it was because Christmas is such a family-oriented time and I was an interloper here to take one of their number away from them. Or had my first instinct been right all along—she *was* out of my league.

I wandered along the beach in the moonlight.

All was in darkness at the Reynard residence.

My naturally inquisitive instincts drew me closer. Was there a garbage can handily placed that I could rummage through to discover Martin's darkest secrets?

I knew there wasn't.

Henri had already shown me how all the trash was mechanically compacted into tightly compressed bales before being placed in a dumpster ready for pickup. Great for reducing the volume of garbage but not much good for snoopy investigators like me.

Nevertheless, I walked off the beach onto the Reynard terrace as if somehow being close by might help me to understand what was going on in Martin's mind.

I wondered if there were any CCTV cameras watching me. I couldn't see any. Martin had already said how safe he felt on Cayman and that crime was rare. However, I would have expected some sort of security at such a valuable property, especially as Martin and Theresa were away so much in Singapore.

I finished my tea and was about to walk back out onto the beach on my way to bed when I heard a noise—a door being opened.

I silently stepped into the shadow beneath one of the casuarina trees and watched as Theresa padded along the path in bare feet from the main house toward the guest cottage. She was wearing a thin white housecoat that billowed open slightly as she moved, revealing her nakedness beneath.

So I had been right about the body language on the plane. Theresa and Bentley *were* lovers.

As she walked, she held her hand to her mouth and furtively scanned from side to side as if she knew precisely how dangerous was this particular Christmas game she was playing. It didn't matter how drunk her husband had become after all that red wine, there was no guarantee he wouldn't wake up and discover her missing from their marital bed.

I smiled to myself as I walked back down the beach to the Coral Stone Club. There was definitely a measure of schadenfreude in me, knowing that my tormentor from the previous evening was being cheated on by his own wife—and right under his nose. And with the creepy Bentley Robertson too.

Henri might be pleased that Bentley's lecherous leanings were currently directed elsewhere. Not that I'd tell her.

She was still sleeping soundly as I slipped back between the sheets beside her. And now I quickly joined her in the Land of Nod.

IN SPITE OF my nocturnal sojourn, I was awake early and I left Henri asleep while I went into the kitchen.

I opened my laptop and checked for any new e-mails, but, not surprisingly over the holiday, there weren't any.

Horseracing paused for just two days before Christmas, and also on the big day itself, then it restarted with fervor on Boxing Day with eight or nine different meetings, the most prestigious being at Kempton Park for the annual running of the King George VI Chase.

The London office of the BHA took the more usual British approach to the season, closing from Christmas Eve right through until the New Year. Not that all the BHA staff had the time off. Far from it. Integrity officers, clerks of the scales, stipendiary stewards and many others were still working at the racetracks, checking horse identities, monitoring weighing rooms and carrying on the other regulatory functions of the authority.

Indeed, this was the first time since I'd joined the BHA that I had not been working on Boxing Day.

I logged on to the *Racing Post* website to see the declared runners for the King George. Unlike the Hennessy, this race was not a handicap but a Grade 1 championship race, where past form made no difference to the weight a horse had to carry. It was an even test, won, without question, by the best horse on the day.

This year, there were ten runners going to post, all of them top-class chasers, aged between six and nine, each due to carry a weight of one hundred sixty-four pounds over three miles and eighteen fences.

I noted that Bill McKenzie had been declared to ride a horse called Special Measures. His collarbone must have mended sufficiently for him to have been passed as fit to ride by the medics.

I looked at my watch. It was just gone seven in the morning in Cayman—midday at Kempton. The crowd would already be gathering in droves at the west London track. The big race was the fifth of the afternoon, due off at ten past three London time, ten past ten here. I could imagine the anticipation of the owners, trainers and jockeys in the run-up to start time, to say nothing of the betting public, who would be eagerly selecting their preferences, if they had any money left to wager after all that Christmas shopping.

I had always been excited by the electric atmosphere that exists at a racetrack on a major event day, and part of me wished I were at Kempton to enjoy it.

I would have to make do with watching the race on my computer, via the Internet, steeplechasing not being rated highly enough to be shown live on the American TV channels available in Cayman.

I made some tea and took a cup to Henri.

"Go away," she said, turning over and burying her head beneath the pillow. "I'm still asleep." Martin clearly wasn't the only one to have drunk too much wine the previous evening.

I went back to my laptop and connected it to my iPhone to download the photos I didn't want to lose.

It took just a few seconds to complete, and I scanned through the files to check that they had transferred safely without being corrupted.

That's strange, I thought.

The photo I had taken of Martin Reynard and Bentley

Robertson, during their heated discussion at Newbury on Hennessy Gold Cup day, didn't appear to have made the transition from iPhone to laptop.

I looked through the *Camera Roll* on the phone.

It wasn't there.

I checked again, but there was no mistake.

The photograph had been deleted.

33

Henri and I ordered a taxi and, with the help of a couple of calls from my cell, we eventually found our way to Derrick and Gay Smith's house for drinks at six o'clock on Boxing Day evening.

They lived on the wonderfully named Conch Point Road in a large house set well back from the road, out of sight behind a stone wall, and with no name shown on the unpretentious gateway. Hence, we had driven past the house twice without realizing it.

"Welcome," Gay said, meeting us at the front door. "Well done, finding us. We like to keep a low profile. Come on in."

We were ushered out to a covered veranda, with its magnificent view northeastward toward the sea.

We were not their sole guests.

Peter Darwin, the Governor, and his wife Annabel were there ahead of us.

"You should have much in common with Peter," Gay said to me. "He loves his racing."

"Just my luck to be posted to a country without a racetrack," Peter said with a laugh. "When I was told I was being sent to the

West Indies, I secretly hoped it would be Barbados. I've always fancied going racing on Garrison Savannah."

"Wasn't that a horse?" I asked, dragging up a distant memory.

"Yes indeed," he said. "It won the Cheltenham Gold Cup back in the nineties. But it was named after the racetrack on Barbados."

"I'm so sorry Cayman is such a disappointment to you," Derrick said, handing around glasses of champagne.

"I've got over it," Peter said with another laugh. "I keep in touch with things on the Internet as much as I can and we go racing whenever we're back home on leave. Don't we, darling?"

"As much as possible," Annabel agreed. "We always try and get to the Cheltenham Festival in March. Peter, effectively, grew up on Cheltenham racetrack."

"There are worse places," he said, laughing.

"And we adore going racing at Stratford," Annabel said, looking lovingly at her husband. "That's where Peter and I met."

"How romantic," Henri said. "Jeff and I met at Sandown races."

"In my box," Derrick said, all smiles.

Annabel beamed at us, her big blue eyes positively sparkling with delight.

"Peter's father was a jump jockey, and I once worked for the British Jockey Club."

"Jeff, don't you work for the Jockey Club?" Gay asked.

"Not quite," I said. "But I do work for the racing authorities."

Derrick again recounted the story of how I had saved his horse from being stolen at Ascot. I'd given up trying to tell him it was meant to be confidential. But if you couldn't tell someone in the diplomatic service a secret, who could you tell? Diplomats were meant to be good at keeping secrets. But they were also meant to be fairly proficient at lying for their country as well.

"When was your father a jockey?" I asked Peter.

"Back in the sixties," he said. "He wasn't famous or anything. He rode only four winners—ever. He'd just started out on his career when he was killed in a car accident."

"How awful," I said.

"I was only an infant at the time. I don't remember him at all."

"I'll look him up in the records. What was his first name?"

"Paul," Peter said, pleased that I had taken some interest. "He was actually Paul Perry. I only became a Darwin when I was twelve and my mother remarried."

"Any relation to . . . ?" I asked.

"None," he replied quickly with one of those wan smiles that told me that he'd been asked that too many times before and he was bored with it.

We watched as the last of the daylight faded away and then marveled as the full moon seemed to emerge straight out of the water, its orange disk appearing unnaturally large and almost frighteningly close.

"Magnificent," Peter said. "Quite enough to drive a man mad."

"Lunatic," I said.

"Exactly so."

THE SIX OF US went for dinner at the Calypso Grill at Morgan's Harbour.

It was everything I had expected, except that there was no sign of Harry Belafonte, and the music being played through the sound system was more steel drum than true calypso. But the bright blues, reds and burnt orange colors, together with the laid-back *No problem, man* atmosphere, were authentically Caribbean.

We were shown to a table out on the open terrace, right alongside the lapping water, and I found myself sitting next to Annabel Darwin and across from Gay Smith.

"How lovely," I said. "I don't think I have ever sat out under the stars for dinner on Boxing Day."

"I hate the winters in England," Gay said. "Give me the warmth any day."

"Doesn't it get too hot here in the summer?" I asked.

"Not too hot," Gay said. "But it does get very humid and it rains a lot. We tend to go away from May to September."

"To England?"

"Mostly, yes, to see the grandchildren. But up to now, we've not been able to spend the whole summer in England. There's a limit on the number of days we're allowed, so we also go to Ireland. And anywhere else that takes our fancy."

"What's the *limit* for?" I asked.

"Oh, it's something to do with residency and tax, but I leave all that to Derrick. The British government has just changed the rules and I think it's now better for us. We used to be able to stay in England for only ninety days per year, but in the future we can stay one hundred and twenty. Something like that."

I chose the chicken liver pâté, which was spectacular, and then the Jamaican curried shrimp, which was hot as hell but delicious.

"I love their crab cakes," Gay said. "They make them fresh from local crab caught right here in Morgan's Harbour."

"Is it named for the pirate Captain Henry Morgan?" I asked. "As in the rum?"

"Probably," she said. "But I suspect it's more for the American tourists than because he ever came here."

We laughed.

I liked Gay Smith.

HENRI AND I were offered a lift back to the Coral Stone Club from the restaurant with the Governor and his wife in their official limousine.

"Are you sure it's allowed?" I asked.

"Positive," Peter said. "But one of you will have to sit in the front. Neither Annabel nor I are allowed to. Protocol. Strange, I know, but there you have it."

I sat up front with the driver, a Cayman Islands policeman in uniform, while Henri was between the Darwins in the back.

"Do you fancy a nightcap, Jeff?" Peter asked during the journey. "I seem not to have spoken to you much all evening."

I turned my head, receiving a nod of agreement from Henri.

"That would be lovely," I said.

"Take us to Government House, please, Christopher," Peter said to the driver.

The driver did as he was asked and he soon stopped the car under the canopy in front of the Governor's residence. He was the first out of the car, opening the rear door for Peter and standing smartly at attention as the Governor stood up.

"Christopher, here, will wait and take you home," Peter said.

"I'm sure we could get a taxi," Henri said.

"We could even walk," I said. "It's less than half a mile."

"I will wait for you, sir," the driver said firmly, putting a stop to our shilly-shallying.

"Thank you," I said to him. "We won't be long."

"Take your time, sir," he said. "I'll be here."

Peter and Annabel went into the house and Henri and I followed.

"Seems like a nice chap," I said to Peter, indicating the driver over my shoulder.

"All the police here are," he said. "They mostly have a good relationship with the community."

"I'm told there's not much crime in the islands."

He sighed. "There's a lot more than I'd like," he said. "Opportunist burglary is the real menace, but we've also had a minor drug war going on recently between some rival gangs. We like to think we're clear of that sort of thing, but we're not."

How about attempted murder, I thought.

Henri and Annabel had a brandy each, while Peter and I chatted amicably about racing over a couple of glasses of port.

"I see that Duncan Johnson trained another King George winner," Peter said. "He seems to have a knack of winning the big races."

"Yes, he does have a remarkable record." I'd watched the race on my laptop. Bill McKenzie had finished a creditable fourth. "Dave Swinton would have probably ridden the winner if he'd still been with us. He rode the horse last time out, when it won at Haydock in November."

"His death is a huge loss to the sport," Peter said. "Personally, I am extremely saddened by it. He was so exciting to watch, even when he rode a raw novice over hurdles. He seemed to have a sensitivity for the horses unlike any other jockey. He could easily have gone on to be the champion for many more years, to become one of the super-greats."

"I agree," I said.

But did I really?

For me, Dave's superhero reputation had been tarnished somewhat by his greed in demanding extra payments from the owners and trainers and then his nondisclosure of such payments to the tax man, while maintaining the pathetic excuse that the payments were merely *gifts*.

Not that he deserved to be murdered for it.

I wondered if his almost godlike standing with the racing public might take a hit when all the sordid details came out at his inquest, or at the trial of Leslie Morris and son, as they surely would. But I wasn't about to burst Peter Darwin's bubble of admiration just yet.

Henri and I finished our drinks and departed, arriving back at our apartment in the back of the Governor's official car, albeit without the Union Jack flying from its pole on the hood, as had been the case earlier.

"Would *Your Excellency* like to come to bed with me for some rumpy-pumpy?" Henri said in an ultraposh voice as we went in.

"I may not be that *excellency* tonight," I said with a nervous laugh. "Not after all that booze."

"Let me be the judge of that," she giggled.

A little while later, she didn't complain.

I WOKE AGAIN in the middle of the night, the bedside clock showing me it was three-thirty.

It was unlike me to suffer so much from jet lag and I wondered if the hyperbaric treatment was somehow to blame.

Or maybe it was just that my inquisitive mind was running on overdrive.

Something that Gay Smith had said over dinner had struck a chord.

I gently eased myself out of bed and went into one of the other bedrooms and closed the door.

I used my cell to call Faye and Quentin.

"I thought you'd call us on Christmas Day," Faye said with a degree of reprimand in her voice.

"I'm sorry," I said. "I was out all day and carelessly didn't have my phone with me." I had decided not to tell her of my diving adventures for fear of unduly worrying her. "Did you have a good day?"

"Quiet," she said. "In fact, it was just the two of us. Kenneth made a late decision to go to France with a new friend."

I don't think she was actually *trying* to make me feel guilty, even though she had.

"Sorry," I said.

"Are *you* having a nice time?" she asked.

"Lovely, thank you," I said. I told her all about the private jet and the fabulous apartment.

"Don't get ideas you can't afford," she said, ever concerned about my welfare.

"Yes, Mother." We laughed. "How are *you* feeling?" I asked.

Such a simple question with so many unspoken overtones attached.

"Fine," she said. "A little tired, as always." She laughed again. "I've been using that as my excuse to get Quentin to do all the dishes."

We chatted a bit more about what we had both been doing.

"How's it all going with Henrietta?" she asked.

"Great," I said. "Very happy."

"Quentin was very taken with her."

I knew. I'd noticed.

"Is he there? I'd like to have a word with him."

I waited while she found him.

"What the hell time is it with you?" Quentin said as he came on the line.

"Half past three," I said. "I couldn't sleep."

"Got a guilty conscience?"

"Slightly," I said. "But that's not why I called. Do you remember you told me about the man who sold his printing business and didn't pay the capital gains tax?"

"Of course. What about it?"

"How did he claim to be a tax resident of the Channel Islands and why did you think he wasn't?"

"He bought a house in Guernsey and established residency there, but he spent too many days in London. He was a fool to think that no one would bother to count."

"What's the limit on days?" I asked.

"They've introduced a new system and I'm not sure of the latest rules, but it used to be if someone spent more than one hundred and eighty-three days in the UK during any one year, or more than an average of ninety days a year during the current and previous three years, then he or she was considered a resident for tax purposes. Those were the rules that applied in this case."

Unlike for American citizens, who are obliged to file an annual IRS tax return wherever they live in the world, the British are required to do so only for years when they are actually resident in the United Kingdom.

"How can you find out how many days someone spends in the UK?"

"It's not as straightforward as you'd think. Passports are now scanned on the way into and out of the country, but that didn't used to be the case. Until very recently, there was no record made when anyone left. Airline passenger lists could tell you, provided they went by air. But there were no passenger lists on the ferries or on the trains through the Channel Tunnel. Then, of course, there's Ireland. There are no passport checks whatsoever for UK citizens going either way across the Irish Sea or when crossing the border on land between Northern Ireland and the Republic. That's where my Guernsey man went—he used cash to buy a ferry ticket from Liverpool to Belfast, took a bus to Dublin, and then returned to London by air, later claiming he'd been in Ireland for two whole weeks. The tax people reckoned he'd gone there and back in a single day. He couldn't produce any hotel receipts or even say where he'd stayed."

Sometimes, Quentin's long answers could be quite useful.

"How do I find the new rules?"

"It's sure to be on the web somewhere," Quentin said.

"If I was so inclined, to whom would I report if I discover that someone has been defrauding the tax man?"

"Directly to Revenue and Customs."

"Not the police?"

"No. The police wouldn't really know what to do with it other than pass it on to the tax authorities. It is they who prosecute tax cheats. They even have a hotline especially for tip-offs from the public."

"Thanks," I said. "That's very helpful."

"Glad to be of service."

We hung up.

Quentin knew better than to ask me *why* I wanted the information or even *who* I was interested in. I would tell him if I needed to.

I went through to the kitchen and opened my laptop.

I googled the rules on determining UK tax residency and discovered that the new system was way more complicated than the one Quentin had described. It took into account far more factors than just the days a person was present in the UK. Available accommodation, family ties and days spent actually working in the country were also now important.

Henri had told me that Martin had been working in the UK to restructure the British end of their organization. He also had a house and a minor child in the country. All of those things would have worked against him, reducing the number of days he was allowed to remain.

From carefully reading the rules on the UK government's website, it seemed to me that Martin would have been allowed to be in the country for a maximum of only ninety days without becoming a tax resident, maybe even less. Yet Henri had said he'd spent much of the summer there, and he'd also been in England for at least a week during the previous month.

I'd seen him.

So had he overstayed his permitted time?

You're a total fucking idiot! You absolutely shouldn't be here. You shouldn't even be in the country. It's far too risky.

And what had Martin then replied to Bentley?

No one will ever know.

But I knew.

34

I went back to bed, but I still couldn't sleep.

I lay on my back in the dark, thinking and asking myself many questions, but I came up with very few definitive answers.

Apart from the one in Dave Swinton's sauna, were the other attempts on my life nothing to do with the blackmailing of jockeys to fix races?

Were they all to do with the fact that I knew Martin Reynard had been at Newbury races on Hennessy Gold Cup day and I'd taken a photograph to prove it?

It seemed rather extreme, as others would surely have also seen him there on that day.

Was it Martin Reynard, not Leslie Morris, who'd sent a couple of London's criminal fraternity to kill me with a carving knife?

Indeed, when those attempts had failed, had he resolved to murder me here in Cayman with the contaminated dive tank?

And perhaps the most important question of all—if I was right, how did I stop him from trying again?

If it had been Martin who had taken the opportunity to delete the photo from my iPhone during the confusion on the boat, was that enough? Was that the end of it? Or did he still feel the need to bump me off?

Could I take that chance?

So far, I'd been very lucky to survive, the doctors kept telling me so.

Could I trust that my luck would hold? I had to be lucky every time, whereas my would-be murderer had to be lucky only once.

I could report my suspicions to Revenue and Customs, but it wouldn't result in an arrest—not yet anyway. There would be weeks, months or even years of investigation.

Maybe not even that.

I suspected that *no* crime had yet taken place, as we must still be in the tax year in question. Any return for the current year would not be due to be filed until well into the year after next, more than twelve months away. A crime would be committed at that time only if a return was not submitted and the taxes due not paid.

A year's income tax didn't seem worth murdering me over, not on the off chance that I might have spotted what was going on, especially as the attempts had done nothing more than make me increasingly determined to discover why.

But Derrick Smith had been constantly telling people that I was some sort of superagent/supersleuth who could spot and then prevent wrongdoing from afar with almost mystical powers.

Had Martin believed it and simply decided to act sooner rather than later?

But murder?

All he had to do was accept his responsibilities and pay his tax like everybody else. End of story.

Other than the minor fact that he may have tried three times to cause my untimely death, I didn't have any particular ax to grind with Martin—after all, I was an investigator for the BHA, not the tax authorities. But would it make it safer for me if I told him that I believed he had become a UK tax resident for the current year and that I had informed many others including the tax people? He could hardly murder everyone, so would he have anything to gain by killing me?

No.

Except, perhaps, revenge.

"TELL ME more about Martin," I said to Henri over breakfast the following morning.

"What about him?" she replied.

"Who was he married to before Theresa?"

"Some bimbo called Lorraine, who he met when he was a student."

"Were they at the same university?"

"Good God, no," she said with a laugh. "Lorraine didn't go to university. She always used to say studying was a waste of time and that she went instead to the *University of Life*. More like the *Reformatory of Life*, if you ask me. I know for a fact that she's been done for shoplifting several times even though Martin provides handsomely for both her and Joshua."

"How did they meet?"

"In Spain, when he was twenty. She was nineteen. He was there on holiday and she worked in a bar on the Costa Brava. Absolute disaster, it was. Met, married and a mother all within nine months to the day. The divorce took a little longer, but not much. Uncle Richard was furious with him."

"Why on earth did Martin marry her?" I said. "She surely could have had an abortion."

"She didn't tell him she was pregnant until it was too late for that, so Martin did the "honorable" thing without even telling his parents. She may not have gone to university, but our Lorraine is no mug. She's far more clever than him, that's for sure. He's been her meal ticket for life."

"He can't be that much of a mug if he's the managing director of Reynard Shipping," I said.

"Uncle Richard has all the brains in the family. While Martin may be called the managing director, it's Uncle Richard who really manages everything. He makes all the decisions. He worries, rightly, what will happen to the firm after he's gone. That's why we've sold the Hong Kong end of the business. I think Uncle Richard is afraid that Martin will lose it all."

How sad, I thought. Richard Reynard had two sons, one an artist who lived in the Scottish Highlands and had no interest in business, the other not quite up to running the family firm.

"Would you say Martin and Theresa have a happy marriage?" I asked.

"What is this?" she said sharply. "The Spanish Inquisition? You asked me that before. Do you know something I don't?"

"No," I lied. "I just wondered. Theresa seems to be quite keen on Bentley."

"I can't think why. He's a horrid little man."

"Doesn't he have any family of his own to spend Christmas with?"

"I know that he has parents," she said. "I've met them. But perhaps they've disowned him. This isn't the first time he's spent Christmas with us."

"If no one likes him, why is he still employed by your company?"

She sighed. "It's only me who can't stand him. That's because he and I have history." She paused and I waited while she worked out in her mind if she was going to tell me about that history. She obviously decided not to. "Uncle Richard almost worships the ground he walks on. And, I have to admit, he's very good at his job and fiercely loyal to the firm."

"Do Bentley and Martin get on?"

"Not really. Martin hates the fact that Uncle Richard talks to Bentley about business strategy more than to him. I know I shouldn't say this but at times I think that Uncle Richard wishes that Bentley was his son rather than Martin."

It was quite a statement.

"How about you?" I asked. "Do you get on all right with Martin?"

"Yes, I'd say so," she said. "Sometimes, I feel a bit sorry for him. It's not his fault that he's not quite up to the job. He tries his best. But God knows what will happen to us when Uncle Richard finally retires. Or dies."

"How about the other directors? The two from the law firm?"

"They don't seem to have much to do with the day-to-day running of things. Their job is more to do with ensuring that we, as a board, comply with all the local regulations."

"You could always bring in more directors," I said. "Bentley, for example."

Henri pulled a face. "Martin won't allow that. He's totally adamant. I think he feels threatened—and for good reason. I suppose we will have to have more directors at some point, but Uncle Richard is keen to keep control in the family for the time being, especially while we are selling off some of the company's assets."

I couldn't argue with that.

"Now, what would you like to do today?" Henri asked.

"What is there?"

"We could go to Stingray City."

HENRI ARRANGED to charter a boat to take us, but we wouldn't be going until later in the day when the cruise ship passengers had all departed.

"It would be a nightmare earlier," Henri said. "Far too many people."

From the beach in front of the apartment we could see five huge liners at anchor off George Town, each of them disgorging thousands of passengers on the island for the day, all of them searching for something to keep them busy.

So we spent much of the day lying on chaise longues in the shadow of a beach cabana while I tried to work out what I should do.

I wondered if I should tell Henri of my suspicions.

The last thing I wanted to do was to ruin our budding affair by further accusing her cousin of trying to kill me. It had caused enough trouble when I'd suggested he'd purposely given me a contaminated dive tank. To now accuse him of also sending the men with the carving knife to stab me to death would probably be terminal for our relationship.

Perhaps I could tell her only that I believed Martin had inadvertently become a tax resident in the UK. But she would likely say *So what? Why are you telling me?* and all the other stuff would all come out.

But I felt I had to tell someone.

It would surely be safer for me if someone else knew.

But who?

Bentley the lawyer must already know. Otherwise, why would he have been so outspoken on the Newbury balcony?

What had he said at the time?

I know, and that in itself is bad enough.

If the company lawyer knew, then surely in due course Martin would *have* to file a UK tax return. Unless Bentley was planning to turn a blind eye.

Henri went down to the sea for a cooling swim while I went back inside the apartment to call Quentin. I needed some legal advice and he was my go-to lawyer of choice.

"I'm not sure what to do," I said to him. "I don't know the law."

I explained the gist of my problems.

"With reference to the tax position, no crime appears to have been committed as yet, so you are under no obligation to report anything to the authorities," he said. "That would only change later if you had firm evidence to the effect that a tax return and payment had not been submitted when due, hence a fraud had been committed."

"So what would you do now?" I asked.

"Say nothing and get out of there as soon as possible. I'd write formally to Reynard Shipping, at their registered address, explaining that you believe that Martin Reynard may be a UK tax resident for the current year. You should copy the letter to their accountants, if you know who they are. You would then be fully covered, from a legal point of view."

It all sounded so logical.

"But I would also contact the UK police," Quentin went on, "to inform them of your suspicions regarding the attacks on you and leave them to deal with it."

Maybe saying nothing and leaving as soon as possible was the sensible thing to do, but did I really want to prematurely end my time in Cayman with Henri?

This was the first holiday I'd had in years.

I decided that I should take my brother-in-law's advice. He hadn't become a top QC by getting much wrong.

I logged on to the Internet and looked up commercial flights back to London. There was a direct one the following evening.

I would stay until then.

I made a reservation online.

Meanwhile, I would say nothing to any of the Reynard gathering and, when I was safely home, I would write the letters Quentin had suggested.

And to ensure my well-being, I would make certain that I was never left alone with Martin Reynard. In fact, I would spend every moment of my remaining time on Grand Cayman in the company of one Henrietta Shawcross.

Little did I realize that it would not be enough.

35

Henri went on working on her tan for the rest of the morning while I sat in the shade complaining that it was far too hot in the midday sun even for mad dogs and Englishmen.

"Would you like a cold drink?" I asked, standing up.

"Yes, please."

"Water or wine?"

"Both," she said. "Together. I'll have a spritzer. With some ice, please."

"Sounds lovely. I'll have the same."

I walked the few yards into the apartment and went into the kitchen to fix the two spritzers, but I didn't go straight back outside. Instead, I went into the master bedroom and took out the packet of Henri's board papers from the bedside drawer where she'd put them.

Atherton, Bradley and Partners, Attorneys-at-Law was printed across the top of an accompanying letter that gave the details of the Christmas Eve meeting to be held at their offices. I found a notepad and copied down the address and telephone number. I tore off the sheet and put it in my pocket.

I skimmed through the stack of papers, looking for any financial accounts that might indicate the identity of the company's accountants, but there was nothing. In fact, the board papers appeared to be very sparse for the main annual meeting of the directors of such a big organization. Henri had clearly been right when she said that most of the discussion and decisions were made at the management level and the main board was only there to rubber-stamp their findings.

I glanced briefly at the documents pertaining to the sale of the Hong Kong end of the business. The amount of money being paid for it made me whistle. I reckoned the Reynard family would soon be moving farther up the *Sunday Times* "Rich List"—some considerable way farther up.

I put the papers back how I'd found them in the drawer and took the drinks out to Henri, who hadn't moved an inch.

"Lovely," she said, taking one of them. "Thank you."

We clinked our glasses. How perfect was this?

I decided not to tell Henri that I intended to go home the following evening. I would make up some work-related excuse in the morning and then try to slip away before Martin even realized I had gone. I certainly wasn't going to spoil our last wonderful day together in this paradise.

STINGRAY CITY was everything that Henri had made it out to be, with not a single street or building to be seen. This particular city's blocks were nothing but water.

In the middle of North Sound, at least a mile from the nearest point of dry land, we stood waist-deep on a barely submerged sandbar while scores of stingrays swam around us, gliding back and forth between our legs like mini delta wing bombers, their soft undersides caressing our skin like velvet.

By holding small pieces of cut-up squid, we were able to make them follow our hands in circles in the water, even to swim right onto our outstretched arms to lie with their prominent, staring eyes just inches from our faces.

A stingray had killed Steve Irwin, the Australian conservationist and broadcaster, and their very name implied danger. But here they were acting like pets, playing with us, seemingly enjoying the experience as much as we were.

Our captain, the weather-beaten local from whom we had chartered the boat, told us that more than fifty years ago, when he was a young lad, the local fishermen used to bring their catch to the sandbar to clean and gut it, where the water was calm and they were able to throw the waste into the sea.

The stingrays would gather to feed on the fish scraps, and soon the fishermen were organizing trips for locals to see them and Stingray City was born. And so it had continued, with both the humans and the stingrays apparently very happy with the arrangement.

"This is now the most visited tourist attraction in Cayman," Henri said. "There would have been masses of boats and literally hundreds of people here earlier, all on organized tours from the cruise ships. It's like Piccadilly Circus at rush hour, from about ten in the morning until about four in the afternoon, almost every day of the year. Then they go back to their ships and sail away."

I looked around us at the empty sea, with only our boat bobbing gently at anchor nearby.

"It was a good call of yours to come later," I said.

It had also given me the opportunity to phone Atherton,

Bradley and Partners, Attorneys-at-Law, and ask them who the accountants for Reynard Shipping Limited were. Not that it had been a satisfactory call.

"I'll put you through to Greg Sherwood," the operator had said.

"And who are you, exactly?" Greg Sherwood had asked when I'd repeated my request to him.

"Just someone who wants to know."

There had been a distinct pause on the other end of the line.

"I am sorry," he'd said eventually. "Cayman law does not permit me to give out that information to persons not directly involved with the company."

I had no way of knowing if he'd been telling me the truth or not. Either way, I would have to be satisfied with just writing to the company at their registered office. They could forward it to their accountants if they wanted.

Henri and I stayed on the sandbar a while longer, enjoying the stingrays, until the sun started dipping rapidly toward the western horizon. Then we climbed back on the boat and set course for the shore as the darkness descended across us like a falling blanket from the east.

Henri and I stood in the bow of the boat, in each other's arms, and watched as the lights in the hotels and condominiums on Seven Mile Beach began to twinkle brightly.

"It's so beautiful," Henri said. "I don't want to ever go home."

Neither did I. And especially not five days earlier than originally planned.

THE PHONE was ringing in the apartment when we arrived back just before seven.

Henri answered it.

"We'd love to," she said. "Shall we meet you there?" She listened. "OK. We'll be ready."

"Who was that?" I asked as she put the phone down.

"Uncle Richard," she said. "He's asked if we would like to go out to dinner tonight with him and Aunt Mary. There's a new restaurant they want to try. They're picking us up in an hour."

"Is Martin coming?" I asked.

"Uncle Richard didn't say. I got the impression it was just the four of us."

Henri hurried into the bathroom to shower and change while I opened my laptop and logged on to the Internet. I was still in the shorts and T-shirt I'd been wearing on the boat, but it would only take me a few minutes to change.

There was an e-mail from Quentin:

Jeff,

A few more thoughts about our friend Martin Reynard. I called a solicitor friend of mine who deals with tax affairs for offshore companies. He says the new rules on tax residency are catching out all sorts of people who thought they were safe and now find they're not, mostly because of how the tax authorities are interpreting the UK ties rule in their new Statutory Residence Test. Some, who thought the new system meant they could stay in the United Kingdom for up to 120 days each year, are actually only allowed to stay here for 90, or even for only 45. There was also something else he said that might be of interest—it seems that some companies are also finding themselves in trouble because of a director inadvertently becoming a UK tax resident.

Good luck, Quentin.

I typed *UK tax residency for companies* into the Internet search engine. The result was most revealing:

> ***A company is generally treated as tax resident in the United Kingdom if it is either incorporated in the United Kingdom or, if not, if the boardroom control is exercised in the United Kingdom, or a majority of its board members are UK tax residents.***

Reynard Shipping Limited was not incorporated in the United Kingdom. Martin had moved its registration to the Cayman Islands three years before.

I could hear Henri singing in the shower.

I went quickly into the bedroom and looked again at the packet of board papers in the bedside drawer. They included the minutes of the last meeting, held in Singapore the previous September. The minutes recorded those board members present: Sir Richard Reynard (Chairman), Martin Reynard (Managing Director), Henrietta Shawcross, Greg Sherwood and Alistair Vickers. There had been no apologies made for absences. So the Reynard Shipping Limited board of directors comprised just those five.

I knew from my earlier phone call that Greg Sherwood worked for Atherton, Bradley and Partners, the local Cayman lawyers, and I assumed that Alistair Vickers did as well. They were the two directors that Henri had said were there just to ensure the company complied with the local regulations.

Sir Richard and Henrietta both lived permanently in England.

A company is generally treated as tax resident in the United Kingdom if . . . a majority of its board members are UK tax residents.

As long as Martin was a nonresident, a majority of the board members were nonresidents, so the company was nonresident.

If, however, Martin had become a UK tax resident, even accidentally, then the company . . .

"What are you doing?" Henri said behind me in an accusatory tone that made me jump.

I turned around with the board papers still in my hands. It was far too late to put them back without her seeing.

"Nothing," I said, smiling at her.

She did not smile back. "What are you doing with those?" she asked, pointing at the papers, the accusation still evident in her voice.

"I just wondered who the other directors were," I said tamely.

"Why?"

"No reason."

I could hardly tell her my true motive. I returned the papers to the drawer and pushed it shut.

She was not happy.

I had grossly invaded her privacy and she didn't like it. Not one bit.

The doorbell rang.

I was relieved, thinking that it had got me out of a spot of trouble.

How wrong I was.

I opened the front door to find Bentley Robertson and Sir Richard Reynard standing there and neither of them was in a friendly mood. They didn't wait to be asked in, they just forced their way through the door as I backed down the hallway. They closed the door behind them.

Henri came waltzing out of the bedroom wearing her bathrobe and with a towel turban on her head.

"What's going on?" she said. "You said in an hour. I'm not ready." She pointed at Bentley. "And what the hell is he doing here? I'm not going anywhere with him." She was almost shouting.

"Henrietta, be quiet," Sir Richard said, taking his eyes off me for only a fraction of a second.

Henri opened her mouth as if to say something more.

Her uncle held his hand up toward her. "I said, be quiet!"

She closed her mouth again.

"Greg called me from Atherton's," Sir Richard said. "Someone's been asking questions about the company and I reckon it's Hinkley. I want to know why."

"He's been asking me lots of questions about it as well," Henri said unhelpfully. "And I've just caught him looking through my board papers."

"Are you some sort of industrial spy?" Sir Richard asked. "Who are you working for?"

"I am *not* a spy," I said. "And you know damn well that I work for the British Horseracing Authority."

"So why are you asking questions about our company?"

I thought about Quentin's advice and said nothing.

"Go and pack your things," Sir Richard ordered. "You're leaving."

I looked at Henri, but if I thought she was going to stand up for me, I was sorely mistaken. She turned away without looking at my face.

Sir Richard followed me into the bedroom and waited while I gathered my things together and put them in my suitcase. It seemed to be the only thing to do.

"Where am I going?" I asked him, putting my wallet and passport in my shorts pocket.

"Out of here," he said. "We will put you on the late Cayman Airways flight to Miami. After that, I don't care."

We went back to the others.

My laptop computer was open on the table and Bentley was studying the screen, which I'd carelessly left still showing the government website on company tax residency.

"He knows," he said, looking up at Sir Richard. There was something about his tone I didn't like.

"You bastard!" Henri shouted, coming up and standing right in front of me. I could see the tears in her eyes. "And to think I was falling in love with you when all you were interested in doing was spying on me. You make me sick."

She hit me hard across the face with her open right hand, making my skin sting. I could taste the saltiness of blood at the corner of my mouth.

She turned away from me, walking over to the window facing the beach.

How I desperately wanted to go after her to explain that it was not true. I was not a spy, my feelings for her were genuine, not fabricated—and I'd fallen in love with her too. Deeply.

But, for now, my best course of action was to get out and catch that late flight to Miami. And, preferably, before Martin turned up with alternative plans.

Say nothing and get out of there as soon as possible.

I should have followed my brother-in-law's advice to the letter.

I was cross with myself for having been distracted by Henri. If those years in Afghanistan should have taught me anything it was to know when to leave a situation, to get out before the shooting started. And yet I had delayed my departure to spend the day with a girl. And it had also been ill-considered on my part to call the lawyers. I should have waited until after I was safely away.

I went over to pick up my computer and phone from the table.

"Leave them," Bentley said. "You're not taking those."

"They're the property of the BHA," I said.

"Then we'll arrange to have them returned," he said, "once we're satisfied there's nothing on them about our company."

Bentley closed the lid of my computer and put my iPhone in his pocket. Short of fighting him for them, there was nothing I could do.

I picked up my bag and walked out of the apartment without a backward glance. I couldn't bear to look at Henri in such an angry state with me.

It was as much as I could do not to cry.

SIR RICHARD drove with Bentley sitting next to him in the front. I was in the back. None of us spoke.

I'm not sure how long it took me to work out that I was not on my way to the airport and the late flight to Miami. When we had arrived, the journey from the airport to the apartment had only taken ten minutes, and we'd already been driving for much longer than that.

The lights of George Town receded behind us.

"Where are we going?" I asked with trepidation.

There was no reply.

The car slowed for some red traffic lights. Time to go, I thought.

As the car stopped, I reached for the door handle and pulled, but nothing happened. It was child-locked.

"Let me out," I demanded.

Bentley turned around to face me between the front seats.

He was holding a pistol and it was pointed directly at my heart.

"How melodramatic," I said.

It was far from being the first time someone had pointed a gun at me, although the last time had been several years ago, in Afghanistan, but there was something about the smirk on Bentley's face that sent a shiver down my back.

"You're a very difficult man to kill, Mr. Hinkley," he said.

36

"Do they still have the death penalty for murder in the West Indies?" I said. "I wonder if there's enough time for your whole life to flash before your eyes between the trap opening and the rope breaking your neck."

I was trying to unnerve my captors, but it didn't seem to be working. They seemed happy to let me babble on without reply.

"Dead bodies are hard to dispose of, you know. Even here. Especially ones with bullet holes in them. The police will be knocking on your door before you know it."

Still no response.

I tried another tactic.

"My brother-in-law is aware of everything I know, so killing me will not stop it being passed to the relevant authorities."

I now wished that I'd sent a few more e-mails, including one to the tax man.

"Why don't you just stop the car and let me out?" I said. "Make Martin pay his taxes and that will be an end to it. I'll make no further complaint against any of you."

Sir Richard went on driving and the creepy Bentley said

nothing. He just continued to smile at me, and the gun in his hand wavered not an iota.

We turned off the main road down little more than a trail, with no visible lights from any nearby houses. What had Henri said? *Most of the eastern half of the island is just deserted mangrove swamp.*

It didn't look particularly promising for my long-term prospects.

Was my good luck finally running out?

But at least now I would die knowing the reason I was being killed.

Did that make me any happier?

Probably not, but maybe it was better than being randomly knifed to death in my apartment without having the slightest idea why.

The trail seemed to go on forever until we eventually stopped at the very end, where it ran into a small beach surrounded by the mangroves. Through the windshield, in the glow of the headlights, I could see a boat with an outboard engine, its bow pulled up on the white sand. This was no spur-of-the-moment plan, not if that boat had been pre-positioned.

The two men got out of the car, leaving the headlights on. Bentley then opened the rear door next to me. He was still aiming the gun at my chest.

"Get out," he ordered.

"No," I replied.

"I said get out."

"And I said no."

"I'll shoot you," he said, lifting the gun to his eyeline and aiming it at my face.

"If I get out, you'll definitely shoot me," I said. "In here, maybe not. Your car, is it? Or hired? Either way, it would take too much explaining if my blood and brains were splattered all over the inside."

"Get out!" He was almost screaming.

"No," I repeated.

He obviously hadn't imagined such an impasse. He looked to Sir Richard for assistance.

"Shoot him in the foot," Sir Richard said without any visible emotion.

"He'll still bleed," said Bentley.

Sir Richard walked around the car to our side and took the pistol from Bentley.

"Get out of the car," he said, pointing the gun at my right leg. "I'll shoot you in the foot first, then in your knee. Get out of the car now. You have three seconds."

It was his matter-of-fact tone that was most appalling. This was clearly a man very accustomed to getting his own way, and I could detect the ruthlessness in him that would have been needed to transform the small shipping company of his grandfather into the multinational corporation it was today.

I could also recall the words of the Special Forces sergeant who had run the *escape and evasion* part of the Army captains' course: *Resist your captors if you can, but try to avoid leg injuries. If you can't walk or run, then you'll not be able to take advantage of an escape opportunity, if it arises. Lack of mobility is a sure death sentence.*

"OK," I said.

I got out of the car.

Sir Richard Reynard smiled broadly. Just like Dave Swinton, he always liked to win.

"Over to the boat," he said, waving the gun to the left.

I walked in front of him while Bentley kept well to the side, out of reach and out of the line of fire.

There was a diver's buoyancy compensator in the bow attached to a common or garden plain gray aluminum dive tank connected to a regulator set.

"Not more carbon monoxide," I said.

"That was Bentley's idea," Sir Richard said, smiling. "And it almost worked."

And it would have, I thought, if it hadn't been for Henri pulling me up to the surface and Carson Ebanks's timely intervention with oxygen.

"Put it on," Sir Richard said.

"I'll wash up somewhere on a beach. How are you going to explain away a diver with bullet wounds? Fish don't have guns."

"You'll not wash up from where you're going," Bentley said with a smile. "Over the wall and down into the depths. They say the sea is three miles deep just a mile offshore in these parts."

Perhaps for the first time I was truly frightened.

I had hoped and half expected that they wouldn't go through with it—that they would come to their senses and work out that the risks outweighed the benefits. But proving murder without a body was always difficult, if not impossible.

In 1660, three people were convicted and hanged for the murder of a local official who subsequently turned up alive and well, having been away abroad. Since that time, English common law adopted the *no body, no murder* rule, maintaining that there could be no conviction for murder without the victim's body. The rule has been overturned in only a handful of cases in recent years when other circumstantial and modern forensic evidence has been overwhelming.

I would have to try to leave some of my DNA and hope it would be found.

"Put it on," Sir Richard repeated.

I leaned over and spat in the bottom of the boat, first scraping the inside of my cheek with my teeth to ensure that there were plenty of my cells present. Then I picked up the scuba equipment. It was heavy.

My abdomen complained, but that was the least of my worries. I knew that from the moment I was in the boat with the equipment on, my time was up. It was not easy to dress a body, even in scuba gear. And lifting my literal deadweight into the boat would be far from easy, especially for a man of sixty-nine and his diminutive sidekick. But once I was in there, it would be a fairly simple task for even just one of them to roll my lifeless form over the side into the water.

I checked the console at the end of the air hose. The pressure gauge read zero. The tank was empty. What's more, I could see that the valve assembly was loose. As soon as this tank was submerged, it would fill with water and provide the necessary ballast to take me all the way to the bottom.

I placed the tank on the edge of the boat and put my arms into the sleeves of the BC jacket.

"I thought Martin would be here to help you," I said.

"Martin is a fool," Sir Richard pronounced. "It was he who got us in this mess. Now Bentley and I have to pick up the pieces."

"Why not pay the tax?" I said. "It can't be that much."

"Shut up," Bentley said.

I ignored him.

"Even the corporation taxes can't be worth murdering for," I said.

Although I couldn't be sure of that.

Martin had stayed too long in the UK, which meant that of the five main-board directors of Reynard Shipping Limited, the majority were now UK tax resident. Consequently, it would be considered by Her Majesty's Revenue and Customs to be a UK-based company subject to British tax on all its worldwide profits, including the eye-watering capital gain realized from the sale of the Hong Kong operation.

The tax would run into many hundreds of millions of pounds. Maybe as much as half a billion.

Was that worth murdering for?

"I need that money for my new yacht," Sir Richard said.

So I was to be sacrificed on the altar of Sir Richard Reynard's new yacht, no doubt a huge multisuite gin palace with every luxury, including gold faucets and a helicopter landing pad on the deck.

Even if Quentin did follow things through and report my suspicions to the tax authorities, it wouldn't save me now from a watery grave.

It made me angry. Bloody angry.

"Hurry up," Sir Richard shouted. "Get into the boat."

"What does Martin think of this little caper?" I asked.

"Martin will do as he's told."

Something about the way he said it made me realize that Martin had no idea whatsoever that this was going on.

I had been wrong.

All this time I'd thought that it was Martin who was behind the attempts on my life, but it had been his father, aided and abetted by his creepy lawyer.

No wonder Martin had been affronted when I'd accused him of deliberately filling the guest dive tank with carbon monoxide.

Bentley must have done it while we were at the Governor's residence watching the carol singing.

I did up the fastening on the front of the buoyancy compensator and stood up, the weight of the tank causing me to gasp slightly at the stress to my chest.

"Get in the boat," Sir Richard said again.

My time was running out fast.

I started to turn toward the boat but then turned back to face him, taking the air hose in my right hand.

"Are you aware that your friend Bentley here is screwing your daughter-in-law?"

He took his eyes off me for just a second to look at Bentley.

It was enough.

I swung the console with all my might at the hand holding the gun and caught him across the wrist just behind the base of the thumb. The impact was hard enough to break the glass face of the depth indicator.

He screamed and dropped the gun and I fell on it like a starving dog on a juicy steak.

Sir Richard reacted more quickly than I would have expected for a man of his age, stepping forward and taking a wild kick at my head.

The weight of the dive tank was hampering my movement, holding me down, and I desperately tore, one-handed, at the fastening on the BC. My other hand was on the gun, but it was stuck beneath me.

Bentley weighed in with some footwork of his own, trying to stomp my neck. Fortunately, all he managed to do was kick the tank valve and hurt his foot.

Finally, I was free of the scuba gear and I rolled it off my back. But the two men had teamed up. Sir Richard was trying to use my head as a football, running up and kicking at it as if to hack it off my shoulders and send it over the goalpost for an extra point, while Bentley had taken to stomping on my now-unprotected lower back.

"Enough," I shouted, but they took no notice.

It had been only three weeks or so since my chest had been open and my heart manually massaged. I was still in no shape to fight, especially when the odds were not in my favor by two-to-one, even though one of them was more than twice my age.

I curled myself into a ball to protect my delicate chest and abdomen.

I still had my hand on the gun beneath me, but I was loath to use it. I didn't want to shoot anyone. Indeed, in spite of my years in the Army, I had never fired a gun in anger and I wasn't keen to start. I'd been an intelligence officer and, right now, I was trying to use my intelligence to stop this madness without any loss of life.

But Sir Richard and Bentley were clearly not reading the same script. They seemed intent on murder, as they continued to rain down brutal kicks.

Then things got more serious.

Bentley went over to the boat and returned holding the anchor, a sort of grappling hook contraption with a central rod connected to four arms set at right angles to one another with sharp-looking points on their ends. There was a rope attached to the central rod and Bentley was using it to swing the anchor in a big circle over his head before aiming it right at me.

I rolled over as the anchor bit into the sand where I'd been lying just a fraction of a second earlier.

I tried to grab it, but Bentley tugged it away with the rope before I could reach it.

He swung the anchor over his head again for another go. I was now lying on my back and far more vulnerable to the attack.

I lifted the gun in my right hand and shot him.

I didn't try anything fancy, I just aimed at the widest part of his trunk and pulled the trigger.

The bullet hit him just below the heart, a red star appearing vividly in the center of his white shirt.

The anchor seemed to stop in mid-swing, falling harmlessly to the sand in front of him, while Bentley himself had a look of immense surprise on his face.

He pitched forward, falling right across the sharp arms of the anchor, his body adopting a grotesquely twisted pose with the crown of his head pointing down into the sand.

Sir Richard stopped kicking me.

He stood, unmoving and staring at Bentley, the look on his face seeming to suggest that he had only now grasped the true enormity of what they'd been doing. It was also a look of intense grief, and I recalled what Henri had said about her uncle Richard wishing that Bentley had been his son rather than Martin.

He went over to his trusted lawyer and pulled him off the anchor, laying him flat on the sand and going down on his knees beside him.

Bentley's eyes were still wide open, but he was no longer seeing.

"You've murdered him," Sir Richard said, looking across at me. His tone of accusation somehow implying that Bentley trying to kill me had been all right, but the other way around was hugely wicked.

I continued to stare at him, holding the gun ready, wary that he might try to complete with the anchor what Bentley had started. But the fight seemed to have drained out of him and he suddenly looked every one of his sixty-nine years.

He stood up and stumbled, wide-eyed, back to the car. I made no attempt to go after him. There was nowhere for him to run to, not on this island.

He started the engine, turned the car around and drove away down the trail, leaving me in the sudden darkness.

I rolled over onto my knees and rested my head in my hands.

In spite of the warmth, I started shivering.

It was the shock of having killed someone, I told myself, and the relief of still being alive when I'd been so sure I would die.

After a couple of minutes, the shivering abated and I reckoned it was time to move. I didn't fancy still being here if Sir Richard came back with reinforcements.

As my eyes adjusted to the moonlight, I could see Bentley lying on his back, motionless, on the sand.

The situation didn't seem real.

I stood up and went over to him.

To be sure, I felt for a pulse on his wrist, and also his neck, but there was nothing. I'd come across dead bodies before, but never one where I'd been so personally responsible for snuffing out the life that had once inhabited the corpse.

I felt his pant pocket for my iPhone.

Who should I call?

The police for sure, but who else?

I might need someone who was an ally.

I punched in Derrick Smith's number.

37

I didn't catch the flight for which I'd made a reservation. In fact, I didn't leave Cayman until four days later, boarding a commercial red-eye to London at seven o'clock on New Year's Eve.

I slept through the actual moment of change from December to January, somewhere over the mid-Atlantic at thirty-six thousand feet.

As a journey, it couldn't have been more different from that which had brought me to the Islands. This was no private jet—more like a knees-to-the-chest charter. And Henrietta Shawcross was becoming a distant memory.

I had spent nearly twenty hours in custody at the Royal Cayman Islands Police headquarters in George Town, answering questions and trying to explain how I had come to be on a deserted beach in the middle of the mangroves with a gun in my hand and a dead body on the sand.

At first, it had been fairly obvious that the police didn't believe a single word I was telling them.

Even to my ears, the story seemed too far-fetched to be true. Things like that just didn't happen in the idyllic Cayman Islands.

"Consider yourself a bit of a James Bond, do you?" one of the local detectives had said as his opening gambit. "Reckon you've got a license to kill, do you?"

"No," I'd replied, "I do not."

"That's not what I've heard from Mr. Smith."

I wondered if calling Derrick had been a mistake. He must have told them the tale of the foiled kidnapping of Secret Ways at Ascot. They were clearly getting me mixed up with the name of the horse.

I'd been arrested on suspicion of murdering Bentley Robertson and had spent a night tossing and turning on a hard mattress in a stifling-hot prison cell.

It was not knowing what was happening outside that was the most frustrating thing.

After an initial interview on that first evening, when I had gone through the whole story from start to finish, I'd been left alone in the cell without any further communication, not only for the rest of the night but throughout the whole of the next morning.

"What's going on?" I asked the police constable who brought me some lunch at noon.

He didn't reply.

I was most concerned about what Sir Richard Reynard might be telling them. What fabrication he had thought up to land me in deeper trouble.

At about three in the afternoon, the same detective came to the cell, opening the metal door wide.

"You're free to go, Mr. Hinkley," he said. "There will be no charges."

I was relieved.

"Have you arrested Sir Richard Reynard?" I asked him.

"Richard Reynard is dead," he said. "He was found this morning in his son's diving store. It appears that he died of carbon monoxide poisoning. A gasoline-driven air compressor was discovered still running in the store with insufficient ventilation for the exhaust."

"Oh," I said. That had been Bentley's idea.

"We are treating his death as a suicide. He left a note."

"What was in the note?" I asked.

He paused for a moment as if deciding whether or not he should tell me.

"It was just four words long: *I am so sorry.*"

Unexpectedly, my overriding emotion was one of sorrow.

Up until last night, I had quite liked Uncle Richard. There had been a kind of magnetism about him, drawing people in under his wing, charmed by the strength of his personality.

But it had all been a façade.

His character had been deeply flawed by recklessness and greed.

And it had been his greed that had ultimately resulted in him taking his own life—that and the folly of imagining that he could somehow cover up Martin's costly error by killing anyone who knew about it.

Part of me was surprised that he had chosen to take such a way out. I had half expected him to be more of a fighter and to tough it out, perhaps blaming everything on his dead lawyer. But Bentley had been like a son to him and maybe he didn't want to further tarnish his memory.

"You will have to remain on the island until the inquests for both Mr. Reynard and Mr. Robertson are opened," said the detective.

I wondered if he had intentionally dropped the *Sir Richard*, reducing him to a mere *Mr.*

"When will that be?" I asked.

"In a few days time. At the very least, you will have to give evidence as to how Mr. Robertson died."

"OK," I said, but I wondered where I would stay. The apartment at the Coral Stone Club was out of the question, obviously, and all the hotels were full to overflowing at this peak time of the Christmas and New Year's tourist season.

"Mr. Smith has indicated that you can stay with him," the detective said as if reading my mind.

WE LANDED at Heathrow in a snowstorm early on New Year's Day and everything was covered in white.

The aircraft was parked out on a remote stand and walking down the steps to the bus was quite a shock to the system. The Cayman Police had been reluctant to return my suitcase from the trunk of Sir Richard's car, as it was still classed as evidence, and I'd been unable to buy anything warmer than a paper-thin plastic rain jacket.

Not surprisingly, there was little demand for thick, warm sweaters, scarves and gloves in the tropics.

Derrick and Gay Smith had been good to me, providing me not only with food and accommodation but also with a pair of pants, a decent shirt, a shaving kit and some friendly ears to listen.

I had told them everything over a welcome glass of wine in their living room on the day I'd been released.

They were both totally shocked.

"I can't believe that it was me who was the cause of everything," Derrick had said. "I introduced you to Richard Reynard and I took you up to the Hennessy suite at Newbury."

But he couldn't have known what I'd hear on the balcony and what Richard Reynard's awful reaction to it would be.

Two days later, Derrick had driven me to George Town for the opening of the inquest into the deaths of both Bentley Robertson and Sir Richard Reynard.

I had been informed that, at this stage, the proceedings would establish only the identities of the dead, provide a brief summary of the actions leading up to the fatalities and confirm the actual cause of each death. Then the hearing would be adjourned, to be resumed only after the forensic and police investigations were concluded.

However, on the grounds that I would soon be leaving the island, the presiding magistrate, who was also acting as the coroner, had required me to give a full and complete account of the events leading up to the shooting of Bentley Robertson, including details of the failed attempt to kill me with the poisoned dive tank on Christmas Day.

Inevitably, under questioning from the magistrate, I'd had to refer back to all the relevant incidents that had occurred since I had first set eyes on Bentley on the balcony at Newbury racetrack and then explain my understanding of the reasons for those incidents.

I'd been on the witness stand for most of the day.

It had been halfway through the morning before I'd noticed Martin Reynard sitting at the back of the courtroom. He was leaning forward and listening intently to every word I said.

There had been no sign of Henri.

I had purposely hung back at the lunch break so as not to run into Martin, but we had accidentally come face-to-face at the end of the day after my testimony was complete.

We had stood looking at each other at a distance of only a couple of feet.

"I'm sorry for your loss," I said to him.

He nodded. And then he held out his right hand to me.

"It was my father's idea to take you diving on Christmas Day. He was insistent that I should ask you. I'm sorry."

I shook his hand.

Nothing more needed to be said.

TWO WEEKS LATER, a BHA disciplinary panel held an inquiry into the race-fixing allegations against Bill McKenzie and Willy Mitchell and the unusual betting practices of Leslie Morris.

Bill and Willy both arrived early at BHA headquarters, each of them wearing his best suit to try to impress the panel members.

Leslie Morris, however, was absent.

On New Year's Eve, while still free on police bail, he had been prevented from driving his car onto a Channel Tunnel train by a member of the border police, who had shown unfamiliar diligence in spotting that he was attempting to travel on an expired passport.

Consequently, Morris was presently remanded to Belmarsh Prison, charged with conspiracy to murder Dave Swinton, and also with violating the terms of his bail.

Mr. Andrew Morris, Leslie's son, was still on the run and believed to be somewhere in Spain. Detective Chief Inspector Owens of the Thames Valley Police had called and told me that he was convinced Morris Senior had been on his way to join his son when he'd been stopped. A European arrest warrant had since been issued for Andrew Morris and, according to the chief inspector, it was only a matter of time before he was caught.

"Mind you," the policeman had said, "Morris obviously thinks we won't ever find his son because he's now blaming him for everything in a misguided attempt to save his own skin. Singing like a canary, he is. Claims that it was his son who shut you in the sauna and also set fire to Dave Swinton. He maintains that he was there only as the driver. Does he think we are idiots or something?" He laughed. "But *he* is one, for sure. He's clearly never heard of guilt by *Joint Enterprise*. Don't worry, we have him nailed for murder."

THE BHA formal disciplinary panel proceedings were short, the details having been discussed and agreed to ahead of time.

Bill McKenzie and Willy Mitchell both pleaded guilty to charges of intentionally riding so that their mounts could not obtain the best possible placing, in contravention of rules (B)59.2 and (D)45.1 of the Rules of Racing.

Both were banned from riding for twenty-eight days and warned regarding their future conduct.

Subject to the outcome of legal proceedings, Leslie Morris was suspended from the *fit and proper person* list and thus could no longer be a registered owner. Furthermore, he was excluded from all BHA-registered premises.

The whole thing took less than an hour.

Bill and Willy were all smiles afterward when I met them in the lobby.

I had been working behind the scenes on their behalf ever since I'd returned from the Cayman Islands and I had convinced the chairman of the Disciplinary Committee that they should be charged only with the most minor of possible offenses and that the penalty should be the most lenient available.

If they had been found guilty of the most serious offense, they would have faced a ban from riding for ten years or more, which would have surely ended their careers.

"I'll take a holiday with my missus," Bill said. "And I'll be back before you know it."

"Is everything now sorted with Mrs. McKenzie?" I asked.

"All fine and dandy," he said with a laugh and without elaborating. "The baby's due in April. We can't wait."

I didn't ask him if he'd told her about his encounter with the French floozy. Somehow, I doubted it.

Willy Mitchell's wife had come with him to the hearing and both of them came up to me.

"Thank you," Amy said. Then she touched Willy's arm as if to prompt him.

"Yes, thank you," Willy said. "I suppose that went as well as we could have expected. At least I'll be able to ride at the Cheltenham Festival. Maybe my gaffer will even let me ride Electrostatic in the big novice chase."

"I think he will," I said.

I'd been down to Gloucestershire to speak with the trainer in question. Initially, he'd been angry that Willy had claimed the saddle had slipped when it hadn't. But I had explained the specific circumstances and, in the end, he had been supportive, and I think I'd convinced him to give Willy another chance.

I wandered reluctantly back to my desk and opened the next

file on the pile, an investigation into the possible blood doping of a novice hurdler at the Perth races in November.

I sighed.

Did I really want to do this for the rest of my life?

Not for the first time, I thought seriously of emigrating to Australia, starting afresh in a new city on a new continent.

There was plenty of racing in Australia. Surely I could find a job.

I checked my phone. No messages. No texts.

I had sent several to Henri, and I'd tried to call her, but all to no avail.

I sighed again and dragged myself back to the topic in hand, reading through the blood report from the equine laboratory.

But my heart wasn't in it.

Maybe I'd feel better in the morning.

"I'm going home," I said to Paul Maldini, putting my head around the door of his office. "I don't feel well. I'll see you tomorrow."

I took the Tube to Willesden Junction and walked along the gloomy trackside path as the feeble mid-January daylight faded into night.

No one attacked me. Did I care?

As I turned into my road, I could make out a shadowy figure half-hidden by the bushes outside my front door.

It was Henrietta Shawcross.

We stood looking at each other in silence, each of us trying to gauge the mood of the other.

"Martin has told me everything," she said finally.

I remained silent, unmoving.

"I'm so sorry," she said.

She started to cry and I reached out a hand toward her. She rushed into my arms and hugged me as if never wanting to let go. I leaned down and kissed her and she responded in passionate fashion.

"At least it isn't *all* bad," Henri said into my shoulder. "You did finally rid me of the creepy Bentley."